DRAGON LORD

MASE EVANS

For everyone who wanted HER to be the badass fighter
saving HIM, I wrote this book for us <3

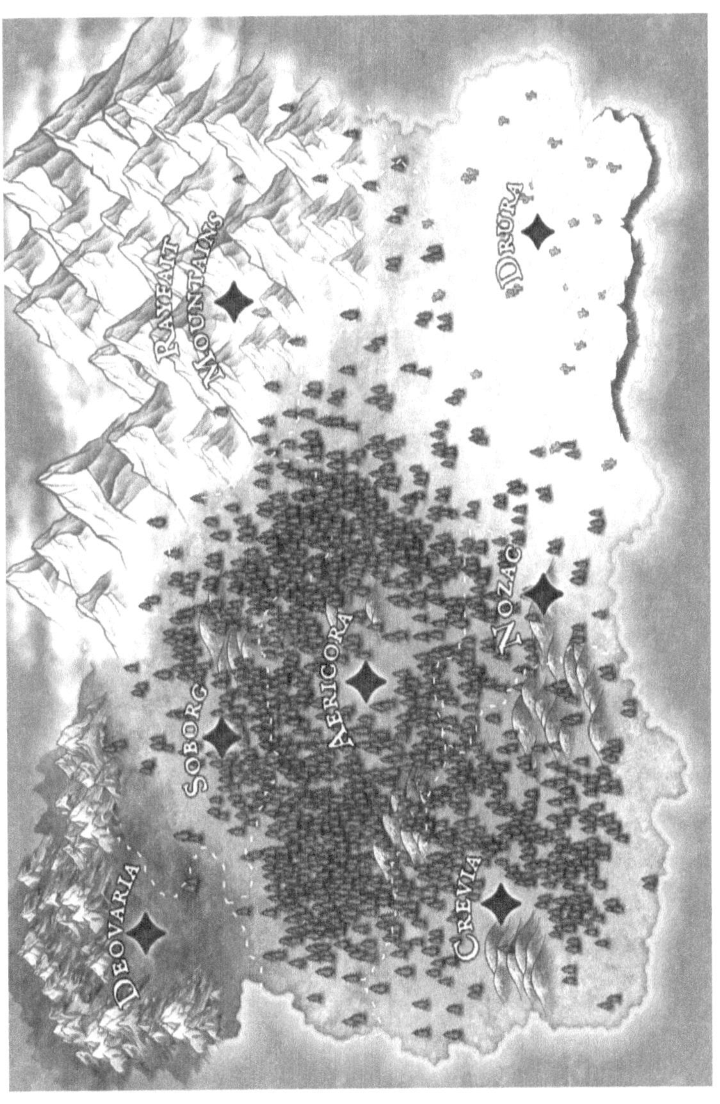

RAYFAIT MOUNTAINS
DRURA
NOZAC
SOBORG
AERICORA
CREVIA
DEOVARIA

Chapter 1

"Ow!" Eryn snapped, clenching the bloodied bandage wrapped around her left shoulder. She froze, glaring daggers at the dragon behind her, who sniffed curiously at the wound. "Why does he keep doing that?"

Caeden rested a hand on her elbow and gave her a gentle tug, pulling her a step closer to him and away from the large beast looming over their group. Now, that she only stood a mere few inches from him, his heart raced.

The dragon had been with them since their fight at the border between Aericora and Deovaria, Aericora's enemy kingdom. A man referred to only as the Dragon Lord ruled Deovaria after assuming the throne fifteen years ago, bringing with him the ability to control the dragons from the Rayfait Mountains. He'd passed that ability to his soldiers when the wars first broke out, and up until last week, no one outside of Deovaria knew where the ability came from or how they were able to use it.

Until Ronan held Caeden's mother's ring with its glowing sapphire stone to the dragon's nose.

They still didn't know how the stone gained them the

dragon's loyalty, but it hadn't left their side since. Despite Ronan being the one who used the ring to tame it, the dragon had taken a liking to Eryn.

"She's a lady," Ronan corrected her from where he sat atop a chestnut mare. Margaid, Caeden's fiancée from Crevia, clung tightly to Ronan's waist from where she rode behind him.

They'd suggested Eryn trade with someone and ride one of the horses to avoid hurting herself any further, but she said the jostling only hurt her shoulder more. None of them pressed the subject, but Caeden worried about her expending too much energy walking when her body could be using that same energy to heal the wound in her shoulder.

Two hundred soldiers trailed behind them. They had been sent to collect the soldiers from the battlefield to help guard the castle after the Dragon Lord and his men attacked. Now that Caeden and Margaid's engagement was official and Crevia had sent some of their soldiers to aid Aericora, they justified bringing some of their own soldiers back to the castle without worrying that they would be spreading their men too thin in the field.

"How can you tell?" Caeden asked, glancing back at the dragon again. It was huge, standing at least fifty feet tall—a good bit taller than most of the trees surrounding them. Its scales gleamed in the afternoon light, blues of all different shades twinkling brilliantly. Its amber eyes lingered on Eryn, who had turned away, her attention focused on Caeden's hand resting gently against her elbow.

Eryn swallowed hard, and Caeden glanced at where his hand laid against her skin before quickly pulling away. They hadn't spoken much since the attack on their camp when Ronan tamed the dragon. After a blow from an enemy sword struck her just beneath her collarbone, she spent days sleeping and giving her body time to heal. In the rare moments she was awake, her pain was so immense that he kept quiet. Though he'd remained by her side as much as possible, he was the prince, and after something as monumental as taming a dragon had taken place, he was needed in meetings with those in charge of the camp. Even if it had made his heart ache to leave her alone.

She'd healed quickly. Far faster than anyone had expected. Especially considering how some had speculated that she wouldn't wake at all.

Their training session right before the attack was still clear in his mind. He remembered her heart racing beneath her skin and the blade he'd held to her throat when he'd won their fight. He remembered the way her cheeks had turned bright red, making her blue eyes even more vibrant. He remembered telling her how he felt, wanting to kiss her when she'd said that she *maybe* felt the same way. He'd seen through the mask of irritation she tried to pull over her features, and his heart had leapt in his chest knowing that the "maybe" was purely part of her mask.

There hadn't been a good moment to mention it again, and bringing everything up now would only provoke a frustrated outburst from her.

Ronan raised an eyebrow at him suggestively. "Look, I know you're tired and stressed and whatnot with all your princely duties or whatever, but I know ya ain't that stupid."

Margaid giggled from where she sat behind Ronan, then buried her face in his shoulder to quiet herself when both Caeden and Eryn looked at the two of them again.

Caeden had forgotten entirely what they'd been talking about. His blank stare must have alerted his friend to the fact that he wasn't paying attention, because Ronan rolled his eyes.

"I ain't goin' into anatomy with ya, princy," he said, and Margaid burst into more giggles.

Caeden felt the blood rush to his face. That's what they were talking about.

Eryn gave him a pointed look, her eyebrows raised and a smug grin tugging at the corners of her pretty lips. "Watching you squirm is the best pain management I've had all week," she teased, nudging him lightly with her unhurt shoulder, all earlier discomfort gone.

His pink-tinged cheeks turned crimson, and he turned away, hoping no one would see it. They were halfway back to the castle by now, but they had at least another day ahead of them before they would be standing outside the castle gates. His father would be waiting for them when they returned. They were multiple days behind schedule, but they would be back before his father sent anyone looking for them. Even if only barely. If they'd stayed another day at the camp and given everyone more time to rest—which he'd wanted to do for Eryn's sake—they wouldn't have been. And no one needed his father sending out rescue parties.

"I still can't believe it worked," Eryn whispered beside him, her eyes trained on the dragon still watching her.

"You're sure it was the ring?" Margaid asked. It was the first time Caeden had heard her speak in nearly a day. She'd been quiet since the attack, but part of that was likely because up until a month ago, she had never seen such a gruesome scene. Now, she'd seen two. Caeden had barely seen more than that, but after hearing descriptions of the massacres taking place on the battlefield, it felt like he'd witnessed countless others.

All eyes turned to the red-haired princess, and she flushed the palest shade of pink, highlighting the freckles dotting her cheeks and nose.

"What else could it've been?" Ronan asked, voicing the question Caeden was sure was on everyone's mind.

Margaid shrugged before turning away and focusing her gaze

on the looming dragon. "Maybe she just liked you."

Ronan threw a skeptical look over his shoulder at the dragon, who glanced momentarily at him before she turned back to Eryn. "She doesn't seem to want nothin' to do with me now."

Margaid was the only one who hadn't known their theory about the ring before Ronan used it. Only Caeden, Ronan, and Eryn knew the suspicion Caeden had about the stone's ability to control the dragons after he'd seen one nearly identical to his mother's ring on the hand of a Deovarian soldier during the attack on the castle. Even though she'd agreed that his theory seemed plausible, Eryn hadn't agreed with the plan that followed.

"We saw a soldier with a similar ring," Eryn explained before Caeden got the chance to. "And we caught a spy trying to take that one." She nodded in Caeden's direction, where the ring sat in his pocket.

Margaid nodded in response, but didn't say anything before she turned away.

"Wonder what the court thinks happened to it," Ronan mused, his trademark mischievous smirk pulling at the corners of his lips.

"They definitely didn't figure it out before we left," Caeden said. "I almost hope my father figured it out while we were gone. I'll be in less trouble if he's had time to think about the benefits of us using it versus the possible costs. Especially since we're all still alive."

"Still can't believe you were going to take that risk."

He could practically feel Eryn's glare boring into the side of his head. Now was definitely not the time to bring up their conversation from last week. He'd probably end up with a dagger shoved through his stomach.

"But he didn't," Ronan cut in. "I'm the one who ran straight to what could've been my very heroic death, remember? Ya forget the part where he dropped the ring and forgot all 'bout it just to check on you." Ronan winked suggestively, and Caeden averted his gaze, looking anywhere but at Eryn.

Bastard.

Eryn rolled her eyes. "Did you miss the part where Aericora's only living heir almost died being an absolute idiot?"

Ronan gave him a look, as if to say there was nothing more he could do, and Caeden would need to make Eryn see reason.

"I wasn't going to send one of my soldiers—or my friends—to their death," Caeden told her, doing his best to keep his voice even. Getting frustrated would only stoke her fire, just like her irritation toward him only ever stoked his own. If she was already angry, he was the one who would have to play the peacemaker.

She turned her fiery glare on him. "So it would've been better for you to die than one of us?" She looked like she wanted to laugh. "Please, someone make that make sense."

Caeden sighed, his hand instinctively falling to the pocket of his pants, where the comforting weight of his mother's ring sat inside. He ran his finger along the jagged edge of the metal. It had been melted and warped in the fires of the first Deovarian attack where both Caeden's mother and his older sister, Amelia, were killed.

"We were already losing the war," he said quietly. "There's no use for me if we're going to lose to the Dragon Lord. I wasn't going to send someone else to their death if the plan didn't work. Even with the soldiers from Crevia, if our theory had been wrong, we wouldn't have any real upper hand. We can use the lavender to dampen the dragon's powers, but that has only prolonged our defeat. We're out of options, and the extra soldiers are only going to be another way of prolonging the fight.

Now that we know what the ring can do, maybe it can help us, even if we only have one."

Eryn shook her head, and gently pushed away the dragon as it started sniffing her bandages again. "If either of you had gotten yourselves hurt," she said, her glare shifting from Caeden to Ronan, then back again, "I swear I would've stabbed you myself."

Ronan laughed. "Don't worry," he said to Caeden. "She told me the same thing 'fore the Dragon Lord took me. She didn't follow through with it."

Eryn pulled her dagger from the holster strapped to her upper thigh and pointed the tip in Ronan's direction. "Never too late to keep my promise."

"Easy there, Reckless" Ronan said, using the same nickname he'd had for Eryn since they were young. Caeden hadn't heard the nickname until earlier that week when Ronan had first come to visit Eryn in the infirmary. She'd hardly been lucid while the medic worked to stop her bleeding, but she'd laughed when he'd called her by it.

Caeden laughed. "Just don't kill him before we get back to the castle. The more people who can recount the story who weren't bleeding out when the dragon was tamed, the higher our chances the court won't think we're insane."

Chapter 2

Aericora's castle came into view a few hours after sunrise the following morning. After spending the past nights sleeping on the hard ground with nothing but a thin bedroll for support, the idea of a warm bed only made the aches and pains throughout Caeden's body more noticeable.

The dragon walked behind their group. Caeden and Eryn discussed her staying back with Ronan to keep the dragon occupied until Caeden broke the news to the guards that the large creature would be walking up to the gates soon after. The last time the guards saw a dragon, it had either dropped a bloody, dying soldier at their front gates and flown off, or had flown straight through their front doors with the Dragon Lord on its back. None of the guards would enjoy the sight of the dragon traveling with them, but he hoped the forewarning would ease the inevitable discomfort and fear.

Caeden rode on the back of the chestnut mare as he, Margaid, and the few hundred soldiers neared the front gates. Margaid rode on her own horse beside him, both attempting to play the roles of the future King and Queen of Aericora. The soldiers had seen Margaid ride with Ronan for a while, but only when the other horses were being used. Caeden hoped it wasn't enough for anyone to get suspicious and uncover the truth about the secret relationship between his fiancée and his best friend.

One of the soldiers beside him unfolded a large, blue Aericora flag that, coincidentally, depicted a large golden dragon billowing out a torrent of flames. He and another soldier held it above their heads between them as they neared the castle gates.

The castle's guards were on high alert when they came into view, but once their eyes landed on the flag and their prince leading the group, their composure relaxed, and a few lowered their readied weapons.

"Alert the king!" one of the soldiers bellowed to another standing beside the closed gates. "Prince Caeden has returned."

The second soldier nodded once before he slipped between the two golden gates that kept the outside world from entering the castle courtyard. He disappeared from Caeden's sight as he followed the curved path leading to the front doors.

Caeden stopped their group near the gates before he dismounted and approached the guard who had given the order to alert the king. The guard bowed forward at the waist before Caeden had a chance to tell him not to bother.

It shouldn't have bothered him to be shown that kind of respect, but he'd done nothing to earn it except be born to the correct set of parents. Maybe once he was king, or when he found a way to help them win the war, it wouldn't feel quite so undeserved.

"Your Highness, the castle has been worried. We're glad to see you've returned safely."

"We ran into some delays," Caeden told him vaguely. "We've returned with a dragon. Please inform the other guards that the dragon means no harm to anyone here, and that you are strictly to ignore it. No harm is to come to the creature while it's within our borders. Ronan will be meeting with all of you later to fill you in once we've spoken with the court."

The guard's face noticeably paled while Caeden spoke, and he nodded his head too quickly when he finished. "Of course, Your Highness."

Right on cue, a collective gasp went up among the guards standing around the front gates as the dragon emerged from the forest with Eryn and Ronan beside it. The dragon snorted, tendrils of smoke dancing from its nostrils into the air surrounding its face before dissipating.

"Quit actin' like you've never seen one of these before and get back to your posts!" Ronan shouted, and the guards averted their gazes. "There ain't a threat here, so all of you get back to where you're supposed to be."

The guard standing in front of Caeden moved to open the gates to allow the group inside, while a few of the others shrank back at Ronan's words.

"Bryn!" Ronan called, catching the attention of one of the guards.

"Yes, sir?"

"Take the newbies to the trainin' field. Eryn and I'll be there soon for an introduction and a quick trainin' session."

The guard nodded, and hung back with the rest of the soldiers, while Caeden and the other three made their way into the castle toward the king's office. His father would be there, given the time of day, and it would be easy to gather the court to meet them there.

Caeden stopped once the castle doors were shut behind them, and turned to Eryn. She raised an eyebrow at him when their eyes met, the start of a glare hiding in the edges of her expression, as if she already knew what he was going to say. She wouldn't like it, but that wouldn't stop him from saying it. "I need you to go to the infirmary. You still aren't fully healed, and we need to make sure your wound didn't get infected."

"We'll get the court assembled," Margaid said. She grabbed Ronan by the arm and tugged him down the hall.

"Good luck with that one, princy!" Ronan called over his shoulder as Margaid pulled him away, a mischievous laugh hiding in the edges of his voice.

Caeden turned back to Eryn, who had her arms crossed awkwardly over her chest in a pose that was supposed to be intimidating. Instead, it only made a pang of worry strike him squarely in the chest at the reminder of her injury, and how much it was likely still hurting her.

He didn't want to argue with her, but it looked like he wouldn't have a choice. He needed to know she would be okay after being wounded. It was already a week old, and she hadn't yet gotten proper medical attention. The supplies in the field were limited, and though the medics out there were well trained, they still wouldn't be able to do as good of a job as the doctors in the castle, given the resources they had.

He reached for her, but thought better of it at the last second and dropped his hands to his sides. "Please, get it looked at," he said, his voice quiet—pleading.

Eryn's expression softened, and she uncrossed her arms. "I'll be fine, you dummy prince," she told him, her voice light when she called him by the same insult she'd used since they met. It didn't bother him to hear it anymore. If anything, he was growing to like it, strangely enough.

His gaze flicked to the bandages wrapped around her shoulder, and images of the sword protruding from beneath her collarbone as tears streamed down her face forced their way to the forefront of his mind. He heard her ragged breathing as they won the fight and he carried her to the medical tent. He felt her cool hands against his chest as she held on to him with barely any strength. He remembered sitting beside her for those first days, waiting for the brief moments when she would wake up, and dreading every second in between that maybe she wouldn't.

Caeden shook his thoughts away, and despite his better judgment, he reached for her hand. Her fingers were warm against his, and it eased the ache in his chest. "I need to know you're really okay," he said, so softly he wondered whether the words even reached her.

Eryn swallowed hard, and when he looked at her, he could see a faint blush had spread across her cheeks. She didn't pull her hand away. "Okay," she agreed, her voice quiet. "I'll have it looked at, but after the meeting."

Caeden wanted to argue, and opened his mouth to do so, but the small smile she gave him and the way she gently squeezed his hand made his breath hitch in the back of his throat and words failed him. He swallowed hard. "Just… don't put it off too long, okay?"

"I promise, I won't."

Chapter 3

By the time Caeden and Eryn made it to the king's office, half of the usual advisors were already gathered. Another arrived just behind the two of them, and more would follow.

The king sat in his usual place behind his large, wooden desk, his hands clasped in front of him. His knuckles were white from holding his hands so tightly together. The only sign his father felt any relief that they had arrived back safely was the way he loosened his grip, the color returning to his fingers.

The king's gaze traveled between Caeden and Eryn as they stepped through the open doorway, taking in the injury on Eryn's shoulder and the lack of any noticeable injuries marking Caeden.

Caeden took a step away from the Dragon Hunter standing beside him, putting a respectable distance between the two of them before anyone could notice how comfortable he was being near her. His father had already picked up on Caeden's feelings toward Eryn before they'd left for the field. He hadn't noticed it at the time, but looking back on his father's parting words and the subtle glance he gave Eryn, Caeden knew he had figured it out.

He was set to marry Margaid in only a few weeks, though. Even though he did have real feelings for Eryn and none for his fiancée, the court couldn't know that. His father shouldn't have known either. No one should've known aside from the woman currently standing beside him, who he'd told directly. The woman who'd said that *maybe* she liked him back, and who he couldn't be with because his marriage to Margaid and the soldiers it would provide his kingdom was the only reason they could prolong the war.

Caeden shook away the feeling as he took in everyone in the room. Another few advisors arrived, and Caeden's father stood as everyone fell into comfortable places throughout the space.

"I'm glad to see you've all returned," the king stated. "And I hear there's more news than just that you've brought back the soldiers we discussed? I was informed of a dragon, as well?" His tone was even, but there was a pinched look to the left side of his father's mouth when he spoke. His father was scared, even if he was trying to hide it from the gathered court members.

"Yes," Caeden responded as he pulled his mother's ring from his pocket. There was no easy way to tell his father the news. He needed to get this over with quickly since his father hadn't yet put the pieces together. "During the first attack on the castle, Miss Gedding and I encountered one of the spies attempting to take Queen Anna's ring. After seeing another soldier in the hall with one that looked identical, we came up with a theory that the ring had something to do with Deovaria's ability to control the dragons. We didn't express the theory to the court for fear of more spies attempting to take it and keep us from testing to see whether we were correct. Once we got to the field and were under attack from Deovaria again, Ronan Atkyn used the ring to tame one of the Dragon Lord's dragons. So far, it appears to be loyal to all of us, despite Ronan having had the stone while near the creature."

Chatter rose in the room, but the voices of the advisors faded away as Caeden took in his father's wide eyes, and how his knuckles had turned stark white again. The king cleared his throat, and the chatter ceased. "That's an impressive discovery," he stated, as diplomatic as he always was in front of the advisors. Caeden would get an earful later, but for the moment, he didn't have to worry about it.

"It could turn the war in our favor. This could mean our victory if we can get more stones and turn their dragons to our side," Fionn, a military veteran with a beard that hung down to his round stomach, said.

Muire rolled her eyes. "We don't even know where to find more. Don't get your hopes up. It could be beneficial, but we only have one stone. That's far from enough to turn the war to our favor."

"The ring came from the Rayfait Mountains," Caeden's father said, so quietly that Caeden barely heard him over the advisors beginning to argue with one another.

"The mountains?" Eryn echoed as the advisors slowly quieted again. There was an edge to her tone that hinted at the fear Caeden saw hiding behind her eyes.

The king nodded. "Anna said it came from somewhere inside. That was all she knew about it, and I never asked more because the only thing special about it before now was that it glowed."

"So, someone goes to the mountains, then," Fionn cut in. "Like Muire said, only having one ring is hardly going to do us any good."

"We can't afford that right now," Muire snapped. "We only just got the soldiers from Crevia. The camps they're going to be dispersed to will need time to train them before we can pull any of our higher-ranking officers for this sort of mission. And our guards certainly can't handle it right now."

"I'll only be here for a couple of weeks training the guards," Eryn said, stopping Muire before she could run any further with her arguments. "I can handle going to the mountains. I've been up there before."

Caeden winced as images flooded his mind of a six-year-old Eryn shivering on a bedroll after waking up alone on the side of the mountain. The only reminder that her parents had been there was the footprints they left behind after abandoning her as a sacrifice to the dragons.

"Your shoulder is bandaged right now," Muire argued. "And I know you injured your side during the attack on the castle, as well. We can't only send you, and no one else is available."

"The four of us will go again, then," Caeden said, feeling his father's gaze boring into the side of his head. "We survived the attack in the field, and if anything, we'll be even further away from Deovaria's soldiers in the mountains. And since we will be in such a small group, the ring should be enough to keep us safe from the dragons."

Muire opened her mouth to protest again, but Fionn interrupted her. "He's got a point. And they did come back alive from the field. We're still in the same situation that put them out there in the first place. I don't see why letting them try would be so bad. The worst thing up there is the dragons, which they have a solution for, and the cold, which is easy enough to prepare for."

The king rubbed his hands over his face and let out a deep sigh. It was the first time in a very long time that Caeden had seen him lose some of his composure in front of the advisors and the court.

He sighed loudly, and the room quieted once again. "Very well," he said without looking up. "You will be sent to the Rayfait Mountains to retrieve the stones. However"—he looked up and his gaze pierced Caeden right to his core—"if anything, and I do mean anything, happens that puts the prince in harm's way, you are to come back immediately and we will find another solution."

Across the room, Caeden caught the slight grin pulling at the corner of Ronan's mouth. He hadn't meant to volunteer them so carelessly, but his friend didn't seem to mind. If Margaid had different feelings about the matter, he wouldn't fault her for staying behind, but he was grateful she didn't voice any concerns now.

Caeden expected the argument to take longer before his father would be convinced, and he stood entirely still as his father finally broke eye contact with him.

They really were losing badly.

There was no possible way the soldiers from Crevia would be enough to win the fight anymore if his father was agreeing to this so easily.

It had seemed like it would be enough back when Caeden was offered the agreement of an arranged marriage in exchange for military training, but they must have been worse off than he ever imagined. The ring was always going to help, and he knew they were losing even with the new soldiers, but he'd thought the soldiers would give them some semblance of a chance. He thought the soldiers would at least prolong the fight long enough for them to find another solution, and that an argument would ensue in favor of that route. But if that had been the case, his father would've opted to wait to put together a different group to go to the mountains. If that were the case, they would've had time to wait for other soldiers to be called back from the field.

"Miss Gedding," the king said, turning his intense gaze on Eryn. Caeden half expected her to cower beneath his father's gaze as every member of the court had done at least once before, but instead, the fire that burned behind her eyes only intensified as she waited for him to speak again. "You will be given three weeks to get the new castle guards trained to fight the dragons. After that, the four of you will depart to the Rayfait Mountains. I'm trusting you to ensure the prince returns home safely."

Eryn nodded once. "Yes, Your Majesty."

She spoke the words smoothly, but Caeden noticed how her hands trembled. It wasn't a task she hadn't already taken upon herself. She had made it her mission to keep him safe long before anyone ordered her to. But something about being given the command now made her seem far more fragile than the woman who'd had a screaming match with the king over a similar topic a few weeks ago.

Caeden had really scared her.

The thought hit him like a punch to the stomach.

He'd known he would scare her when he left her side to attempt to tame the dragon. It was why he hadn't wanted to look back at her. He hadn't wanted to see the fear and the hurt in those blue eyes of hers.

Even though he hadn't been the one to tame the dragon, he'd still hurt her. He'd still scared her.

And she was scared he was going to do it again.

His heart broke at the realization that he'd done the one thing he'd never wanted to do to her. She cared about him, and he'd run off to what could've been his death right in front of her. Knowing that she hadn't wanted him to.

He'd vowed to never abandon her, and in a way, he had.

"Very well," the king said, shaking Caeden from his thoughts.

"You are all dismissed, except for Caeden."

Caeden cringed.

The courtiers and advisors each bowed to the king before disappearing. Ronan and Margaid followed quickly after, Eryn directly behind. She gave Caeden a backward glance, and he fixed her with a look.

The corner of her mouth twitched and she nodded her head once, confirming she would hold up her end of their earlier agreement and have her shoulder checked.

The door closed behind her before Caeden turned to his father. The king hung his head over his desk, his hands holding the small box that Caeden's mother's ring had sat in for most of Caeden's life.

"I thought Colm took the ring," his father whispered. He chuckled to himself, but there was no amusement in it. "I thought he wanted some sick trophy for killing her." He shook his head. "Why didn't you tell me? You did a good thing, Caeden. You figured out how they control the dragons. It could be enough for us to win the fight if you can collect more from the mountains."

Caeden sighed, his heart aching for yet another reason as he took in his father. It had taken so long for the war to affect him, but now that it had started, it was breaking him quickly. Every time he looked at his father over the past weeks, he looked worse. His voice sounded broken. His shoulders were slumped. The bags beneath his eyes were so dark Caeden wondered if they could ever fade entirely again.

"I'm your father above all else, Caeden," he whispered, and it sounded like whatever he'd been doing to hold himself together had finally shattered. "I worry about you. I'm not trying to keep you from helping our people. I want you to stay safe. It's your duty as the heir to the throne, but you are also my son.

I love you and I want you safe." A tear slipped down his father's cheek and fell onto the wooden desk he sat hunched over.

He sounded so broken.

He hadn't only hurt Eryn when he'd made those choices; he'd broken his father, too.

"I couldn't ask anyone else to risk it," Caeden answered, his voice barely audible. "Ronan only ended up with the ring accidentally. I couldn't ask anyone to go out there when we didn't know for sure that it would work. I didn't tell you because I didn't want to scare you."

It was the first time it had truly occurred to him since he had first planned to use the ring while in the field. He'd known his father would worry, and he'd kept it a secret partly for that reason, along with the possibility of another disguised spy attempting to steal the ring and take it back to the Dragon Lord.

Maybe he'd made the wrong choice. Maybe everything would've worked out better if he'd been honest with him.

More tears streamed from the king's eyes when he glanced up.

"I'm sorry," Caeden whispered, his own tears pooling in the corners of his eyes and blurring his vision as he looked at his father.

The king swallowed hard. "I miss your mother," he said, his voice hitching at the end with a light sob. "And your sister. I miss them so much."

Caeden had only seen him cry once, right when his father had told him what happened at the festival, and that his mother and sister would never return home.

All of the grief, fear, and hurt he felt from their deaths and everything that had taken place over the past weeks hit him at once, and he couldn't hold the tears back anymore. He walked around the desk slowly as silent, warm streaks ran down his cheeks, burning his skin. He approached his father like he would approach a wounded animal in the woods, unsure if he would allow him to help or if he would only lash out.

His father stood as still as a statue when Caeden stepped up beside him and wrapped his arms around him. He felt so thin beneath his thick clothes, and it only made Caeden's heart ache more. The last time he'd embraced his father, the man had been strong and muscular. Now, he felt as frail as someone twice his age.

The king didn't move, and Caeden contemplated simply letting him go and stepping away. Then, he felt his father's sobbing continue, and he hugged him tighter.

Chapter 4

The next few days passed quickly. Eryn began training the new guards with occasional help from Ronan. Caeden joined in a few times, but after his first day sitting in, he realized he'd covered what she was teaching during his own training. If anything, the many books he'd read had gone more in depth.

It was good to sit in and listen to her training. The repetition was helpful, even if he'd learned the material already. It had been a few weeks since he'd last picked up one of those books, and he didn't want to forget the information. After sitting for a few hours with the guards, all of the details from his reading and from her training sessions came back to him.

She only had a few hours each day with the guards, since Ronan wanted to ensure they were well spread throughout the castle during the day. She split them into two groups and alternated between teaching the first group one day and the second group the next. When she'd trained Caeden, they hadn't had much time to work with either, but they'd had around six hours a day. She was assigning reading to the soldiers just like she'd done for him, but they had as much time to complete it as

Caeden had, if not less.

Caeden sat near the edge of the assembled group as Eryn showed off one of her hand-drawn diagrams, this one of a wyvern. She told them about their illusion magic, the songs they sang to the soldiers fighting on the battlefield, and their lack of aggression compared to the other dragon breeds.

He'd chosen to sit out this session and only arrived near the end. As a result, he stood a decent distance away from everyone else. He wanted to hear what Eryn had to say, but didn't want to distract the soldiers. Eryn's voice reached him clearly from where he stood, but only barely.

"A'right!" Ronan called to the group as Eryn finished explaining an overview of wyverns to the guards. "That's the trainin' for today. Go get lunch and be at your posts in an hour!"

The group dispersed, and Caeden approached where Eryn and Ronan stood huddled together, discussing plans for the following day's training. Ronan leaned heavily on his cane, unable to apply much weight to his injured leg after having been on it for most of the day, but that didn't stop the look of frustration from playing clearly across his face as he listened to Eryn.

"I can't make this lesson fit into only four hours," she was telling him as Caeden approached and their words met his ears. "I need at least six for tomorrow. I have to run them through precision, and making sure they can hit moving targets. They can't learn how to hit a dragon's weak spot in only four hours, and I don't have days to dedicate to it."

Ronan sighed, his hand absentmindedly reaching for the flask that, for the first time outside of a court meeting, wasn't hanging from his hip. "I'll see what I can do, but they're on my ass 'bout the schedule since the attack. Thought it'd be better with more guards, but no luck. Didn't care for two years when I told 'em we needed more soldiers guardin' the castle, and now they won't leave me alone 'bout it."

Caeden snorted a laugh, and the two of them turned to face him. "They still wouldn't be listening if we hadn't been attacked."

Ronan rolled his eyes, but a smirk pulled at the corners of his mouth less than a second later. "This is why I drink, princy."

Eryn gave him a look as she crossed her arms over her chest, her eyebrow raised. "Not just so you can get the bravery to sleep with pretty women?"

Caeden laughed as Ronan waved a dismissive hand at her. "You know I never needed alcohol to do that. Besides"—he glanced at the castle to his left, as if he could somehow see Margaid through the stone walls—"I 'specially don't need it for that now."

A blush broke out across Ronan's cheeks as he spoke, and Caeden could practically hear all the words he left unsaid. Caeden gave him permission to be with Margaid before he knew she would end up his only choice left for a wife.

Ronan had a crush on Margaid from the moment they met, and because it hadn't seemed like a big deal at the time, Caeden allowed him to spend his time with her. Since then, his friend and his fiancée had fallen for each other, though he hadn't asked either of them point-blank. It was a subject he preferred to avoid, seeing as how no one outside of their group could ever learn of it. If anyone found out, it would result in serious consequences for all three of them.

Ronan glanced at his injured leg. He tested his weight on it before seeming to decide that it wasn't worth it and balanced his full weight between his uninjured leg and cane. "Mostly just for the pain management now." He said it like a joke, but the pain he referred to wasn't only the physical pain that he was left with after his injury three years ago. It was also the mental anguish he'd suffered after having been tortured at the hands of the Dragon Lord for nearly a month before Eryn had rescued him.

Caeden cracked a smile at the attempted joke either way though, ignoring the darkness that hid beneath it. He pulled a small flask from his pocket and handed it to his friend. "I figured you'd want a drink while you're on your lunch break."

"You're a terrible influence," Eryn muttered as Ronan took the flask and drank at least half of it in one go.

"Says the one who drinks tequila like it's water," Caeden retorted, the grin on his face growing.

Eryn snorted. "At least I don't prioritize it over my training, like some dummy prince I know."

Caeden opened his mouth to argue that he'd gotten his reading done in the end, but Ronan snorting into the flask of whiskey and choking on air as he tried to catch his breath interrupted him.

"It went up my nose!" Ronan whined, unable to quiet his laughter.

Eryn laughed in the way only a sibling ever could as Ronan continued to choke, and Caeden couldn't help it when a laugh escaped him as he watched the two of them.

It took a moment for all three of them to quiet, and Ronan handed him back the flask.

"You say that like ya didn't get the nickname Reckless while drunk off your ass," Ronan said, smirking at her.

Eryn rolled her eyes. "Only because you dragged me into that tavern."

Ronan shrugged innocently. "You have free will. All I did was tell ya where I was goin', and lo and behold, there ya were, right at my side when I walked through the door."

Eryn raised an eyebrow at him before she turned to Caeden,

pulling her dagger from the holster strapped to her thigh in the process. "Hey princy," she whispered, her tone serious despite the mischievous glint hiding in her eyes. "You wanna learn how to gut someone in under a minute?"

Caeden laughed as Ronan held up his hands in surrender. "A'right, a'right. Thought your specialty was killin' dragons, but I ain't testin' that today."

Despite Caeden being sure it wasn't Eryn's intention to make Ronan leave, he sloppily turned on his heel and headed in the direction of his small shack on the far end of the training field.

Margaid wouldn't be there yet, but with the sun setting in a few short hours, she would be sneaking her way through the castle halls, draped in her black cloak, and out to the field soon.

"Do you want to train?" Eryn asked suddenly, catching Caeden by surprise. He turned to face her as she put her dagger back in its holster. "I have free time in the evenings since I get so little time with the guards. You're finished with the basics, but you still almost died in the field and during the attack. And since I'm stuck here, anyway." She shrugged a single shoulder, her ocean-blue eyes meeting his emerald ones through thick eyelashes.

A time not long ago when she would've given anything to avoid training him—or even looking at him, for that matter—popped to the forefront of his thoughts.

He hadn't liked her very much at first either, but he'd grown fond of her fast. And now, well, he knew he had feelings for her, but he still wasn't sure what that meant, or if it could mean anything at all.

"Sure," Caeden responded, not sure what else to say. He needed to learn everything he could from her before she was sent back to the field for good. He'd managed to gain extra time to learn from her since she'd offered to train the castle guards, but he doubted he'd get that lucky again.

He wanted to train with her, but that wasn't the thought nagging at him as she grabbed her bow and arrow from where they sat haphazardly on the ground nearby and shouldered both. He wanted to talk to her again. He wasn't sure what good would come from it, or if anything could, but he wanted to know where he stood with her.

As much as he wanted to speak to her, he held his tongue as they walked to the archery range on the far side of the field, opposite the castle. Only five targets were set up, likely because the others were still being repaired before the soldiers would need them in the coming days. The weapons in the armory, along with the targets and other equipment set up, hadn't been used in three years, since the last round of soldiers were brought to the castle for training. He'd broken more than a few of the things himself over the couple years he and Ronan had trained together in secret, too.

Eryn nudged him in the shoulder with the end of her bow, and he took it from her.

"Let's see if the break you had somehow made something click in that head of yours," she said, as she unshouldered the quiver of arrows and handed it to him.

Caeden snorted a laugh and readied the bow and arrow in his hands before hearing Ronan's words from weeks ago replay in his mind. He widened his stance before aiming the arrow at the center mark of the target.

For a moment, he remembered how he had felt in the field when he'd been fighting against the Deovarian soldier. When the world slipped away and it was just him against his attacker. His movements had felt automatic, his muscles remembering the things he'd learned when practicing with Eryn and putting them into action before his mind had time to register he was doing it.

Maybe he could do something similar with the bow and arrow. He focused his gaze on the center of the target, allowing everything else to fade away. He ignored the birds chirping in the trees. He ignored the way his leg throbbed from the still-not-fully-healed stab wound he'd sustained several weeks ago. He let the world fall away momentarily, until all he could see was the dot on the target.

For a moment, he did it, but then the moment ended and his concentration broke.

Lavender.

Eryn's scent filled his lungs, leaving his mind hazy as his thoughts filled with only her. Her scent made it as hard to focus as the strongest alcohols Ronan kept in his shack.

He could feel her gaze on him as the memories of their night in the safe room resurfaced. The way she'd laid her head on his chest.

But then the darker moments sprang forward, pushing past the memories of how his heart had raced and how perfectly she'd fit into his arms.

The blood he'd woken up covered in from the wound across her ribs. The sword protruding from her shoulder. Her slurred words. Her cold hands on him. Her pale face as her eyes had closed. He'd worried he'd never see her open them again.

Caeden cleared his throat, shaking himself from his thoughts. He lowered his bow as he turned to face Eryn.

The doctors cleared her after they returned from the field. They'd said her wound wasn't infected, and that it only needed time to heal. She'd been gentle with it since getting injured, and it would be difficult for her to get worse at this point in her recovery.

"Where's your head at, princy?" Eryn snapped, her usual

impatience making its way into her voice.

He'd never wished he could avoid a question as much as he wished he could every time she asked him that.

He cleared his throat. "Could you step back a little?"

Eryn frowned. Confusion settled over her features, momentarily replacing the irritation. "Why?"

"Just… please?" he asked, not wanting to give away where his thoughts had been. She knew he worried about her, but there was something very different about her knowing it and him outright telling her. Especially since he shouldn't care for her like he did.

He was marrying Margaid.

Caeden expected Eryn to argue with him, but instead, she only looked more confused as she took several steps away.

He turned back to the target again. It was harder now to push away the thoughts, but with her being farther away, her scent didn't distract him. After an agonizingly long moment, he focused his full attention on the center of the target and drew the bowstring back again.

Caeden loosed the arrow, and for only the second time since Eryn first arrived at the castle to train him, the arrow struck the center of the target.

Eryn whooped behind him as he stared wide-eyed at the target and the arrow he'd shot.

Before he moved to face her, he felt her arms wrap around his neck as she crashed into him, laughing happily. She released him just long enough for him to turn around. "Finally!"

Caeden's face warmed as he slowly hugged her back. He tried not to think about how perfectly she felt against him when he stepped away from her a second later.

Eryn's smile was wide when his eyes focused on her face, and her bright blue eyes shone with a kind of happiness that made him feel like he could do anything.

"Eryn," he said, not allowing himself enough time to think better of it.

Her smile faded slightly. She expected him to be happy about his accomplishment like she was, but he couldn't find the ability to give it a second thought when all he could think about was her.

"Is something wrong?" She looked concerned, and he caught the twitch of her hand as she started to reach for him before she pulled it back to her side.

"I…"

Whatever words he was going to say died on the tip of his tongue as one of the soldiers approached them from behind Eryn.

Eryn noticed when his attention shifted, and turned around to face the young man as he called for her from across the field. She turned back and offered Caeden an apologetic smile. "Talk later?"

Caeden swallowed hard. Part of him hated the distraction, given that he hadn't had time to talk with her in nearly two weeks, but another part of him was glad, considering he wasn't sure what he hoped to achieve.

"Yeah," he agreed. "Thank you for the extra practice."

She grinned. "The extra three minutes?"

Caeden nervously rubbed his hand over the back of his neck, but a smile pulled at his own lips. "Every second of it."

Chapter 5

Caeden made his way to his sister's bedroom late that night. It took him an hour to finish painting the walls in her favorite shade of yellow, like he'd planned to do weeks ago in time for the anniversary of her and their mother's deaths. He was late, but he hoped that if she could've been here today, she would've appreciated the project being finished.

He reorganized the paint cans and brushes into a neat pile like they'd been when he arrived. They'd sat beside the large, floor-to-ceiling window that overlooked the training field outside ever since she died and the painters abandoned their project. He caught a glimpse out the window as he set one of the cans down on top of another, and he saw Eryn training one of the groups of soldiers.

She and Ronan must have worked out the schedule so she would have the time she needed. She probably wasn't happy about it, given that it was dark out now and the only lighting was from the torches set up every ten or so yards away from one another.

They'd trained in the dark every day when it was just the two of them, and nearly every one of those days a complaint had slipped from her lips. It was the worst right before his official engagement ceremony. He'd promised to spend extra time with the two princesses who remained in the castle, which left him with only a few hours after dinner for training.

Images of a very similar setup flashed through his mind as he watched Eryn in the field with the soldiers. She fought with the soldier who had come to find her earlier in the day, swords glinting in the air as she ruthlessly threw blow after blow in such quick succession, he was barely able to defend against them. The others practiced throwing daggers at small wooden boards that other soldiers threw into the air for them.

It hadn't been light out either when he'd watched her train during a class the previous Head of Security put on a few years ago. He hadn't paid attention to any of the individual faces, but it was hard not to notice her long black hair in the group.

Most soldiers—both male and female—either cut their hair short or kept it up in a tight bun when training. She'd worn hers loose or in a sloppy ponytail the whole time, just like she still did. He remembered thinking it was going to hinder her abilities when she'd stepped up to practice with the teacher, and then being surprised when she didn't make a single one of the mistakes he'd been expecting.

He'd watched dozens of training groups by then, which was the only reason he knew what to look for. The group Eryn was in had been the last one brought to the castle before the man retired and Ronan took over. They hadn't had a new group of soldiers come to the castle since then.

Caeden had tried to learn what he could from watching their techniques, but too much time passed between the last group and when he and Ronan had started training together for him to remember many of the lessons he'd watched. The books he'd read hadn't been the same as physically doing it, either.

A light knock came on the door to his sister's old room, and just as his eyes snapped to the doorway, Ronan pushed it open and hobbled inside. His steps were slow as he approached from the other end of the room, and though he tried to hide it, Caeden noticed how his leg troubled him by the way he leaned on his cane and shifted his weight to the opposite side.

"We spyin'?" Ronan asked with a light chuckle as he stepped up beside Caeden and peered out the window.

"Painting," Caeden answered, gesturing to the still-damp wall to their left.

"Paintin' as an excuse to spy then, got it." Ronan glanced at him as a sly smile pulled at the corners of his mouth, clearly looking for a reaction.

Caeden rolled his eyes, doing his best not to give one, even as his heart rate sped up at the implications that were hidden beneath Ronan's words. He hadn't told his friend how he felt about Eryn, but he was sure he'd noticed, just like Caeden's father had. "I'm not spying," he told him. "I just glanced out the window while putting the cans away. I got stuck when I remembered seeing Eryn training out there one time when I really was spying."

Ronan laughed, startling Caeden.

"Too pretty of a face for ya to forget about?" Ronan teased, wiggling his eyebrows suggestively before pulling his flask from his hip and taking a long drink from it.

The heat in Caeden's face grew tenfold, and he was thankful for the darkness blanketing them. Hopefully, Ronan wouldn't be able to see the crimson coating his cheeks through it.

"She wears her hair loose," Caeden said, ignoring Ronan. "Not many soldiers do."

Ronan shrugged, a chuckle escaping him while he did. "Yeah,

she's cocky like that."

Ronan offered him the flask, and Caeden took it despite his better judgment. He planned to be up early in the morning and sneak in some practice with the throwing knives before Eryn needed the field to train the soldiers. He wasn't good at knife throwing, and he needed to be much better before he would feel comfortable wielding the weapons against an enemy. The chances that he'd get up early enough after putting alcohol into his body at this hour were slim, which he only realized after gulping down multiple mouthfuls of the peach-flavored brandy he'd taken a liking to.

"So," Ronan started as he sat down cross-legged on the floor, tossing his cane haphazardly to one side, "what's goin' on with the two of ya?"

Caeden raised an eyebrow at him, even as his heart skipped a beat in his chest. "What do you mean?"

Ronan fixed him with a look that was eerily similar to the one Eryn was so good at. "You and Eryn have been off ever since the field. I can't read her with this sorta thing 'cause this is new, but I know ya like her, so spill."

Caeden sighed and glanced out the window again. Eryn stood at the edge of the training field now, her dagger in her hand. She tossed it up into the air and caught it between her thumb and first finger, a trick he'd watched her do countless times, yet it still impressed him. She continued to play with the dagger as she watched her trainees practice with daggers of their own. Most hit their targets well, but only the ones who managed to land it perfectly received any praise from their Dragon Hunter trainer.

"We had—" Caeden paused, searching for the right words to describe whatever it was he and Eryn had during their training session out on the battlefield. "A talk of sorts in the field."

"Oh?" Ronan asked, his eyebrows disappearing into his

honey-colored curls hanging down over his forehead. His hair had grown in the past few months, and it was longer now than Caeden had ever seen.

Caeden shrugged a shoulder and leaned against the wall directly next to the window so he could see Eryn outside. He pulled Ronan's flask to his lips again and swallowed another mouthful before handing it back.

"I like her, she likes me, *maybe*. Her words. She was mad that I said anything at all because I'm engaged to Margaid, but I don't know if she still is or not. The attack started right before we got a chance to say much else, and she was hurt, so I haven't brought it up again." He swallowed hard, his eyes flicking to Eryn outside again before settling back on Ronan's face. "I don't know if it's worth bringing it up. Enough people have already been hurt in various ways because of the decision I made."

Ronan's smile was tight, and Caeden's chest ached at the sight. Hurting his friend was the last thing he ever wanted to do. He'd told Ronan it was fine for him to pursue Margaid if he wanted to, but he hadn't expected at the time that both of his other options for a wife would opt to leave. He should've seen it coming, with how distant Ceana was and with how Kylana felt ignored, but he hadn't. Kylana had all but laughed in his face when he'd attempted to propose to her as a last resort so he wouldn't have to hurt his friend.

Ronan shrugged, a sympathetic look on his face. "I wish I had some advice for ya, but I haven't exactly been engaged to a woman and had feelin's for an entirely different one."

Caeden sighed. "I'd give just about anything to break off this damn engagement," he mumbled, though the words weren't as true as he wished they were.

He could've opted out of marrying Margaid, but it would've cost his kingdom the soldiers, and they desperately needed more people if they were going to have any chance in this war, though at this point, it likely still wouldn't be enough. He wouldn't sacrifice his people's lives for it. He hadn't been willing to attempt to prolong the decision and find another solution because it would've cost more lives.

Ronan nodded and held out the flask to him again. "More alcohol to drown your sorrows? Always works for me."

Caeden snorted a laugh, but took the flask from his friend, regardless.

Chapter 6

Eryn swirled her tequila in her glass absentmindedly, the clear liquid nearly spilling over the edge multiple times in the span of a few seconds. Caeden was dimly aware that he shouldn't be staring at her or anything she was doing so openly, but with the alcohol in his blood dulling his thoughts, it was hard to care.

He still hadn't talked to her. Each time he'd wanted to bring it up since their last conversation, he'd either thought better of it or they'd been interrupted again. He still wasn't sure what he wanted to say to her, and when he realized a week ago that bringing it up without having a solution would get him nowhere and likely leave her as frustrated as she'd been with him on the battlefield, he stopped trying. He either needed to figure out a solution or forget what was said between them.

The latter was simpler, but so far it had proved harder than he wished.

Caeden sat on the far end of the couch beside Ronan, who was pressed up against Margaid, leaving him with nearly half of the couch to himself. Eryn was perched on the edge of the glass coffee table, halfway between him and Ronan, and close enough to both of them that one of each of their knees would brush hers if they shifted.

Ronan, Margaid, and Eryn were talking, but Caeden had tuned out of the conversation when his focus got stuck on Eryn.

A splash of tequila finally spilled over the edge of her glass, and she glanced at her now-wet hand.

"Fuck," she swore beneath her breath as she set the glass down and licked the alcohol off the back of her hand. "Can't let that go to waste."

Ronan laughed. "Damn, Reckless. You could do what normal people do and get a napkin from the kitchen, but instead you've gotta bring your uncivilized ass in here and do that."

Margaid gave him a sideways glance. "I don't believe you wouldn't have done the exact same thing."

Ronan shrugged. "I probably would've, but that doesn't mean she's gotta act like an animal in my house."

"Isn't the first time, won't be the last." Eryn grinned. "Even when you try to escape me by taking a job at the castle, you'll never truly get rid of me."

"And I tried so hard, too," Ronan said with a dramatic sigh as he sank deeper into the couch. The movement jerked Caeden's attention back to the real world and away from the way Eryn's sweat-soaked tank top clung to the curves of her hips.

"Where's your head at this time, princy?" Eryn asked teasingly, the hint of a smile pulling at the corners of her mouth. "His drama isn't ever that surprising."

Caeden fought the urge to shake his head to clear the fog away. It was ridiculous how good she was at catching him every time he was focused only on her.

"The mountains," he lied, but he was sure the others weren't oblivious. No one pointed it out, though. "We only have three more days until we're supposed to leave."

"Yeah." Eryn sighed. She tested her shoulder and winced before she even rotated it halfway. "It's gonna be fun."

"Buzzkill," Ronan muttered beneath his breath. Margaid swatted his arm, and he laughed.

Caeden heard his friend's words, but he couldn't focus on them. His mind drifted back to the battlefield again. To the sword sticking out of Eryn's shoulder. Her scream that had pierced the air, causing him to trip and drop the ring.

Had his mother sounded like that when she'd been killed? If he hadn't been so close to Eryn when it happened, would she have been the next person he cared for to die by the hands of a Deovarian soldier?

The thought made bile rise in the back of his throat, and he swallowed hard.

Any of them in that room could die in the next few days. Maybe not by the hands of the Deovarian soldiers, but by the cold up in the mountains, or by the dragons who resided within them. Could he watch Ronan, his best friend of nearly three years, meet that fate? Or Margaid? He didn't love her like he should've loved his fiancée, but he cared about her.

His fingers found the ring through the fabric of his pants as Ronan and Margaid teasingly bickered about whether Margaid's small swat could be considered abuse. He traced the jagged edges absentmindedly, his thoughts still racing until a hand came down on top of his and he froze.

Caeden glanced up, and his eyes met Eryn's. She offered him a tight smile and squeezed his fingers between her own, drawing his attention away from the ring in his pocket. Lavender filled his senses, mingling with the faint tequila on her breath. It left his thoughts hazier than the alcohol in his veins ever could.

Her eyes were all he saw. The deepest blue that he wanted nothing more than to drown in for the rest of his life.

"We're going to be all right," she whispered, her thumb making slow circles over the back of his palm, burning his skin in a way that left him craving more.

He didn't believe the words entirely, but between her scent and the whiskey he'd had to drink, his mind was too foggy to argue.

♥ ♥ ♥

"Caeden! Caeden, wake up!" someone whisper-yelled while shaking his shoulder so violently that he nearly tumbled out of his bed.

Margaid's bright red hair was the first thing he saw when he opened his eyes. His head throbbed terribly from the start of a hangover, though he wasn't quite sober yet.

Caeden shook himself. His eyes focused on her face in the dim light from the moon and stars outside for a split second before her features swam in front of his eyes and he tried again. He barely had time to register that it was odd for her to be in his room, especially in the middle of the night, before she was yanking on his arm and pulling him from beneath the covers.

"Come on," she hissed back at him, worry and fear etched into every inch of her face. "They'll find us. We have to hurry."

She pushed open his bedroom door and he stumbled after her, unable to form a coherent thought through the haze.

He shook his head again as she pulled him through the halls, clinging to the edges and peeking her head around each corner before dragging him along behind her into the next hall, and the next after that.

She was scared, but he couldn't think clearly enough to discern what was causing it as he stumbled after her.

"What's going on?" He slurred the words horribly, and he

shook his head again. Why couldn't he talk? He hadn't drunk enough to still be out of it.

"The Deovarians," Margaid whispered, her words rushed and urgent. She was breathing heavily, her eyes wild as she glanced around again. "We're under attack."

That wasn't what he'd expected to hear.

For a split second, the fog cleared and his mind raced back to the last time the Dragon Lord and his men attacked them. He and Eryn had snuck through the Grand Hall just like they were doing now. They'd ran past soldiers in the halls. They'd fought off more than Caeden cared to remember. The dragon had roared in the distance as they'd sealed themselves into the safe room.

"It's quiet," he said, the haze blurring his thoughts again and ridding him of the fear he was dimly aware he should have felt. "They can't attack if it's quiet."

She gave him a confused look over her shoulder, and it took Caeden a moment to realize he hadn't said the words he'd intended.

He shook his head for what felt like the hundredth time and rubbed his temples with the thumb and forefinger of his free hand. "It's too quiet. If we were being attacked, it would be louder."

The words were just as slurred as his others, but at least they made more sense. Or at least, he hoped they did.

"They've already taken most of the castle. The fighting has slowed. Ronan found me and told me to get you. They're coming to this side next."

Caeden frowned. He'd slept through an entire attack and hadn't even stirred. How much had he had to drink? He must have blacked out before he'd even left Ronan's shack.

As he thought over the events of earlier that night though,

he couldn't find any missing pieces. He remembered everything clearly. He even remembered climbing into bed and falling asleep. He'd come back to his room late, and since he, his father, and Margaid hadn't continued to have regular meals together, his food was waiting for him. He'd eaten and gone to sleep.

The missing piece clicked into place, though it wasn't where he'd expected it to be.

"They drugged me," he slurred as he continued to stumble after the princess. "The food. I didn't drink a lot. Had to have been the food. Right?" He cringed at his own words, even as the panic he should've felt long ago washed over him.

They were under attack again.

The Deovarians had drugged him so he would be out cold while they overtook the castle.

Were they planning to kill him and his father while they slept? Was that why he and his father weren't being escorted somewhere by the castle's guards together? Had they drugged them both so they could overtake the castle without giving anyone time to come up with a plan to fend them off?

His head spun, and he lost his balance. He tripped and fell, his head connecting with the tile floor and sending a wave of agony ten times worse than the hangover flooding through him.

"Caeden!" Margaid hissed quietly, bending down to tug on his arm again. "We have to go. We really have to go."

His movements were difficult, and he slipped when he tried to stand. Whatever the Deovarians had drugged him with was still taking effect, and the haziness was becoming harder and harder to push through with every second.

It took three attempts before he was finally able to pull himself to his feet.

Pain split the back of his skull, reverberating through his bones. He was dimly aware that nothing should have been above him that he would've hit his head on as his vision went dark.

Chapter 7

Eryn

Eryn tossed her dagger into the air over her head as she lay in bed late that night. She watched it spin end over end through the air before she caught it between her thumb and first finger.

"Hmm," she hummed to herself, as she took in how close the tip of the dagger had come to her stomach. Good thing she hadn't missed this time.

She'd come back from Ronan's shack hours ago, but sleep hadn't yet found its way to her. She was still buzzed from the alcohol, but the drunkenness had worn off. She hadn't had a lot to drink, all things considered, compared to the others. She still had to train the guards tomorrow and couldn't risk being hungover for it.

The way the alcohol turned her stomach toward the end wasn't what kept her up, though. Her mess-up in front of Ronan and Margaid was what had her mind racing since she'd returned to the solidarity of her room.

She shouldn't have grabbed his hand. He was worried, and she cared for him enough to try to ease those worries, but that had been a step too far. She should've made a joke and handed him more alcohol to calm his nerves like she would've any other person. She shouldn't have shown that kind of affection, especially not when others could see.

But the way his skin had felt against hers…

She'd felt something when she'd touched him before, but she hadn't been expecting it earlier that night. She hadn't even expected to touch him until she caught herself with her hand placed over his. But she had felt something. That same something that she never should've felt for the man she'd been brought here to train; Aericora's future king.

Maybe that same feeling was what made her get out of bed and wander through the halls toward Caeden's room without so much as a second thought.

Eryn took a deep breath and rapped her knuckles against the door. She stood anxiously, fidgeting with the hilt of the dagger strapped to her thigh, but even after several minutes, there was no response.

She waited a few more before she decided it wouldn't feel too rushed to knock again. When no answer came the second time either, her burning impatience took over, and she pushed the door open. His room was dark inside, but she could make out the outline of his large bed, a bookshelf against one wall, and a writing desk with countless papers tossed haphazardly atop it. Aside from the writing desk, his things were neatly organized as if he'd never touched anything other than some of the books on the bookshelf.

Eryn closed the door quietly behind herself before she tiptoed over to the edge of his bed. She didn't even make it all the way across the room before her eyes adjusted to the darkness and she made out the askew sheets. Caeden wasn't in his bed. There was a raised portion of sheets on the bed she had thought was him when she'd first entered the room, but she'd been wrong. It was only the comforter that looked as if it had been hastily tossed to the side when he'd gotten up.

That was strange. It was the middle of the night.

Worry pooled in the pit of her stomach, but she pushed it away, blaming it on the cloud blurring her mind from a combination of being tired and the remaining alcohol in her system. She left his room and went out to the training field. The only places she'd ever seen him so late at night were out training, or in Ronan's shack. It wasn't likely he'd gone back to see Ronan, considering they'd been there earlier, so she checked the training field first.

It was cool outside when she opened the small wooden door. A shiver ran down her spine as the breeze washed over her, tousling the ends of her loose hair. No sound reached her when she walked through the seemingly empty field, and there was no sign that Caeden had been out here at all. She wandered to the opposite end of the field and tried the door to the armory. She gave it a hard tug, but it didn't budge. It was locked, just like she'd left it earlier in the evening.

Maybe he really had gone back to see Ronan.

She glanced at Ronan's shack for the first time since she came outside, but the lights were dim. Not all of the candles were blown out, but she knew she would never see him sleep in total darkness again.

Her heart pounded loudly in her ears at the sight of the dim lights. He wouldn't be there. Dim lights meant Ronan was already asleep. But where else would he have gone?

Despite herself, Eryn ran across the field as images she would've done anything to never see flashed through her mind. The fear she'd seen in his eyes during the first attack. The soldier standing over him, ready to make the killing strike. The knife in his leg. His back to her as he ran off to test their theory about the ring.

None of those things were happening now.

They were within the castle walls. The chances of the Dragon Lord getting in again after so many guards were stationed here were nearly impossible, never mind how extremely unlikely it was since they'd just attacked during Caeden's betrothal ceremony.

She took in a deep breath as she reached the door to Ronan's shack and knocked. Wherever Caeden was, he was fine.

Of course, he was fine.

Ronan's muffled groan reached her through the thin walls of the shack. "I'm comin'!" he called, his voice raspy from sleep. His bare feet padded against the floor in time with his wooden cane.

The door opened a moment later and her shirtless brother stood before her, his hair a tousled mess on top of his head and his eyes only half open. The anxiety working through her made it impossible to worry about having woken him.

"He's not here," Eryn said, taking Ronan in. The words weren't a question.

Ronan blinked at her, his brow furrowing in confusion. "Who? The princy?"

Eryn nodded, her eyes flicking to the door that led into the castle. He must still be inside. But where inside if not his room? "He wasn't in his room, and he's not out here. I thought he might have come back to see you."

He raised an eyebrow at her, his lips quirking to one side despite the tiredness written across his face. "Worried about the princy again, I see."

Eryn rolled her eyes. "I'm not worried about him," she snapped, but even she could hear the lie in her words. "I just need to talk to him and I can't find him."

Ronan gave her a knowing look, and it struck her for the first time that he was able to see right through her. He'd teased her relentlessly plenty of times before, but this was the first time she was seeing this kind of look on his face—the kind that told her he *knew*. There was nothing teasing hidden in this expression. Nothing that told her he was trying to get under her skin because of a suspicion he had. There was only love there, worry, and maybe even a bit of pity. He'd seen her slip up earlier that night, and no matter what she said or did now, he knew exactly how she felt about Aericora's prince.

Eryn's face heated against her will.

"And it can't wait till mornin'?" Ronan asked, stifling a yawn as he leaned his full weight against the doorframe.

Eryn shook her head. "No."

Another lie. It could easily wait until morning. She'd put off talking with him for weeks, and one more day wouldn't change anything. But her worry was too much. She needed to know where he was. She needed to know he was safe. She wasn't sure when she'd started caring about him enough to worry, but she did. And despite whatever these feelings for him were, she was still his teacher—still one of Aericora's soldiers. She was responsible for him.

Ronan groaned and dropped his forehead against the edge of the door. "Always so damn impatient. Thought you grew outta that."

"Are you going to help me find him, or are you going to stand there and give me one of your talks about my personality traits that, as I continue to remind you, saved your life? Kind of thought you grew out of those, too."

He smirked. "Ya thought I would, but here we are."

She rolled her eyes. "Where else could he be?"

"Hang on." He sighed and stood up straight. "Lemme at least get a shirt, and I'll help you look for him."

Ronan disappeared back inside. She waited for him impatiently, tapping her foot rhythmically against the damp grass as images she wished she could ignore swirled through her mind again.

Eryn tried to shove them away. He was safe. Caeden was somewhere inside the castle, and he was safe.

No matter how much she tried to convince herself though, the nagging doubt in the back of her mind wouldn't quiet.

"A'right, let's get this over with so I can get back to sleep," Ronan grumbled when he returned, this time fully dressed.

The two of them split up to search the castle. Ronan took the kitchen, where he said Caeden enjoyed sneaking to once in a while when he wanted a drink or a snack, along with the hallway where the king's office and meeting room were. Eryn began in the garden before she planned to search the library. Aside from those few places, they couldn't think of many others where Caeden was likely to spend his time.

After searching both the garden and the library and coming up with nothing, Eryn waited for Ronan near the castle's grand entrance. It was the only place halfway between where they searched that wouldn't disrupt anyone in the castle.

She twirled her dagger between her fingers as she paced impatiently through the large space. Ronan would've found him if she hadn't, but when she heard the distinct sound of Ronan's footsteps and cane approaching without the sound of a second set of feet against the floor, her stomach plummeted.

"No luck," Ronan said with a shrug. He was playing it off as though the situation wasn't serious, but she could see the slight pinch to his lips that told her he was worried, too.

Despite her personal reasons for worrying, Caeden was still

the heir to the throne. If he was anyone else and had been missing for a few hours, it wouldn't be concerning, but he wasn't. He was important. He was the next ruler of their kingdom.

Even if all she could focus on was her worry for a man who made her heart race when his eyes met hers.

"We have to wake the king," Eryn said, slipping back into the role she was comfortable with. She may have been a girl with a crush, but she was a soldier first. She was a First Rank Dragon Hunter. She'd learned to push her feelings aside when they didn't help a situation long ago. She'd done it with Ronan when she'd saved him from the Dragon Lord, and she would do it now.

An agonizing two hours later, the king sat at his desk with his hands clasped firmly in front of him, his back straight. Despite the calm façade the king put on in front of the gathered court members, Eryn saw the tears threatening to spill from his eyes as he delivered the words she'd been dreading to hear.

"Prince Caeden is missing."

Pain sliced through her chest as his words cut her heart in half.

She'd been trying to convince herself that he was fine. He was somewhere in the castle, and he was safe.

He wasn't, though. They'd woken every one of the castle's staff and searched the entire place up and down for the past hour and a half. They'd practically turned the place inside out, and Caeden was nowhere to be found. Neither was Margaid, which caused the same look of anguish she was sure she wore on her face to cross over Ronan's when he heard the news.

It didn't take long for the court to come to the same conclusion that Eryn had suspected since she'd first found his bed empty: Caeden had been taken by the Dragon Lord.

"There must have been more spies," Muire stated calmly, as if the situation was barely a minor inconvenience.

Eryn could've shoved her dagger through the woman's chest had she not prepared herself for exactly that tone from her. She'd gone through the same thing with Ronan. Ronan wasn't the heir to the throne, but she'd known before coming into this that despite Caeden's title, there would be court members who wouldn't be bothered by his disappearance.

If Aericora didn't have a future ruler, then one of them would be the next choice. They would be given the entire kingdom once the king could no longer rule. It was the only logical way to ensure there was still a competent ruler, and none of these people would be here if they weren't at least a little power hungry.

The king nodded, but his words were quiet when he spoke. "They've taken both Prince Caeden and Princess Margaid. My best guess is that they either wanted to…" He paused for a moment, and his next words were strained when they left his lips. "Remove Aericora's next rulers entirely, or they want something else from us, and are using them as a bargaining chip."

"Likely the second," one of the other courtiers said. Eryn couldn't tell who it was, with how they were all crammed into the small space.

"There were no signs of forced entry," Ronan stated. He'd fallen back into his own familiar role, but Eryn could hear the pain beneath his voice, despite the tone he tried to convey and the stiff way he stood. His face had been pale since they first learned Margaid had disappeared as well, and it hadn't faded.

"Also no sign of a struggle from either of 'em. They must've known whoever took 'em, but we haven't figured out who it was yet. We're roundin' up the servants now, but there were a lotta new hires, according to Teafa. It's gonna take some time."

Eryn balled her hands into fists, her right hand falling around the hilt of her dagger, gripping it tightly. Whoever was responsible was going to meet the end of her blade.

Chapter 8

Ronan

Ronan stared up at the ceiling. The court had opted to wait and see what the Dragon Lord had to say about Margaid and Caeden's disappearance. The only guess anyone could make was that they'd been kidnapped to use as a bargaining chip, and the court would rather wait to hear if Deovaria would send a proposal offering them the two royals back before planning a rescue mission.

He hadn't unclenched his fists since he left the court meeting earlier that night. He cared about Margaid, but he hadn't been able to admit to himself that he'd fallen in love with her until he'd heard she was missing along with his best friend.

He hadn't realized how much she meant to him, how much he relied on her being around each evening to get through his days. He'd taken her presence for granted. Even though he'd known their days together were numbered, he hadn't appreciated them like he should have.

He should've told her he loved her rather than being afraid and assuming he would be able to do it the following evening, or the evening after that.

He had tried to dull the pain with whiskey earlier that night, but after he poured the glass, he hadn't been able to drink it. No matter how much he wanted an escape, the alcohol wouldn't provide it. He was sober now, and had been since before Eryn had woken him up with that panicked look on her face. He'd thought it was an overreaction until less than half an hour later.

Eryn would be going crazy, and as much as he disliked the court's decision—as much as he wanted to lose himself in the insanity every bit of him begged to give in to and run after the woman he loved—he had to keep his head straight. He had to be here for Eryn, to keep her from doing the same things that had crossed his mind countless times.

She was on the couch in his living room, likely still awake like he was.

She'd paced around for hours until she finally lay down, the light creaking of the couch beneath her weight confirming that the lack of her steps against the floorboards didn't mean she'd slipped out the front door when he wasn't paying attention.

He'd been grateful for her pacing earlier. Silent tears still rolled down his cheeks, but earlier—when he couldn't keep them as silent as he wanted—the light thumping of her footsteps was enough to drown out his sobs as he thought of the red-haired princess who held his heart, even if she never should've.

Chapter 9

Caeden's head throbbed with an intensity that felt like an ax was splitting his skull. Bright sunlight assaulted his eyes before he even opened them fully. He lay in the back of an open wagon. The only things he could see were the worn wooden slats and the glaring sky above.

He blinked repeatedly as he took in the ropes encircling his wrists and ankles, binding him so tightly he couldn't do much of anything. The sound of horses' hooves against the uneven ground sent mild stabs of pain through his head in time with the jostling of the wagon. His body thumped against the wood beneath him, which only added to the pain.

Bits and pieces of memories drifted back to him. He remembered drinking in the shack with his friends, and Margaid waking him up in the middle of the night.

He shook his head, trying to push through the haze wrapped around his thoughts.

Margaid was scared.

They'd been under attack.

He'd hit his head when he'd stood after tripping over his own feet.

Or maybe, he hadn't hit his head after all.

He glanced around the wagon again, and fear seized him as the full realization of his situation sank in. He'd been kidnapped. He'd been taken from the castle, and was who-knew-how far away.

He'd felt foggy-headed when Margaid woke him. He'd had a bit to drink with Ronan and the others, but not so much that his head should've still been spinning when she found him. But then he'd remembered the dinner waiting for him when he'd returned to his room.

It hadn't tasted how he expected. He'd assumed it was because he was drunk. He shouldn't have written it off so quickly. His father had been poisoned once before, and though Eryn had been training him for weeks, they hadn't gotten to that category.

Where was Margaid, though? The kidnapper would've needed to take her with. She would've seen everything.

Unless they hadn't.

Bile rose in the back of his throat as images of what likely happened to her since she wasn't in the back of the wagon with him flooded his head.

They could've easily killed her and left her there. It wouldn't have been a good plan, considering that leaving a dead body behind would alert the kingdom immediately to what happened, but it had been the middle of the night and no one would've found her until first light.

"About time you woke up," a voice from the front of the wagon called.

Caeden blinked in the direction of the driver, trying to see any details through the sunlight assaulting his eyes. All he could make out was a dark cloak.

That voice, though.

He knew that voice, but he was still so out of it from whatever he'd been drugged with that he couldn't place it.

He groaned as he sat up, the world spinning around him with another wave of pain. Leaning back against the edge of the wagon, he tried to massage his temples with his fingers. The ropes binding his wrists made it more difficult than he expected, but not impossible.

"If you'd just given in to the sedative, that headache would be ten times better than it is," the driver said, amusement clinging to her tone.

Her. It was a woman driving the wagon.

She shrugged, still facing ahead. He hadn't seen when she turned to look back at him, or he could've figured out who she was by now. "I came prepared, though," she continued, holding out a long pole that looked like it was cut away from the handle of a castle servant's mop. "Drunks always hold out longer against the sedative, so I wasn't surprised."

"Where are you taking me?" Caeden said through gritted teeth. Anger burned in his veins, and the restraints she'd put on him combined with the cloud hanging over his thoughts only stoked the flames. "Where's Margaid?"

The wagon jolted to a stop, and he fell onto his side. The driver's laugh rang in his ears when the agony in his head dulled again. She laughed so loud and long that she clutched her stomach as she doubled over from it. "I know Eryn calls you 'dummy' all the time, but I didn't think she meant it so literally."

Caeden's stomach felt like it dropped through his body to the ground beneath.

She turned around and pushed the hood of her cloak back with the broken mop handle, revealing a smirk and a head of curly red hair.

Caeden's head spun, but for an entirely different reason this time. What reason did the Princess of Crevia have for betraying and kidnapping him?

"There it is," Margaid crooned, as if she could somehow read his thoughts. "She didn't have any reason, because I'm not actually Margaid. Remember that lovely little sob story about how I was attacked on the road to Aericora? That wasn't all a lie. I just wasn't the one who got attacked." She shrugged a single shoulder, as if it was a simple miscommunication. "Poor girl was sweet, but I couldn't have her running back to her little kingdom and ruining the whole plan. I made it quick. I disguised myself as her and played the part once I got back to the carriage. It wasn't hard to convince the carriage driver I'd escaped the mad woman who dragged me into the woods, since apparently, the real Margaid had some military training up her sleeves. Wasn't enough to save her, though. Then it was off to the castle to get information out of you."

He swallowed hard, his mind racing. Margaid—no, not Margaid, some crazy woman who worked for the Dragon Lord and disguised herself to look identical to the Princess from Crevia and pretended to be her until she'd turned into his fiancée—turned back to face the road ahead of them and jolted the horses into a trot.

The pieces slowly clicked together as they rode down the path. He remembered the odd sort of determination he'd seen on her face the first day they'd met, the way she always clenched the ruby necklace at her throat when she was anxious, how she'd known all the details of his mother's death and why she'd used them to connect with him. It explained the questions she'd asked; the eager curiosity he always saw lighting her face when he'd answered those questions.

"I honestly thought you would've figured it out sooner," the mad woman continued. She clucked her tongue, feigning disappointment. "I certainly didn't think I'd be here this long. It was only supposed to be a week. I was supposed to make those girls dislike you, then leave. Not end up your only damn option left. Aside from the other *benefits*, I even created a whole relationship with your best friend to avoid that happening." She shuddered lightly. "A fake betrothal is one thing, as disturbing as that whole scene was, but I would've been sent down to the dungeons and executed before that wedding or… well, you'll get it soon enough."

Caeden clenched his bound hands into fists so tight he felt the warmth of his own blood seeping beneath his fingernails as they bit into his skin. Her rambling did nothing to ease his headache. "You never answered my question," he snapped, every ounce of anger making its way into his tone.

"Oh, princy." The mad woman sighed. She shook her head as if disappointed he was asking. "I'm taking you to the Dragon Lord."

Chapter 10

Caeden wasn't sure how long he'd been unconscious by the time he woke in the back of the wagon, but considering they only traveled two more days when they finally reached the front gates of Deovaria's palace, it must have been a few days.

They'd traveled nearly nonstop, only taking a few hours each night for the madwoman to nap, and occasional breaks along the trail for the horses. Caeden tried to get away each time she slept, but it proved useless. He'd gotten the bindings off once, but she'd heard him and promptly put them back on. He'd tried to run, but was exhausted after his body fought off the sedative. Now that tiredness was also combined with the weakness from his lack of food. She'd given him water to drink, but he hadn't so much as glimpsed anything edible since he'd woken the first time. The water alone wasn't enough to give him the energy to fight her off when she caught him trying to escape.

They'd entered Deovaria a day and a half ago, but only around twelve hours ago had Caeden started to see signs of starving citizens like Eryn had told him about. The towns were broken down, and most of the people living in them wore worn clothing. Stores were stocked with minimal food, and the food they did have was either stale or on the verge of growing mold.

The only sign any of the small villages had any sort of wealth was the grand dragon statues constructed at the entrance to each one. They were lavish; each one was at least three stories high. They were built of pristine crystal, and he couldn't make out a speck of dirt on any they passed.

Despite the lack of food and finery in each town, cakes, gems, jewelry, and even large bouquets of wildflowers were laid at the base of each statue in tribute to the large beasts the townspeople worshipped.

The contrast between the towns and the palace was staggering. Where the towns were rundown, the palace was easily twenty stories tall, and made entirely from black marble that glittered purple hues in the bright sunlight. Large windows lined the walls, showing off grand ballrooms and pristinely decorated hallways.

If the Dragon Lord claimed that the favor he was supposedly granted by the dragons had led to all of the finery he lived in, it made sense why Eryn's town wanted to make a sacrifice to the creatures living in the Rayfait Mountains.

The gates outside of the palace were painted black to match the high walls; dragons' heads carved from amethyst rested atop each end. Deovaria's purple and red crest depicting a dragon's wing rested at the center of each of the two large gates.

It struck him for the first time how similar Deovaria's crest looked to the golden Dragon Hunter pin Eryn wore.

Two guards dressed in full battle armor blocked the entrance with two spears crossed over one another when the wagon approached

The mad woman sighed. "Let us in," she stated simply, flashing the ruby necklace resting at her throat. "We have an audience with the Dragon Lord."

The two guards glanced at one another before exchanging a slight nod, and opening the gates to allow the redheaded wagon driver and her captive inside.

She parked outside the palace's main entrance. The large dragon heads painted onto the doors stared down at them as she unlocked the back of the wagon and yanked Caeden out by his bound wrists.

She was stronger than he'd expected, but given that she was disguised in the body of an entirely different woman, Caeden wondered if there was anything about her that hadn't been a lie.

He couldn't keep his footing for more than a second when his feet hit the ground due to the bindings still tied around his ankles. His face connected with the hard dirt, and blood poured down the side of his face from a gash he'd sustained during the fall. He turned onto his back and glared up at the woman.

She smirked before pulling a dagger from a holster beneath the hem of her long dress. "Seeing as I don't feel like dragging you all the way up there," she stated, nodding at the staircase leading up to the palace entrance. Whatever she was about to say was cut short as she flicked her wrist, sending the dagger flying from between her fingers toward the rope binding his ankles.

Caeden forced himself not to flinch as the ropes tightened painfully before the dagger sliced through them and embedded itself into the ground between his feet. He stared up at her instead, refusing to break eye contact. She was toying with him, and he wouldn't let her win. "Would it have been so difficult to untie the rope?" he asked lazily, his tone indifferent despite the fear that hadn't stopped working its way through him since he'd woken in the back of the wagon. He could feel his resolve dwindling after the days of travel, but he couldn't let her get to

him.

He'd tried to come up with a plan to escape, but his few ideas had all failed, and now that he was fully in his enemy's territory, there was no possible way he could see out.

The only thing keeping him sane was that they clearly didn't want him dead. If they did, the woman standing before him would've killed him a long time ago. No, whatever their plan for him was, it wasn't death.

That fact only made it slightly easier to fake boredom each time she pulled something like the knife trick.

The woman's smirk widened, and despite the disguise she still wore, she looked nothing like the redheaded woman he'd had to propose to a few weeks ago.

Everything she'd done to get him here, lying bound on the ground at her feet, struck him all at once. She'd killed the real Princess Margaid, she'd stolen her identity and pretended to be her for weeks, she'd lied to him and tried to manipulate him into giving her information, which he likely had, though he couldn't remember how much he could've accidentally let slip.

And Ronan.

His heart broke for everything his friend would feel when he found out the truth.

Ronan had never outright said so, but he had fallen in love with the woman standing before Caeden now, even if she hadn't truly been real. He hadn't fallen for the real person behind the freckled face and red hair. He'd fallen for a woman who didn't exist; a woman who had been murdered before he'd even met her impostor.

"I know you can walk," the fake Margaid snapped. She bent down and grabbed the rope securing his wrists, yanking him up to his feet.

She was barely up to his shoulders when they were standing

side by side, yet she lifted him with hardly any visible signs of a struggle.

He glared at her with what he hoped was the kind of intensity Eryn always managed. She was so small, yet she held every advantage in this situation. He could try to fight her, but his hands were bound. He hadn't seen her abilities with a sword or her fists, but they wouldn't be lacking if she'd been assigned to kidnap him, even if it hadn't been her original mission. He was good at hand-to-hand fighting now—good enough to win against Eryn occasionally, at least—but that was when he could use all of his limbs, never mind the stab wound in his thigh that had yet to fully heal itself since he'd refused to rest after he first got it.

The woman yanked him a step closer, and Caeden tripped over his own feet. She glared at him, but the same look of amusement quickly replaced it. "If you think you're going to somehow escape, I'm afraid you're sorely mistaken, Prince."

"If you think trying to intimidate me is going to keep me in line, I think I've given you the wrong impression," he said, keeping the same easy tone he'd used since she took him hostage.

"That's right. I forgot you're only afraid of women you have a crush on." A smug grin sat upon her lips, and despite how much he tried to hide it, pink covered his face at the mention of Eryn. Her smirk widened, and she pulled him close enough that he felt her breath against his ear when she spoke. "Give me too much trouble, and I might make her my next guest in the dungeon."

Caeden stilled as her threat rang in his ears, sending ice through his veins. He swallowed hard. Eryn would never be as oblivious as he was. If they tried to take her, she would catch on to it long before they got her too far from help. She was smarter than he was. She was more capable, too. Even if they managed to get her alone, she could fend them off.

She was safe. They couldn't hurt her.

"Captain," a voice called from the top of the large staircase. A guard stood there, clad fully in battle armor identical to what was worn by the soldiers at the front gates.

The woman's grip loosened on Caeden's bound wrists, and he stepped as far away from her as he could.

Making no attempt to fight her had been the right choice. She didn't look it with her disguise, but she was better trained than nearly everyone else in Deovaria would be. She wasn't just another spy or soldier. She was the captain of Deovaria's army.

"The Dragon Lord is ready to meet with you," the guard informed her.

The woman nodded once. She looked to another guard standing a few paces away before she shoved Caeden forward. He stumbled to the ground again, this time hitting his head hard against the bottom step of the staircase.

Stars drifted across his vision as his head collided with the marble, and pain radiated through his skull and down his spine.

"Escort the prince," she ordered, her words like ice against Caeden's skin. "I've dealt with him long enough."

Both guards nodded to the woman before hurrying down the steps and yanking Caeden up to his feet again. His head spun as his body was forced upright too quickly, but he refused to show it as she offered him one final glance over her shoulder before she walked ahead of him and the two guards.

The guards dragged him up the stairs behind her. He couldn't get his footing with the rough treatment, and his shins connected with the edges of the steps repeatedly, bursts of pain erupting through his legs each time. By the time they reached the top of the steps, he wasn't entirely sure he could stand on his own anymore, and he was almost thankful that they didn't give him the opportunity to try. Instead, they continued to forcefully pull him through the hallways.

How had Ronan survived through his time here? Caeden wasn't even being tortured and already he could feel himself breaking with each failed attempt to get his feet under himself. He was trapped, but he grasped onto the fact that they wanted him alive. No matter what they did to him moving forward, they wouldn't kill him unless they couldn't use him for whatever they were planning. Ronan hadn't had the same luxury. He'd likely heard the dying screams of his fellow soldiers who'd been taken to the dungeons with him. He'd likely thought his own death was next after he'd heard each one of them take their last breaths.

The throne room wasn't far from the palace's main entrance. They walked down a long hallway directly into what Caeden assumed were the doors to the Grand Hall before they veered left. The throne room's entrance was on the opposite end, only a short distance away from the entrance to the Grand Hall. Chandeliers hung above their heads every few yards to light the expansive space, and expensive paintings of dragons and small statues resembling those built at the entrance of each of the towns they'd passed rested along the walls.

The guards slowed enough for Caeden to get his feet beneath him as the front of the throne room came into view. One of the doors was propped open, silently beckoning them inside.

The Dragon Lord sat somewhere behind the open door.

The man who had killed his mother and sister, who had tortured his best friend for a month, who had brainwashed the people of Deovaria so much that it led to the woman he cared for being abandoned up in the frigid mountains as a sacrifice to the dragons lurking inside.

More anger flared through him as the thoughts pressed in like a vice—images of what the cruel man sitting somewhere behind that open door did to those he loved.

There was no way he could kill the Dragon Lord in the confines of his own palace while he was alone and weaponless. He would suffer an arrow to the back, an ax to the neck, a sword to his throat. But if he got the chance, he wasn't so sure he could stop himself from trying despite the risks.

"Move it, Prince," the guard hissed at him, kicking him in the back of the knee so he fell forward once again. Without his feet beneath him to keep him planted where he was, the guards dragged him forward again.

The woman who kidnapped him walked through the door first, followed by the guards, who carried Caeden's limp and bruised body between them.

Caeden's eyes landed on the Dragon Lord immediately, as if he knew the exact layout of the inside of the room and where the cruel king would be. He sat in a large, amethyst throne that swallowed him. Like everything else in the palace, a dragon's head was carved above where the Dragon Lord sat, fire pouring from its mouth and falling down the arms of the large chair, as if caressing the man sitting in it. Large spikes of stone jutted out in every direction on top, creating the vague shape of an unfinished crown that looked strikingly similar to the one resting atop the Dragon Lord's head.

"The mission is complete, Father," the woman said, bowing her head to the Dragon Lord. Her voice was even and sure, but her hands were visibly shaking at her sides. A hint of amusement curled Caeden's lips.

The woman may have been the Dragon Lord's daughter, but she clearly wasn't above his cruelty. She was likely just as brainwashed as everyone else in the kingdom to see past his actions. The Dragon Lord had ordered her to do everything that led to Caeden standing here, but it didn't ease the satisfaction he felt from watching the woman's demeanor change from cool and collected to nothing more than a cowering soldier who was all too aware of the power her king held over her.

She was aware of his cruelty, yet she still shrank beneath it and obeyed his every command.

The Dragon Lord waved his daughter off, hardly sparing her a glance before his emerald eyes landed on Caeden. A slow smile spread across the Dragon Lord's face. "Welcome, nephew. It's good to finally meet you." His voice carried through the room, striking Caeden like a blade through his chest.

Chapter 11

Caeden's heart raced as the words replayed in his mind.

He was lying. Neither of Caeden's parents had siblings. He couldn't have a long-lost uncle. Especially not the man sitting in front of him.

But then Ceana's words from weeks ago resurfaced. The Dragon Lord had a sister before he'd assumed the throne. She disappeared from Deovaria's history right before the Dragon Lord took over ruling the kingdom.

She'd disappeared from their history right before Caeden's mother and father got married.

The Dragon Lord offered him a smile. It was gentler than anything he thought the man was capable of, and something about it sparked another flare of rage inside him. "I assure you, though you may not believe me, I am your uncle, Caeden." He said the words so easily as he leaned back into his enormous throne.

Caeden tried to come up with a reason—any reason—why the man before him would come up with that sort of lie, but he couldn't. There was no benefit he would get from telling Caeden that information, regardless of the truth. Being related to the man in front of him didn't make Caeden want to shove a sword through his chest any less than he had when he'd walked through the throne room's doors.

Caeden took a deep breath in and let it out, doing his best to ensure the others wouldn't notice when he did.

The Dragon Lord gave a slight nod, and the guards on either side of him released their hold. They shoved him forward hard enough that he once again fell forward against the marble floor. The gash he'd gotten on his cheek only a few moments ago reopened, and blood dripped down the side of his face.

His cheek burned as he lifted his head, the copper taste of more blood pooling in his mouth. He spat it onto the floor in front of him, feeling a mild wave of satisfaction as he noticed the faint pinch to the Dragon Lord's lips.

"Is telling me that supposed to make me hate you less?" Caeden snapped. His bound hands made it hard to get to his feet, especially with the pain still radiating through his legs, never mind the starvation making his entire body weak. That didn't stop him from shoving his way up into a standing position, though.

The Dragon Lord let out a low chuckle. "Feisty young thing, aren't you?"

The woman huffed beside Caeden, and he suppressed a grin. He hadn't been able to get to her the whole way here, but her father didn't even have to try before she grew visibly agitated. She was the captain of his military, but she was still only his errand girl, even if she was his daughter. Caeden didn't need to see anything other than the way she stood to know that for certain.

"On the contrary, I'm hoping it will make you more susceptible to accepting my proposal."

"I find that possibility unlikely," Caeden said through clenched teeth, his hands balled into tight fists that made the ropes around his wrists bite into his skin.

The Dragon Lord waved the guards away, and the door shut softly behind Caeden as they left the room. He never took his eyes off the Dragon Lord. "You see, your mother and I were never very close, but we had an arrangement when we were younger. She wanted the throne, and I wanted to travel to the mountains to study the dragons. It was a fine plan for years. I knew she would be better with our people than I was capable of being, and I was far better suited to increasing our kingdom's knowledge, starting with the Rayfait Mountains and the secrets they hold. That all changed when she met Aillin, though."

The Dragon Lord said Caeden's father's name with a bitterness that suggested it left a bad taste in his mouth.

"I was summoned back from the mountains to rule Deovaria, but I lacked the training necessary to do so. Your mother spent the last ten years learning the ins and outs of ruling, while I shied away from it because of our deal. I hadn't yet learned much from the mountains when she left, but my people were starving. I prolonged it as long as possible, but we decided to war with Soborg to expand our borders. I hoped to find a magic up in the mountains that could help my people grow enough food to survive, or at least to find enough relics to sell to other kingdoms to grow our wealth. All we found were more of the gems that allowed us control over the dragons, as I've heard you and your friends have done as well. I'd learned of them before then, of course, but that knowledge hadn't proved useful until years later.

"The people started to rebel when that plan failed, but they've always held a deep love of the dragons. It wasn't hard to convince them that the dragons' magic could grant extraordinary favors. It boosted morale and kept them from blaming their suffering on me. They decided on their own that I was untouchable because I held the dragons' favor. I didn't go out of my way to correct them, since it gave us more time to find a solution.

"I arranged to meet with Anna at the festival in Silran. I wanted to rule our kingdoms together—tap into some of Aericora's wealth to help my own people and in exchange we would live under Aericora's flag, so long as she agreed that I would retain a sizable say over what happens to my people." The Dragon Lord sighed heavily, as if lost in a distant memory, before shaking his head disappointedly at whatever happened that day. "She laughed in my face, calling us a charity case that she long ago escaped. She told me we may have grown up together, but that the well-being of Deovaria was no longer her responsibility. That she had a family now in Aericora that needed her, and that taking on the responsibility of a whole separate kingdom and their safety wasn't something Aericora could handle. Lies. Aericora could've handled it very easily. She didn't want to give up her control over the land. And well, you know what happened next."

The Dragon Lord shrugged a single shoulder, as if it was an unfortunate turn of events that couldn't be avoided, when murdering his sister in cold blood most certainly could've been.

"I hope that you will see more sense than your mother," he continued. "I'm offering you a very similar arrangement. Seeing as you and your kingdom are already losing this war, I want primary control over the joined kingdoms. I'll allow you to remain on my council. However, Aillin will have to go, seeing how he would never allow that to happen. But after him, no one else will have to die. We can end this war right here and now, nephew."

Caeden wanted to scoff at him. "Your people are

brainwashed," he snapped, his words coming out louder than he'd intended them to, fueled by the anger he felt at every word that passed through his uncle's lips. "They believe the dragons will save them after all of this is over—that you're some sort of saint because you can control them. I don't understand how they haven't seen through your twisted lies or how they can think anything will ever be okay with you leading them. You claim you have no riches, yet you sit here surrounded by precious stones and gems that you could sell and your people could gather from the mountains now that you've overtaken Soborg. But instead, you sit here, wanting to take over my kingdom because you're too lazy to find a real solution on your own. Or is it even that? There are a thousand other things you could do, yet you choose to war with us because my mother refused you."

The Dragon Lord rose to his feet, his glare boring right into Caeden as he stepped down from the dais and closer to the prince. "My people were starving long before I assumed the throne." His words were a deadly whisper in the surrounding space. "My people needed something to believe in, and the dragons were the easiest to turn to. It's the only thing that's kept them from rioting and killing each other, especially since they believe me to be so powerful after I revealed the powers of the gems. I can't send my already starving people off to the mountains to die. Because they will die. They are too weak—too frail. If they aren't killed from the physical labor, they will freeze in the cold."

"If you really cared about your people," Caeden hissed, his tone matching his uncle's, "you wouldn't care who ruled the kingdom as long as they were safe. If you really cared about your people and weren't only spinning lies, you wouldn't require that my father be killed before any deal can be reached. If you really cared, you wouldn't have started a war that puts your people in harm's way every single day. You would've tried to work something out with my mother if that was the real reason you went to that festival. You wouldn't have killed her. You only did that because she went back on your arrangement. You only did that out of pure spite and nothing more."

The words struck him as they fell from his lips, and he fought to keep the surprise and fear from showing on his face.

His heart pounded loudly in his ears, and he fought to ignore it; to push down the feelings welling inside until he wasn't standing face-to-face with his enemy.

His uncle did all of that for revenge.

It wasn't the same kind of revenge that Caeden wanted against him for murdering his mother and sister, but it was a mirror of it. The Dragon Lord killed his sister because she'd wronged him; because she'd gone back on their arrangement and thrust an entire kingdom he'd never wanted into his hands. And now Caeden wanted revenge against him for having done it.

He thought back to his time with the princesses, and how he chose the one who was a disguised spy because he didn't take the time he should've to get to know them. All because he was too blinded by his want to kill the man now standing before him.

A slow smile spread across the Dragon Lord's face, and fear spiked through Caeden's veins. As much as he'd tried to hide it, his uncle saw the expression that crossed over his face. He didn't say anything about it when he continued, though. "I want my people safe, Caeden," he said slowly, deliberately, as if Caeden hadn't already seen the lies hidden beneath those words. Maybe there was some truth laced in there as well, but it certainly wasn't the Dragon Lord's reason for going to war with Caeden's kingdom. "But I will not see that Aillin is the one to rule them when he can't even rule his own people. Less than half of

Aericora even receives any kind of real assistance from the castle unless they are literally dying. I will not turn my kingdom over to a man who is so occupied with a single war that he can't ensure his people's needs are met while he does it. And you?" His smile turned to a smirk. "Well, you can't even seem to find the time to entertain three women properly, so I imagine you wouldn't be any better."

The barb in the words hit him harder than he wished it would've.

The woman, Caeden's cousin, snorted a laugh beside him.

Disgust flared through him as he glanced at her, still wearing the red hair of the woman his entire kingdom expected him to marry, and her words from when he'd woken in the wagon resurfaced.

As disturbing as the situation was, at least she'd made it clear she never would've allowed the situation to become any worse.

A shudder ran through him, and he forced the thoughts away before turning back to the Dragon Lord.

His reasoning wasn't as sound as it seemed, considering he acted as if he wasn't also unable to tend to the needs of his people, even before the war started. At least Caeden's father did his best to send aid when he knew his people needed it. The Dragon Lord let his people starve for so long that a family traveled up into the mountains and attempted to sacrifice their daughter to the dragons to fill their empty stomachs. And while knowing that was happening, he opted to go to war with a second kingdom.

Caeden shook his head. "You're mad if you think I will ever turn my kingdom over to you," he spat. "You think my father is a terrible ruler, but it seems you haven't taken a good look at your kingdom, or a look in the mirror."

The Dragon Lord sighed and took a step away from him. "It

seems you haven't taken a good look at your own, either."

Something about his words sent a chill through Caeden's bones. He knew his father sent money to the towns to aid them. He'd been in the meetings when it was discussed. He'd helped determine just how much would be sent, who would transport it, and when the transport would leave. Yet, the Dragon Lord spoke as if Caeden's people were suffering. Was there something else going on that he was missing? Were the Deovarians interfering with the transfer of money and supplies as well? But if they were, why wouldn't the Dragon Lord come out and say so? Why blame it on Caeden's father instead?

The questions swirled in his mind, making him dizzy. He wanted to sit down. This was all too much. He knew he shouldn't believe the words of the madman standing before him, yet something about the way they were said gave him pause. He'd been kidnapped less than a week ago, been tied up in the back of a wagon the whole way here, practically starved, would be imprisoned for who knew how long, and was now offered a second arrangement in only a few months.

He couldn't agree to the Dragon Lord's terms, though. He wouldn't. If this was how the Dragon Lord chose to rule his kingdom—if this was what he'd resorted to in the name of keeping his people safe—he wasn't fit for the role. He wasn't fit to rule a kingdom, and he would leave Caeden's people far worse off than its current ruler ever could.

Caeden shook his head, clearing away the haze, the confusion, the anger, and the fear mingling together inside of him. "You're mad," he whispered, not having any other words. "I won't agree to those terms."

The Dragon Lord shrugged. "I didn't think you would so easily." He turned to his daughter, still standing silently beside them with her hands clasped stiffly behind her back. She still wore the disguise of the dead princess, and the wide-eyed look she gave her father when she noticed his attention on her was so strangely familiar it made Caeden's heart hurt.

The woman standing there with the red hair and the ruby necklace around her throat wasn't the woman he'd grown to be friends with. She wasn't the woman his best friend fell in love with.

"Dealla, escort the prince to his room for the night. Maybe a night of rest will help him see reason."

The Dragon Lord turned away from him, and Dealla grabbed him roughly by his bound wrists. It would take much more than a night in a dungeon cell before he would ever sentence his people to a living nightmare, and his father to death.

Chapter 12

Dealla pulled him through the halls and to the dungeon in the same manner as the guards who dragged him inside. He stumbled repeatedly, barely catching his footing since she refused to slow. The only reason his shins weren't taking a beating this time was because there was only one of her, and fully dragging him along by herself would've been more difficult than letting him walk. Though he was sure if she wanted to, she would've.

Unlike any other palace Caeden had heard of, their dungeon was near the top story of one of the highest towers.

An escape from this high up would likely be harder than one from the basement, considering if he were to attempt one, he would need to go down ten stories before he would reach the ground floor. And would likely be caught long before making it all the way there.

"Lucky you," Dealla muttered as she reached to light an oil lamp hanging on the wall at the top of the staircase. It wasn't as dark as a basement dungeon would've been, but it still lacked proper lighting compared to the rest of the palace. "You get one of the special rooms."

Caeden glanced at her, only able to make out the red curls framing her face in the dim light of the lamp. "What's that supposed to mean?" he said in the most bored tone he could manage.

His wrists hurt from being yanked by the bindings, the coarse rope biting into his already raw skin every time she pulled him or he moved. His body ached from spending so many hours in the back of the wagon. His head throbbed from a combination of the lack of food and likely still from the sedative she'd dosed him with.

"You'll get to see the space your friend spent his time in while he was here," she answered. She tried to make her voice sound light and cheery, but he heard the lump in the back of her throat.

Caeden swallowed hard, a new kind of fear settling deep into his bones.

She wasn't just taking him to any dungeon cell. She was taking him to the rooms where they tortured soldiers they took from the field. She was taking him to the room where the Dragon Lord had kept Ronan and beaten him so badly he was barely lucid from blood loss and starvation when Eryn finally rescued him. The same space where he'd lost his ability to walk properly because his leg was shot clean through with an arrow.

Three doors waited for them at the top of the stairs, and a single guard was posted outside. The doors were made of thick metal, with a small window cut into the center of each with bars to ensure no one tried to escape through the opening. Not that they could, even if they tried.

A shutter was attached to the door so they could easily leave the prisoners alone in total darkness.

That was why Ronan's shack was always lit.

Caeden's stomach clenched, and bile rose in the back of his

mouth.

Caeden had known that he was afraid of the dark, but he never knew exactly why. He was afraid of the dark because they'd left him alone in a pitch-black room between bouts of beating him half to death.

"Cell number two," Dealla told the guard, her words clipped and her tone ice cold.

The guard moved to the center cell, selecting a key from the ring tied to his belt before opening the door and stepping aside.

Dealla ushered him forward, but Caeden's legs were suddenly too heavy to carry the weight of his own body. He felt sick; his body felt weak and limp. He closed his eyes tightly, and the world spun. She dragged him forward and into the cell, the only indication they'd passed through the doorway the sudden echoes of their footsteps against the stone floor.

Dealla kicked him in the back of the knee, and Caeden tumbled forward. He caught himself, but his bound hands did little to ease his fall. His palms scraped against the floor, jagged stone biting into his skin and making his hands damp with his own blood.

He dared to open his eyes as he sat up, and his heart stopped. Blood.

There was so much blood.

The walls were covered in it. The floor was stained with it. The whole room *smelled* like it.

His stomach turned again, and Caeden doubled over against the floor. He heaved, but his empty stomach had nothing to offer but bitter acid as he coughed. His breaths came in short, shallow gasps as he spat the foul liquid from his mouth. His eyes darted around the room again, meeting the same countless red splotches he'd seen before.

The stones were chipped in places, and the blood that

smeared those areas was thicker.

They'd tried to escape. The soldiers who were in these cells went so mad they'd tried to claw their way out.

Something else caught his eye in the very corner of the cell on the back right side. There were scratches in the stones, but they weren't done by someone making a futile attempt at escape. Instead, a small rock sat beside the scratch marks, even more blood-covered than the rest of the space. The tip was worn, and the size matched the scratches in the stone walls, but with the darkness around, Caeden couldn't make out what the scratches were.

"Most of this was courtesy of your friend," Dealla said, her tone still holding the false lightness it had when she'd spoken of Ronan the first time. "He held out far better than any other soldier I've tortured, I'll give him that. I was so close to cracking him when that godforsaken Dragon Hunter you love so much took him."

Images filled his mind as she spoke. A bloody Ronan with injuries that matched the soldier who was dropped at the castle gates. He clutched the small rock in his damp, scarlet hands, sitting pressed into the corner as he scratched nonsense into the stone walls.

He'd been here. He'd been in here for a month.

How had he survived?

"You're a monster," Caeden spat, whipping around to face her. He pulled himself to his feet despite his still-bound hands.

He couldn't fight against her and win—he could hardly do anything without a weapon and with his hands bound together. But he didn't care. He didn't care if she killed him. He didn't care if she beat him as badly as she had his best friend.

He needed her to pay for what she'd done. He needed her to feel the pain she'd inflicted on a man who never deserved such horrors.

Something flickered in Dealla's eyes then, but Caeden was too angry to care or take the time to decipher what he'd seen. "It's war," she said, her voice stern, as if trying to convince herself as much as she was him. He hadn't seen her unsure of her words aside from when she spoke to her father, but he was seeing it now. "This is my job. Anyone else would do the same if their king had asked it of them."

Caeden shook his head, a maniacal laugh leaving his mouth. He wasn't sure where it came from, but in that moment, he didn't care. The last of his resolve crumbled as the panic he'd felt since waking in the wagon turned to nothing more than blinding anger.

He wanted blood for what they'd done.

He wanted her blood.

Without allowing himself time to think, he lunged for her, his hands balled into tight fists that connected with the side of her face before she could duck away.

Dealla stumbled back, spitting blood from her mouth. Her lip was split and bleeding, her cheek already puffy from the hit.

Seeing her like that felt good. It was wrong, but she deserved it. She deserved so much more after everything she'd done.

She'd killed an innocent woman in the woods. She'd tortured his friend—tortured hundreds of others. She deserved so much more than he could ever do to her with his bound wrists.

Caeden lunged again, but Dealla was anticipating it this time. He was being reckless. His moves weren't calculated. They were sporadic, sloppy, and she was waiting for every single one of them.

He didn't even care.

She blocked his fist when he tried to punch her in the stomach, grabbed his ankle when he tried to kick her, and landed hit after hit when he tried to dodge beneath them. She knocked him to the floor quickly, his breaths coming in short gasps as pain flared through his stomach from the kick she'd landed there a second before.

But the pain didn't stop him.

He was back on his feet before realizing what he was doing. He tried to kick her again, but she grabbed his leg and punched him in the face before his hit connected. Stars broke out across his vision, distorting Dealla's face as she shoved him to the ground again.

He forced himself back to his feet, only to be knocked to the ground just as quickly. They repeated that cycle at least ten times before Dealla finally grew fed up with him, and Caeden's body was so bloody and bruised he wasn't sure he could stand.

"Enough!" Dealla shouted. Aside from her lip and cheek, he'd failed to land any other hits. The only other sign they'd fought was her raw and bloody knuckles. "Stay down, before I have to break both of your legs to keep you there."

If it weren't for the fact that he couldn't get up on his own, he would've ignored her.

She turned to walk away as Caeden finally pulled himself up against the wall. "Were you there?" he demanded. The blood pooling in his mouth made his words nearly impossible to understand.

Dealla turned back and looked at him over her shoulder, confusion hiding behind her bright green eyes that were nearly identical to her father's—identical to Caeden's.

Caeden spat blood from his mouth. "Were you there?" he demanded.

He needed to know. He needed to know if she'd had a hand in killing his mother and sister, too.

"I'm not a mind reader," she told him evenly. "Was I where?"

"The festival," he snapped. "Were you there? Did you kill them?"

Something flashed in Dealla's eyes, the only sign she felt anything at all, but the look vanished before he could place what he'd seen. Instead, a smug smile curved her lips. She reached behind her neck and unclasped the necklace hanging there before letting it fall away from her skin.

All at once, her disguise faded, revealing a woman who looked eerily similar to the way he remembered his sister. She had the same eyes—the ones most of Caeden's family seemed to share and that the disguise clearly couldn't hide—but there were other things, too... Things that only Caeden's mother and sister had. She had the same blond hair, the same arch to her nose, the same V shape in the center of her upper lip, the same dusting of freckles across her cheeks, nose, and forehead that were so faint they were easy to miss. She could've been Amelia's twin, if Amelia had lived to be a woman in her early twenties.

"I was too young to be there," she said, knocking Caeden from his trance and back into the cruel, real world where his sister was gone, and the woman standing before him wasn't her or Margaid, but his cousin he hadn't known existed until she'd kidnapped him and thrown him into a prison cell covered in his best friend's blood.

She said the words so softly, and if her eyes weren't a window into her true emotions in the same way Eryn's were, he might have missed the sadness on her face. It was an apology of sorts, though if she hadn't been there, it didn't matter whether she apologized.

"You look just like her," Caeden whispered, his voice cracking as the words left his lips. Tears he hadn't felt prick his eyes silently fell down his face, stinging his split cheek.

He hadn't cried in front of anyone in so long, and he wasn't sure if it was the fact that she looked like his sister, or if it was because of everything that had happened in the past few days that caused it now. Whatever the reason, they poured down his cheeks. He wasn't able to stop them or muster up enough strength to care to try. Instead, the longer he sat there, the faster they fell.

As memories began to surface, the silent tears turned to pained sobbing. It was the kind that shook his entire body, made his chest ache, and his breathing come in short, shallow gasps that would never be enough to fill his lungs no matter how hard he tried. This was a sadness that swallowed him from the inside out and kept him paralyzed there on the floor, sobs shaking his entire body as his cries echoed against the blood-covered stone walls.

He wasn't sure when Dealla left him alone in the cell, but when his sobbing finally calmed, he was surrounded by only silence and utter darkness.

Chapter 13

Dealla

Dealla pushed the door to her father's office open without bothering to knock. It wasn't like he would answer if she tried to, anyway. "The prince is in his cell," she said, her tone even despite the nervousness she'd felt since being back in the palace.

It'd been months since she'd been home, and the fact had worked its way under her skin in a way that left her feeling on edge from the moment she pulled the wagon up to the front gates.

The Dragon Lord gave a single, stiff nod, but didn't turn away from whatever he'd been working on before she'd entered. Instead, his gaze remained focused on his work on top of his large desk. There were a few stacks of paper, but his desk was mostly covered in mini dragon sculptures—just like the rest of the palace—carved from the mysterious stones from the Rayfait Mountains. The purple stones that made up his crown were the same, but their magical abilities were far from as strong as the blue ones, or the red one she currently held in her hand.

Frustration flared through her when her father didn't so

much as glance up.

She'd been gone for months on a mission that could've seen her hanged at any turn, yet he couldn't be bothered to bat an eye in her direction.

She shouldn't have been surprised. It had been like this ever since she was young. She'd never known the luxury of having a father who praised her accomplishments, even when she spent every waking moment of every day doing what he asked of her, and then some, in an attempt to earn that pride from him.

It hadn't been enough. It never would be, but she wasn't sure why it still angered her when she'd accepted it long ago.

Dealla tried to push down the anger, but she didn't stop herself from marching straight to her father's desk and slamming the necklace down on the edge of it.

She flinched despite herself when her hand connected with the wooden desk, preparing for the glare that would eat into her very soul when he looked up at her.

The Dragon Lord set his pen down slowly before turning to face her, rage flaring in his green eyes.

She shouldn't have done that. She should've bitten her tongue and walked away.

The mistake was already made, though.

"He didn't believe you," Dealla said, the edge to her tone she'd tried to have faltering before she got the first words out. Instead, she said them gently, like a child afraid of being too loud and waking the monster lurking beneath their bed.

She wasn't afraid of him. She would never consider herself afraid of him, but she did respect him. He was her father—her king—and the respect she held for him was the same as anyone else in Deovaria.

"He will, soon enough," her father said calmly, despite the fire still raging behind his eyes.

She wanted to protest. She wanted to point out that there was hardly anything to believe. There had been truth in her father's words, but lies laced everything he'd told the prince. He was trying to scare him into agreeing to the deal, but Caeden hadn't fallen for it. He may have been an idiot who hadn't seen through her despite the numerous times he should've, but he wasn't dumb enough to believe her father outright.

"The cell will help," Dealla said, pushing away the feelings that welled inside of her when she thought about that cell and the man it held three years ago. "But I don't think it will be enough for him to agree. He agreed to marry one of the princesses in exchange for training from Eryn Gedding. He wants to kill you for his mother's and sister's deaths. He's not going to agree to his father being put to death as well."

"She'll change his mind," her father said easily, as if Dealla's concerns were irrelevant. He turned back to the papers on his desk and picked up his pen once again. "We'll give him a few days in the cell first, but once he sees her, he'll change his mind."

Dealla swallowed hard. It was cruel, but it would likely work. Maybe not right away, but eventually. If he came to his senses, maybe he would agree that the end of the war would be worth it, even if he would be trading his father's life to get it.

"Very well," she said stiffly, letting the necklace fall from her hand and stepping away from his desk, leaving the glowing red gem sitting on the edge. "When will you take him to her?"

"A few days. Four or five, depending on how he's behaving. I'll let you know when." He waved her off without looking at her again.

Dealla gritted her teeth, but took the hint. She turned on her heel and strode from the room.

Chapter 14
Eryn

Eryn's nails dug into her palms, stinging as she listened to the King's Court speak so casually about Caeden's disappearance over a week ago. They had argued like this already after both royals had disappeared, only to wind up deciding to wait and see if Deovaria would send a proposal for their release. Nothing had come yet.

"We should wait longer," Muire stated, her tone even, as if the prince's life wasn't the one they were debating saving or letting the Deovarians do with as they pleased. "It takes time for a message like that to travel. They would've had to take them to the palace before the Dragon Lord could send out a message to begin with. It could be another few days still before we hear anything. And if we send out a rescue party now, we may only end up making the Deovarians feel backed into a corner and kill them."

"Or they're already dead," Ronan muttered, his words nearly drowned out by the other members of the court who shared the same opinion.

Eryn glanced at him. He'd been quiet since Caeden and Margaid's disappearance, only speaking when necessary. He was holding it together for her, just like he always did. He always played the part of the one who was strong; who could get through any situation, even if it killed him. Even when it required him to drink himself to the brink of death to keep up the façade.

This was the first time she'd heard him utter something like that since last week, and though part of her was glad to see he wasn't entirely bottling it up anymore, it also worried her. If he was saying things like that, he truly wasn't as okay as he pretended to be. At what point would he break so much that the cracks would be beyond repair?

"We've already waited so long they've probably killed them both!" Fionn yelled. He was a military man who likely wanted to be out fighting to get his kingdom's prince back as badly as Eryn did, though her reasoning wasn't as straightforward as Fionn's would be.

She felt his words deep in her heart, making her stomach clench at the thought. It was possible Caeden was already dead; it was equally possible that they'd killed him and Margaid rather than doing anything else with them. Though it was unlikely a spy had snuck into the castle to kidnap the prince and his fiancée only to kill them in the forest just outside of the castle walls. If that were the case, they would've tried to kill the king, too. No, whatever the reason they'd taken the two of them, it wasn't to kill them. At least, not immediately.

They had time, but every day that passed made the weight crushing against Eryn's chest grow increasingly heavy. It was hard to catch her breath when she thought about Caeden, bloody and tied up in a cell like she'd found Ronan multiple years ago.

"It makes no sense for them to do that," Muire argued, still as calm as before. "No attempt was made on the king's life, and given that the spy was so well hidden that we haven't uncovered who it was, they could've easily killed the prince and princess in their sleep and left the castle. It would've been easier than sneaking them both out."

"And what if they don't send a messenger?" Ronan asked, surprising Eryn again. His words were sharp. He tried to keep himself calm, and from ripping the woman across from him in half with his own two hands, but a fraction of it slipped into his voice. The piercing gaze he held on Muire and the way his clenched fists trembled in his lap confirmed it.

"What else would they do?" a young courtier whose name Eryn learned was Neill put in. He had an anxious air about him, as though weighing which opinion he wanted to believe.

"They know we learned how they control the dragons," Cormac, another military veteran Eryn recognized, offered. "Maybe they want the stone and the dragon back?"

Eryn rolled her eyes, her temper rising with every second she continued listening to those around her. "Why would they steal the prince for that?" she snapped, all of her worry and fear turning to anger and spilling into her voice against her will.

"It's unlikely," the king cut in. He said it softly, but she heard the warning in his tone. She'd blatantly ignored that warning before, but that was when it was only the two of them, not in front of the whole court. She didn't have enough sense not to have a yelling match with the King of Aericora, but she did have enough sense not to argue with him in front of his court.

She pressed her lips together tightly before a string of unsavory words could slip out.

"It's unlikely," Muire agreed. "I believe it has something to do with the discovery of the magic in the stone. However, I don't think it's quite that simple. I believe they want to dampen our resources since we learned of their magic and can now use it as our own. By taking our future king and queen, we are left with no one to rule the throne, should something happen to our current king. They've hung a threat over our heads; all they have to do is kill the king and take over before we can find a replacement. But it's far more likely they will resort to asking for gold or other resources before resorting to murder. If they take away our wealth, they'll have taken away our chances of winning the war. If we go after the prince before they send a messenger, chances are they'll resort to the former and kill them both before we have time to save them."

It was the exact argument she'd made a week ago when they'd held a similar meeting. It made sense, but the risk wasn't worth it. If Deovaria asked for gold or resources in exchange for Caeden and Margaid, they would ask for so much that Aericora's people would starve and they would lose the war in a heartbeat, anyway. The logical part of her knew that it may be worth it to wait another day or two to see what Deovaria would end up asking for before making such a decision, but the reckless part— the part where feelings for him had started to blossom multiple weeks ago—didn't want to wait. It could damn him to death, but after how Ronan was tortured, after seeing the shape his body and mind were in when she'd carried his limp form from the Dragon Lord's prison, maybe a quick death was better. But maybe—just maybe—she could save him before either happened. Maybe, if she took the risk, she could get him out of there alive and in one piece.

It was foolish, but once the thought formed, she couldn't shove it away.

The court muttered around her, quietly agreeing with Muire's points, just as they had before, but Eryn hardly heard them. It didn't matter what verdict they came to. She wasn't going to wait around while the Dragon Lord tortured the man she cared for. Not again.

She'd tried that with Ronan. The military officers had told her to wait until a specific number of soldiers volunteered for the rescue party, and she had. It had helped, but in the end, they could've left sooner with fewer soldiers and still been successful. She wasn't going to make that mistake again.

The king sighed heavily, his Adam's apple bobbing as he swallowed his emotions. "Very well," he said, his voice still quiet, his words strained as he forced them past the lump in the back of his throat. "We will wait another three days. If we hear nothing from Deovaria, we will ready a rescue party."

The king dismissed them, and Eryn relaxed her fists as she exited the room and made her way through the halls toward her bedroom. Three days was plenty of time. She could be back by then if she was fast enough.

Chapter 15

Days passed, but with the lack of light in his cell, Caeden lost track of exactly how long he spent in the prison before the Dragon Lord came to find him. He had been given four meals since he first arrived in Deovaria, and his best guess was that the number of meals correlated directly with the number of days he spent there, given the hunger pains. He was used to them by now—only pausing occasionally when his stomach grumbled loudly after eating. The food wasn't filling, consisting of mostly stale bread and cheese, which he would slowly eat until his hunger got the better of him and he lost the self-control to eat it slowly.

The reminder of his mistake the first day when he'd eaten his meal far too quickly and heaved until his stomach was empty still sat in the corner of his cell. He stopped noticing the smell a long time ago, but he avoided stepping in it, which was far harder than he wished in the total darkness blanketing him.

He'd been in darkness and total silence for longer than his sanity liked. The only thing keeping him from losing his mind was the scratches on the wall in the corner of the cell. Each time the claustrophobia and the need for an escape became so intensely overwhelming that tears slipped from his eyes and he found himself scratching welts into his own arms, he would find the corner of the space and trace the marks his best friend made when he'd been trapped here.

Ronan had come out of this alive, and it gave him the strength to hope that maybe he would, too.

Thoughts of Eryn plagued his mind as he paced the cell for hours on end. Their night alone in the safe room was never far from his thoughts, or their training session in the field before the attack when he'd admitted his feelings to her. The blush he often saw on her cheeks, that occasional smile, or her deep, ocean blue eyes that pulled him in each time he met her gaze. All of it was a welcome distraction from the reality surrounding him.

His body ached from the numerous times he'd lunged at Dealla and she'd won. His wounds were healing far more slowly than he'd ever experienced from his lack of food, water, and sleep.

He hadn't managed to sleep for more than a couple of hours at a time. Nightmares plagued him each time he drifted off, and he always woke in a cold sweat and shaking, which did nothing to help his injuries. The first time he'd woken, he'd sat up so fast he'd sent a wave of pain through his abdomen from one of the times Dealla had punched him and knocked him to the floor. He'd been careful to avoid making that mistake again.

"Comfortable?" the Dragon Lord's—his uncle's—rough voice asked through the small slot in the door where his food was slipped inside. Caeden heard the wicked grin in his voice, and he ran his fingers over the marks in the wall to keep himself from attempting to claw the man's eyes out through the small hole.

"Very," Caeden lied, keeping his tone even. He wasn't going to appear shaken. He wasn't going to let the evil man outside his cell get to him, no matter how he tried.

"Glad our accommodations are up to the Prince of Aericora's standards." He sounded so amused that Caeden clenched his hands into tight fists against the marks in the wall.

"What do you want?" he snapped.

The lock on the cell door clicked, and the Dragon Lord pulled it open. The light assaulted Caeden's eyes, and he blinked several times before his eyes finally adjusted to the sunlight he hadn't seen in days. "I wanted to see if you've come to your senses about my proposition yet."

Caeden laughed, a loud, borderline hysterical sound slipping past his lips. He threw his head back against the wall, hard enough to leave a bruise, but he hardly felt it. His whole body was numb as the laughter shook through him. He hardly felt the bumps, bruises, gashes, and scratches along his body anymore. "You're insane."

Maybe he was starting to go a little insane himself, but he didn't let his uncle see the doubt the thought caused him.

The Dragon Lord set his jaw. "Your people are dying, Caeden. You should be grateful I'm offering you anything at all instead of ending this war in a far bloodier way."

Caeden's laughter came to a sudden stop. He had no doubt that the man before him would have ended the war in the bloodiest of ways if he had the power to do so. "I will not see you spill my father's blood. You've hurt enough of my family. If you really were able to win this war so easily and so quickly, you would've already done so a long time ago. It's not helping your people to war with us any more than it is us. You're acting like you have a huge upper hand, but the truth is, you don't. We have too many soldiers, and your dragons' abilities are weakened by nothing more than a simple flower we have in abundance. And we just learned how to take control of your dragons. We may only have one gem, but we know your secret. That alone is enough to be a problem for you."

The Dragon Lord shook his head, an amused smile pulling at the edges of his mouth again. "You're far more naïve than you think, young prince."

He stepped further into the cell, stopping when he was in front of Caeden, who remained crouched in the corner of the cell with his fist pressed against Ronan's markings in the stone. When they were both standing, the Dragon Lord stood only a few inches taller than Caeden, but with Caeden pressed into the corner of the cell, the Dragon Lord seemed far taller.

"Soldiers and dragons aren't the only means I have to use against you," the Dragon Lord said as he knelt before him, his piercing green eyes boring into him. "Can you stand?"

The question was gentle, and if Caeden didn't know any better, he would've mistaken it for genuine compassion. But he knew better than to think the man before him was capable of that kind of emotion.

"Yes."

A sneer twisted the corner of the Dragon Lord's lips before he stood and stepped back. "Prove it, then."

Caeden glared up at him, anger flaring through him hotter than he'd ever felt. He clenched his fists tighter, blood seeping beneath his fingertips, though he didn't feel the same prick of pain he usually felt when the crescent shapes pierced his skin. He pressed his fists into the floor and forced the weight of his body forward onto his feet. It was hard—not because it hurt, but because his body was still so weak. He wasn't sure how he managed to get to his feet without staggering.

The Dragon Lord's smirk widened. "I have something to

show you," he said, and without giving Caeden time to respond, he left the cell without so much as a backward glance to ensure Caeden followed.

Caeden stumbled after him, his eyes taking a moment to adjust to the even brighter light outside. His limbs were heavy as he walked, but he kept his pace a few feet behind the Dragon Lord. He could've easily turned around and tried to escape, given that he hadn't bothered to shackle him in any way other than the rope still binding his wrists—or even spare him a glance—but something about his tone sparked Caeden's interest. That, and the chances of him escaping in his current state were slim at best. He was too weak to run even if he tried.

"I have more to offer you than just the end of your people's bloodshed," the Dragon Lord said as they walked down multiple hallways. He spoke to the space ahead of him, as if Caeden didn't even exist.

He led him down two stories to a large hallway filled with various trinkets and other expensive objects. There were more crystal dragon sculptures here, along with silk tapestries embroidered with strings of gold and silver, delicate paintings, and hundreds of other things that Caeden could've spent the rest of the week looking at.

Something at the very end of the hallway caught Caeden's eyes as they walked. From where he stood, all he could make out was the blue glow and the edge of a rectangular object that looked to be made of crystal or glass.

The Dragon Lord stopped in front of it, his eyes locked on whatever was depicted on the front of the glowing piece.

Caeden stumbled his way there, his legs feeling heavier as he neared his uncle.

His eyes widened, and his stomach clenched so painfully he was sure he would throw up again when he laid eyes on the glass.

Or, more accurately, what was inside.

Caeden tripped over his own feet, his heart pounding so wildly in his chest he couldn't hear anything else as he fell to the floor. He looked up quickly, the pain from the fall not registering in his mind as he took in the sight before him.

"You…you…" he stuttered, unable to get the words out.

Amelia.

It was Amelia inside of whatever the crystal material was.

Her blond hair, her frightened eyes, her mouth open in an almost scream—all of it was frozen on her eleven-year-old face.

The nausea increased, and Caeden heaved, but nothing came up. He tried to pick himself up off the floor, but his limbs refused to cooperate as he stared into the features of his sister's face. "You-you kept her body?" he asked, his voice high past the lump in the back of his throat, making the words fall from his lips in a nearly indiscernible squeak.

The Dragon Lord shook his head, but Caeden hardly saw it. He couldn't turn his gaze away from the sight of his sister.

"She's not dead," the Dragon Lord told him, his tone calm and unfeeling. "She's frozen in space and time. It's another magical ability we discovered the stones are capable of. I killed your mother, but she was so young, I didn't have the heart to. But I also couldn't leave her as she was."

Caeden's hands shook as he pushed himself up to his feet. It took a few tries to get his limbs to cooperate, and his body was rigid when he finally managed it. He stepped up to the strange magic encasing his sister.

He would kill him.

He would sink his dagger into his heart and end the life of the man beside him the moment he got the chance. He would rip his throat out with his bare hands. He would tear him to shreds bit by bit, and he would enjoy the sounds of his uncle's screams as he tore each limb from his body.

The sounds of the guards approaching behind them was the only thing preventing him from trying right then and there.

If his sister was alive, he needed to live to get her out of here. No one here would do it. If he attacked the Dragon Lord, the guards would kill him. They would plunge a sword right through his heart, no questions asked.

Caeden placed his hand on the material holding his sister, right above where her own hand rested inside. It was cold beneath his touch, and the sensation sent a shiver down his spine. She was still so small. He hadn't realized he'd grown so much until now, as he gazed at his sister who was the exact same as when he'd last seen her eleven years ago.

She was alive inside. Somehow, there had to be a way to break the magic holding her. She could be free. She could still live her life.

He couldn't attack the Dragon Lord, but if he agreed to his deal…

Caeden shook his head, pulling his hand away despite every bit of him protesting the movement.

No.

He couldn't sacrifice his father. Nothing would make him do that. Amelia may still be alive, but she was frozen in space and time. She'd already been in there so long that waiting to find a different solution wouldn't make a difference.

Caeden would never damn his father to that. He would never damn his people to a life under the rule of his tyrannical uncle.

He loved his sister, but he would find another way to save her.

For now, at least, she was safe where she was.

"So, do we have a deal?" the Dragon Lord asked. "Your sister and the lives of your people in exchange for the joining of

Deovaria and Aericora beneath my rule?"

Caeden swallowed hard before ripping his gaze away from his sister's scared, green eyes, and instead looking up at his uncle. "Nothing you can offer me would make me agree to your proposal."

The Dragon Lord's eyes darkened, but rather than say anything, he gestured to the guards standing down the hallway. The clanking of their armor filled Caeden's ears as he held his uncle's gaze. Rough hands grabbed him beneath the arms, but rather than the pain from their tight grip, all he could focus on was the relief at no longer needing to support the weight of his own body.

"Escort the prince back to his cell," the Dragon Lord commanded. He said Caeden's title like it left a bad taste in his mouth.

The guards each gave a curt nod. They turned with Caeden held between them and half carried, half dragged him through the hallway they'd come down.

"Oh, and Caeden," the Dragon Lord called to him. "I could've easily sent my dragons to burn down your entire kingdom. The only reason I haven't yet is because it would kill thousands of good people. People who could be living happily if you simply agree to my terms. But you're beginning to force my hand. My proposition still stands if you decide to come to your senses, but I don't know how much longer I'll be willing to wait."

His uncle's words rang loud in his ears long after Caeden returned to his cell.

Chapter 16

Eryn

The cool metal of Eryn's dagger against her thigh sent a shiver down her spine as she pushed open the door and stepped outside. The cold night air hit her along with the chirping sounds of the cicadas and the hoot of a nearby owl. Ronan's shack was brightly lit ahead of her, indicating he hadn't gone to sleep yet.

The court meeting had been the previous day, and she'd tried to listen to them. She'd tried to be patient—to force the burning anger and overwhelming sense of dread away and find that place in her that had turned everything numb the last time the Dragon Lord took someone she cared about.

But she couldn't wait any longer.

She walked through the grass quietly, sticking to the shadows to avoid any prying eyes from inside the castle as she snuck her way to Ronan's front door. Her bag rested over her shoulder, along with her bow and a quiver of arrows. Her sword hung from her hip, and her dagger was strapped to her upper thigh. Three other daggers were strapped to various parts of her body, ready to be grabbed and used at a second's notice.

She rapped her knuckles gently against the door to the shack, and she heard Ronan slam into what sounded like the kitchen counter before she heard his steps against the floor.

Eryn expected the smell of whiskey to punch her in the nose when he opened the door, but instead, she was hit with nothing. It was even more jarring than the scent of whiskey would've been, and her heart ached as she took him in. She may have cared for Caeden and wanted him to be safe, but Ronan fell in love with Margaid, and the fact was written clearly across his entire body.

He slumped forward heavily, the full weight of his body resting on his cane. Dark bags hung beneath his half-closed eyes, as if he hadn't slept a second since the two went missing. His hair was greasy, the limp curls sticking to his forehead. His eyes were red and raw as if he'd been crying, and the usual glimmer in them was gone. The smirk that usually pulled at his lips had vanished with it.

"Yeah?" he asked.

He didn't make a joke about the late hour. There was no amusement written across his face. No mischief. Nothing.

Eryn swallowed hard. She hadn't seen him like this in a long time, and she'd hoped she never would again. At least back then, he'd relied on the alcohol and the arms of strangers. This time, he was using nothing to drown out the pain, and that scared her so much more.

She gritted her teeth. All of this was because of the Dragon Lord and his war. Everything that happened always led back to him. Every single image that plagued her mind when she slept: her parents, the mountains, every death she'd witnessed, Ronan's bloody and beaten body, and now the possibility of Caeden's, too.

She pushed the sadness away, letting it harden inside of her like she always did until there was nothing left but anger. "We're getting them back," she said through clenched teeth. She pulled her pack from her shoulder and held it out to him. "Put your stuff in here. We're leaving tonight."

Ronan stared at her. Something like longing flashed across his face, but he pushed it away as quickly as it appeared. She hated watching him do that. She hated watching him push away what he wanted because he thought it was what was best for her. Because he needed to be the strong one who kept her from doing something crazy when he wanted to do it just as badly.

"The court said—"

"I don't give a fuck what the court said," Eryn snapped, cutting him off despite herself.

That tone used to work with her. He used to be able to make her second-guess her decisions with nothing more than a look, but this wasn't the same as those scenarios years ago. This wasn't just any other mission she wanted to jump into. This was Aericora's future king. This was Caeden, and even though she never should have thought of him as anything more than the prince, she couldn't help when her heart fluttered just because he glanced in her direction.

Her heart ached, and she pushed the feelings she never should've had away. "The soldiers are well-trained enough that they can protect the castle while we're gone. The court is too stupid to realize that even if the Dragon Lord does plan to release Caeden and Margaid to us, they're still going to try to beat something out of them first. We've seen what they've done to everyone else they've taken. They would only try to bleed us dry of our wealth by offering them back to us. But that doesn't match how the Dragon Lord has gone about this war for the past eleven years. They'll resort to that last, if they can't get whatever it is they want out of them first. And that's only if they decide killing them wouldn't be more beneficial, which I doubt would happen. And they may not even wait that long with Margaid. She could already be dead."

So much emotion flashed across Ronan's face that Eryn almost hated herself for saying the words. He needed to hear them, though. He wouldn't be convinced if she didn't throw it in his face.

"There's only two of us," Ronan argued, even as doubt played across his face. "And I can't walk." He gestured at his injured leg, his anger flaring to match hers.

"Doesn't matter," Eryn said, stepping into the shack past him. "You won't need to walk, anyway."

"Reckless…" There was a warning in his tone when he said her nickname, but she ignored it. "We don't even know where they are. They could've taken them anywhere."

Eryn rolled her eyes. "They took them to the palace, Ronan. They wouldn't have taken them anywhere else. They're hardly taking prisoners anymore, and they wouldn't take their enemy's future leaders somewhere else. Deovaria hasn't taken anyone since you and the others, so they won't have them in the dungeon. They'll have them up in the prison cells where they kept you."

Fear like Eryn had never seen before fell across Ronan's face, and his hand gripped his cane so tightly his knuckles turned stark white.

"Are you going to keep arguing with me, or are we going to get them out of that hellhole?"

She said the words softly this time, knowing she wouldn't hear another argument from him.

Eryn handed him the pack again, and he took it, all doubt gone from his features. He didn't say anything before he turned and walked to his room to get his things.

"Do you still have the ring?" Eryn called after him as the sounds of him rummaging through his clothing filled the small space.

The rummaging stopped, and Ronan poked his head around the doorframe. "What are you plannin', Reckless?"

Eryn rolled her eyes again. "You know what I'm planning. Do you have it or not?"

He shook his head. "Caeden had it last. Gave it back to him while you were recoverin' in the infirmary."

She nodded, but didn't say anything as she unfastened the sword on her hip and set it on the couch along with her bow and quiver before she left the shack again.

Ronan didn't turn to face her as she disappeared through the doorway and back toward the castle.

The halls inside were dark, aside from a few lit candles every so often to help see, though they did little in the end. She nearly stumbled over her own feet in the darkness. She'd never been good at being sneaky. That was Ronan's thing until his leg was injured. But she could do it well enough when she needed to, and she certainly needed to now, given that Caeden's room was down the same hall as the king's.

He hadn't heard her the night Caeden went missing, but earlier that night he'd looked like he'd gotten as little sleep as Ronan had since the discovery of their kidnapping. Chances were, if he was asleep at all, he would wake up easily with everything that happened.

She snuck down the hall silently. Her body was rigid as she turned the doorknob to Caeden's room and pushed it open slowly, the hinges creaking with the movement. Once the door was barely wide enough for her to fit through, she slipped inside and closed it behind herself once again.

Caeden's scent struck her as she entered the room: strong

and crisp like the scent of pine, though there was something uniquely him about it.

It made her heart ache, and she clenched her jaw in an attempt to push away the sudden wave of emotion that crashed into her as she walked further into the room.

She would get him back.

She had to get him back.

She tried his desk first, pulling open each of the drawers and pushing aside the papers and other stationery littering the inside of each, but it wasn't there. The bookshelf and his nightstand were just as fruitless. She tried his bed last, out of pure desperation, but even after pulling off the sheets and shaking them out, the ring was nowhere to be found.

"Damn it," she muttered. Where else would it be if not in his room? Did he have it on him when he was taken?

"I highly doubt rummaging through my son's belongings will bring him back," a voice said behind her, and Eryn stilled.

Fuck. She'd been caught.

She turned slowly, her eyes landing on the king standing just inside the doorway. He could've been a spy himself with how silently he entered the room, given she hadn't heard him until he spoke.

Eryn took in his expression. She expected to see anger, but curiosity played across his features instead. He stood with his hands at his sides, not crossed or in fists like they should've been, and his eyes held no fire.

Words slipped out of her mouth before she could think better of it. "I'm looking for something," she told him truthfully, though she wasn't entirely sure why she opted for the truth over a lie. She was digging herself a deeper grave.

The king offered her a smile, but the sadness he'd had in his features since she'd first met him had grown so much since

Caeden's disappearance that the smile did nothing to wipe it away. He reached into his pocket and produced the ring, its sapphire gem glowing brightly in his hand and illuminating his palm as he held it out for her to see. "For this, I take it?"

Eryn swallowed hard. "Yes, Your Majesty."

She'd had a screaming match with the man before her only a few weeks ago, but all the fire she'd felt then was gone. He'd caught her. And, worst of all, he'd caught her rummaging through the crown prince's room.

The king sighed, his already slumped shoulders falling farther forward. He looked so weak standing before her. He was so thin, so frail a light breeze could've blown him over where he stood. "I know where they're coming from," he said softly, and it took Eryn a moment to realize he was talking about the court. "But he's my son." He held the ring in his palm out to her, and though he looked like he was offering it to her, his face told her this was something very different.

She was going against the court's wishes, and she expected to be in trouble, but the look her king was giving her demanded it of her. He wasn't offering her the ring to take if she wished to. He was commanding her to save the prince. To save Caeden. To save the man she was scared she was growing to love.

"Bring him back," he said to her. He was commanding her as her king to do what she had already planned to with or without his permission, but a king shouldn't have made that command. The man before her didn't speak as the king, though. He spoke as Caeden's father. His tone wasn't demanding. It was pleading. "Bring my son home to me," he whispered.

She took the ring slowly, gripping it in the palm of her hand. "Yes, Your Majesty," she repeated, her voice even as she bowed to him like any soldier would.

"There's no need for that," the king said, a laugh beneath his tone.

Confusion struck her when he said the words, but she stood straight and looked up at him, regardless.

"You've already done so much for this kingdom, if you bring my son back to me alive, I should be the one bowing to you."

"I'll take my dying breath before I'll see him harmed," she told him, her voice quiet. The truth lacing her words felt heavy on her tongue, as if she was saying far more in that single sentence than she ever should.

The king's smile was knowing, and her heart skipped a beat. "I'm sure you would."

He didn't give her the chance to say anything in response before he turned and strode from the room.

"Did you find it?" Ronan asked when Eryn reentered the shack. He sat on the couch with her overstuffed pack beside him. He'd changed while she was gone. Rather than his usual tattered clothes, he wore a plain black shirt and pants that fit close to his body. He'd replaced his usual cane with a different one too, and she could just make out the thin line near the top of it where it split in two, the bottom likely concealing a sword inside.

"Yes," she responded. "It'll take us about a day and a half to get there. Did you pack enough?" She didn't tell him about the king, or how he'd given her the ring along with the command to rescue the prince. They would no longer be in trouble when the court found out or if something happened, but the look the king had given her left her shaken.

He knew. There was no other explanation. But if he knew, how many others did too? How many servants were walking through the castle halls gossiping about her and the prince's secret relationship that didn't exist? How many of them were single-handedly ruining her reputation despite her having done nothing wrong? Did she even care?

The memory of Caeden's hand in hers from nights ago resurfaced, followed by their night in the safe room, and when he'd told her he liked her right before the attack in the field. She'd blamed her behavior in the safe room on the blood loss. She'd blamed it on the fact that she hadn't been in her right mind, but even if no one but Ronan saw them together, that didn't make it the truth. She'd wanted to be close to him. She'd wanted to touch him. She'd wanted to feel the warmth of his body against hers. Just like she'd wanted to hold his hand the other night. Or how she'd wanted to admit to him, truly admit to him, just how much she was beginning to care for him, too.

If rumors were spreading through the castle about her, part of her worried that maybe some of them weren't entirely wrong. She had feelings for a man who was engaged—for the prince and heir to Aericora's throne when she was only a soldier in the military. There were so many things about it that were wrong, and yet that hadn't stopped her that night. It hadn't stopped her any of the times she'd done something like grab hold of his hand.

"Eryn?" Ronan snapped his fingers in front of her face, and her attention turned to him. "There you are. I have everythin' packed. We need to get the dragon and leave 'fore the sun comes up."

His words were so straightforward they struck her like a slap across the face. She already missed him; longed for the day he would be back to his normal self again. It had been so long before she'd heard him so much as crack a joke last time, and she hadn't seen him like his normal self again until she'd been brought to the castle to train Caeden. How long would it be this time if they couldn't get them back?

She shook her head, clearing away the thoughts. "Yeah, let's go."

Eryn gathered her weapons from off the couch and strapped them back onto her body before the two of them left the shack. The dragon was being kept in a large offshoot of the stable that was hastily set up after they first arrived back from the field. It wasn't entirely covered, but it had a small roof and three walls that gave the dragon some protection from the weather, and bedding was laid inside to keep her comfortable. The dragon wasn't chained aside from a rope tied around her ankle that wouldn't do anything to hold her if she tried to escape. So far, she hadn't bothered to try.

"There's a shift change at sunrise," Ronan whispered as they neared the stables, keeping quiet and to the shadows as they snuck through the castle grounds. "We can't wait that long or too many of them will see us leave."

"We can lie," Eryn said casually, though what they were doing wouldn't be a lie. "You're on the King's Court and I've sat in since I got here. We can say the order came from him. They'll believe it."

Ronan stayed silent for a moment, and she could almost see his furrowed eyebrows as he thought over her words. "Okay."

They veered away from the shadows as they neared the stable. The guards stood at attention as they approached, and the dragon's head peered over the top of the building. Her orange eyes stayed on Eryn, and her skin crawled uncomfortably beneath the creature's gaze. The dragon had paid her the same level of attention the whole way back from the field, too. She hadn't done anything to hurt anyone, but after the many days spent with the dragon at her side, Eryn couldn't shake the fear that she would decide to swallow her whole, or engulf her in flames.

Eryn fixed her eyes forward, ignoring the feel of the dragon's gaze boring into her.

"General Atkyn." The soldier farthest to the right of the stable entrance bowed his head respectfully as they approached. "Miss Gedding."

Eryn rolled her eyes. She outranked Ronan, yet because she was a Dragon Hunter, she'd never had the luxury of a title other than Miss.

Four guards were posted outside of the stable tonight, opposed to the single guard who had been there since Eryn first arrived a few months ago. They'd brought back enough soldiers that Ronan could nearly triple the number of guards at every station. In places like the stable, he'd opted for four times the number of guards, seeing as the dragon was kept inside. The castle entrance was guarded by eight soldiers now instead of two, as well.

"Anythin' to report?" Ronan asked the young soldier. He looked no older than Eryn, but he lacked the years of experience she'd gone through. His movements were twitchy, and his gaze scanned the perimeter too fast, not taking in any of the small details because he was too scared of missing something large instead. All but one of them shared his same composure, and she was glad to see at least one of them had enough experience to notice if something or someone tried to sneak up on them.

The soldier whose attention hadn't left the perimeter since they arrived shook his head. "Nothing yet, General." His eyes flicked to the two of them quickly before going back to the edge of the forest. "It's been quiet all night."

Ronan nodded firmly. All signs of his depressive state, aside from the bags beneath his eyes and his greasy hair, vanished as soon as they approached the guards. He stood straighter now, taking on the façade of the castle's Head of Security, and a soldier who wouldn't let anything get to him—who had lived through hell for so long nothing could. "Good," he responded and began to walk past the soldiers. "The king has sent us to look over a few things. We will be inside for a while."

The guards nodded in unison, and just as Eryn suspected, none of them dared to question them as they stepped inside and closed the stable doors firmly behind themselves.

The stench hit her nose as Ronan closed the doors, and a wave of nausea washed over her. She'd always hated the smell of the stables.

A door at the very back was barred from the inside and led out to the extension that was built for the dragon. The door hadn't existed a couple weeks ago, and it was as hastily built as the structure the dragon slept in. The harness the dragon had worn when Ronan tamed it was set beside the back door.

Blood marked the jagged edges of the contraption. It wasn't built for comfort. It was built to inflict pain, and it made Eryn's stomach twist into knots. She didn't like the creatures, but they didn't deserve to be tortured for no reason. Especially not when they were already under the Deovarians' control because of the stones. She could've understood it more if it were a harness used on a drake, given their aggressive nature, but not a Royal Talon like the one just beyond the door.

So far, since they'd been back at the castle, the dragon hadn't done anything to harm any of the people responsible for tending to her. She hadn't destroyed anything and hadn't tried to escape. She seemed perfectly content to spend her days lying in the sun outside, or curled up comfortably on the pile of bedding beneath the large covered area they'd built for her.

"We're not using the harness," Eryn said, and Ronan tossed her a questioning look over his shoulder. "It's cruel."

"Have you ever ridden a dragon without a harness before? Better yet, have you ever ridden a dragon at all?" he asked, though they both knew the answer.

It was a valid point, but she wasn't going to hurt the creature when she'd seen plenty of Deovarian soldiers simply hold on to the spines along the dragons' backs before.

Eryn pulled the pack off her back and produced a long length of rope—something she always carried with her on missions, proving useful far more times than she could count. "I'm not putting that thing back on her," she stated. "We'll just have to make our own."

Ronan sighed. "Fine."

His lack of excitement for the challenge set her on edge. The memories she wanted so badly to forget crept in again, and she did her best to shove them away as she pushed open the back door.

The Royal Talon stood directly in front of her when she stepped outside, her brilliant blue scales shimmering in the starlight and eyes like fire boring into Eryn's very soul.

Eryn froze dead in her tracks.

Suddenly, she was up in the mountains again. Soft, white snow blanketed her in her small sleeping bag as it fell against her face and stuck to her eyelashes. A dragon roared inside the mountain above her as she shivered and pulled the bag around herself. She glanced around. The fire was still lit, but her parents were gone. Only a few of their footprints remained in the snow.

She swallowed hard, holding the dragon's gaze. The dragon wouldn't eat her. She had plenty of chances to do so on the way back from the battlefield. If she wanted to kill humans, there had been enough opportunities to since she'd been in the stables. What if she changed her mind, though?

Eryn's hands shook at her sides, and a cold sweat broke out

along her brow and upper lip. Her heart pounded so loudly in her chest she could hear it beneath the ringing in her ears. Her breathing came in shallow gasps, and no matter how hard she tried, she couldn't catch her breath.

A hand rested on her shoulder, and she flinched beneath Ronan's touch. "You're in the castle, Reckless," he whispered beside her. "I'm with you." His hand slid down her arm until his fingers intertwined with hers, and he gave them a light squeeze. He pressed the back of her hand against her thigh, and she could feel the jagged edge of the ring inside her pocket. "Just breathe. You've got the ring, remember? The dragons won't hurt you when you've got the ring."

Eryn's breathing slowed as he slipped his hand free, and she reached into her pocket to hold the ring in her palm. The dragon wouldn't hurt her with the ring. It wouldn't hurt anyone who held the stone, and it rested in the palm of her hand.

"We're goin' to get Caeden, remember?" Ronan said.

The mention of Caeden's name snapped her from her trance, and she dropped the ring back into her pocket. She pushed the fear aside as a different kind of worry filled her once again. They had to get him back before the Dragon Lord hurt him, or worse, killed him. She wasn't going to let that happen, and she wasn't going to let her fear stop her from saving him before it did.

She gripped the rope in her hands and let out a deep breath before she stepped up to the dragon. It stared down at her, its gaze unwavering. She held the rope out to it as she took in the scars marking its sides from the saddle the Deovarians used. The corners of its mouth were scarred and still scabbed over from the bridle that had been between her teeth and strapped to her snout when they'd first tamed her. The wounds were healing quickly, but she would forever have scars from the rough treatment the Deovarian soldiers had put her through.

The dragon bent slowly, sniffing the rope in Eryn's hand. Her large breaths sent Eryn's hair flying out of her face, but she kept her footing as she allowed the dragon to ponder the rope. When it finally pulled its head away, she stepped alongside it slowly.

She was incredibly tall, but she seemed to know what Eryn wanted her to do. She lowered herself to the ground, stretching out her wing and leg to create a sort of double step for her to climb up onto her back. She stepped up, letting the dragon adjust to the weight of her before she continued the rest of the way. She didn't so much as flinch as Eryn maneuvered herself onto her back between two of her large spines.

"I don't know if I can do that," Ronan said quietly from where he stood on the ground, now beside the dragon's wing and leg.

Eryn tied the rope around one of the dragon's spines before twisting it around her waist to hold her in place. She reached a hand over the side of the dragon and held it out to Ronan. "If you can get up the first step, I can pull you up the rest of the way."

He gave her a skeptical look, but once she fixed him with a look of her own, he sighed and climbed up onto the dragon's leg. He wavered, but he didn't fall. He held the end of his cane up to her, and she grasped it tightly to help brace him as he struggled up the next step onto the dragon's wing. It took a few agonizingly long moments for Ronan to stagger his way up to sit behind her, and once he did, she quickly tied the end of the rope around him to keep him atop the dragon with her.

"Ouch," Ronan said as she tightened the last bit. "Not so tight, Reckless."

She smirked up at him, but he still didn't return it. "It's got to be tight to keep you on," she told him, turning away from his gaze as she faced forward again. She let out a deep sigh as the dragon stood to her full height again and the ground beneath them moved farther and farther away.

The dragon spread her large wings as Eryn nudged her gently with the heels of her boots like she would a horse. She took off so suddenly Eryn's stomach lurched, nearly enough to make her throw up her last meal as they rose higher and higher into the night sky.

The guards shouted to one another as they flew away, but whatever words they said were lost to her ears as the wind whipped past. She wasn't sure where the gesture came from, but she patted the dragon gingerly on the back of her neck. "Let's get that prince and princess back," she whispered, so quietly she was sure her words were lost on the wind.

The dragon seemed to nod in response either way, and she sped up as she flew through the black night ahead.

Chapter 17

"Good morning, cousin." Dealla's voice came through the open slot in the door to Caeden's cell. There was a smirk in her voice, and the way she sang her words was mocking. "Feeling better after your little tantrum last week?"

Caeden clenched his hands, his nails reopening the wounds he'd inflicted on himself a couple days ago when the Dragon Lord came to collect him. He'd been here for a week. One week, and his sanity already felt like it was slipping away more and more by the minute; the thoughts of his home, Ronan's blood surrounding him, Eryn's ocean blue eyes, and now his sister trapped in space and time in a magical prison consumed him.

He chose to ignore her, instead unclenching his fists and tracing the marks in the stone again. One, two, three, four, and a fifth that slashed through the other four. There were six groups in total, but the last one, the one closest to the bottom of the wall, only had two marks. He'd figured out a long time ago that it must have been Ronan's way of keeping track of the days he was trapped.

"You dead in there already?" Dealla mocked, tapping lightly

against the edge of the door. The thrum of her fingers on the metal reverberated through him, loud enough that it hurt his ears after the hours upon hours of silence. "Didn't even last half as long as that soldier friend of yours."

"Ronan," Caeden corrected, his voice hoarse. It could've been from lack of use, or from the hours he'd spent screaming at the walls the previous night, as if that would get him out of here. Or maybe he'd dreamt that. He wasn't entirely sure anymore which memories were real and which were concocted in his own mind.

Nightmares still plagued him, but now they were beginning to be of the cell he was trapped in, too. Repeatedly, he thought he'd woken from sleep, but wasn't entirely sure since the world around him was exactly the same. Just a dark, empty void with walls hidden behind the blackness.

"You spent more nights in his bed than I can count," Caeden continued, the raspiness subsiding the more he spoke. Maybe he really had screamed in his dreams. "You know his name. Stop acting like you don't so you can avoid saying it."

He shouldn't prod her. It wouldn't get him anything from her but anger, but he wanted to hear her admit it. He wanted to hear her admit the cruel things she'd done. He wanted to see if there would be even an ounce of remorse in her tone when she said the words, or if she really was as unfeeling and evil as her actions suggested.

Dealla scoffed outside, and despite himself, a smile touched Caeden's lips as he pictured the flustered expression on her face. She didn't have Margaid's face anymore, but not all of the person she'd portrayed when acting as the Princess of Crevia was fake, and her scoff was all he needed to confirm it.

"What do you want?" he asked. The same anger he'd felt for the past week slowly seeped back into him, and the smile on his face faded.

The lock clicked, and the door groaned on its hinges as she pulled it open. The light from outside flooded into his cell, and Caeden blinked repeatedly until his eyes adjusted to the harsh light.

Dealla stepped inside, holding a platter with scraps of food that were a worthless excuse for a meal. She was dressed in a tank top and leather pants with a sword loosely tied around her waist. Her hair was down, falling in golden waves. Her green eyes scanned over his body, taking in the countless bruises and scrapes covering him from the wagon ride and his repeated lunges at her his first day here. Dried blood covered him from head to toe, but not even half of it was his own.

He pulled his hand away from the wall and rested it in his lap. He kept his knees pressed to his chest though, and his body pressed into the corner of the room. She wasn't worth forcing himself up.

"I brought you food," she said simply. She set the tray down in the center of the room, over a particularly large spot of dried blood.

She was mocking him again by leaving it there. She knew his body ached, and that his limbs were so weak that climbing to his feet would be one of the hardest things he'd done in his life.

Dealla watched him expectantly, her hands on her hips and a curious look on her face.

Caeden stayed where he was.

"Are you going to eat, or are you going to wait for it to grow legs and walk to you?" she taunted.

It probably could've if he waited long enough, given that mold was already growing on patches of the hard loaf of bread.

Caeden glared at her, his eyes locked on hers. He didn't look away. "Say his name."

Amusement twitched the corner of her lips upward, but it didn't reach her eyes. He saw a flash of fear behind them instead. She scoffed. "What?"

Caeden smirked back at her, but unlike her, the amusement he was letting slide onto his face was real. "Say his name and I'll get the tray. You can watch me struggle like you want, all you've got to do is say it."

Dealla raised an eyebrow at him, something like shock combined with pure fear flashing across her features despite the mask she tried to force into place. Just like Eryn though, all of her emotions showed in her eyes. "You're acting like you have something over me, but you don't. You're the one stuck in the cell, remember?"

She said it so forcefully it only made him more sure he really did have something over her.

His smile widened. "It's not hard. It's two syllables. Ro-nan."

"I never said it was hard to say," she snapped, her irritation flaring, though the fear behind her eyes remained.

She opened her mouth to continue, but Caeden interrupted her. "Then why won't you say it?"

Dealla scoffed again, but he caught the way her knuckles turned white as she dug her fingers into her hips out of frustration. He had something over her, and even though it didn't seem like much, the way she was acting suggested he had more than she ever wanted to admit.

"You fell for him, didn't you?" Caeden teased, his voice light and playful, disguising the threat he was hanging over her head with only those words.

Ronan was a mission. She'd been sent to collect information from Aericora, and when she hadn't gotten any from Caeden, she'd gone to Ronan for it. But he was still a source of information. If the Dragon Lord found out she'd caught feelings for the man she was supposed to be using for what he heard in court meetings, Caeden wondered how much trouble he could cause her.

"I did not," Dealla said too quickly. Her cheeks were suddenly bright red, either from her anger or from embarrassment. Whichever it was, Caeden found it amusing.

"That's a lie."

"Eat your food," she snapped, kicking the tray to him so hard the glass of water fell over onto the stone floor.

He didn't care, though. It was the smallest win he'd ever accomplished, but it was still a win. He'd beaten her in this small mind game. He hadn't gotten her to give in to his demand—she'd given him the food without saying Ronan's name—but she gave up a secret he shouldn't have known instead.

Caeden picked up the piece of bread on the edge of the tray and took a bite from one of the few areas that looked safe. The smile on his face hadn't faded.

Dealla rolled her eyes and turned her back on him before leaving the cell.

"He really did love you," Caeden told her, hoping it would twist the knife just a little more. He wanted her to feel the pain, even if she would never feel the same level Ronan would once he found out the truth. "He loved you, and you betrayed him. Not to mention that you were the one who tortured him when he was here. That fact alone might be enough to crush him entirely when he finds out."

He watched her swallow hard, but she didn't say anything as she closed the cell door and left him alone in the darkness once again.

"Caeden," Eryn's voice whispered, so softly it hardly registered in his mind.

He heard the sound of the door opening, but didn't bother to turn toward it. He'd grown so used to the nightmares by now that he couldn't bear to look. She would be bloody, her fingers and toes missing, her eyes cut out, teeth pulled, gashes drawn into her flesh. Her voice would turn raspy as she choked on her own blood, just like the last time she'd appeared in his dreams. He would watch the sword embed itself by her collarbone, and watch the life leave her eyes as she fell to the floor.

It hurt too much to turn to face her, even as every part of him begged to. He wanted to see her face, her beautiful blue eyes, the way her smile tilted the left side of her mouth up ever so slightly more than the right. He missed her so much his heart ached, though he shouldn't have felt that way. She was his trainer, a soldier from his kingdom's military. Yet she was everything he'd ever dreamed of. She was everything he wanted, but he could never have her.

Silent tears spilled from his eyes, as irrational as they were.

He was losing it. He was going to go insane in this small cell, and no one back in his home kingdom would ever know what happened to him.

"Caeden," Eryn's voice came again, and he hated himself for whimpering like a child when he heard it.

It rang through his mind, slicing through his heart and soul. She'd only spoken his name a handful of times, but the emotion his mind crafted in her tone broke him a little more.

"Will you please look at me?" she asked softly.

Caeden swallowed hard. "You aren't real," he bit out, harsher than he ever wanted to speak to her. But this wasn't her. He had to remind himself of that over and over again. The voice he heard didn't belong to the woman he loved. It was his mind playing tricks on him. It wasn't real. *She* wasn't real.

"I'm here, Caeden," she whispered.

Against every part of himself that told him not to, he faced her. His eyes landed on the candle she held between bloodied hands, then the parts of her it illuminated in its faint orange glow. The gash she'd had on her ribs weeks ago poured blood, and the sword she'd been impaled with in the field stuck out of her shoulder on her left side. Her bright blue eyes were missing, as if they'd been cut out of her head, and all that was left behind were two gaping, bloody holes.

It was everything he'd expected to see, but his stomach still lurched at the sight.

Caeden woke with a start, and his stomach heaved. Nothing came up but bile, and he spat it from his mouth before he lay back against the stone wall again, hot tears spilling from his eyes.

Not real. Not real. Not real.

His fingers found the scratches on the wall again.

One. Two. Three. Four. And the fifth that slashed through the others.

He counted them over and over again, trying to picture Ronan sitting right where he was now. Thoughts of his friend eased the terror that gripped him.

He remembered their long nights in Ronan's shack together, the talks they'd had, the bottles and bottles of alcohol they shouldn't have finished but did. He remembered Ronan's crooked smirk, his laugh, his rosy cheeks when he was drunk. He remembered spending many of those late nights with Eryn, as well. An Eryn whose eyes weren't missing, whose wounds had healed rather than continued to bleed endlessly. He remembered the look she gave him when he said something stupid, the feel of her hand against his, the warmth of her against him when she sat beside him on the couch, the scent of her each time she was near and the way it lingered on his clothing long after their training sessions together ended.

He thought of his father, who he'd hardly seen these past years. He thought of how tired he was because of the war. How broken he'd started to look in just the past few months. He remembered a time when his father was the strongest man he'd ever known. He remembered playing with him and Amelia in the garden for hours, practicing with swords in the training field before there was ever a need for the skill, and the picnics they had together as a family before his mother was murdered and his sister was taken as some sick trophy.

Those things were real, even if the memories hurt.

They kept him grounded. They kept him from losing himself entirely in the cramped cell with only the surrounding darkness for company.

He would get out of here. He didn't know how, but he had to believe it. He had to believe it, or it might just be enough to push him over the edge.

He needed to get back to his kingdom. He needed to get back to his father, to Ronan, and to Eryn. He needed to get back to his people, as well. He needed to help his father ensure the kingdom was okay, especially after he'd been kidnapped. He trusted his father wouldn't fall apart entirely, but he worried that even if he held himself together on the outside, he would be too broken on the inside to do what he needed to ensure they won the war in the end.

And they had to win.

Their people would die if they didn't.

Everyone would die if they didn't.

And even if the Dragon Lord's crazy deal wasn't as ridiculous as Caeden was sure it was, he wouldn't agree to it. He could never agree to seeing his father put to death. He would have to find another way to save the lives of his father and his people from the monster ruling Deovaria.

Chapter 18
Eryn

It took Eryn and Ronan just under two days to get to Deovaria's palace. It would've been roughly a day and a half, but they discussed stopping at one of the outer towns. Luckily, they'd found guards like they'd hoped for, and had easily and quietly disposed of them and stolen their uniforms.

They didn't have a well-constructed plan. They would have to get in and out of the palace with Caeden and Margaid quickly, but if that was everything planning a rescue mission required, she could've single-handedly won the war by now. So far, getting out seemed like it would be easier than getting in. Getting in required either finding a still intact tunnel that Eryn could recall from the maps she'd pored over before the rescue mission to get Ronan, or figuring out something else. But since the tunnels were already used to infiltrate the palace once, the chances of that working again were slim to none.

"Keep your pack hidden when you get down there," Ronan called to her as the courtyard and the palace came into view.

They hadn't planned to drop in very close, but they also

didn't want to waste time. If the dragon swooped low enough over the trees, she could jump off without any guards at the gate noticing her. The smartest thing to do would be to drop her at the edge of the town surrounding the palace, but that would require her being sneaky for longer, and she doubted she could keep up the façade. Instead, they would drop her in the trees. There would be guards around, but if she hid there long enough, she could find a time to sneak out when no one was looking and march up to the front entrance like she belonged. Or so they hoped. If that plan failed…

"Easier said than done," Eryn called as she pulled the last few things from the pack, tucking them into the extra space in the Deovarian armor she wore over her usual clothing. It was big on her, but hopefully it wouldn't be noticeable. It gave her enough extra space to store what she needed, at least. She tossed the pack at Ronan's back, and he barely caught it over his shoulder before it plummeted to the ground a hundred yards below. "Hold on to it for me."

"Could've asked nicer," Ronan mumbled beneath his breath, the words nearly getting lost on the wind howling past. "We're going in now. Get ready for the dismount."

"Way ahead of you," she responded. Her legs hung over the edge of the dragon, carefully hidden behind the dragon's wing so she could slide down it and into the trees. The soldiers could notice her if they cared to pay attention, and she hoped they had seen enough dragons near the palace that they wouldn't bat an eye in their direction.

The dragon swooped low over the trees, and Ronan angled the creature at just the right moment for Eryn to slide off.

Eryn held her breath as she pushed off the dragon's spines and plummeted toward the treetops below. The fall wasn't far, considering how high they'd been moments before, but the dragon was large, and it was a good ten to fifteen feet from the dragon's back to the tops of the trees.

The air rushed past her as she slid into the treetops. Branches scraped her arms and legs as she fell, biting into the bare skin of her hands and ankles, and she was grateful for the light armor protecting the rest of her body. Her arms flailed for an agonizingly long second, searching for a branch to grab onto before she fell too far into the trees and the noise became too noticeable. The dragon roared above her as she got a grip on a medium-sized branch and found her footing on another beneath it.

She grinned.

The silhouette of the dragon grew smaller and smaller as Ronan veered away from the palace. He would be back in roughly half an hour, and would begin making laps around the high tower where she'd rescued him from. It didn't leave her much time to get up there.

Eryn climbed down the tree and edged her way near the palace entrance as stealthily as she could with the clinking of the metal from her various weapons and the thin armor pinging against itself with every step.

Two guards stood by the doors, chatting to one another as she neared the entrance. Part of her hoped they wouldn't notice when she approached, but as she drew closer and her covering of trees fell away, their attention shifted to her and she stiffened beneath their collective gaze.

The one to the right gave her a suspicious once-over. "Who are you? I thought Danielle was taking over my shift?"

Lucky timing.

Eryn tilted her head, twisting her features into something that resembled surprise. "Is she?" She frowned. "Maybe I got mixed up. I thought I was." She said her words cryptically, steering clear of saying anything too specific as she walked up the steps and stopped in front of the pair.

"Pretty sure it was her," the guard said. He looked her over again. "You new? You aren't dressed for this post."

Eryn laughed sheepishly and shrugged a shoulder. "Yeah. First day." She shrugged again and moved to walk past the two of them. Neither stopped her. "Sorry about the mix-up. Guess I'll go find the boss and get it sorted."

"You should probably do that," the guard agreed, and didn't pay her any more attention as she slipped inside, shutting the doors behind herself.

Her heart stopped as she took in the space in front of her once the door was firmly closed. It looked exactly the same as it had the last time she was here. Black marble tile with veins of white snaking through it stretched out before her, the small dragon head statues still lined the walls, and not a single one of the tapestries or paintings had changed.

The only difference was the blood.

The last time she'd been in this room, Ronan's arm was slung over her shoulder and she'd supported the weight of his body on hers as she hauled his barely conscious form out of the palace. His leg hadn't been shot yet, but he'd been covered in wounds already. Some of them were still open and bleeding. His clothes were a tattered mess, and his hair was matted with dirt and grime.

She'd glanced behind herself to make sure her fellow soldiers remained behind them before she'd ventured beyond the doors that now stood beside her to the tunnels down the hallway behind. The only thing her eyes had been focused on was the trail of smeared blood against the marble floor from the only person she truly loved in her life. She'd watched someone else she'd thought could one day be a friend die before her eyes here, too. That was when the reality of their situation hit her. It instilled the same level of fear she'd felt when she'd found herself alone in the mountains as a child.

Caeden was up in those cells now.

They wouldn't have taken him down to the usual dungeon. He was too important. It would be easier to guard him up in the tower where she'd found Ronan all those years ago.

Eryn gritted her teeth and pushed herself off the doors. She forced down the fear threatening to overflow and render her limbs and mind useless. She held her head high as she walked through the hall she remembered as well as the back of her hand, ensuring she emanated an air of importance as she walked. No one would question her if she looked like she knew exactly where she was going and what she was doing.

It was easier this time than the last time she'd snuck through these same halls.

She passed multiple palace guards, but none of them batted an eye in her direction.

She walked up ten flights of stairs before she reached the correct floor. Her heartbeat was loud in her ears as she rounded corner after corner, making her way through the maze of hallways like she'd done it a thousand times before.

Her fingers found the hilt of her dagger hidden inside the plate of armor strapped to her thigh. She pulled it free and held it at the ready as she turned the final corner.

A single guard stood in front of the center cell; the same cell Ronan had been kept in.

Bile rose in the back of her throat, and she swallowed it down despite the sickness welling in the pit of her stomach.

The guard turned to face her, giving her a curious look. "What are you—"

Anger pulsed through her, and he didn't have time to finish

his sentence before her dagger pierced the tender skin of his throat. His eyes were wide when he fell. Sickening, gurgling noises reached her ears as she stepped up to him and watched the life leave his eyes. She pulled her dagger free from his neck, hot, sticky blood coating her fingers.

Her hands shook as she pulled his keys from where they were strapped to his belt. She was dimly aware that having only a single guard posted outside of the cell holding Aericora's heir to the throne was odd as she selected the correct key and slid it into the lock.

She turned it slowly. An entirely irrational part of her was scared that it wouldn't open, but the lock clicked and the door swung inward.

The cell was dark inside, and the lack of extra light in the hall made it nearly impossible to see anything. It took her eyes a long moment to adjust before she finally caught sight of Caeden sitting on the floor in the very corner of the room.

"Caeden," she whispered. Her voice cracked through the lump in the back of her throat. Against her will, tears pricked her eyes as she adjusted to the darkness around her and could make out more of his features.

He ran his fingers over the marks Ronan made on the wall years ago repeatedly. His fingers were bloody—likely from the rough stone. Bruises bloomed across his skin, and scratches and scrapes lined his arms and legs. They weren't fresh and bleeding like Ronan's had been, though. He'd gotten them days ago, maybe even longer for some. Whatever they'd been doing to him in here, it hadn't been physical torture.

He didn't turn to face her when she said his name. Instead, he ran his bloody fingers across the marks on the wall again, this time faster. One. Two. Three. Four. And the fifth mark that slashed through the others before he repeated it. He kept his eyes firmly shut.

"Caeden," Eryn whispered again, stepping closer.

"Not real. Not real. Not real." Caeden repeated the words again and again, and something inside of Eryn's chest broke as she listened.

They hadn't physically tortured him, but they'd done something to him. They'd probably left him alone in darkness for days, maybe even given him so little to eat that he was becoming delusional.

"I'm real, Caeden," she said softly as she knelt beside him. She pushed her now bloody dagger back against her thigh and rested her hand on top of his. His skin was sticky with blood, and his hands were cold. "I'm right here."

He startled beneath her touch and turned to face her. Tears shone in the corners of his eyes, and she squeezed his hand tighter as a single tear of her own slipped down her cheek.

"Eryn." He said her name so softly the sound hardly reached her. "What-what are you doing here?"

A slight smile tugged at her lips despite there being nothing funny about their current situation. "I'm here for you, you dummy prince."

"You're here?" he asked quietly, as if she would disappear into thin air at any second. He lifted his hand slowly and placed it against the side of her face. He ran his thumb along her cheek, wiping away the tear that fell. "You're crying."

A small part of her wanted to deny it, but instead, she closed her eyes and leaned into his touch.

He was alive.

He wasn't safe yet, but he was alive.

Eryn took a deep breath and swallowed down the rush of emotions flooding her. She had to get him out of here. They had to find Margaid, and they needed to leave. Quickly.

"Can you stand?" she asked, gently guiding his hand away from her face, though every bit of her protested.

"I think so," he answered, but he didn't sound sure.

Eryn took his hands in hers and helped him to his feet. He was unsteady, but he was able to hold up the weight of his own body, which was a good sign. He wasn't quite to the state Ronan had been in, at least. He tried to take a step forward, and nearly stumbled into her, only managing to catch himself at the last second.

"You're okay," she told him as she held tight to his arms and helped him balance. "I'm right here."

It took him a few more steps to get the hang of walking, but she was able to let go of him after a moment and he stood on his own. He was slow, though. It would be hard to get out quickly enough to avoid being caught, especially since they needed to find Margaid, and Eryn wasn't sure where they would've chosen to keep her if not here.

When she'd rescued Ronan, there were soldiers held hostage in each of the cells. There was one guard per hostage, but today, only a single guard stood post. Wherever they were keeping the princess of Crevia, it wasn't up here.

"Do you know where they have Margaid?" she asked as they exited the cell and entered the hallway.

Caeden went stiff beside her and froze dead in his tracks. His eyes were wide and his gaze stayed frozen ahead. He shook his head after a long moment before he finally spoke. "She's not Margaid," he said slowly, as if he knew the words wouldn't make sense.

Eryn frowned. "What do you mean?"

He swallowed hard. In the darkness, it was hard to see his expression, but she caught something like fear as he worked out how he wanted to go about answering.

"She was a disguised spy," he settled with. "She found the real princess while she was on her way to the castle and she killed her. She disguised herself as Margaid and played the part to try to get information out of us. Her real name is Dealla. She's the Dragon Lord's daughter and my cousin."

Eryn's mind raced with the information he'd given her. Questions swam through her mind, but they didn't have time for her to get the answers she needed right now. If they didn't have to find Margaid, they could get out of here faster and there were fewer chances for him to get hurt in the process.

"Okay," she said, though everything he'd told her made their situation the furthest thing from okay.

Especially since the man who had fallen in love with the disguised woman was currently waiting for them outside and would definitely notice when they escaped without the redheaded princess beside them.

Chapter 19

Every inch of Caeden's body ached as they descended the stairs. Eryn supported most of his weight with his arm slung over her shoulders, and he braced himself on the other side with a hand against the wall. Their steps down the stairs were slow, and with each passing second, more and more adrenaline worked its way through him at the high possibility of being caught. His steps became less labored, and it was easier to ignore the pain temporarily the longer they walked. It didn't push away the fog hanging over his thoughts, or how his vision refused to focus, but he could walk on his own by the time they reached the base of the first staircase.

"Not much farther," Eryn whispered, her words rushed. "Just a couple more halls and we'll be safe, okay?"

She gripped his arm tightly as they veered left and hurried down the hall.

He couldn't remember the exact path Dealla brought him down days ago, and he was thankful Eryn seemed to know exactly where she was going. He kept pace with her, as impossible as it seemed.

Caeden's heartbeat was loud in his ears as he thought of the Dragon Lord sitting somewhere inside of the palace, no doubt with plans to find Caeden again to ensure he'd decided to agree to his insane arrangement. He had no way of knowing what his uncle would do once he learned Caeden was no longer in his cell. He had no idea what he would do if he found them attempting to escape, either.

If they were caught, it would likely result in his death along with Eryn's. If they made it out alive, it would result in the deaths of thousands more on the battlefield and likely the attempted—if not successful—death of his father too, if the Dragon Lord and his threats of burning the kingdom to the ground were to be believed.

"Don't go down the rabbit hole," Eryn said through clenched teeth. Her fingers bit painfully into his arm as they turned the corner. "Let's get you out first, then we can worry about the consequences."

"Or you could consider them now, since you're about to receive them," Dealla's voice said from the hall ahead of them. "You didn't think I'd only leave one guard to watch him, did you?"

Bright light shone into the hallway from a large, floor-to-ceiling window where the hall ended, but Dealla was nowhere in sight. He'd know that voice anywhere, though. Hers and her father's would plague his nightmares for the rest of his life.

"Take this," Eryn whispered, so softly he could hardly make out her words as she forced the hilt of a dagger into his hands. He wasn't sure how she'd grabbed it without him noticing.

"That's her," Caeden told her quietly, his hands shaking as his fingers wrapped around the dagger's hilt.

Footsteps echoed around them, and Dealla appeared from around a corner ahead. She held a sword and a smug smirk pulled at the corners of her mouth. "You really thought you'd get away with taking another one of my prisoners?" Anger laced each word as they fell past her lips, and Caeden's skin crawled as the sound of her voice echoed through the hall.

Eryn went rigid beside him. "That's her?" she asked, her voice wavering. "You're sure that's her?"

Dealla's smile grew, and she answered before Caeden got the chance. "Miss Gedding," she said playfully, curtsying to mock the Dragon Hunter. "Long time, no see. Or, so you seemed to think. Your face healed nicely. I was going to tell you sooner, but I'm sure you can guess how that would've ruined the whole disguise and all."

Eryn's hand traced the faint scar across her left cheek. Caeden had noticed it once before, when she'd sat close to him on the couch in Ronan's shack. He'd assumed it was just another scar from years of fighting in the war, but maybe it was more personal than he'd realized.

"Maybe if you'd tried harder, the cut would've been deep enough to leave a real scar," Eryn said easily. "Wait. No. If I remember correctly, that was you trying when I beat you last time. How's your leg? Bet you would've had trouble keeping your secret from Ronan if you hadn't been disguised when you spent your nights naked with him."

Dealla's face turned a dangerous shade of red.

A smug, condescending grin pulled at Eryn's mouth. "So it did scar then?"

Dealla's movements were so swift Caeden would have missed them if he'd blinked. She charged toward the two of them, her sword raised high above her head, anger and hatred etched across her face.

Eryn shoved him so hard he stumbled back against the wall to his right. His back connected with the rough stone, sending a shock of pain up his spine. He braced himself against the stones, barely managing to stay upright as his head spun from the impact.

"Break the window!" Eryn shouted as Dealla collided with her, slamming her sword against a dagger Eryn pulled from wherever it had been hidden on her.

Dizziness washed over him as he pulled himself to his feet, but he pushed the feeling aside and ran to the window. The dagger was cool in his hand as he brought it up to the window and slammed the pointed edge of it into the thick glass. The hit should've been enough to break it, but his body was weak and so were his movements. Instead of shattering the glass, it only chipped away a small shard from the window. A crack split through the glass from the indent, no thicker than a sheet of paper.

He pounded the hilt of the dagger against the window as the sounds of the fight happening behind him reverberated through his bones. The window didn't break, but the crack deepened and snaked higher.

Eryn grunted behind him from the effort of fending off Dealla. Their weapons scraped against one another, and the sound of their quick feet against the tile floor followed.

His body begged him to turn and face the fight, to lift the dagger and throw himself into the middle of it. He couldn't win in the state he was in. He would make it worse. He would be a liability. Eryn would spend her energy trying to protect him instead of protecting herself and doing whatever needed to be done to defeat Dealla.

His hands shook as he lifted the dagger again, his knuckles white as he gripped it with every ounce of strength he could manage. He beat it against the window again and again, and the crack spread out farther and farther with each hit until, eventually, it shattered.

Glass rained down on him, biting into his skin as he stumbled back. He shielded his eyes with his arm until the glass stopped falling.

"Jump!" Eryn said from behind him.

Caeden turned back to face her. Dealla had her pressed against the wall, her sword perpendicular to Eryn's dagger. She fought against the full weight of Dealla's body as she leaned into her.

"I'm fine!" she screamed. Her gaze was steady when she glanced at him, before she refocused on her attacker.

She would be okay. He had to believe she would be okay.

She would win.

Caeden swallowed hard, pushing back the feelings welling inside and instead focusing on the task she'd put in front of him. "Jump to where?"

The question sounded ridiculous, even to his own ears. She was fighting for her life. He shouldn't be asking dumb questions when he knew she had a plan. The plan seemed like it might very well end in his death, though.

"Stop asking questions and just trust me!" she snapped as she pushed Dealla off. They squared off again as they both found their footing on the tile. Eryn's back was to him, blocking Dealla from making an attempt to keep him from escaping.

Caeden forced his eyes away from the scene and turned to the empty space where the glass used to be.

He didn't give himself time to think before he jumped through the open window.

Chapter 20
Eryn

"I see the feelings haven't gone away," Dealla taunted as she lunged for Eryn again, and she pivoted out of the blond-haired princess's reach.

She'd seen that face once before, and she hadn't wanted to see it again. She'd been the one to torture Ronan. She'd been the one to corner Eryn when they'd rescued Ronan, and had nearly killed her. If the strike hadn't scarred her cheek, it would've gone straight through her eye.

She was one of very few Deovarian soldiers who kept Eryn on her feet. Not many were trained at the level that the woman before her was, which made so much more sense now that Eryn knew this was the Dragon Lord's daughter. Dealla was still easy to distract, though. It was the only way Eryn had managed to beat her.

"Clearly, yours haven't either," Eryn responded as Dealla's sword connected with her dagger. She leaned into her weapon, using the full weight of her body to keep the sword's edge from nearing her.

She needed to end the fight quickly. Soldiers would find them here and she'd be captured if they got to her before she defeated Dealla. The princess could be useful to them, though.

Eryn had learned quickly last time that once Dealla was angry, her fighting turned reckless and predictable. It was fast, and hard to block if she attacked in the right order, but it was her best chance to win.

Dealla set her jaw and pushed harder against Eryn, putting all of her weight into it like Eryn had.

Good.

Eryn smirked as she released the pressure against her blade and ducked to the side. Dealla fell forward, tumbling to the tile floor as she tripped, and Eryn lunged after her, practically falling on top of the other woman as she hit the ground.

Dealla grunted as her forehead connected with the tile, the air whooshing from her lungs.

She'd be fine, but she was disoriented and that was all Eryn needed.

She held the dagger to the back of her neck, and Dealla stiffened. She angled herself so she could kick Dealla's sword away from her hands, and it skidded across the floor before bumping the wall on the other end of the hallway.

Dealla breathed heavily beneath her. She spat blood from her mouth as she tried to lift her head off the floor and her neck pressed into the tip of Eryn's dagger. "Bitch," Dealla snarled. "Either kill me or escape, but you're wasting your time."

Eryn grinned again as she reached for the length of rope tucked into the breastplate strapped to her chest. She yanked Dealla's wrists behind her back. The princess grunted again and Eryn bound her wrists so tight the rope bit into her skin. She didn't care whether it was comfortable. She deserved every ounce of pain she would receive for the things she'd done.

"I'm going to get out of here, but I think it's time you endured a little of that torture you seem to enjoy putting others through."

She climbed slowly off the other woman, yanking her up by her bound wrists while keeping her dagger pressed firmly to the back of her neck.

"Walk," Eryn demanded, and after a moment of struggling against the rope, Dealla eventually did.

The broken glass crunched beneath Eryn's boots as they approached the window. Ronan waited outside with the blue dragon a short distance below them. Caeden was on the dragon's back just behind Ronan, though he looked like he wouldn't be able to keep himself on much longer. She kept Dealla pulled far enough back that she wouldn't be able to see the creature, or the two men on her back.

"Don't scream," Eryn taunted, and didn't give Dealla time to comprehend her words before she pulled her up to the window and pushed her through the opening.

She screamed on her way down, and Eryn almost laughed at the sound. It was cruel, and if not for all of the things the woman had done, she would've hated herself for enjoying it so much. She'd tortured Ronan for a month, though. She'd disguised herself as a princess from Crevia and made the same man fall in love with her. Then she'd kidnapped the man Eryn was beginning to love, and kept him in the same bloody cell his best friend was trapped and tortured in.

Eryn could throw her out the window another thousand times and it wouldn't make up for the cruelty.

The sound of Dealla's body hitting the dragon below reached Eryn's ears right before she leapt off the edge of the windowsill. She landed gracefully on the dragon's back, just behind Deovaria's Princess. The air was loud around her as the dragon flapped its wings to keep them suspended in midair, and the wind against her skin sent a chill down her spine.

"What's she doin' here?" Ronan demanded as he angled the dragon away from the palace and in the general direction of the border to Aericora. "Where's Margaid?"

Eryn's heart thudded loudly in her ears and pain tore through her chest. Dealla's eyes widened as she stared at Ronan, who hadn't turned away from facing Eryn. Caeden flinched.

She couldn't tell him now, and it broke her inside that she would ever have to. She shook her head slowly. "Not now," she yelled. Ronan set his jaw, but he didn't say anything as they headed for Aericora.

Chapter 21

Caeden gripped the rope tied around his waist tightly as they flew. His whole body was weak, and his head spun as they made their way back to Aericora. He almost slipped off the back of the dragon more times than he could count, but Ronan caught him each time before he plummeted to the ground beneath.

They flew for hours before finally landing in the forest near the border. The dragon came to an abrupt stop when she landed, sending a jolt through him that reverberated through his bones and made his head ache.

The moment the dragon was still, Ronan spun around. His gaze bore into Dealla, hatred and pure anguish mingling in his features.

She was the same woman he'd fallen in love with weeks ago, but he didn't know that yet. All he saw was the face of the woman who tortured him for information. She'd spurred his drinking problem, she'd given him his fear of the dark, she was the reason he could hardly walk without leaning on a cane. And that wasn't even the worst half of it.

Ronan turned his gaze on Eryn, the anger he felt mingling

with the fears of what Margaid not being here meant. He didn't know the truth, but he knew something was wrong if they hadn't come out with the Princess of Crevia. "What's she doin' here?" he demanded, an edge to his voice Caeden had only heard once or twice in the years he'd known him. "Where's Margaid, Eryn?"

Eryn tensed, and her knuckles turned white. Her fingers bit into Dealla's arm hard enough that her skin turned red around Eryn's fingertips with the start of bruises.

Caeden reached to put a hand on his friend's shoulder, though it wouldn't do anything to lighten the blow of the words he had yet to say.

His hand never made it to Ronan's shoulder. Instead, the movement paired with the suddenly noticeable lack of adrenaline made his vision so blurred and his body so dizzy that he fell forward. He would've slipped off the dragon's back if not for Ronan catching him for what had to have been the hundredth time.

"Fuck, princy." Ronan lifted Caeden into a sitting position while Caeden blinked to clear away the fog clouding his vision. The anger that was in his tone before had disappeared, at least momentarily.

It took longer than Caeden wanted it to, but after a few agonizingly long moments, his vision cleared and his body was no longer quite so out of his control.

"This is your doin', isn't it?" Ronan practically growled the words, turning his once again angry gaze on Dealla.

She had enough grace to look ashamed. "It's my job," she bit out. Her cheeks were red, and she couldn't seem to lift her head high enough to look Ronan in the eyes.

Caeden had been right. She had fallen in love with Ronan.

"Don't make you any less of a murderer," Ronan spat. He looked at Eryn, who hadn't moved an inch since Ronan first spoke to her when the dragon landed. "What's she doin' here, Reckless? This better be part of the plan to get Margaid out."

Eryn swallowed hard. "I'll tell you after Caeden is taken care of. He needs food and water, and it would look bad if he walked into the castle like that." She gestured to the state of his clothing, likely referring to the smell rather than the dirt and blood covering him.

"Reckless," Ronan warned.

Eryn's face softened. "Trust me, okay?" Her voice was pleading.

"You don't want to know yet," Caeden whispered. His words came out strained and slurred around the edges.

Ronan threw his hands up, his anger coming back. "I don't give a damn how bad it is. I wanna know what happened. Where's Margaid, and why is she here? Just tell me what the hell you were thinkin' kidnappin' the—"

"Ronan!" Eryn snapped. Dealla winced, and Eryn looked close to breaking her arm.

The two siblings stared at one another, their glares so identical Caeden wondered if they were biologically related after all.

"Fine," Ronan snapped. He faced forward on the dragon, and before Caeden had time to realize what he was doing, his head snapped back and he fell into Dealla and Eryn behind him as the dragon launched into the sky.

The dragon flew for another hour, and Caeden nearly passed out more times than he could count.

They landed at the bank of a small river, and Eryn helped him off of the dragon's back while Ronan tied Dealla up between two trees with an extra length of rope. He backed her against a tree before binding her wrists around it, and tying her legs together right above the knee and again at her ankles. From there, he took another section of rope and tied her bound ankles to another tree a few feet away so she couldn't bend her knees and get her feet beneath herself.

"A little overkill, don't you think?" Dealla mumbled as Eryn slung Caeden's arm over her shoulders and helped him walk toward the river's edge.

Pain shot through his limbs as he tried to keep up with Eryn's footsteps in the grass. His head still spun, and the pain in combination with the dizziness made him want nothing more than to curl up in the grass and sleep.

"Prob'ly could've gone for another few ropes," Ronan responded as he cinched the rope around her bound ankles and she winced. "Lucky for you, I ran out."

"Do you have her?" Eryn called over her shoulder as she and Caeden stumbled past them.

"I've got her," Ronan said. He turned to face them with the same expression he'd had when they'd refused to answer his questions. "The second you're back, I want answers, Reckless."

Eryn nodded once before she turned forward.

Caeden stumbled, and Eryn shifted her weight to catch him before he hit the ground. The relief the ground would offer almost made him forget to use his remaining strength to help her steady him back to his feet.

"We're almost there," she whispered, and he wasn't entirely sure if she was talking to him or to herself.

Mud squished beneath his shoes the closer they got, and the rushing of the water along the shore and across the stones at the bottom filled his ears. Water seeped into his pants as Eryn helped him kneel in the damp dirt. The cold settled deep into his bones, making a shiver run up his spine.

She reached around him and her fingers found the hem of his shirt. She gave it a light tug, gently peeling the blood-soaked fabric from his raw skin.

His cheeks heated at her closeness as her lavender scent washed over him. The pain subsided as he took her in—her bright blue eyes shadowed by long lashes, the way her lip quirked slightly higher on one side, the small, jagged scar running along her cheek. He'd remembered she was beautiful, but he'd forgotten how truly stunning the woman in front of him was. He'd forgotten the way her closeness made his heart race, the way his face grew hot, and the way his body reacted to even her slightest touch.

"Lift your arms," Eryn said quietly, and he really must have been far more out of it than he'd realized, because before he remembered to feel self-conscious as she undressed him, he did as he was told.

His face grew hotter as she pulled his shirt over his head and set it aside.

Eryn swallowed hard, her eyes trailing along the bruises and scratches marking his torso and shoulders. The injuries were mostly from his first day in the cell, but a few new ones blossomed across his skin since his waning strength made it hard for him to climb to his feet without falling straight back to the floor.

She reached for him and ran her fingers along the edge of a particularly jagged and long scratch beneath his collarbone. Her eyes met his again, and he would have been content to let the tiredness take him into a dreamless sleep if the last thing he saw were those eyes.

"Did she do this to you?" she asked, a fierceness in her tone he'd never heard before, despite the words themselves being gentle. The look in her eyes could've been enough to kill a man where he stood.

Caeden didn't answer. Instead, he only blinked a few times

to clear the fog from his head and reached for the bloody shirt she'd set beside him.

"Caeden," Eryn said, halfway between gentle and demanding. He turned back to face her. "Who did this to you?"

"It doesn't matter," he responded, because it truly didn't. Ronan had been tortured for a month, and while Dealla was the reason for his condition, none of that compared to the pain his friend was about to face within the hour.

"It does," she insisted. "If this was her fault too, I swear I'll kill her now."

Caeden shook his head. "She's too useful. We can use her to bargain with the Dragon Lord. I don't know if he has a heart, but if he does, his daughter is likely the way to hurt it. She could help us win the war."

"I don't give a damn about the war right now, Caeden," Eryn told him. She lifted her hand from where it still rested on his chest and placed it against his cheek, making him look into her eyes. "I'm worried about you."

Her gaze was so intense he froze in place, pinned by the depth of whatever it was she felt behind those beautiful oceans of blue.

Eryn shook her head, breaking their gaze and letting her hand fall away from his cheek before she shoved her hair out of her face. "It doesn't matter. Let's get you cleaned up."

She reached to take his shirt from his hands, and Caeden didn't have the strength to stop her. "Eryn," he said quietly, as her hands grasped the fabric.

She looked up. "Hmm?"

"You're beautiful."

Eryn's eyes widened, and her breath hitched. She stayed frozen for several seconds, her face a few inches away from his and her hands still gripping the fabric of the shirt.

He wasn't sure what he'd expected from her when he'd said the words, but he wasn't at all surprised when she swallowed and turned away from him with the shirt before she began washing it out in the river beside them.

Once it was clean, she used the wet fabric to dab at the wounds marking him. She rinsed it out repeatedly, but they didn't have any better options given their current situation. She didn't say anything while she worked, and he wasn't sure what he could say to her to lighten the mood again. So instead, he kept quiet.

Halfway through cleaning him, she handed him a bag of dried fruits to eat. He ate them slowly, chewing them more than he normally would before swallowing to keep his stomach from heaving.

It took her around half an hour to get him clean and his shirt wrung out enough that it was no longer dripping water.

Caeden struggled to get it back on, and it stuck to his body as badly as it had before. The wind blowing past was brutal, sending waves of cold crashing into him, but it would be better to enter the castle with at least a clean shirt rather than a bloody one.

Ronan waited impatiently for them when they finally finished, and Eryn helped Caeden hobble back to the clearing. She helped him sit against a tree, and he collapsed against it once her arms were no longer around his body to help support his weight.

"Where is she?" Ronan demanded before Eryn had time to stand up straight.

Eryn visibly tensed, and Caeden felt his own body do the same. They couldn't put it off any longer, but he would've given anything to never say the words he forced out of his mouth. "That's her," Caeden said softly, nodding in the direction of

Dealla still tied between two trees.

Confusion fell over Ronan's face as he glanced at the blond-haired woman who had tortured him for a month. He looked at Caeden and opened his mouth to say something, but Caeden cut him off before he could.

"She was disguised as Margaid," he said quickly, the words falling from his mouth before he gave himself too much time to think them over. If he thought too long about it, he wouldn't be able to force them out, and he couldn't do that to his friend. He had to tell him the truth before he found out in a way that would inevitably be worse. "She's the Dragon Lord's daughter, and also my cousin. She was sent to kill the real Margaid and take her place so she could get information from me while the princesses were staying in the castle. She killed the real princess on the trail before she ever got to the castle. When she didn't get anything interesting from me…" A lump formed in the back of his throat, making it hard to breathe.

"When she couldn't get anything from Caeden, she used you," Eryn finished, her words hardly above a whisper on the breeze.

Ronan only stared at them. His gaze flicked from Caeden to Eryn, then back again. For a moment, he looked like he wanted to call them out on a lie, but that moment ended and instead he shook his head. He clenched his jaw tight; the only sign of the betrayal he felt hidden behind his hazel eyes.

He glanced at Dealla, and both Caeden and Eryn did the same. She had the decency to keep her eyes downcast and her head bowed. Her hands shook against the rope keeping them bound around the tree.

She looked broken, as if she'd endured a kind of torture herself.

Caeden almost felt bad for her. Despite being sent to gather information, she'd caught genuine feelings for Ronan. But whether those feelings were real or fake, she'd still betrayed him. She was still the one who held the keys to his cell and inflicted all kinds of pain on him.

The small part of him that almost felt empathy for her vanished, replaced with the same anger he felt toward her father.

"Ronan," Eryn said softly, taking a step toward him. Her hand was outstretched, like she was about to rest it on his shoulder, but he turned away from her.

"I'm too sober for this," Ronan stated simply as he strode to the dragon and carefully climbed onto its back. He struggled to get himself all the way up, but he managed it despite his injured leg.

Eryn didn't make a move to follow him, and Caeden wasn't sure he could even if he wanted to.

"Whenever you're ready, let's get back to the castle," Ronan said, not looking back at any of them. He tied the rope around his waist and ran a hand along the dragon's neck tenderly. It nickered softly like a horse and leaned its head back farther, enjoying the attention.

Caeden moved to climb to his feet, but Eryn shot him a warning look over her shoulder and he stayed put.

She turned back to Ronan, the mask of a soldier she wore often falling back into place. "Caeden needs to rest a little longer," she said firmly, but not unkindly.

"I'm okay," Caeden argued, which only earned him another warning look.

"You're not. You need to eat some more and drink something, then we can talk about leaving."

Ronan glanced back, but was careful to avoid looking at Dealla. "Listen to her, princy. I've been there, remember? You ain't gonna be as okay as you think."

His words struck Caeden like a knife, and all he could do was nod.

Chapter 22

The dragon landed smoothly on the ground half a mile away from the castle. They flew low over the treetops the rest of the way back, hoping to avoid the gazes of the guards. They couldn't risk causing a panic so soon after Caeden was taken and Eryn and Ronan went behind the court's backs to take the dragon and rescue him.

They remained on the dragon's back as they walked down the path closer to the castle. They dismounted near the forest's edge, and Eryn helped Caeden down the dragon's wing to the ground. He was wobbly on his feet, but after the food and water Eryn had offered earlier and the first rest he'd gotten in days that wasn't laced with adrenaline coursing through him, he felt much better.

"Eryn stays with Dealla," Caeden said as strongly as he could once they dismounted and Ronan had Dealla firmly tied to another pair of trees like she'd been earlier in the day. "Ronan comes back with me. We'll alert the guards so we don't scare anyone. I'll have them send a couple of guards to help you back."

Eryn fixed him with a look, but Ronan only nodded his head once. He'd been silent since they left the riverside, only communicating with head nods or grunts that were mostly lost to the wind.

He was hurting after finding out what really happened to Margaid, and that Dealla was a spy trying to get information from him, though hurting didn't seem like a strong enough word to describe it. He'd loved her, and she was the same woman who had spent a month torturing him.

If Caeden could make every bad thing Ronan went through disappear, he would've done it in a heartbeat.

"You're hurt, and he can barely walk," Eryn argued, glaring at him with an intensity that could make an army cower.

"Exactly," Caeden agreed. "You're the only one who can make sure she doesn't escape."

He hadn't expected her to like his plan, given she hadn't taken her eyes off either him or Ronan since they left Deovaria, but it was the only reasonable way they could do this without terrorizing the guards.

Surprise flashed across her features, and she set her jaw. "Fine," she bit out through clenched teeth.

Ronan turned and shouldered a small pack. He struggled to get it on since he couldn't lean against his cane for balance while doing so.

"Caeden," Eryn said softly, stepping closer to him. She reached for him but seemed to think better of it and pulled her hand away quickly. Pale pink blossomed across her nose and cheeks, but she didn't break eye contact.

He swallowed hard, unable to look away from her eyes. Those eyes were what had kept him sane. The memory of her touch, her scent, her small smiles, her laugh, even her unwavering irritation. It had been her.

"I know we're back, but promise me you'll be safe," she whispered, so quietly her words hardly reached him.

Caeden forced a smile. Nowhere was safe. Deovaria attacked the castle only a few weeks ago, and he'd been tricked into being kidnapped when he was asleep in his own bed. It didn't matter if they were home. They could've been in the middle of Deovaria still, and he would've felt as safe there as he did now.

The worry hidden in her eyes lodged itself into his heart. Even though she knew as well as he did that they weren't any safer here, he spoke the words she needed to hear. "I will."

Eryn smiled. It was genuine, but sadness clung to her features. "Thank you."

Ronan cleared his throat from a few feet away, and Caeden jumped at the sound before he turned to face him. "We leavin', or you two need another minute?"

Usually, a comment like that would've been paired with a mischievous grin, but the question was asked with a kind of seriousness Caeden rarely saw from his best friend. It made his stomach twist into even tighter knots.

"We don't need 'minutes,'" Eryn said, rolling her eyes, even as Caeden's face grew warm at the suggestion behind the comment.

"Well, then let's get goin', princy. The longer we're gone, the madder that damn court is gonna get."

Caeden nodded, and Ronan started down the trail ahead. "We'll be safe," he promised Eryn, before turning to follow Ronan.

Their walk back to the castle was mostly silent. Ronan walked with his eyes forward, his jaw set, and his hand gripping the top of his cane so tightly his knuckles were white.

"Did you ever think she was hidin' somthin' before all this?" Ronan asked quietly, just as the castle gates came into view. The guards posted in front held their maces high, their eyes trained on them as they approached since they wouldn't yet be able to determine who they were.

"No," Caeden answered honestly. "She asked a few questions and said some things that threw me off, and looking back it makes sense, but in the moment, I only thought she was asking because she could've ended up being Aericora's queen. I never thought anything more than that."

Ronan grunted. He nodded slowly, his eyes downcast, but didn't say anything as they approached the gates.

"Prince Caeden," one of the guards said loudly once they could make out the two men standing before them. The guard's attention flicked from Caeden to Ronan standing beside him. "General Atkyn." He blinked several times, his eyes going between the two men, then back again. "You-you're..."

The guard trailed off, and Ronan interrupted any chance for him to figure out what he wanted to say. "Yes, we're alive. Inform the king that we require an audience with him." He turned to the other guard, and the first one sprinted inside of the castle so fast Caeden would've missed him if he'd blinked. "You. Eryn Gedding is down the trail with a prisoner from Deovaria." He pointed in the direction they'd come from, and the guard's eyes followed his gesture. "They have the dragon with them. Find the two guards from the southeast post and ensure they are brought back to the castle safely and that the dragon is escorted to her shelter."

The second guard nodded quickly, and she turned to head to the post Ronan mentioned as he and Caeden stepped through the gates and into the courtyard.

Caeden's heartbeat matched their rhythmic steps up to the main entrance, where a second pair of guards waited for them. They bowed their heads politely to the two men before stepping aside and allowing them entrance.

It felt strange being back in the castle. He was only gone a week and a half, yet stepping through those doors—though he'd done it hundreds of times before—felt impossible. It hadn't occurred to him when he'd been the Dragon Lord's prisoner, but he hadn't thought he would ever see the inside of his home again. He'd known they would attempt to rescue him, given the title he held, but he hadn't expected it to be successful. He'd expected to have to find his own way out, or to die in that cell before anyone from Aericora could get inside of Deovaria's palace.

He shouldn't have been so quick to underestimate Eryn and Ronan.

The walk through the halls to his father's office was automatic, but his limbs were heavy. He told himself it was the residual weakness from his time spent in the cell, but he couldn't believe the lie. He hadn't thought he'd see his father again, and he had no idea what he would say to him when he did.

He didn't know how to tell him about everything he'd learned. How was he going to tell him he knew the Dragon Lord was his uncle? That he'd been kidnapped by his cousin who had posed as the woman the rest of the world expected him to marry?

How would he tell him about Amelia?

"You okay, princy?" Ronan asked. He stopped walking and glanced back with a worried look on his face.

Caeden swallowed hard and forced himself to nod. He wasn't, but there was no point in prolonging this. The faster he got to his father's office and spoke with him and the court, the faster this would be over. As much as the fear of seeing his father's reaction to everything made a sharp pain lodge itself into his chest, it needed to be done.

Voices reached him as they rounded the final corner and stepped into the hallway leading to Caeden's father's office. His father's voice, along with multiple of the usual advisors, rang through the hallway, and Caeden's heart clenched as the fear of what he would walk into grew tenfold.

Ronan let out a breath and seemed to steel himself against his fear, likely of the king being enraged that he and Eryn had snuck out of the castle with the Deovarian dragon to rescue him without the support of the court.

The chatter from inside ceased as Caeden stepped through the doorway with his friend by his side.

"Your Highness!" Muire practically squeaked, sounding equally surprised and confused at the sight of him.

His eyes landed on his father sitting behind his desk, ignoring the advisor's words.

The king hadn't looked well in months, but he'd never looked so frail. His cheeks were hollow, dark circles hung beneath his eyes, and he'd lost so much weight Caeden could see the bones in his hands. He looked like he'd aged thirty years in the time Caeden was gone.

Tears pricked the corners of Caeden's eyes, but he willed them not to fall as his father's eyes widened and he stood. Before Caeden had time to say anything, or register what he was doing, his father was in front of him and wrapping him in a hug with a strength that shouldn't have been possible in his current state.

"You're safe," his father breathed, his breath warm in Caeden's hair. The king's breaths came in ragged gasps as Caeden wrapped his arms around him in return, and he realized for the first time that his father was crying.

"I'm here," he whispered, the weight of it crashing into him all at once. He'd been so worried to tell his father everything he'd learned that he hadn't stopped to think how his father would react to the fact that he was back—that he was still alive and hadn't been lost to the Dragon Lord and his armies like the rest of their family had.

His father's tears wet the top of Caeden's head and the king held him tighter, crushing Caeden's already bruised frame, though he couldn't have made himself care about the pain.

"You're alive," the king whispered, his voice cracking.

He pulled away from his father just enough to look him in the eye. Tears streamed down his father's face, and he looked so broken Caeden wished he could avoid telling him everything he learned in Deovaria and simply keep it locked away inside. "Dad, I'm here."

It'd been so long since he'd referred to his father that way. He'd grown used to thinking of him as the king in recent years, and sometimes he forgot that he was also his father. The king was gone as he looked into his father's watery eyes, though. This man didn't bear the weight of the kingdom on his shoulders. For just a moment, he was only a father who thought his son had been taken from him like his wife and daughter had been.

His father nodded his head slightly before he hugged Caeden again.

They stayed like that for longer than Caeden was sure any of the court was comfortable with, but he didn't care. They could feel how they wanted. They could say his father was weak for worrying, or for letting tears fall down his cheeks. But none of it mattered right now. They would deal with it when it came. And if the court was wise, they would keep their mouths shut.

Eventually, his father's crying eased, and he stepped away. He wiped the tears from his eyes before giving him the kind of smile Caeden only remembered seeing from him weeks ago when they left for the field. There was so much love in his smile that Caeden felt the walls he'd built up between himself and his father over the years crumble beneath it.

The king walked back around his desk and took a seat, his usual composed expression falling across his features as he gestured for both Caeden and Ronan to sit in the two chairs opposite him at the desk.

They did as he asked.

Muire sat in a chair a few feet from his father, and Fionn, Cormac, and Neill stood awkwardly around the room as well. No one else was present, and he was thankful the assembled group was small with everything he still needed to say.

"I'll speak to you and Eryn separately," the king said to Ronan.

A warning hid in his tone, but only for the court's benefit. Everything about his father's expression said that he was nothing short of indebted to them for the risk they took.

His father turned to him. "What happened?"

"Yes," Muire cut in. "And where is Princess Margaid?"

Caeden glanced at her before turning back to his father. "The real Princess Margaid was killed before she ever got to Aericora," he explained. "The Dragon Lord's daughter, my cousin Dealla, was disguised as Margaid and sent here with the intention of gathering information from me during her stay for the Deovarian army. As far as I'm aware, she wasn't able to gather anything devastating. If she had, I doubt she would've kidnapped me and taken me to her father."

Caeden watched his father's expression as he said the words, but no surprise flashed across his features when he mentioned Dealla. He'd kept it a secret that Caeden's mother was a Deovarian princess, but he'd certainly known about it.

Heavy silence filled the room. Caeden couldn't see the looks on any of the other courtiers' faces but Muire's, but if her expression and the silence were any indication, the information he'd shared left them stunned.

Countless questions hung in the air around them, but when the silence finally broke, none of the ones Caeden expected were asked.

"Did they get any information out of you while you were held prisoner?" Fionn asked, his voice gruff. His expression was serious when Caeden faced him, but fear laced his words.

Caeden shook his head. "The Dragon Lord attempted to persuade me to work with him. He wanted me to agree to having my father killed and join our kingdoms under his rule. He said he would end the war and the bloodshed, and give me power on the court of the joined kingdoms. I refused, so he left me locked in a cell. I wasn't tortured for information. They only wanted me to agree to their terms and join the kingdoms."

"Damn it, Colm," the king muttered beneath his breath.

"What reason would they have for that?" Neill, the youngest of the courtiers, asked.

"Less bloodshed all around," Fionn answered. "They dangled power in front of him as if our defeat is inevitable, likely to pull it away the second he agreed and the king was dead. It would be an easy way to ensure they won, even though they don't have as much power over us as they think. It would also be easy to kill the prince, after he saw to it that his father was dead, since he would walk right back into their hands."

"Luckily, our prince ain't that stupid," Ronan stated. There was an edge to his tone, and Caeden wasn't sure what part of the conversation caused it.

"We've taken Dealla as a hostage," Caeden told them, getting back to their earlier conversation. "Eryn has her now and they are being escorted to the castle by a few guards. I don't know how much she knows about the stones, but I think she could help us. We know the stones are from the mountains, but she might know more specifically where we can find them, if we can get the information out of her.”

The king nodded. “Ronan, have a cell prepared for her.” Ronan gave a curt nod, and the king turned to face the other court members. “Fionn, I want you to interrogate her in the morning. Give her time to let her situation sink in so she’s more likely to give up the information. The prince and I will join you.”

“Yes, Your Majesty,” Fionn replied.

Caeden’s stomach twisted itself into knots at the thought. The hate he felt for his cousin was strong after everything she’d put him through and everything she’d done to Ronan, but he wasn’t sure he wanted to be present for whatever measures the interrogation would lead to, either.

The meeting ended soon after, and Caeden’s father dismissed the others in the room.

Their shoes thudded against the floor before the sound of the door closing left him and his father alone.

He’d dreaded this part the most.

“You should get cleaned up,” his father said gently, offering Caeden a warm smile from the other end of the desk.

Caeden swallowed hard, his father’s words hardly registering as his mind raced. Before he gave himself enough time to think over the words he wanted to say, they spilled from his mouth. “Amelia’s alive.”

His father’s eyes widened as if a dragon had just burst through the door behind Caeden. He shook his head a moment later, and the expression vanished. “What kind of lies did he spin?”

Caeden shook his head. “None,” he said quietly. “I saw her with my own eyes.”

His father didn’t look convinced, and somehow, that was worse than any of the emotions Caeden anticipated seeing on his face.

"He took her as a trophy," Caeden whispered. "They figured out how to use the dragon's magic to keep an object frozen in space and time. He has her held in a space that looks almost like a block of ice." His throat felt tight. "She's still eleven."

The king shook his head. He reached across the desk and rested a hand on Caeden's arm. "Son, you were held prisoner for a week. I don't know what they did to you, but I assure you that was a tactic to get you to agree to their terms. She isn't alive. We already know they have magic that can manipulate a person's appearance. I know it's hard to hear, but what sounds more realistic: that Amelia is still alive, frozen forever as an eleven-year-old girl, or strange lighting and a child disguised to look like your sister?"

Caeden's heart stopped.

He hadn't even considered that possibility.

How had he believed the Dragon Lord so easily when the truth could be something so simple?

It would've been easy to disguise a person and set up the weird bluish hue he'd seen around Amelia's body. They could've simply constructed a wall of crystal and placed a young girl disguised as his sister inside.

A sadness he hadn't felt since he'd first learned of Amelia's death hit him, and the tears he'd attempted to keep at bay slipped from his eyes.

"I'm sorry, my son," his father whispered. "She's gone. They're both gone."

Chapter 23

Dealla

A rustling in the woods caught Dealla's attention as she struggled against the bindings securing her wrists and ankles to the two trees nearby, just like earlier in the day when they'd tied her up the first time.

When *Ronan* had tied her up the first time.

The thought sent a pang of hurt through her chest, and a flare of anger surged through her before she pushed it away.

Another rustle came from somewhere behind her, and a slow, wicked grin pulled at the corners of her lips. She'd been waiting for them to find her.

Eryn stood twenty feet away, patting the neck of the large blue dragon tenderly, despite the way her rigid shoulders hinted at the fear she felt toward the beast.

Traitorous creature.

More footsteps reached her, but she couldn't so easily distract the Dragon Hunter like she'd done on the way to the battlefield weeks ago, though maybe the distraction was more from Caeden's presence than her less-than-subtle actions.

Falling off her horse had hurt, but it was worth it if it kept them from hearing the assassins hiding in the woods. They were beginning to figure it out now, but she'd gained them more time if nothing else by pulling that stunt. And though Eryn was suspicious of her after, she hadn't figured out her secret until it was too late.

The assassins didn't know of her disguise, which was why she opted to cause a distraction and get the group on guard in the first place. The assassins were given strict orders to only attack unassuming groups, so their numbers wouldn't dwindle quickly.

If they'd still chosen to attack, she would've removed her disguise and they would've recognized her, considering she had assembled the group herself, but it wasn't worth giving up the possible information she could still uncover.

The dragon let out a low growl, but she would be powerless to stop the assassins since Dealla had ensured each wore a stone.

Eryn's attention snapped to the woods behind Dealla. She tried to appear unfazed, but her hands dropped to the daggers strapped to her thighs, fingers tightening around the leather hilts.

"Your friends somewhere out there?" Eryn asked, her distaste seeping into her tone, though her gaze never left the edge of the forest.

She was smarter than Dealla had given her credit for when she'd first met her in the halls of the palace three years ago. She hadn't expected the Dragon Hunter would lead two successful missions into the palace and free two separate men Dealla was interrogating.

Her rage toward the woman in front of her resurfaced at the thought.

Dealla plastered on an expression of confusion. "What friends?" she asked, the sweetness dripping from her tone like the deadliest kind of poison.

That same fake sweetness got her into Ronan's bed more times than she could count.

The thought hurt her heart in a way it never should've, and she pushed it away before giving herself enough time to linger on it.

Eryn tossed her a glare as she pulled a dagger from the holster.

More footsteps.

Five assassins were in the woods: two behind Dealla, and another three somewhere behind Eryn.

Dealla's lip quirked to the side again. Eryn was a good fighter, but four against one was an uneven match, never mind her still-healing shoulder. She would lose quickly, and the realization gave her a sweet thrill of joy, even as she pulled against her bindings again.

She wouldn't be trapped here much longer.

Eryn's body visibly tensed, and her knuckles turned white as she gripped her dagger tighter. The severity of her situation seemed to dawn on her, but the fear in her eyes hardened quickly.

"Your little prince can't save you," Dealla sneered, just as two figures cloaked in dark green stepped around the trees behind her, and two more appeared behind Eryn. The fifth appeared in front of the dragon, holding a blade to the tender part of her chest. The dragon bared her teeth, but she couldn't move from where she was if she wanted to keep her life.

The Dragon Hunter's gaze flicked from the assassins behind Dealla to the two standing twenty feet behind her. She swallowed before her eyes landed on Dealla for the first time and remained there, unwavering as the assassins closed in around her. She returned Dealla's smile before a loud laugh left her. "Even if he were," she said, her words hardly audible through her laughter, "he's not trained enough to fend off even one of these assassins." She shrugged a single shoulder, but her eyes hardened again. "I'll die either way, but I'm taking some of you with me."

Dealla didn't have time to blink before a second knife—one no bigger than the palm of her hand—appeared in Eryn's hand. Where it came from, Dealla could only guess as Eryn spun the blade through the air with such precision it sliced through the jugular of the assassin standing to her right.

The man grabbed his throat, but the bleeding was too severe. Only a few seconds passed before he fell to the ground in a lifeless heap.

The other assassins charged at the Dragon Hunter, their swords outstretched. Yells permeated the air, causing her ears to ring, but her eyes never left the sight in front of her. Blood flew from the tips of blades, but in the mess of bodies, it was hard to tell who caused what injury.

Another assassin fell, and when she caught a glimpse of Eryn again, a large gash ran the length of her leg. Her shirt was split in two along her stomach, but only a thin slice cut through her midsection, not enough to cause any real damage.

"Leave her alive!" Dealla screamed over the fight.

The assassins offered no response to her order, but they wouldn't dare disobey their princess and face the wrath of her father.

The fight was over a minute later. Eryn stood stock still with a blade to her throat as one of the assassins held her firmly from behind. The second assassin held his sword to Eryn's side, just in front of her lowered arm, where she gripped her blade so tightly her knuckles were stark white. She could shove her blade backward and strike down the assassin who held his blade to her throat, but she would be killed by the other without a second thought.

"Disarm her and untie me," Dealla ordered the second assassin—the one with the blade pressed to Eryn's hip.

The assassin nodded, but no words left his mouth. Not that any could. Most assassins in Deovaria's army cut their tongues out once their training was finished as a way to show their loyalty to the crown. They were silent, unfeeling beings only made to kill. If they uttered a word of complaint, refusal, or anything of the kind to the Dragon Lord, they were killed on the spot. The Dragon Lord never required them to cut out their tongues, but it became a ritual only soon after Dealla was born.

The assassin pried Eryn's dagger from her fingers with the tip of his sword. She refused to let it go for so long that blood poured from her hand by the time the blade finally dropped to the ground. Droplets of red leaked from between her fingers, and the satisfaction Dealla felt from watching the scene was palpable.

He bent to cut Dealla's bindings, but just as his knees hit the dirt, an arrow struck him in the temple, and he fell against the ropes securing her in place. They tightened around her wrists and ankles, sinking into her skin and cutting off the blood to her hands and feet.

She sucked in a breath through gritted teeth as the pain struck her. If he'd been standing when he'd fallen, he would've hit the bindings hard enough to break her wrists. The pain was so intense that if not for the fact that she hadn't heard a crack when the bindings tightened, she would've assumed they had broken without a second thought.

"Let her go," a woman's voice said from just down the path. Dealla couldn't see her from where she sat tied between the trees, but she was sure both Eryn and the assassins holding her could.

The assassins lowered their weapons.

Fuck.

Her heart sank. More than one soldier was standing down the trail. Or these were truly the most worthless assassins she'd ever encountered. But she wasn't stupid enough to allow them this kind of responsibility if they were. Surely, her father never would've allowed her to place them in the woods if they were, either.

"Lower your weapon and step away from her," the woman's voice continued, and the assassins did as she instructed.

Eryn reached for her dagger immediately after the assassin stepped back, and two more arrows flew through the air, piercing one assassin in the neck, and the other in the chest.

"Are you okay, Miss Gedding?" the woman's voice came again as she ran down the trail, and Dealla fully laid eyes on her.

Anger surged in her at the sight of the woman.

No. Not a woman. A girl.

No older than maybe seventeen.

She'd killed two of her people. Two of her kingdom's most trained assassins in a matter of a minute. Part of it was luck, but the rage flaring through her didn't care that it was purely because she'd taken them by surprise.

Eryn clenched her dagger tightly, blood spilling from between her fingers. She nodded. "Yes, I'm fine," she answered the girl, before turning back to Dealla with a new kind of hardness in her eyes. The rage Dealla felt for her was reflected in the Dragon Hunter's gaze as she lifted the body of the man who fell against the ropes and threw his limp form to the side.

Eryn knelt on the ground in front of her, and Dealla refused to break eye contact, even as Eryn pressed the tip of her dagger to her windpipe and a trickle of warm blood flowed down her throat. She didn't so much as flinch.

"Try to kill me again, with your soldiers or by your own hands, and I swear you will meet death with more pain than any other person ever has," Eryn whispered, her voice so low Dealla hardly heard it.

Dealla smirked. "You forget again that I gave you that scar." She nodded to the side of Eryn's face, ignoring when Eryn's dagger sliced her skin open further.

Eryn matched her expression. She pulled the dagger away, and before Dealla could process what she was doing, Eryn sliced a cut into her shoulder and collarbone, deep enough that the wave of agony that washed through her made her suck in a sharp breath.

It was far from the worst pain she'd endured—nothing could compare to the torture she'd undergone to ensure that if she was ever imprisoned, she wouldn't give up information—but her bone was visible through the gash Eryn cut into her flesh.

"And now you have another one of your own," Eryn said slowly. "Don't test me, Princess."

Dealla opened her mouth, but Eryn turned to the girl standing behind her and spoke before Dealla got the chance.

"Unbind her and help me transport her to the dungeon," she instructed the girl as two more guards came into view from wherever they'd been standing further down the trail. "Make sure she isn't too comfortable. People like her don't deserve the luxury of food or water unless they've earned it."

The three soldiers nodded, none of them daring to look up too high and meet the fierce gaze of the Dragon Hunter. "Yes, Miss Gedding," the girl squeaked, before the three rushed over and untied Dealla from between the two trees.

Chapter 24

Caeden pulled the bowstring tight, aiming the arrowhead for the center of the target fifty yards away. His muscles ached, and every inch of his body protested as his fingers gripped the string. He was stiff, and though it likely wouldn't help his injuries, hopefully some movement would prevent his body from aching each time he dared to do anything more than breathe.

Lining the shot took far longer than usual, since he couldn't keep his hands still while aiming. When he finally loosed the arrow, his whole body tensed as it flew across the field straight for the target.

It hit the center.

His eyes widened, and he shook himself before looking ahead at the target again, making sure his mind hadn't continued to play tricks on him since his time in the prison. It had hit the bullseye.

An arrow flew past his head, striking the target in front of him and splitting the arrow he'd just shot in half.

Caeden spun on his heel, every inch of his aching body tense, but it immediately relaxed when he found Eryn standing behind

him.

She lowered her bow with a self-satisfied smile pulling at the left side of her pretty lips.

Caeden grinned in return. "Show off."

Eryn's smile widened. "I can't let you get too full of yourself," she teased. She eyed the target again, then turned her attention back to him. "But in all seriousness, that was probably the best shot you've ever made. Where was that skill weeks ago?"

He snorted a laugh. "I guess all it takes is a little imprisonment and mild psychological torture to make me good with a bow and arrow."

He'd meant the words as a joke, but Eryn's face fell, and he wished he could take them back. He hadn't fallen back into a normal routine since they'd been back in the castle, but it had only been a day so far, and it was easier than he'd expected to pretend everything was okay.

Eryn took a step closer to him, lowering her bow to her side slowly, though he didn't think much of it until he noticed her favoring her right leg over her left, then the bandage covering the palm of her hand as she stepped closer to him, and he remembered her still-healing shoulder in addition to the two new injuries.

"Are you okay?" she asked. Her expression was serious, but concern hid beneath those stunning blue eyes of hers.

He glanced at her leg, where he could just make out the outline of a thick bandage hidden beneath the fabric. He met her gaze again. "Are you?"

She fixed him with a look. "You first."

Caeden swallowed hard. "I don't know," he answered honestly.

He'd been surprisingly fine overall, but he hadn't yet gone up to his room. The thought of being alone in an enclosed space with the door shut made a shiver run down his spine and fear work its way through his veins.

Instead, he'd opted to come out here, though he wasn't sure where he would go once it got later and he needed to get to sleep. So far, he hoped Ronan might let him sleep on the couch in his living room. If that didn't work, he hadn't figured out what he would do.

Eryn offered him a sympathetic smile that made his heart ache. She opened her mouth to respond, but he cut her off before she could. "What happened to your leg?" She made a fist around her bandaging, and his gaze followed. "And your hand?"

She sighed as she shifted her weight from her right leg to her left, then back. "I may have confirmed the disguised spies who never made it to the castle were, in fact, hiding out in the woods along with a group of assassins. They found me with Dealla after you and Ronan left, but the guards showed up in time and we…" She cleared her throat awkwardly and refused to meet his gaze. "Disposed of them."

Anger flashed in him and his nails bit into his palms.

She was more than capable of taking care of herself, but a mixture of fear and anger swirled together at her words. They shouldn't have left her alone. They should've taken the risk and brought the dragon and Dealla with them to the front gates. They had no way to know Eryn would be attacked, but they should've assumed something would happen. They'd been speculating for weeks that assassins were hiding in the forest.

Eryn dug the toe of her boot into the grass, still refusing to meet his gaze, and his anger disappeared. Instead, it was replaced by a wave of relief that made a lump form in the back of his throat.

She reached for the flask tied to her hip and unscrewed the cap before pressing it to her lips. She took a sip before pulling it away, wiping her mouth with the back of her hand, and offered it to him.

Caeden smirked at her, but took it. "More tequila?"

She fixed him with a look, the almost shy air she'd had before entirely gone. "You got a problem with my tequila, princy? You don't have to drink it."

He laughed and shrugged in surrender. Taking a quick sip of the foul liquid, he winced as it burned his throat on the way down. A shudder ran through him as he pulled it away, goosebumps rising along his arms and legs.

Eryn bit back a smile of her own. "It's not that bad."

Caeden shook his head, another shiver making its way up his spine. "It really is. Worst thing I've ever drank."

"Hits you fast, though," Eryn said, a light laugh escaping her.

A smile touched his lips. "Yeah," he agreed, unable to tear his gaze away from her face.

He hadn't heard that sound in what felt like forever. In reality, it had been only a few weeks since Eryn had last laughed in front of him, but it was one of the things that had replayed in his mind when he'd been in that prison cell.

Her laugh, her smile, her eyes, the look she gave him when he said something she thought was ridiculous, the blush that spread across her cheeks when she was nervous, the feel of her warmth when she touched him; there were so many little things he'd grasped onto. He hadn't realized just how much he thought he'd never see her again.

"Caeden?"

Eryn's voice pulled him from his thoughts and he shook his head to clear away the spark of fear the memories caused.

"Yeah?" he asked, gripping the bow tighter in his hand, still unable to look away from her face. If he was ever taken and held in a prison cell again, he wanted to remember every single detail.

"What are you doing out here?" she asked softly, her voice barely audible above the chirping of the cicadas.

Caeden swallowed hard. He didn't want to answer that question, but he couldn't bring himself to lie to her either. "I haven't gone up to my room yet," he whispered, unable to meet her gaze when he said the words.

Eryn frowned, confusion settling over her features before her eyes widened and understanding seemed to dawn on her.

He looked away from her finally. He couldn't force himself to see the pain hidden beneath her gaze. Seeing Ronan struggle after he'd been trapped had been hard on her. Now, she was seeing him go through something very similar, which he was sure brought back emotions he didn't want her to have to feel.

Eryn shifted in the grass, and he felt her fingers intertwine with his before he realized that she'd stepped closer.

He took in a sharp breath as the warmth of her hand seeped into his skin, sending a wave of electricity surging up his arm. Eryn squeezed his fingers. "You're safe," she whispered, her voice wavering. "You're home, and you're safe."

He wanted to believe those words. He wanted to go up to his room and sleep through the night like he always used to. He wanted to believe nothing bad could happen so long as they were sheltered within these walls. But that wasn't true. It never had been.

"I thought I was safe the night she took me," Caeden told her.

Eryn's breath hitched and her hand tightened around his.

"I know the Dragon Lord won't try to kidnap me again, but what if they just kill me and my father in our sleep instead?" He met her gaze for a brief second, and a new kind of fear flooded him. "What if they take someone else as a bargaining chip?"

"Hey," she whispered, placing her free hand against his

cheek. His face burned beneath the warmth of her hand. A small smile touched the right side of her mouth, but only barely. "They already tried that with you. They can't so easily do that with your father." She almost sounded like she wanted to laugh at the idea.

Caeden swallowed hard, turning away from her again. "They wouldn't waste their time with that. He wants my father dead, if anything."

"Then there's no one else they could take," she said, running her thumb over his cheek and bringing his gaze up to hers. "They already took you, and Ronan is going to ensure both of you are guarded even more heavily than you were before. They won't be able to get to either of you."

He offered her a sad smile. She was right that they couldn't hurt either him or his father easily, but that didn't mean there was no one else the Dragon Lord could use.

He could kill the king or he could try again to convince Caeden to agree, but the Dragon Lord wouldn't be able to use his father as a bargaining chip over Caeden in the same way he could use Caeden over his father. He wouldn't bother trying, considering how much the Dragon Lord wanted him dead.

But Caeden's father wasn't the only person he cared about.

They could use Eryn.

If Dealla knew how much he cared about Eryn, she'd likely told her father.

And if they took her and hung the threat of her death over Caeden's head…

He would never agree to his father's death in exchange, but he would figure out a way to convince his father to agree to the Dragon Lord's terms in some other way. His people may not be as kindly ruled, but they would no longer die in a war. Maybe they would suffer in other ways, but he couldn't know for sure, and he would take that risk if it meant Eryn's safety.

It was a terrible thing to consider, and even worse that he would take that sort of risk with his kingdom's safety for a single woman, but he couldn't deny how true it was.

"They could take you," he said softly.

Eryn's hand froze against his cheek, and she stayed silent for so long he wondered if she would say anything else at all.

"Caeden," she whispered finally.

He looked at her again.

"I'll be fine," she promised. Her lip quirked upward. "They'd have a hell of a time trying to kidnap me."

She meant the words as a joke, but the images circling through his mind made it impossible to share in her amusement.

What if they knocked her out? What if they gave her a sedative like they'd done to him? What if they beat her until she couldn't so much as lift an arm to fight them off?

"What if they did it, anyway?" he asked, though he wasn't sure what he hoped to hear in response.

She swallowed hard, her hand falling away from his cheek. "So what if they did?" she asked. She shrugged her non-injured shoulder, her eyes finding the ground between them. "I may be a high rank, but I'm not high enough that anyone would risk sending a rescue party after me. Maybe if I was taken with multiple others like Ronan was, but not if it was only me. There are plenty of others who can do what I can. I'm not vital on my own like you or your father. I wouldn't pose a risk to the kingdom if I was taken."

Her words almost made him want to laugh. He'd confessed his feelings to her all those weeks ago before he'd been taken, but it hadn't meant anything back then. It couldn't mean anything back then. Now was different, though. He didn't have to hide how he felt about her from anyone. If she was taken—even if their circumstances were the same as they were weeks ago—he wasn't sure he wouldn't be reckless enough to go after her.

"You are," he told her honestly, forcing the words out past a lump in his throat. "Dealla knew it, and I'm sure the Dragon Lord found out too, but you are exactly the bargaining piece they would need."

Eryn looked up at him and met his gaze. "Caeden, what do you mean by that?"

He took in a breath and let it out slowly. He'd told his father and the court, but he hadn't told her any of what the Dragon Lord attempted to get him to agree to while he was held captive.

"The Dragon Lord wants me to surrender Aericora to him in exchange for letting our people live. He wants to kill my father, and me to transfer my title as king to him. He offered me a spot on his council, as if that would make any difference." He said the next words so quietly he almost hoped she wouldn't hear them. "I refused then, but if Dealla told him about my feelings for you and they used you, I don't know if I would be able to refuse again."

Eryn's face burned bright red, and she pulled her hand away from his. "You can't say that," she said, taking a step away from him. "You'll be king one day. You were about to marry your future queen to help your people. You can't so easily say you'd hand the entire kingdom over to that tyrant for one person."

Caeden sighed again, the weight of his own words settling on his shoulders. "That's why I need you to stay safe," he told her. "Because as much as I hate it, I can't promise I wouldn't."

The anger written across her features before softened, and the redness in her cheeks deepened. "Why not?" Her words were so soft they hardly reached him from where he stood a few paces away.

His heart skipped a beat. He didn't want to answer that

question. He was sure she knew the answer, but they hadn't talked about his feelings toward her so directly since they were on the front lines weeks ago. And now that he was no longer engaged, it did matter how he felt. It could matter.

And that alone scared him more than anything else.

"Because I'm falling in love with you, Eryn Gedding," he whispered.

He half expected her to laugh at him once the words passed through his lips. Instead, before he had time to register what she was doing, her hands were on either side of his face, and her lips were pressed against his.

For a moment, he stood there frozen. Then, slowly, the unbelievable reality sank in.

Eryn Gedding, his irritable, brutal, harsh teacher who hadn't been able to stand him, the one woman he'd thought he'd never be able to be with, was kissing him.

His hands traveled to her waist as his lips softened against hers, and he pulled her closer. Her arms wrapped around his neck, her fingers intertwining in his hair as he deepened their kiss, drawing a moan from her lips.

Her warmth seeped into him as he held her close, every thought gone from his mind except for her and the way her body fit so perfectly against his own.

Eryn pulled away slowly until she met his gaze, her fingers still tangled in his hair and her body pressed against his. "Promise me you would choose the kingdom," she whispered, her breath warm against his face, the faint scent of tequila mingling with her ever-present scent of lavender.

Caeden swallowed hard. He didn't meet her gaze, and instead focused on the arch of her eyebrows, the blush across her cheeks, and the curve of her lips. A stray piece of her long black hair fell across her forehead as a breeze blew by, and he tucked it behind her ear. "Eryn, I can't… I can't promise that."

Her hand trailed from the back of his neck to his cheek again, forcing him to gaze into her eyes. "I need you to," she said softly. "I have the luxury of risking everything to go save you. You'll be the king one day, and your kingdom and its people are your greatest responsibility and burden. I need you to promise me that if it came to it, you would put them first because that's what they deserve." A sad smile pulled at the corners of her mouth. "I made my choice when I started falling for the future king of Aericora, and I can accept that its people will always come first. I need you to accept that as well."

Caeden sighed, his shoulders slumping. He pulled her closer, and rested his forehead against hers. He hated how right she was, but he couldn't deny the truth behind her words. He couldn't deny that no matter how much he would want to pick her, he couldn't if it truly came down to it.

He didn't want to think about those possibilities right now, though. All he wanted was to stand there with her for all of eternity if he could, because even if there was a war raging only miles away, he didn't want this moment to end. Standing here with her—even if it didn't change anything—made everything in his life feel okay. He felt safe in her arms, as if being here with her could keep anything bad from happening in the world ever again.

"Okay," he whispered, holding her tighter. "I promise."

Eryn sighed, her shoulders relaxing as she leaned into him further, her head resting against his shoulder. "Thank you."

Chapter 25

"Rise and shine, princy."

The combination of Ronan's yell and a semi-gentle nudge against his shoulder startled Caeden awake. He sat upright and looked around. In his half-dazed state, he expected to be met with darkness, but instead, he took in the familiar walls of Ronan's living room.

His heart raced as his eyes roved over the space. A blanket rested over his body, and a pillow sat beneath where his head had been at the back of the couch.

For a moment, he was entirely convinced this was another trick of his mind. Another dream or illusion his head crafted to trick him into thinking he was safe before the blissful fantasy was brutally yanked away.

Eventually, the night before came rushing back, and he recalled choosing to set the pillow on that end of the couch so he could keep an eye on the door even after he was lying down. The terrible headache pulsing in his temples reminded him of the tequila he'd sipped when Eryn had found him out in the training field.

Eryn.

Their kiss.

Everything snapped into crystal clear focus and he tossed his legs over the edge of the couch. He pushed the blanket aside, despite the pain in his head intensifying from the movement.

"Calm down," Ronan said, his voice softer than Caeden expected.

Ronan stood across the small hallway separating the living room from the kitchen. A glass of water rested in his hand and he eyed Caeden with an intensity he'd very rarely seen from his friend.

After looking Caeden over, he averted his gaze and took a tentative step closer, offering him the glass of water. "It takes a second to remember where you're at," Ronan muttered. Emotion laced his voice, though Caeden was sure he hadn't meant it to. "Can't say for sure whether it goes away, but it gets better after a while."

Caeden nodded and took the water slowly. A few drops slipped over the rim from his shaking hands as he pulled the glass to his lips and took a tentative sip.

He'd come to Ronan's shack maybe six hours ago. It was later into the night than he'd intended, but after Eryn found him and everything had happened with her, they'd stayed in the field for a long time. They hadn't talked anymore about the promise he'd made to her or his confession that he'd choose her over his kingdom if he was faced with the choice. They hadn't talked about what their kiss meant either or how they'd both confessed to beginning to fall for each other.

He'd blamed it on the alcohol last night, though when everything happened, he hadn't yet felt the effects of it. But now that Eryn no longer stood in front of him, he could admit to himself that the real reason was because he was scared. He didn't have a marriage hanging over his head anymore. They could be something to each other if they chose to.

That fear in and of itself felt debilitating, though not necessarily in a bad way. But his promise to her scared him more. He'd already allowed himself to fall in love with her; he couldn't undo that, but if something happened to her, if she was taken by the Dragon Lord like he was, if she was hurt, if she was *killed*...

He'd already lost people he loved.

He couldn't undo falling for her, but it was too much to admit he loved her and talk about whether it meant something for their future in the same night. Not with all of the fears circling through his mind. They would need to talk again at some point, but for the time being, he liked how far it had gone, and she seemed to be content with it, too.

Caeden finished the water and set the glass on the coffee table, ignoring the way Ronan studied his movements.

"You sleep a'right?" Ronan asked.

Caeden shrugged. "Better than I expected."

"That tequila prob'ly helped."

He expected to see the usual mischievous smirk hiding in the corners of Ronan's lips, but it was nowhere to be found.

Caeden swallowed hard. "Are you doing okay?" He kept his eyes on his friend, who refused to meet his gaze and instead focused on the end of his cane as he shifted his weight from right to left.

Ronan shrugged a single shoulder, matching the gesture Caeden made before. He still refused to look up. He stood straight and went to the kitchen without saying a word.

Caeden stayed quiet, hoping that if the silence stretched on long enough, Ronan would opt to answer.

Ronan grabbed a glass from the cabinet above the sink, but

instead of reaching for one of the multiple bottles of alcohol lining his countertops, he held it beneath the spigot and let the water fill the glass to the brim.

Ronan still hadn't had even a sip of alcohol since they'd been back. He was sober the previous night when Caeden finished with Eryn and came here to spend the night. He wasn't drunk now, either. The usual rosy tint to his cheeks wasn't there, and neither was the ever-present sheen of sweat that coated his forehead when he was drinking.

Given different circumstances, Caeden would've viewed the situation in a positive light. Ronan drank so much he could use at least a break every once in a while to let his body rest, but given everything that happened since Dealla kidnapped him, he doubted anything positive was associated with the sudden change.

"I didn't think she was capable of lyin'," Ronan said suddenly, a light laugh hiding in his tone. He stared blankly at the countertop in front of him, the half-empty glass still in his hand. He took another sip and set it down in the sink. "Turns out everythin' she ever said was a lie."

Ronan looked lost in thought as he spoke, and for the first time since Eryn revealed the truth to him, Caeden saw just how broken Ronan was beneath the façade he put up. The walls he'd built were beginning to crumble. Maybe that was part of the reason he'd stopped drinking. He was having a hard time keeping them up when he was sober, and the alcohol only made it harder.

Caeden opened his mouth to respond, though he wasn't sure what he would say, but Ronan held up a hand. "It ain't important, princy," he said softly. "No one knew, and there's nothin' anyone could've done. It's just still sinkin' in, is all."

That didn't take away from the pure hurt hidden in his

friend's gaze, but Caeden chose not to point that out and only nodded.

"Are you coming with for the interrogation?"

Ronan laughed, but there wasn't any humor in it. "I ain't got much of a choice, princy."

♥ ♥ ♥

Caeden and Ronan met the king and Fionn just outside the door to the dungeon where Dealla was being held. As far as Caeden was aware, they hadn't discussed an interrogation plan the previous day, but he wasn't present for much with the court after arriving back. His father offered to reiterate the information Caeden gave those who were present yesterday to the rest of the court so he could have time—even if it wasn't much—to get comfortable being back inside the castle. Those few extra hours hadn't cleared his mind, but he was grateful he wasn't thrown straight back into his day-to-day routine. He'd needed the afternoon of rest, even if he hadn't allowed himself much time alone with his thoughts.

"Our goal is to uncover what we can about the stones," the king said, forgoing any introduction as usual. "We already know why they took Caeden, and even if that story is only a cover-up for the real reason, it's unfortunately too believable to disregard. If we get more information about why, or any information about their strategy on the front lines, that would be ideal, but it's not our goal and not what we will be focusing on. We already know the stones work, but we need to figure out how to get our hands on more. We know they came from the mountains, but if we can determine whether she knows a specific location or not, or whether there are even any left to mine, that is the most pressing. Knowing their strategies won't help us if we can't combat them well enough to turn the field in our favor."

The king glanced at each of them, his eyes lingering the longest on Caeden, before flicking to each of the other two for confirmation. The three of them nodded their understanding.

"It would likely be best to avoid any topics but the stones for today. She'll be reluctant to speak, especially since she's only been here for a day. If we ask her too many questions, she's more likely to not answer anything at all," Fionn put in, which earned a nod from Ronan. "Or only answer whatever will be least helpful."

Caeden had long forgotten what Fionn's position was when he'd been in the military, but it sounded like he knew his way around an interrogation better than the rest of them did, and he trusted the man wouldn't offer the information unless he was confident in his words.

"How was she treated overnight?" Ronan asked. Though his voice was calm, Caeden could hear the fear beneath his words. Despite everything Dealla had done to him, Ronan still cared about her.

"When Miss Gedding and the guards arrived with her, she was placed in the cell and has been there since. No one has spoken to her, and she hasn't been given food or water yet," Fionn answered.

Ronan nodded once, his lips pressed together in a thin line, but said nothing else.

"Bring her something to eat once we're done," Caeden said firmly, before giving himself much time to think over the words.

He didn't have experience in this area, and his words wouldn't carry much weight in the eyes of his father and Fionn, but if Dealla was being put through too much, it would be hard for Ronan to think rationally about the situation. And if she'd been trained to withstand such things, it would likely make her even more reluctant to answer their questions. But they couldn't risk the consequences if anyone found out Ronan and Dealla had been in a relationship. If Ronan saw Dealla being tortured in any way, that fact would be harder to hide.

Both Caeden's father and Fionn turned to him with the same confused expressions he'd prepared himself to see, but he stood his ground. "Deovaria trains its soldiers to keep quiet when they're being interrogated or tortured. She's the Dragon Lord's daughter and was chosen to impersonate the Princess of Crevia to get close to me. No one would assign that task to someone who wouldn't be able to withstand the possible torture they would endure if they were found out."

Surprise flashed across his father's features, and Fionn looked like he wanted to argue, but Caeden pressed on before he could.

"She's an aggressive captive," he stated bluntly, knowing that to be true even if he hadn't laid eyes on her since she'd been put into the prison cell. If her attitude while they'd been on the way back was any indication, the chances were slim that she would be any less difficult now. "Starving her won't get us anywhere since Deovaria trains in that area and their soldiers always opt to pass out from starvation before they opt to talk. And it will only make her temper shorter if she's starved. She already tried to kill Miss Gedding, and I doubt that's all she'll try while she's here. I don't want anyone to get hurt over such a slight chance she'll give up information in that state."

Fionn didn't look convinced, but he nodded regardless. "We already sent word to the Dragon Lord that we have his daughter. We can tell him we are willing to trade her for information about the stones."

"We'll get the information from them somehow," Ronan agreed with a shrug.

The king finally turned away from Caeden. The surprise in his features disappeared when he turned to the other two. "Very well," he stated, pulling his shoulders back and standing at his full height, a trait Caeden had noticed himself implementing in his own stance when he wanted his words to be final. "It's not worth the risk for now. Fionn also has other methods to get the information from her before resorting to starvation."

Ronan stiffened beside him, and Caeden noticed when he had to force his shoulders to relax.

No one said anything else before Fionn opened the door to the dungeon and the three of them entered the dark hall that descended to the underground prison cells. They had only been used a handful of times since Caeden was born.

The air surrounding them was damp and foul-smelling, a combination of still water, blood, and waste permeating the air and leaving Caeden's head spinning. Sconces lined the walls on either side of them, but only every third or fourth held a lit torch. Mold and algae grew between the lower bricks the farther they descended the stairs, and if not for how uneven the jagged stone floor was, it would've been slick from the surrounding dampness.

Fionn picked up one of the torches as they reached the bottom of the staircase. Two guards stood post in front of the only way in or out of the dungeon, and they stepped to either side to allow them to pass. They quickly fell back into place beside each other not a second after the four passed.

Dealla was alone in her cell, three doors down from the entrance. In the darkness, Caeden could make out the first few cells lining both sides of the long hallway, but couldn't tell how far back the cells went.

Ronan took in a stiff breath beside him as Fionn held the torch up to see inside the cell. With the light to illuminate the space, the four of them laid eyes on the woman who'd disguised herself and hidden among them for weeks.

Dealla sat with her legs pressed to her chest and her chin resting on her knees. She rocked back and forth, muttering something so faintly beneath her breath that Caeden couldn't make out the words. She glanced at them as the light from Fionn's torch flooded over her, before squinting and turning away.

"That's bright," she muttered. Her voice was raspy, as if she hadn't spoken in weeks and hadn't had anything to drink in even longer, though it had only been a day.

Fionn pressed the torch closer, until the bright orange flames licked the rusted metal bars keeping Dealla firmly trapped within the confines of the cell. "The faster you answer our questions, the faster you can get back to your coping mechanisms." He said the words softly, but the edge to them was sharper than a sword.

Dealla laughed suddenly, so loud it made Caeden jump, and Ronan flinched beside him.

Her laugh lasted a good thirty seconds before she finally placed her hand over her side and calmed down.

Maybe she wasn't as well-trained in being held prisoner as Caeden guessed. She was acting suspiciously like he had when their positions were reversed. He was more familiar with that maniacal laughter than he ever wanted to be.

She focused on them again, nothing but hatred hiding behind her eyes as she took in each of them. She looked at the king first, then Fionn, before her eyes lingered on Caeden for a beat longer than the other two. She tilted her head slightly to see Ronan standing behind Fionn, and the hatred Caeden saw before was replaced with a flicker of fear when her gaze landed on him. It was gone in a split second, but not quickly enough that no one noticed.

"What do you want?" she bit out, her words sharp enough to slice through brick.

"The stones," Fionn stated. "We know they come from the mountains."

Dealla raised a mocking eyebrow at him and made an impatient motion with her hand for him to continue. "Okay, and?"

"How did your king get his hands on so many of them? Where were they? They are a rare commodity, or we would've learned of them long before now."

Dealla sat back against the wall again, her eyes fixed on the ceiling above her head. "I don't know. Maybe he did this fascinating thing called 'looking for them.'" She made air quotes with her fingers before dropping her arms back at her sides, as if the interrogation was a waste of her precious time.

"Enough," the king snapped, his voice echoing against the dungeon's stone walls.

Caeden flinched. The severity of his nerves hit him then, and he swallowed hard. He took in the small cell she was locked in—the woman who brought him his meal each day, who held the keys to the room where he'd been trapped only days ago.

He shook his head, forcing away the wave of panic beginning to take hold.

Now wasn't the time. He could be afraid of his own room; he could be afraid to sleep facing away from the door. Those things were fine. But he would not let Dealla or anyone else see how much being held prisoner affected him.

"Where did Colm find the stones?" the king demanded. His words were ice, and they sent a chill down Caeden's spine. His father never spoke to anyone with the level of hatred that laced his words now. Not even the Dragon Lord himself.

"The Rayfait Mountains, as your helpful assistant already

stated," Dealla answered, her head still lying against the wall and her eyes focused on the ceiling above. The hint of a smirk hid at the edges of her mouth, and it made a wave of anger flood Caeden's veins.

She was toying with them again, and it was infuriating.

The king gritted his teeth.

"Where in the Rayfait Mountains?" Ronan asked, stepping around Fionn and taking his first real look into the cell. His body tensed as he took in the woman sitting inside. She was the woman who stole his heart weeks ago, but she wore a different face now. Ronan didn't let any of his emotions show across his features. Instead, he kept his eyes focused on hers and his jaw set.

Dealla flinched at the sound of his voice. "I don't know," she said. Her voice was softer this time, and a hint of fear laced her words.

"You do," was all Ronan said in response.

"You're the Dragon Lord's daughter, correct?" Fionn asked.

Dealla raised an eyebrow at the ceiling. "Yes."

"And you expect us to believe you don't know the answers to our questions?"

"Yes," Dealla said again. "Believe it or not, I can't magically acquire information I was never given access to."

"She's nothin' more than a soldier," Ronan explained to the group, turning away from her. He didn't explain how he knew this fact, but neither of the other two asked. "She was trained and sent on missions as soon as she was capable of holding her own." His gaze found Caeden's, and Caeden realized where he was going with his statement.

"The Dragon Lord doesn't trust her to handle much," Caeden agreed. "She was sent as a spy, but that was likely only convenience, since he knows he can trust her to report back accurately and not turn on him. He only trained her to fight because he didn't want her handling any other responsibilities."

"I'll have you know I've overseen hundreds of missions as Deovaria's Military Commander," Dealla spat.

She'd taken the bait.

Caeden grinned, and both his father and Fionn looked between him and Ronan with bewildered expressions. Ronan's expression remained unreadable as they turned back to face the woman in the cell.

"To what? Gather information from the field? Move soldiers from one camp to another? Do things a 'Military Commander' would do?" Caeden taunted, though he kept his tone as genuine as he could. He turned back to the others. "She holds the title, but he wouldn't have sent her here as a spy if she were necessary. He wouldn't have sent his Military Commander on a mission that could've been handled by any normal spy if he needed her."

Dealla gritted her teeth, and Caeden's grin spread across his face again despite himself.

"I'll have you know," Caeden continued once he got his expression under control and turned back to face Dealla, "as someone with far less training, I was given the responsibility of a similar mission." His next words spilled out before he decided whether they would hit like he needed them to. It would be too easy if it worked, but then again, if there was anything he suspected he could manipulate her with, it was her relationship with her father. "I suppose I believe you," he said. "He hardly trusts you to talk. He certainly wouldn't send you to the mountains on that kind of mission, and since you weren't sent, there was no reason for you to be given the specifics of what they did while they were up there."

Dealla opened her mouth to speak, her eyes flashing with hatred, but closed it so quickly Caeden almost questioned whether she'd done it at all.

She rolled her eyes at him. "You won't get an answer from me that easily," she bit out.

Caeden expected to hear a note of amusement in Ronan's voice, something to hint that he was satisfied with their victory, but there was nothing. "We already did."

Chapter 26

"She was part of the group sent to retrieve the stones," Ronan stated, anger lacing each of his words. His hands were clasped around the armrests of his seat, and his jaw was set.

"What proof do you have of that?" Muire argued, raising a curious eyebrow from a few chairs away.

They'd been in a meeting with the court for over half an hour, and so far, they'd only determined that they would continue their original plan of sending Caeden, Eryn, and Ronan to the mountains to collect the stones.

Muire had argued that they could have Aericora's soldiers steal the gems from enemy soldiers wearing them, but they'd been doing that since they first learned what the stones were capable of, and they'd heard no news from the field that they'd acquired even a single stone using that method. It was possible it was working and they simply weren't receiving the information, but the possibility wasn't a good enough reason to put off traveling to the mountains. They would need more time for that strategy to make a difference, even if it was working.

Eventually, the court agreed that sending them to the

mountains would be faster than stealing the stones from enemy soldiers during attacks.

Now, they were on the topic of whether Dealla should be brought along with them or not. On one hand, she could overpower them if she was smart enough, but on the other, she could provide information. But she could also be useful as a bargaining chip against the Dragon Lord, though Caeden had little faith it would pan out the way the court seemed to think.

Ronan gritted his teeth angrily, but didn't offer an answer to Muire's question. He couldn't answer her truthfully and risk them learning about his past relationship with Dealla. But that was the only reason he knew how to read her expressions and body language so well.

"She didn't outright say it, but she led the mission," Caeden stated firmly. He couldn't read Dealla like Ronan could, but he trusted his friend knew the gravity of his conviction and that he wouldn't have said it unless he was sure it was true. "She was there. Her body language was the only answer we got."

"It's too risky to send her with," Cormac put in, his hands clasped thoughtfully in front of him and his eyebrows scrunched together. "Even if she really did lead that mission, she's more likely to kill you while you're there than help you."

Eryn rolled her eyes, not bothering to hide her dislike for the man since he'd blatantly insulted Ronan before they left for the field weeks ago, and Muire nodded in agreement. "Yes. She could also be far more useful here if we offer her to the Dragon Lord in exchange for our land back, or even an end to the war," Muire said.

"Unlikely," Caeden muttered, but it was drowned out by Fionn's response.

"I agree with Muire," he stated. "I think we should see what we can get from the Dragon Lord for her rather than send her with.”

“There’s no point in going to the mountains if this is where we’ve ended up,” Eryn cut in, crossing her arms and rolling her eyes again as she sat back further in her seat. “If we try to get the Dragon Lord to agree to peace in exchange for her, we might as well wait here instead of leaving.”

“Yes,” Muire agreed. She turned to the king. “I believe that is our best course of action, Aillin. The kingdom would be better off negotiating peace than planning for more combat.”

“And what if that doesn’t work?” Caeden argued. Not a single part of him believed the Dragon Lord would trade anything of importance for his daughter. Not only had he not seemed to care about her presence when he’d been kidnapped, but he’d sent her on the mission to begin with. It was dangerous to send his daughter directly into the enemy kingdom, and she could’ve been killed if she had been found out. Nothing he’d seen from the Dragon Lord so far indicated he loved his daughter enough for a plan like that to work. Never mind the fact that they’d taken her days ago, and he’d done nothing.

The king held his head in his hands, massaging his temples with his fingers as everyone looked to him for a response.

“I agree with the prince,” Eryn said after a moment of silence. “What if it doesn’t work? What do we do then?”

“We go back to the original plan,” Ronan answered with a shrug, when it became clear the king still hadn’t formed a response.

The room grew entirely silent. No one said anything as they waited to hear what the king’s final word on the matter would be.

Caeden swallowed hard as he watched his father. The king’s hands shook as he lowered them to the table and took in the faces of the gathered court. They’d been backed into a corner for a long time against Deovaria, even if some of the court refused to admit it. If they made the wrong choice, it could mean their defeat in the end. Even with the soldiers from Crevia, they were only postponing it. One wrong step and they would meet the end of their enemy's blade.

Muire's plan wasn't bad, but after everything Caeden had seen from the Dragon Lord, he worried it would only waste their time.

The king nodded slowly, his eyes returning to the table in front of him. "We'll send word to the Dragon Lord today," he stated, his words coming out strong despite how fragile he looked. "If we don't get a response in the next two weeks, Caeden, Eryn, and Ronan will leave for the Rayfait Mountains to collect the stones, and Dealla will be sent along with them."

No one looked particularly thrilled with the king's statement, but at this point, it was the usual response from the room when their meetings ended.

Caeden stared at the ceiling late that night. The small cracks in the stones above him blurred before his eyes until he couldn't tell where one brick ended and another began. He was tired, but his body ached as he lay on the hard floor just outside of his bedroom. He'd gone in there to grab a pillow and blanket, but hadn't been able to stay for longer than it took for him to rip them off his bed before he turned around and ran back out. He had half a mind to ask Teafa to grab them for him, but he didn't want the kind of gossip that would come of it to spread around the castle.

At least this way, he didn't have to be alone in the confines of his dark room and could easily wake up before anyone caught him on the floor.

Sleeping out here hadn't proven easy. He'd gone to Ronan's shack earlier, but he hadn't been home. He'd thought about waiting, but part of him didn't want to fall into a cycle of spending his nights on his friend's couch. He needed to overcome his fear, even if, for now, the closest he could get was sleeping on the floor in the hallway.

"That can't be comfortable," Eryn's voice said from somewhere down the hall, making Caeden jump.

He sat bolt upright and spotted her near the corner of the hall ahead of him. He hadn't heard her footsteps when she'd approached, but that wasn't out of the ordinary for her. She was stealthy even when she wasn't trying to be.

A yawn escaped him against his will before he shook his head to clear away the fog. "It's not," he answered honestly, but didn't offer an explanation as to why he was out here. She would figure it out on her own quickly enough. She'd already watched Ronan go through something very similar—though far worse. He couldn't make whatever she would feel go away, but he would prolong doing that to her for as long as he could. Even if she figured it out from his odd behavior, he didn't want to say it out loud.

Eryn raised an eyebrow, but didn't question him before she walked over and sat down on the tile floor a few feet in front of him.

Caeden's cheeks suddenly felt hot as he looked at her, the memory of their shared kiss the night before replaying in his mind. He still wasn't sure what it meant, and he wasn't sure whether she did either. The subject felt off limits, despite the fact that nothing was stopping them from having such a conversation. He wasn't getting married anymore.

Eryn smiled at him, and he felt his face heat even more.

"What?" he asked, hoping that if he just ignored it, the blush would go away.

Her smile widened, and her eyes flicked down to his lips before traveling back up to meet his gaze. "I want to kiss you again," she said softly, the slightest bit of color blooming across her nose and cheeks.

He swallowed hard, and though he didn't feel an ounce of bravery when he looked into her eyes, he leaned in and kissed her before he could stop himself.

Eryn took in a sharp breath as his lips met hers, and he felt her smile before her mouth softened against his and she deepened the kiss. Her hands found the back of his neck, and she wove her fingers through his hair.

The smell of her and the warmth of her skin flooded through him, making his heart race and leaving him craving more of her. His hands fell to her waist, and he pulled her body against his. The moan that escaped her lips sent a thrill through him like he'd never felt before. He wanted her closer. He wanted to feel every inch of her skin against his, memorize every curve and dip of her body.

Eryn pressed herself against him, forcing him back against the blanket and pillow lying on the ground until she was lying on top of him.

She moaned into his mouth again, and it was the most beautiful sound he'd ever heard.

He broke their kiss, and his lips trailed along her jaw to her neck. Her pulse was quick beneath his touch, and her fingers tightened in his hair as she pulled him closer.

Eryn kissed his cheek before pulling his mouth back to hers. She kissed him deeper this time, and he could've spent the rest of his life lost in that kiss.

Every inch of her felt perfect—her warmth, her scent, her

lips, the curve of her hips beneath his hands. He never wanted to let her go.

"Caeden," Eryn gasped, breaking away from their kiss and meeting his gaze. She cupped his face in her hands, and he took in every inch of her, from her flushed cheeks to her swollen lips, to those deep blue eyes that somehow consumed his every thought.

"Yeah?" he asked, transfixed by the sight of the woman in front of him; the woman he could say without a single doubt in his mind that he had fallen in love with more times than he could count.

The redness on her cheeks deepened. "Maybe we should take this somewhere other than the hallway," she said, a giggle escaping her as she said the words.

Caeden couldn't help it when he snorted a laugh, until the realization of what she meant dawned on him.

As much as he wanted to continue this with her, he wasn't sure he could. The last thing he wanted was to be closed inside his bedroom. The thoughts that swirled in his head when he thought of going back in there were too much.

"Caeden?" Eryn asked again, her hands falling away from his face as she examined his expression like she could see into his very soul.

He forced himself to meet her gaze again. "I can't," he said, the words coming out quieter than he'd intended.

Eryn's eyes widened when she realized what he was saying. She climbed off of him and sat on the ground a few inches away, her leg pressed against his. He sat with her but refused to meet her gaze, even after she placed her hand tenderly over his, tracing her thumb back and forth against his skin. Another shiver ran up his spine as the warmth of her fingers seeped into him.

"Is it the dark?" she whispered. Her voice sounded broken, and something inside of him shattered. Tears pricked at the corners of his eyes. How could he make her go through this again?

He shook his head, but didn't answer.

He wouldn't lie to her, but he couldn't make her live through the emotions she'd felt when she took care of Ronan after he was held prisoner. One time was more than anyone should have to live with, and it wasn't her job to fix him. It wasn't her responsibility to make sure he was okay.

"Caeden," Eryn whispered again, her voice still broken. "Please, don't shut me out. I don't want to do that again." Her free hand found his cheek again, and she gently turned him to face her. "I care about you, and I want to make this as easy as possible for you. If I can help, I want to. I want to be here for you."

Caeden swallowed hard. He thought back to the night the redheaded woman had found him in his room. He thought about the drugged feeling that overwhelmed him, along with the fear of being under attack again from Deovaria. He thought of the blinding pain in his skull when she'd hit him over the head and knocked him out. He thought about waking up with his limbs bound in the back of the wagon, of the cell, the darkness, the dried blood, the scratches on the wall that were left from his best friend. He thought of the closed door, the sound of the mechanism locking into place each time Dealla shut him into that hellish place where he'd feared he'd be left to die.

"Caeden."

The sound of his name on Eryn's lips pulled him from his thoughts again.

His cheeks were wet—silent, hot tears rolling down his face. He wasn't sure when he'd started crying, but he couldn't make the tears stop.

Before he realized what she was doing, Eryn had her arms wrapped around him, and his face was buried against her neck as he breathed her in. It wasn't enough to distract him like it usually was, but it eased the fear working its way through his veins.

He was safe with her.

She was the *only* place he felt safe.

Eryn held him there until his tears finally eased, and the hazy fog settled back over him again, begging for sleep. He wasn't sure how much time passed when she finally pulled away just enough to kiss the top of his head.

"We should get you to bed," she whispered into his hair.

"I can't go in there," he told her softly, the words coming out rough when they passed through his lips.

Eryn glanced at the door to his room, and the full truth seemed to dawn on her. "It's because of Margaid, isn't it? Well, Dealla."

He nodded against her, unable to pull his head off her chest in his tired state.

Her grip tightened around him before she sighed and it loosened again. "Come on," she mumbled, her voice hardly carrying through the hall. She shifted him so he was sitting up on his own and climbed to her feet. She offered a hand to help him up, and he was sure his confusion was written across his face because the smile she gave him was enough to break his heart. "You're sleeping in my room with me," she explained. "Does that sound okay?"

Caeden swallowed hard. It was still a small space with a locked door, but anything sounded better than going into his own room. At least this way, he wouldn't be alone and he wouldn't be in the same space where he'd been woken in the middle of the night and kidnapped. "Okay," he agreed, and took her outstretched hand.

Chapter 27

Ronan

Ronan pushed the bottle of alcohol away and replaced the glass in the cupboard above the sink. As much as he wanted a drink, it wouldn't help him ignore the reality of the world he'd found himself in.

So far, since learning that everything about the woman he'd fallen in love with was a lie, he hadn't dared to have a drink. On one hand, it might help, but on the other, it ran the risk of him having an even harder time pushing her from his thoughts. And if he was impaired—if the thoughts of her started swirling in his mind—he wouldn't be able to distract himself. He would lose himself in a loop of sorrow he didn't want to deal with.

Not having a drink was better than having one, but the burning ache inside of him longed for some form of escape.

He was angry, far angrier than he'd ever been, and none of his usual vices would help this time. Drinking would leave him even more heartbroken, and even if he'd never had trouble talking to women in a way that led to them ending up in his bed... he wasn't sure he was ready for that either.

So instead, he found himself in the armory late that night after the court meeting finally ended and everyone else turned in for the night. It was dark out already, but trying to fall asleep would only lead to the kinds of thoughts he wanted to avoid.

She would flood those thoughts.

And he wasn't sure if it would lead him to shove a sword through her heart for all the hurt and pain she'd caused not only to him, but his kingdom and his best friend as well, or if he would find himself falling apart with an even more shattered heart. Maybe that sword would end up in his own chest, and he didn't want to entertain those thoughts. Not again.

Ronan grabbed a handful of throwing daggers from the rack, along with a quiver of arrows and a bow that he slung over his shoulder. It was hard to manage with how he needed to lean on his cane, but he was determined to push through the pain aching all the way through his leg up to his hip.

It had been years since he'd given any weapons a real try. He'd attempted to use fighting skills only a handful of times after he'd first gotten his injury. He could still fire a bow and arrow, and he could use a sword if he had to, but he hadn't tried throwing knives again, and he hadn't tried as much as he should've with the sword. He hadn't been able to do much of anything right after the injury happened, and it quickly led to him finding solace in a bottle of alcohol or in the arms of a random stranger rather than trying again.

They'd been quick to inform him that his career in the military was over when he hadn't been able to wield a sword or a bow and arrow within a couple weeks of recovery, which only pushed him to promptly give up. There was no point if they were going to send him home, anyway. Maybe things would've been different if he'd continued trying, but his vices sufficed up until a couple days ago.

Now, he wasn't sure what else he could do but throw himself into what had been his distraction from the world for most of his life.

The target stood ten yards away, far closer than he'd ever practiced with it when he'd been training years ago. He set the bow and arrows down on the ground a few feet away, along with two of the three throwing daggers he'd brought with him. Next, he dropped his cane, which thumped softly against the dirt when it fell to the ground.

His leg ached when he placed his weight on it, and he sucked in a breath through gritted teeth. It hadn't hurt this badly in a long time, but then again, he hadn't been without alcohol in his system in a long time either.

He stumbled when he tried to take a step, but managed to avoid falling face-first into the dirt. Pain radiated up to his hip, and it took everything in him to ignore it and focus on the painted stripes of the target ahead.

If he could regain the skills to fight, maybe that could be his distraction. Maybe he could leave this life at the castle behind and return to the field until the war was won, or until he met his end at the hands of an enemy.

Ronan tested the weight of the dagger in his hand, leaning awkwardly on his uninjured leg as he readied himself to make the shot. He took an uneasy step forward and loosed the knife toward the target. Pain sliced through him as he placed his foot against the ground, and his knee buckled, sending him tumbling to the dirt as the dagger soared through the air.

"Fuck," he muttered, spitting dirt and grass from his mouth as he pulled himself into a sitting position. The dagger lay in the dirt a few feet to the right of the target. It'd been thrown so badly it barely made it eight yards away from him before connecting with the ground.

He balled his hands into fists as he climbed unsteadily to his feet. He grabbed another dagger from his small pile and tried again. The dagger didn't hit the target the second time, but he didn't fall to the ground either.

His third try wasn't much better. The pommel of the dagger hit the trunk of a nearby tree, thudding loudly before disappearing in the long grass.

Ronan tried a few more times with the daggers without much luck before moving on to the bow and arrow.

He hit the bullseye with every single arrow he shot, but the usual satisfaction he felt from it wasn't there. Instead, he stared at the twenty arrows stuck into the center of the target ahead, some having split through others to fit, and felt nothing but numb as his eyes traced the lengths of each of the wooden shafts.

He could still be out in the field right now if it hadn't been for her. If he hadn't been captured by the Dragon Lord's spy and imprisoned by his evil, heartless daughter for a month. If she—the woman who disguised herself years later and had the audacity to make him fall in love with her—hadn't tortured him to the brink of death, he could be out there. If he'd been able to walk when Eryn rescued him, he wouldn't have been shot. If Dealla, the cruel, cold woman locked in the cells beneath the castle, had even an ounce of a heart and given him a single glass of water in those last days he was trapped in that cell, he would've been fine. He would've walked out of there. He would be able to use both of his legs. Pain wouldn't consume his every waking moment.

Tears pricked the corners of his eyes against his will. Anger, rage, and hatred so intense filled him. The tears burned his cheeks as they flowed down and dripped onto the collar of his shirt.

Ronan wavered on his feet, and when he tried to step to righten himself, he fell to the ground again when his knee buckled beneath him. His leg hurt. His body ached. His mind was a blur of rage and pain and hurt like he'd never felt before.

And his heart… his heart felt like it had been ripped from his chest, torn into a million pieces, and the remains had been scattered on the ground just out of his grasp.

Chapter 28

The following days passed with no word from the Dragon Lord, which came as no surprise to Caeden or many of the other court members. He, Ronan, and Eryn met with the court earlier in the day to discuss the next steps of their arrangement if they didn't hear from the Dragon Lord by the following morning.

Their plan was to leave late tomorrow afternoon. Dealla would be drugged with a sedative until they were high enough in the mountains that she wouldn't be able to escape them and have any chance of surviving on her own if she did. They hadn't yet determined how they would get the information out of her, but for now, they would resort to attempting to get inside the mountains through one of the many cave entrances near the top. Their hope was that by the time they got that far, she would either give up the information or be close to doing so. The weather conditions in the mountains wouldn't be pleasant, but with only the four of them, they could lug the supplies needed to remain safe and as comfortable as possible. They would ride the Royal Talon Ronan tamed in the field up to the top, which would at least make the journey shorter and hopefully more manageable.

The biggest concern was surviving if the dragons attacked them. Most were docile unless provoked, but the drakes wouldn't hesitate to tear them to shreds. That was mostly where Eryn and her training came in, and so far, that along with the small numbers they would be traveling in was enough to convince the court and Caeden's father that they could make it out alive. The injuries they'd sustained were healed enough now too, that the court hadn't so much as bothered to question them.

And since Dealla would be drugged until then, the dragons were their only real concern.

"Will you be okay being around her for that long?" Eryn asked suddenly, breaking the silence that had filled Ronan's shack for the past few moments and allowed Caeden enough time to wander into his thoughts. She said the words tentatively, running a nervous finger along the rim of her half-empty glass of tequila.

The tequila was likely the reason she'd dared to broach the subject at all. Caeden hadn't dared ask the question that had prodded at the edge of his thoughts since they'd decided they would still be going to the mountains, but now that the alcohol was working its way through his veins and clouding his better judgment, he'd thought about it.

Ronan, who hadn't had a single drink, only shrugged before taking another slow sip from the glass of water he'd gotten himself a moment before. "I'll be fine," he said. His body was rigid, and Caeden didn't believe a single word from his mouth.

He'd been different since they'd rescued Caeden from the Dragon Lord and revealed Dealla to him. He hadn't seen his friend drink since they'd been back, and he hadn't seen even the slightest mischievous smile pull at his lips, either. Everything about how he acted lately was so out of character that Caeden was surprised by nearly everything he said.

Ronan was still in there, and every once in a while he caught a glimpse of the man he'd gotten to know so well over the years, but then he would disappear into himself again. The worst part was that no one could fix it. He wished more and more each day that he could go back in time and never tell Ronan that he could spend his time with Margaid.

Ronan shrugged again when no one said anything, and he put his glass down on the coffee table. "She'll be outta it for most the time we're gone, anyway. It ain't gonna be a big deal."

Caeden cringed.

The Dragon Lord's words to him from when he'd first been taken prisoner rang through his mind more than he wished they would. He hadn't discussed it with Ronan or Eryn yet, but now seemed like the best time to bring it up.

Caeden cleared his throat uncomfortably, and Eryn turned to face him with a raised eyebrow. "I want to stop on the way there to see at least one of the towns near the border," he told them.

Eryn's confusion only increased, and the crease between her eyebrows deepened. Ronan looked up from the glass he'd set on the coffee table for the first time and gave him a similar expression.

"Why?" Eryn asked.

"The Dragon Lord said something about how our towns are faring because of the war," Caeden explained. "I don't trust him, but I want to make sure he was only trying to get under my skin and that there isn't actually anything wrong."

Eryn moved to place her hand against his leg, but caught herself at the last second and pulled it away, her face turning red. "The towns haven't struggled much throughout the war," she told him. "The kingdom provides them with plenty of supplies and money, especially the ones near the border that help house soldiers when the camps are attacked and the soldiers need somewhere to go."

"She ain't wrong, princy," Ronan put in.

Caeden wished their words were enough to ease his growing worry, but they weren't. No one reported on the well-being of the towns' people. Not since the beginning of the war when messengers weren't going missing constantly. They had no way of ensuring their people were faring as well as they assumed. It wasn't hard to imagine that the supplies they sent were no longer enough, or that they weren't being received like their messages.

"When was the last time either of you visited the towns?" Caeden asked. The words didn't come out harshly, but he still flinched at the implications the other two could take from them. He hadn't meant them like they sounded, but he didn't have a better way to word the question.

Ronan shrugged again, but the truth of Caeden's words seemed to weigh on his shoulders. "Not since after this happened," he answered, gesturing weakly at his injured leg.

Eryn clenched her jaw before she sighed. "Me either," she admitted, sinking deeper into the couch like the same weight that Ronan felt had fallen over her.

Caeden nodded slowly.

Ronan's injury had been three years ago. Back then, they hadn't had such an issue corresponding with those on the battlefield. If the assassins in the woods were tampering with their shipments to the towns, it wouldn't have gotten bad until after Eryn was already back in the field and Ronan was at the castle accepting his new job.

"It'll put us behind schedule," Ronan stated, but the defeated look on his face told Caeden he'd already concluded that checking on the towns was necessary.

"The king won't be happy with that," Eryn said, but the edge to her voice matched Ronan's.

Caeden raised an eyebrow, unable to keep a smile from pulling at the corners of his mouth. "When has that ever stopped you?"

Eryn snorted a laugh into the rim of her glass and shrugged. "It hasn't."

"I can get more of the sedative they're gonna use on Dealla in the morning," Ronan told them.

"Do you know how to administer it?" Caeden asked. "I can't imagine it's hard, but I've never done something like that."

"I have," Eryn answered. "It's not hard, but there are techniques that make it easier and places you can administer it that'll have a quicker effect than others. I'll teach you both before we leave, so any one of us can do it if we need to. Ronan can testify that I can get someone knocked out with that stuff pretty quickly."

Eryn giggled at her own words, but Ronan only nodded in response, a dark shadow falling across his features before he shook his head and it subsided. Eryn didn't seem to notice, but her cheeks were already dark from the tequila, and Caeden doubted she was sober enough to pick up on something so subtle.

"Wait. How are you going to get your hands on the sedative?" Eryn asked, her amusement gone from her voice. "The nurses aren't just going to give that to you without a reason."

Ronan shrugged a single shoulder, but refused to meet her gaze and instead focused his attention on the flickering candle on the coffee table. "I have my ways," he said cryptically.

Ronan's lack of amusement seemed to dawn on Eryn, and she cleared her throat. It was the first time Caeden had heard him talk about sleeping with someone without a mischievous glint in his eyes, and by the look on Eryn's face, it was hers, too.

"You don't need to do that," Caeden told him. "It wouldn't be hard to convince my father to let us take some just in case. I doubt I'd even have to tell him about the extra stop."

Ronan looked confused, then shook his head. "One of the nurses owes me a favor," he clarified. "I wasn't gonna trade sex for it, though that'd prob'ly work, with the reputation I've given myself."

"Oh." Caeden felt his face heat, but Ronan didn't seem to notice. Probably because he had gone back to intently examining one of the lit candles.

"You two ready for the mountains?" Ronan asked, effectively changing the subject. He glanced between Caeden and Eryn before looking away again. Concern and hurt flickered across his features when he looked at Eryn, but he hid that quickly, too. Caeden knew exactly what that kind of worry felt like.

Caeden glanced at Eryn sitting beside him, and he felt her whole body tense at Ronan's words. She downed the tequila that remained at the bottom of her glass, tossing her head back when she did. She shuddered when she swallowed and placed the glass on the coffee table next to Ronan's water glass.

She looked between the two of them. Despite the question being directed at Caeden too, all three of them knew she was the one expected to answer.

Eryn acted fine with the idea of going to the mountains, but she was good at hiding her true feelings. Despite Ronan taming the dragon, proving that she didn't mean them any harm, Eryn still went out of her way to avoid her after they'd returned to the castle. If she needed to go outside for any reason, she steered clear of the stables and the dragon's large enclosure. If she needed to go to the armory, she returned to the center of the training field quickly—not far enough away from the main area that anyone would bat an eye, but far enough that it was noticeable to those who knew she was trying to put more space between her and the dragon.

It was surprising that she'd opted to use the dragon to get to Deovaria to save him, rather than figure out some other way to go about it.

Eryn sighed and sat back further on the couch. "Don't look at me like that. I'll be fine. That was a long time ago."

Caeden and Ronan exchanged a look, and Ronan raised an eyebrow, as if suggesting Eryn would respond better if Caeden prodded her for the real answer.

Now wasn't the time for that, but he worried he wouldn't get the chance to talk to her tomorrow either. She was already drunk, and irritated that they'd pressured her for an answer at all, so instead of pressing her further, Caeden placed his hand over hers and squeezed her fingers between his.

Eryn's cheeks reddened, but she squeezed his hand back, and her shoulders relaxed.

The corner of Ronan's mouth quirked upward slightly as his gaze fell to their clasped hands, before he grabbed his glass off the table and went to the kitchen to refill it.

It was the first genuine smile Caeden had seen on his face in days.

Chapter 29

The court had received no word from the Dragon Lord by the following afternoon. The sun was high in the sky when Caeden met Eryn and Ronan in the dragon's makeshift stable. The king and Muire were the only two who arrived to see them off, aside from the castle staff who were assigned to drug and wheel Dealla out on a stretcher.

Caeden's sword was heavy on his hip, and the bag he'd packed that morning weighed him down, yet he couldn't sit still as Eryn fastened a harness on the dragon's back with a grim expression on her face.

Nothing but surprise flashed through him when he'd learned that Eryn had requested the harness be remade so it wouldn't hurt the dragon during their flight.

Ronan held Eryn's things while she worked, and Caeden paced around the space anxiously. Caeden's eyes flicked to Dealla to ensure she was knocked out and not only faking it. Each time, he expected her to shift on the stretcher beneath the blanket covering her and the straps holding her down, but she was still, aside from her even breathing.

Ronan had collected the sedative late the night before after Caeden and Eryn left his shack, and it was currently tucked into a pocket on the belt Eryn wore. Many of her pockets were filled to the brim with various objects and vials that Caeden couldn't possibly imagine they would need during their journey, but it was better to be safe.

"She won't be comfortable if she wakes up, but there's enough space for us to tie the stretcher to the back of the saddle along with all of our things," Eryn said, jumping down from the dragon's back and landing flawlessly on the ground. Her eyes flicked up to the dragon's large face before she took a few tentative steps away and placed her hands awkwardly in her pockets.

The saddle she'd strapped on the dragon's back was huge— made to carry at least ten soldiers with handles for each to hold on to while the dragon flew. They could easily fit even if Dealla woke up, but he hoped it wouldn't come to that.

The dragon snorted a puff of smoke through her nose before she shifted a step closer to Eryn and bent her head low to sniff near her arm where she'd been struck in the field. It had yet to fully heal, but it was much better. It hadn't stopped her from training the soldiers since they'd been back.

Caeden hadn't interacted with the dragon much, but everything about her personality so far reminded him strangely of a cat.

Eryn tossed the dragon an irritated look over her shoulder and stepped away again. The dragon looked unfazed this time and turned away from her, but her tail slowly snaked around until it was curved on the ground around Eryn, trapping her inside of a large circle between the dragon's body and her tail. Eryn tensed, but kept her expression neutral.

"She deserves to be tied to her tail," Caeden muttered,

refusing to look in the direction of his cousin again.

Ronan stayed quiet.

"She was dosed with enough sedative to keep her out cold for the next eighteen to twenty-four hours," Muire said, mostly to Eryn.

They'd discussed as much the week before.

"You'll arrive in the mountains very late tonight if you fly all the way through," the king stated simply, cutting off whatever Muire would have to say next. He said the words to Caeden, only seeming to remember to speak to the other two after the words were already out of his mouth. "Ideally, we want you to return within the week. We don't have a lot of time before Deovaria will win this war, even with the aid from Crevia. They're attacking us with too much force for us to hold out much longer. We can't risk the loss of time if you are gone much longer than that. For now, our soldiers will continue trying to recover stones from enemy soldiers. Hopefully, they will have more luck moving forward."

There was no way to know how long it would take them to find the stones once they were in the Rayfait Mountains, even if they could convince Dealla to help them once they got there. But Caeden understood what hid beneath his father's words. He wanted them to hurry, but he understood the uncertainty of the mission as well as the rest of them. The hidden truth behind his words was that he wanted Caeden to return quickly, just like he had when they traveled to the battlefield. That wasn't something his father could say out loud though, just like he couldn't back then.

Caeden hadn't told his father their plan to stop at one of the towns to avoid worrying him anymore. If they found anything helpful there, he intended to bring it up, but mentioning the detour now would only cause more tension, which wasn't necessary.

Ronan and Eryn began mounting on the dragon's back in front of the stretcher tied to the back of the saddle. Eryn slipped on her way up, but the dragon's nose was only a few inches behind her back foot. She startled when her foot landed on the dragon's snout, and the dragon helped her righten herself and climb the rest of the way into the saddle.

"Dragons are a good judge of character," the king said, barely loud enough for Caeden to hear. He had a soft smile on his face when Caeden looked at him, and his eyes lingered on the Dragon Hunter with her usual irritated expression on her face as she made herself comfortable in the saddle. "They tend to gravitate toward those who know what they want. They like loyalty and determination." The king's smile grew slightly, a hint of amusement twinkling in his eyes. "They like stubbornness, essentially."

Caeden raised an eyebrow at his father. "I didn't know you knew much about dragons."

The king's smile faded. "Your mother learned quite a bit about them from Colm. She shared those facts with me." He glanced back at Eryn seated atop the dragon, but he didn't look like he was seeing her as much as seeing through her. He had a faraway look in his eyes. "Dragons always liked your mother, too."

Caeden's heart clenched painfully at his father's words. The king shook his head, clearing away the glassy sheen in his eyes before focusing once again on his son and the mission Caeden and the others had ahead of them.

"Be safe," his father told him, placing a firm hand on Caeden's shoulder.

He wasn't expecting it, and he nearly jumped. His father had showed affection to him in front of the court only twice before now—when he'd left for the battlefield, and when Eryn and Ronan rescued him—but he still wasn't used to the new, open way his father was displaying it. He liked it, though.

His father had felt like nothing more than the king to him for so long, and he'd missed being able to look at him and see his father beneath the crown resting on his head.

Caeden nodded, his eyes flicking to Muire, who made an active attempt to avoid looking in their direction, though her eyes flicked up to Caeden's briefly before she turned away again. "We will," he responded.

His father gave his shoulder a gentle squeeze before he removed his hand, and Caeden turned away. He climbed up onto the dragon's back behind Eryn and tied a piece of the rope around his body to keep him firmly in the saddle. Even with the handles, none of them were comfortable enough to forgo the extra step.

"We ready?" Ronan asked, grabbing the reins running down to the bridle fastened on the dragon's face.

"Ready," both Caeden and Eryn said simultaneously.

Ronan nodded once, and flicked the reins gently. Before Caeden was ready, the dragon leapt into the air.

His heart pounded loudly in his chest as they took off, and if he hadn't known it was impossible, he would've thought his stomach fell straight through his body and remained behind them on the ground. He wrapped his arms instinctively around Eryn's waist rather than the handles on either side of him. She tensed beneath his touch before her body relaxed just as quickly. Her hand rested over his, and she held his arm against her stomach as they continued to rise into the bright pink sky.

They flew for hours before finally landing just outside the small town of Dalelry. It was thirty miles away from the Rayfait Mountains, and it would be easy to continue their trip the following morning. The town was far enough away from the castle that they would arrive long after dark, so they wouldn't cause a panic with the dragon. The sun had set hours ago, but it wasn't late enough that they would struggle to find lodging for the night or coordinate an audience with the town leaders. They wouldn't be happy about being woken, given that the only people who would be awake were those stumbling home from the taverns, but they wouldn't be able to refuse a member of the royal family, either.

Ronan and Eryn dismounted in front of Caeden and slid down the dragon's outstretched wing to the ground. Ronan stumbled when his bad leg connected with the hard earth, but he rightened himself quickly. Caeden followed after the other two, landing as smoothly as he could on his stiff legs.

Eryn climbed halfway back up to untie the stretcher Dealla was on from the back of the saddle, and Caeden helped her maneuver it off the dragon's back to the ground.

"We'll have to take her with," Eryn said after jumping down once again and landing beside Caeden. She gave the stretcher an apprehensive once-over, her nose scrunched in distaste as she took in the face of the Deovarian princess.

Caeden suppressed a grimace at her words. They hadn't discussed in detail what they would do once they arrived near the outskirts of the town, but it was inevitable that she would need to come with. They'd only discussed that the dragon would remain in the woods, hidden away from the eyes of the townspeople. From there, they'd known Dealla would wake up since her sedative only lasted up to twenty-four hours, but they hadn't planned on how they would sneak her in and out of the town without drawing suspicion.

"Here," Ronan said, pulling a blanket from his bag and handing it to Eryn. His eyes flicked to Dealla, then back up to Eryn again as she took the blanket. He stepped away as soon as she did, as if to put as much space between him and Dealla as possible, despite her being unconscious. "She'll still draw attention, but that'll keep anyone from seein' her face, at least."

Eryn gave him a skeptical look as she turned the blanket over in her hands.

Caeden shrugged a single shoulder as Eryn seemed to decide that Ronan's idea was better than nothing, and draped the blanket over Dealla's face.

"We'll go straight to the inn. We'll get a room and get her locked in there before we try to find anyone," Caeden said.

"They'll probably find us on their own after we're seen walking around with what looks like a corpse," Eryn muttered, but she clearly didn't have any better ideas or she wouldn't have placed the blanket over Dealla. She moved around the back of the stretcher to push it along with them while they walked.

The road into the town was almost entirely unlit at this hour, and the uneven ground beneath them only made their journey take longer than it would've in the daylight. Dealla's stretcher nearly toppled over more than a few times, but between the three of them, they kept it upright. Part of him wouldn't have cared if they needed to drag her limp form along behind them with nothing but the blankets to protect her from the jagged rocks on the ground, but it would cost them more time.

It took them nearly an hour to walk into Dalelry. The wooden shops and homes in the town were worn down. A few lanterns were still lit, giving the streets an eerie glow, but not providing enough light for them to easily tell the difference between the buildings. People milled around in the streets, but they were few and far between, and most appeared to be homeless, judging by their hollow faces and dirt-covered hands.

Dalelry wasn't a poor town, at least not as far as Caeden was ever made aware, but the sight in front of him suggested otherwise. Where was the money the towns were being sent if this was how their people were living?

Aericora was one of the richest kingdoms, and his father hadn't skimped when sending aid to their people. The town should've received more than enough to fix the rotting boards lining their homes, light their oil lamps, and prevent their people from resorting to living on the streets in the cold. How had the court not heard of this? The severity of his people's situation hadn't simply happened overnight. It would've taken years for Dalelry to turn to this, and yet Caeden hadn't heard so much as a whisper in the hallways to suggest this level of need from his people.

It made his heart ache.

Could this simply be a result of the years of war? It seemed unlikely, given the kind of wealth Aericora still had. But it made perfect sense if the aid never reached them.

"We're drawin' attention already," Ronan muttered, just loud enough for Caeden and Eryn to hear him over the sound of the stretcher's wheels in the dirt as it rolled along the uneven ground.

Caeden glanced at the buildings lining the street around them. There weren't many people out, but all of their eyes were on the small group entering their town. Curtains were pulled aside in windows, and eyes hungry with questions gazed out.

Caeden's stomach churned at what could be running through their heads as they watched the three of them walk through the streets with Dealla pushed between them. Very few, if any, would recognize him as Aericora's prince. They were more likely to recognize Ronan and Eryn, but neither had been stationed near this particular town. To those watching, they probably looked more like a group of Deovarian spies than Aericora's prince and two of their most decorated soldiers.

None of them had the foresight to bring clothing that would dissuade the thoughts likely running through the townspeople's heads, and Caeden swore beneath his breath for not having thought of something so simple. Ronan and Eryn brought their pins to identify themselves by their military ranks, and Caeden brought his ring embossed with his personal crest, but all three of those were too small for anyone to see given the wide berth they were giving the small group.

"There," Eryn whispered, pointing to a crooked sign hanging in front of a building twenty yards from where they stood. The paint on the inn's sign was faded and difficult to read from where they were, but the small image of a bed beside the faded words was unmistakable.

Caeden forced himself to ignore the weight of the gazes watching them as they reached the inn. Caeden entered first, making a show of straightening the collar of his shirt to show off the ring encircling his finger before Eryn and Ronan pulled Dealla's stretcher through the doorway.

Ten people occupied chairs and stools inside, and all of their heads turned in unison as the thumping of the stretcher going over the step in the doorway echoed throughout the room over the quiet chatter. The voices quieted. Half of the people stared at Caeden's hand, visibly attempting to make out the seal on his finger, while the sight of the stretcher and the covered body atop it transfixed the other half.

His nerves stood on end as he walked through the now silent space, his steps against the uneven wooden floors deafening in his own ears. The innkeeper stood behind the bar, a glass in his hand that he'd been about to fill before Caeden and the others interrupted him. He was an older man, and wore a perplexed look that made the wrinkles on his weathered skin deepen. He set the glass down on the counter as Caeden neared him, and his confused expression turned to a forced welcoming smile that had been perfected over many years of practice.

"What can I do for ya, lad?" the innkeeper asked. A trace of fear hid in his eyes when they flicked to Ronan and Eryn standing behind him with Dealla on the stretcher before he turned back to Caeden, but his smile never faltered.

Caeden forced a smile that he hoped matched the older man's. He would need to explain, but now wasn't the time. They wouldn't remain in the town for long, so the townspeople knowing who they were didn't pose too much of a threat, but they couldn't afford anyone knowing what their mission was. Not even the town leaders. As far as anyone here needed to know, they were simply sent to check on the town's wellbeing. But that would leave a lot of questions about Dealla unanswered.

"We need a room for the night," Caeden explained as Eryn and Ronan stepped up beside him.

The innkeeper took in the faces of the group again. His eyes widened for a split second when they landed on Ronan before moving on. He turned his back to Caeden again. "For all three of ya?"

"Four," Eryn corrected. She motioned toward Dealla with a hand. "She caught something on the way here. She hasn't been up for travel, but we were too far away from the castle to turn around. She's been out cold most of the trip."

The innkeeper looked suspicious, and Caeden couldn't blame him. The excuse was good, but it lacked an answer for why Dealla's face was covered with a blanket and why she hadn't so much as stirred beneath the covers since they'd arrived.

"'Fraid I don't have a room big enough for the four of ya," the innkeeper stated, picking up the glass again. He moved to a nearby spigot and filled it with whatever alcoholic beverage the customer had ordered before they arrived. "Only have two rooms, but they're both singles. Two can fit on a bed, but it's a tight fit."

Caeden glanced at the other two, who shrugged halfheartedly. It wasn't ideal, but they couldn't afford to waste time trying to find an inn with a room that could accommodate all of them. "That'll be fine."

The innkeeper nodded and pulled out a large book and pen. He flipped to a blank page. "Names?" he asked, his pen hovering just over a blank line on the paper. His gaze flicked to Ronan before returning to the paper. "The others. I remember you."

Questions swirled in the back of Caeden's mind even as his stomach turned at the question. A lump lodged itself into the back of his throat. It was one thing to show the ring in public. Very few would be able to make out which seal was engraved into the gold, but announcing his name to the entire room felt different.

"Eryn," Eryn answered, before Caeden got the chance to decide if he wanted to give the man the truth or come up with a fake name on the spot. She gestured to Caeden. "And Prince Caeden. This is Margaid." She gestured to the cot behind them, and Caeden hid his surprise at her using Dealla's impersonation when she'd opted to give his name. "I doubt you need any of our last names for this transaction."

The man glanced up quickly. "I don't."

He turned back just as quickly to his book, but the ice in his voice sent a chill down Caeden's spine. He hadn't considered what other effects the towns not receiving aid would have until now, but the man's icy tone made it impossible to ignore it any longer.

This man blamed Caeden's father for the state their town was in, and by proximity, Caeden as well.

Caeden couldn't fault him for it given that any person would've made the assumption that the king stopped sending aid if they weren't receiving any, but it stung to have it thrown in his face when he knew full well that his father hadn't. He'd been present when this specific town was discussed only a few months ago.

He couldn't say that to the innkeeper, though. He didn't know what happened yet, and arguing something like that without having an answer wouldn't end well. It would only make things worse.

So instead, he pulled what he owed the man for their stay from the small bag tied to his belt before he showed them to their rooms on the second story of the small building. The three of them thanked him in the hallway as he handed Ronan a key to each room before he turned and left.

"I'll see about getting the town leaders to meet us here," Eryn said, once the innkeeper disappeared down the hallway. "It shouldn't be hard, and I don't want to leave her alone in case she wakes up." She tossed a look at Dealla that would've sent any conscious person running.

Caeden didn't like the idea of her going alone, but she would draw less attention by herself than if they went together. Still, it worried him to think of her by herself when everyone in the town seemed angry with him and his father over what their town had fallen to because of the war. A war she played a large part in, even if she had no real say in any of it.

"We'll figure out what to do 'bout the rooms," Ronan responded, before Caeden got a chance to say something similar.

Eryn nodded and turned to leave. She only got a few steps before Caeden caught up to her. He gently grabbed her by the elbow, pulling her to a stop. She turned to face him, her cheeks turning the slightest bit pink in the faint orange light of the lamps lining the hallway.

"Please be safe," he whispered, so quietly he wondered whether she would hear him. Ronan knew exactly how he felt about Eryn, but there was something about showing it openly that made his stomach twist itself into knots. They cared about each other, but he still wasn't entirely sure where they stood with one another either.

Eryn placed a hand over his and offered him a small, almost teasing, smile. "You know I've led missions into Deovarian territory that were successful despite everyone saying they were impossible, right?" She squeezed his hand lightly.

Caeden felt his face heat at her words as the sound of Ronan attempting to fit one of the keys into the locked door filled the hall. "That will never be enough to keep me from worrying about you."

Eryn's smile widened. She glanced over Caeden's shoulder at Ronan, who was bent over the lock, still trying to fit the key into it, though he certainly knew it belonged to the other door by now and was only trying to look busy.

"I'll be fine. I promise," Eryn whispered, placing a hand against his cheek and pulling his attention back to her. Before he had time to register it, she lifted herself up onto her tiptoes and planted a quick kiss to his lips that made his heart skip a beat.

"Okay," he breathed, his lips brushing hers when he said the word. He pulled away just far enough to look into her eyes, allowing himself to get lost in the deep blue that had captivated him since the moment he met her. Three words rested on the tip of his tongue, but even as much as he wanted nothing more than to say them, he couldn't force them out. Not yet.

Eryn offered him another smile before she pulled away and disappeared down the hallway.

Chapter 30

"How does the innkeeper know you?" Caeden asked once Eryn disappeared around the corner. Ronan had gotten the door open with the correct key, and it was ajar in front of him. From where Caeden stood, he could only make out darkness inside of the room.

Ronan didn't look at him as he pushed Dealla's stretcher through the doorway. He struggled to avoid falling since he only had the support of the rolling stretcher, and Caeden rushed to help before Ronan ended up on the floor.

They got Dealla inside of the room before Caeden found an oil lamp resting on a table near the doorway. He lit the lamp, and the orange glow of the flickering flame provided enough light to make out the small bed in the center of the room along with a writing desk pushed to the far corner. The entire room was ten feet wide and ten feet long, maybe a quarter of the size of his own room back at the castle, but it would be more than enough space for them for the night.

The innkeeper was right about the size of the beds. There was enough space for two people, but it would be tight, and there wouldn't be room left over to shift around without falling off the edge of the bed.

"You and Eryn take the other room," Ronan said, still not bothering to face Caeden as he finished pushing Dealla into the corner beside the writing desk.

Caeden knew better than to assume Ronan hadn't heard his original question, but chose not to press him for an answer yet. "Are you sure?" His eyes flicked to Dealla, and the bubble of anger he felt toward her resurfaced along with the memories of the hurt across Ronan's face when he'd learned the truth. She'd broken something inside of him, and he didn't want to make Ronan endure a moment alone with her if he could avoid it.

Ronan finally looked up, but whatever emotions he felt were hidden firmly behind the wall he'd built up to keep them at bay. "She's knocked out, princy," he said, trying too hard to make the words sound casual. "She ain't supposed to wake up again till tomorrow mornin'. Plus, I know Eryn's been stayin' with ya at night."

Caeden's face heated. He hadn't known it was that obvious.

Eryn had stayed with him every night since his second day back at the castle. He'd stayed up late each night, and once everyone was asleep, he'd come back to his room to find her waiting for him in the hallway. The sleep deprivation was wearing on both of them from getting to bed so late and waking up so early to avoid anyone seeing Eryn leave his room, but he was thankful to her for doing it. It was hard enough to sleep in the same room Dealla had kidnapped him from when he'd first done it a week ago, but having Eryn beside him made it easier.

How Ronan figured out she was sleeping in his room was beyond him, though. They'd been careful to make sure no one saw, though he wasn't sure why it mattered anymore. His engagement was off, and even if it wasn't, they hadn't done anything but sleep, anyway. But that wasn't how it would appear to anyone else, and it would cause unrest in the court if anyone but Ronan knew, since Caeden hadn't made any sort of official announcement about their relationship. But he didn't know how he would begin to do that. He wasn't even sure what their relationship was.

"It's not how it looks," Caeden explained, the words falling from his mouth too quickly. He wasn't sure why he argued. If there was anyone he didn't need to explain the situation to, it was his best friend.

The corners of Ronan's mouth quirked upward, but there was something like pity hiding in his gaze. "The two of ya ain't subtle," he told him. "And I know the reason ain't sex." Ronan turned away again and dug the toe of his shoe into the edge of the rug blanketing the hardwood floor. "Nightmares? Or the dark?"

He hadn't truly broached the subject of his kidnapping with Ronan. Compared to what his friend went through, Caeden's single week of being held in that cell was practically nothing. They'd attempted to play mind games with him, but he hadn't been physically tortured. He hadn't lain in that cell while his fellow soldiers were slaughtered. He hadn't lost his friends while he'd been kept in there.

Caeden swallowed hard. "I don't like being alone if I'm closed into a room."

Ronan nodded slowly. "I had that," he said quietly. "It didn't last as long as other things did for me."

"Are you sure you want to be alone with her?" Caeden asked again.

Ronan looked at the stretcher for a beat too long before he shrugged. "I need to know she doesn't have power over me," he whispered finally. "She can't hold me bein' scared of her over me. We're at war, and even if I hate her for what she's done, I can't say I would've been above doin' similar things. I was sent on missions as a spy, too. I get it more than I want to." He shook his head. "But I can't let her win the mind games. I won't let her have that power over me."

Caeden nodded. Part of him wanted to argue that Dealla would be knocked out for the night and that she would never know if Ronan chose to spend the night in the other room, but the look on his friend's face gave him pause. Determination hid behind his eyes, and he could see from it that Ronan's reasoning had less to do with what Dealla perceived and more to do with proving to himself that she couldn't affect him.

He stayed silent long enough for Ronan to plop himself down on the edge of the bed and drop his cane against the wall. He pulled open one of the drawers in the nightstand and rummaged inside before pulling out a second small candle and another box of matches to light it with.

Outside in the hallway, a door to another one of the inn's rooms slammed shut, and a man's voice called down the stairs for the innkeeper. It was followed closely by the sound of his loud footsteps thumping down the stairs.

Ronan lit the candle and placed it on top of the nightstand as the man's footsteps faded.

"How does the innkeeper know you?" Caeden asked again, remembering again the innkeeper's reaction to Ronan when the four of them walked in. The man said he recognized Ronan, but he hadn't appeared happy to see him, and Ronan hardly acknowledged the man at all.

Ronan's shoulders tensed, and he fumbled with the matches as he replaced them in the still open drawer. He stayed silent for so long Caeden was sure he wouldn't answer, but eventually, he spoke. "I traveled with his daughter," he said, so softly it took

Caeden a moment to piece together the words. He said each of his next words slowly, as if the weight of the situation was placing itself onto his shoulders all over again. "She was part of my unit when we were taken by the Dragon Lord. I wasn't leadin' the mission, but I was high rankin'. She was young and still new, so her father came to see her off for her first mission. He knew I was ranked above her, and he pulled me aside 'fore we left and told me to look after her. I told him I would. We weren't even close to the capital and Deovaria doesn't keep too many of its soldiers in farther towns, but that didn't change anythin'. She died, and when Eryn got us out, we ended up back in the town she grew up in and I had to explain what happened to her. He must've moved since then."

Caeden's heart hurt as he listened. Her death couldn't have been Ronan's fault, but that didn't change how guilty Ronan still felt over it. "That doesn't sound like it was your fault," Caeden said softly, unsure how else to respond. His words wouldn't help Ronan feel any better, especially not with everything else going on, but they felt necessary.

"He doesn't see it that way," Ronan said with a quick glance over his shoulder at the door. He turned back, his shoulders sagging even further. "It doesn't matter to him that I tried, only that I failed. That I got out alive and she didn't. Nothin' I can do to change that, though."

Caeden sighed, but said nothing else in response. There was nothing more he could say. He hadn't been there, and though he wanted to help Ronan, there wasn't anything he could do to change the circumstances or wash away the guilt.

Silence stretched between them. Caeden wanted to break it, but no good words came to mind, and he wasn't ready to change the subject either. If Ronan wanted to talk about it, he didn't want to close the door and make him feel like he couldn't.

It was a painfully long moment before Ronan finally cleared his throat and stood unsteadily on his feet. He offered Caeden the key to the other room. "I'll stay here with the madwoman. You and Eryn take the other room."

Caeden took the key from him, understanding the hint to give Ronan time alone to collect his thoughts. "Do you want to speak with the town leaders, or would you rather Eryn and I handle it?"

Ronan glanced at Dealla still passed out on the cot. "Someone needs to stay with her."

Caeden nodded, but didn't say anything before he left the room. The sound of Ronan's heavy sigh as he sank back onto the bed followed him out into the hallway as he pulled the door closed behind him.

Eryn returned shortly after Caeden got his few things situated in their room and changed into a fresh pair of clothes before they would meet the town leaders downstairs. The room was just as small as the one Ronan would spend the night in with Dealla, but theirs had a slightly larger bed which resulted in even less space to walk around.

The town had three people who ran it, but given the late hour, only two of them had woken and made their way to the inn. The first of the pair was a middle-aged woman with hair falling down her back in two thick braids. She had creases at the corners of her eyes that deepened when she smiled, and a softness to her that Caeden wasn't used to seeing in those who held positions of power. She'd hastily changed into a loose-fitting shirt and pants with a thin jacket slung over her shoulders to protect her against the chill of the night air. The second was a tall, older man who lacked the warmth the woman emanated. His expression was cool and calculating, and when he attempted to force a smile, it only succeeded in sending an uncomfortable shiver down Caeden's spine.

How many people in this town blamed him and his father for the war and the state they ended up in? How many of them would be as quick to see him dead as they would any of the Deovarians? The court attempted to send aid, which the town leaders must have known, but it clearly hadn't been received.

Caeden took a seat at the table beside Eryn, across from the two town leaders, who nodded politely in greeting, but said nothing else. They hadn't been expecting their arrival to begin with, and Caeden couldn't blame them for the confusion hidden in the edges of their expressions.

"I apologize for waking you so late," he told the two across from them. "I'm sure Miss Gedding has informed you that we are in a hurry and would like our arrival here to be kept as quiet as possible."

"You've made that pretty impossible," the man stated, his tone gruff as he crossed his arms over his chest. He looked annoyed, and his eyes kept flicking to the door, as if looking for any way to get out of here and back to the warmth of his bed. "Strollin' 'round with a dead body's gonna draw attention no matter what ya do."

The woman's eyes widened as she turned to the man beside her, her jaw dropping open before she was able to catch herself. She snapped it shut.

Caeden sat a little straighter at the man's tone. He cleared his throat before he spoke, attempting to keep any animosity from slipping into his own voice. "I don't expect you to undo what we've already done ourselves," he explained. "I only ask that you not tell anyone who isn't already aware the identities of those who arrived in their town with the supposed dead body."

"Supposed?" the woman asked, raising an eyebrow. She shook her head quickly, as if to strike the question away with an expression that reminded Caeden of a mother not wanting to know the kind of chaos their child got into in her absence. "Never mind. My name is Eilise. I handle interpersonal connections within the town: festivals, parties, and all the likes. And this"—she gestured to the man sitting beside her, who hadn't yet uncrossed his arms—"is Nioclas. He handles the town's treasury and trade."

"The exact person we needed to speak with," Eryn said coolly, her tone matching the one Nioclas used only a moment before. She sat back in her chair and crossed her arms to match as well, her gesture a challenge Caeden almost found amusing. She raised an eyebrow at Nioclas, who took the hint and uncrossed his arms. He took on a more pleasant demeanor, but his expression remained hard as steel.

Eilise glanced between the two before she shook her head and turned to Caeden. "What sort of assistance can we offer you, Your Highness? Miss Gedding told us that you've come to gather information on the town, but didn't offer specifics."

Caeden turned away from the Dragon Hunter and back to Eilise. "The King's Court has been attempting to send aid to every town in the kingdom, especially those closest to the border where the war is having the most effect on our people."

Nioclas snorted softly, his eyes flicking to the door again before turning back to Caeden.

Eryn gave the man a warning look, but Caeden ignored him and pressed on. "We opted against asking for confirmation that the supplies were delivered a long time ago, since it would put more messengers in danger, but it crossed my mind recently that we haven't checked up on the status of any of the aid we've sent in the last few years. I mean no offense to either of you by saying so, but it doesn't appear that the town has received our shipments. Or at least, not all of them."

"We—" Eilise started to speak, but Nioclas cut her off.

"We haven't received anything from you lot in years," he bit out. He said the words softly to avoid the attention of anyone else in the room, but a man seated a few tables away still turned in their direction. The innkeeper, who was standing behind the bar glanced up as well, but only momentarily before he got back to whatever task he'd been completing. "Our roads haven't been fixed in years, our buildings are rottin', our food is minimal, and people are starvin'."

"We missed a few shipments here and there," Eilise stated calmly, attempting to take over the conversation from Nioclas. "Every few months supplies and money wouldn't show up, but we haven't received even a single silver coin from the castle in nearly three years."

Nioclas scoffed again. "It's 'cause they're lyin'. They haven't been sendin' aid. They've been keepin' it all for the royals holed up in the castle."

"The castle can't function on its own," Eryn said through gritted teeth. "The towns are necessary for the kingdom to function. Why would they opt to let the towns starve if they can help it?"

Caeden bit his tongue to keep himself from saying anything. He hadn't wanted to go on the defensive with Nioclas. He was already angry, and pushing the blame for it onto them was the only thing that made logical sense. He wasn't going to give up the stance unless they could prove that they'd sent aid, but Caeden hadn't had the foresight to bring any of those documents with them. Not that it would've been a wise decision to do so in the first place.

"So it's all just magically disappearing?" the man said, gesturing wildly around them. He glanced at the door again, but when he looked back, he refused to make eye contact with either Caeden or Eryn and instead focused his attention on the woman seated beside him.

"Our communication has gotten worse," Caeden explained. He didn't miss Nioclas' almost frantic air as he spoke, but he didn't have time to consider what caused it right then. "We're only trying to gauge how badly the same thing is affecting our supplies and money. If we need to send more, smaller deliveries that are harder for the Deovarians to detect, then we'll switch to that tactic. Or if we need to ensure the supplies is more heavily guarded along the roads, then we will do that. We are simply gathering information so we can report back to the King's Court and make the necessary changes to ensure you and everyone else here are getting the aid you need."

Nioclas's eyes flicked to the door again, but this time, when he turned back, he met Caeden's gaze. He nodded once, but said nothing else.

"We appreciate you taking the time to come out here," Eilise said quickly, eager to bring the conversation to a quick close. She didn't look any more comfortable with Nioclas' tone than Caeden and Eryn felt.

Caeden nodded. "We'll be leaving early in the morning, but I'd appreciate it if you could work up a list of the biggest necessities the town has right now. It may be a few weeks before we are able to send a shipment to you, but I will personally ensure it is sent and received. And, as unlikely as it is that there was some sort of mix up since we've been sending generally the same aid to each of the towns, I will also look back at our records to see if I can find any possible reasons aside from Deovarian interference that could've caused the supplies to go missing."

Nioclas didn't look pleased with Caeden's words, but Eilise nodded politely and gave him a kind smile. She stood from the table, pulling Nioclas up beside her when she did, and bowed her head. "I'll ensure it is delivered to the innkeeper for you by first light tomorrow morning. Thank you, Your Highness."

They exchanged polite goodbyes, aside from Nioclas who didn't bother to say a word before he turned toward the door and strode from the inn without so much as a backward glance.

Eryn turned in her seat to face the innkeeper and waved at him until she caught his attention. She made a few gestures that made no sense to Caeden, but the innkeeper seemed to understand and grabbed two glasses from behind the counter before he filled them with ale.

"Is drinking the night before we leave for the mountains really a good idea?" Caeden asked, though he wasn't opposed to the idea of a quick drink after the awkward encounter.

Eryn gave him a half grin, but the amusement twinkling in her blue eyes faded quickly. She stayed quiet until after the innkeeper placed the glasses in front of them and Eryn handed him a silver coin. He walked back behind the counter and out of earshot before Eryn picked her glass up. She swirled the liquid around and took a long drink, gulping down half of the glass's contents before she spoke. "Eilise knows more than she's letting on," she said beneath her breath, her eyes flicking across the different faces in the room around them before they met Caeden's again. "And I'm willing to bet that whatever she knows, Nioclas is in on it."

Chapter 31

Caeden swallowed hard and reached for the glass of ale the innkeeper set in front of him. Following Eryn's lead, he pulled it to his lips while showing as little surprise as he could manage after hearing her words. He'd gotten a strange feeling from the two town leaders, but neither of them said or did anything beyond Nioclas directing his anger at Caeden for the shipments of supplies never arriving.

"What do you mean?" Caeden asked softly into the edge of the glass. He only pulled it away once his surprise faded enough that he no longer felt he needed it to help him keep a straight face.

Eryn gave him a sideways glance. She squinted at him, as if trying to determine whether he was serious before she realized he was, and halfheartedly rolled her eyes. "They really do keep you cooped up, don't they?" There was a hint of a smile playing at the corners of her lips, and a teasing glint in her eyes, but Caeden didn't find as much amusement in the situation. Her smile faded, and she turned serious again. "When you see enough spies and liars, it's easy to tell them apart from the ones telling the truth. Unless they're really good." Her eyes flicked to the staircase leading to their bedrooms for the night, where Ronan was still with Dealla. "I rarely miss them anymore."

"Luckily, I haven't gotten many opportunities to spot spies in the castle," Caeden answered, the corner of his mouth quirking upward despite the heavy weight of their situation pressing down on his chest. There was nothing he could do about it right now.

Eryn smirked and pulled her drink to her lips again. "I don't know, princy. You missed the courtier when he was babbling on like an idiot in front of you."

Caeden opened his mouth to retort, but he couldn't get an argument to form on his tongue, and instead he only shrugged. "In my defense, I'm sure most people miss something like that when they first see it."

She snorted, and her gaze landed on him over the rim of her glass. Amusement twinkled in her eyes. "Only the idiots."

She tossed him a grin, and though her words should've been entirely insulting, there was nothing but fondness in her eyes. Her words should've stung, but all he felt was a familiar warmth flood him when her eyes met his. He'd fallen in love with that crooked smirk, the teasing tone, and her deep blue eyes that held nothing but warmth and kindness despite the words that passed through her perfect lips. The lips that, in that moment, he couldn't tear his gaze away from.

He wanted to kiss her again.

"You're staring," Eryn teased.

His eyes flicked up to hers again. "I know. Is that a problem?"

The smirk pulled at the edge of her mouth again, and Caeden's heartbeat quickened. "Not unless you have a problem when I return the favor."

"I don't."

Eryn's smile widened. "Good."

A comfortable silence fell over them as Eryn reached for her drink again, and against Caeden's wishes, their earlier conversation flooded back to him. They had no way to prove for certain that Eryn's suspicions about the two town leaders were true, but he would have to look into it once they returned to the castle. There was nothing they could do from here, especially after they left for the mountains the following morning. But once they returned to the castle, he could get the information of those responsible for the deliveries and see if he could uncover anything. He would figure out how to go about it, and what exactly he would be looking for when they got back.

"You got serious again," Eryn commented, breaking the silence and tearing Caeden's thoughts away from the path they'd wandered down. She said it as if she was commenting on the dim lights in the bar, or the crooked oil paintings hanging on the wall.

"Are you sure you'll be okay when we get there?" he asked quietly. He had to force the words out, as if even his body was protesting saying them. She wouldn't want to talk about it, but he needed to know she would be okay. If she wouldn't, he would find a way to make her stay back, even if she argued.

Eryn shrugged. "It was a long time ago. I'm scared, but I've faced things I've been more afraid of before." She set her glass back down on the table before she reached over to place her hand gently against his leg, squeezing lightly as if that simple act could prove everything would turn out okay. She met his gaze again, her deep blue eyes searching his—willing him to believe her. "I'll be fine. I promise."

He gently placed his hand over hers, their fingers slowly intertwining until the warmth of her skin melted into his. For a moment, the world around them faded, the constant flood of memories quieted, and all he could focus on was her.

They stayed like that for a moment that felt too short before Eryn pulled her hand from underneath his and finished her drink. He did the same before the innkeeper returned, taking both glasses back behind the counter and adding them to a large bin of used dishware.

"We should get to bed," Eryn said, pushing her chair back with a quiet scrape against the hardwood floor. "We have a long day ahead of us tomorrow."

Caeden nodded and followed her lead.

They walked side by side up to their shared room for the night. Maybe it was the silence filling the inn, but Caeden was sure even a mouse's steps could've been heard with how loudly the floorboards groaned beneath their weight.

"I'm gonna check on Ronan," Eryn said when they reached the top of the stairs, and disappeared into Ronan's room before Caeden could respond.

Ronan and Eryn's muffled voices reached his ears, but he couldn't make out what they said as he pulled the key from his pocket and pushed it into the lock to the other room they'd purchased for the night. The lock clicked softly, and he pushed the door open before stepping inside. He didn't bother to close it behind himself, knowing Eryn would be following behind shortly.

He lit the candle on the table by the door, and the soft orange glow filled the room. It wasn't enough to see by, but it helped him make out vague outlines of the objects in the room so he could navigate his way to the edge of the bed. The mattress wasn't as soft as the one he was used to, but after their long ride on the dragon's back, it felt like the most incredible thing as his body sank into it. He pulled off his shoes and set them aside before he lay back against the bed.

A light thud against the window made Caeden jump, and he instinctively reached to his waist where his sword hung. Panic settled over him until the sound repeated again and again in quick unison. Each thud was a different pitch, and he calmed down when he realized it was only rain, and not an intruder trying to break into his room to drag him back to Deovaria, or slit his throat.

He sank back down against the bed again, his heartbeat still wild in his chest as the adrenaline began to subside. He hadn't truly allowed himself to be afraid since they'd left the castle. After the Dragon Lord attacked them in the Grand Hall during his betrothal ceremony to the woman who turned out to be Dealla in disguise, and then being kidnapped from his own bed by the same woman, anywhere that wasn't the four walls of the castle felt safer than his home. There was no logic to the feeling, given that here, he had no idea what kind of threats awaited him, especially once they arrived in the mountains and were likely to come across more than a few dragons along with the harsh elements the Rayfait Mountains had a reputation for.

All of it felt easier than being back home, though. The bed beneath him was more comforting than his own had been in days. It wasn't in any way an option, but a selfish part of him had wanted nothing more than to run away from all of it since his first night back from the Dragon Lord's prison.

He had nowhere to go, and he could never abandon his responsibilities, but it was all he ached for while he'd been alone in the hallway that night with only the darkness for company. Until Eryn had found him.

He couldn't explain how her presence could wash away the fears clinging to his every waking moment, but he loved her all the more for it.

"The rain is nice," Eryn said from behind him as she closed

the door softly behind herself and came farther into the room.

Caeden startled at the sound of her voice, but relaxed just as quickly. He nodded in agreement, but he wasn't sure whether she saw it. She didn't seem to look as she passed him, and approached the window on the far end of the room. She pulled back the curtains, revealing the dark night outside, and the hundreds of raindrops sliding down the glass pane set into the side of the inn.

"It always feels safer when it rains," Eryn continued, her voice somber as her eyes trailed down the length of the window, following the slow progression of a single droplet sliding against the glass. Her shoulders slumped, and her voice was quieter when she continued. "Battles have stopped because of the rain more times than I can count. The fires go out. The dragons won't fly. Soldiers are able to flee under the rain's cover. Even if we aren't in a fight, when it's raining, everyone knows we won't get attacked until the clouds disperse. It provides a brief, fleeting moment of peace for everyone out there."

He could picture it clearer in his mind than he ever wished. The flames, the screaming soldiers, the blood running through the grass, and then, the total silence as the Dragon Lord's armies retreated at the first droplets of rain from the clouds above. He hadn't known that about Deovaria's dragon army. It was another small piece he added to the growing puzzle he hadn't been able to see from within the castle walls. It wasn't until after they'd been attacked and after he'd been in the field for those few days that he began to gather pieces of what his soldiers went through every single day the war persisted.

Caeden stood before he gave himself time to think over his actions. His steps weren't quick, and when he wrapped his arms around Eryn's waist, his touch was gentle, but she still flinched when his arms encircled her. Her body relaxed after a split second, and she leaned into him. She rested her head back against his chest as a soft sigh escaped past her lips.

The weight of her against him felt like perfection in his arms, and the tension in his own body eased.

"You're safe with me," he whispered into her hair, his gaze following hers out into the dark, rainy streets of the town. "Even after the rain stops."

Eryn let out a light laugh, and he swallowed hard at all of the things that small laugh meant. She wasn't safe with him. She was probably safer on her own than she would ever be with him beside her. She was a trained warrior with years of experience over him. She'd gone through so much, and none of that made her pause for even a moment. She was incredible, but it made something in his heart ache knowing that he could never truly keep her as safe as he wanted.

Maybe she was right to laugh. Despite how true he wished his words were—despite how he would throw himself at the feet of the Dragon Lord and accept death without a second thought if it meant her safety—what he said didn't matter. They weren't safe. They wouldn't be safe until this war was over.

The thoughts swirled heavily at the forefront of his mind, and his heart cracked beneath the weight of them. He held her tighter, as if that small gesture could make his words true.

Eryn's hand found his, and she intertwined her fingers with his. She squeezed his hand lightly, and leaned further into him, holding him to her. "I know I am."

Caeden swallowed hard. Her words felt like a lie, but they still lifted some of the weight off his cracked heart.

She wasn't safe with him.

She wasn't safe anywhere. None of them were.

But he was glad he could provide her with at least a single, fleeting moment of peace amid the crumbling world around them.

Chapter 32

Ronan

Raindrops hit the window as Ronan listened to Eryn's footsteps retreat down the hall toward the other room. The droplets pounded against the glass in time with his racing heart.

He could practically feel the dampness against his skin, feel the ice-cold water the unconscious woman on the cot beside him had thrown over him to wake him as it seeped into the open wounds covering his body.

Ronan shuddered at the memory. Goosebumps flared along his skin, but they only served to remind him that the stinging agony of the acid-laced water was a thing of the past.

She couldn't hurt him anymore.

She was unconscious now. Once they arrived in the mountains, she would wake up, but there were three of them to keep her in line. Once they were safely back within the walls of the castle, she would be kept under lock and key within the confines of cement and steel walls.

She couldn't hurt him.

Thunder boomed outside the inn, and he was thrust back

into the memories of his days inside that cell.

The thunder echoed again, but this time, it wasn't thunder anymore.

It was the sound of the bucket of acid-laced ice water hitting the stone floor and rolling to the side.

It was the pounding of the blond woman's footsteps as she stepped closer to where he lay, huddled into the corner as rock bit into his arms and legs.

It was the crack of the whip they'd beat into his flesh more times than he could count.

It was the bloodcurdling screams that tore from his throat no matter how hard he tried to keep them at bay.

It was every time the whip, acid, poisons, and knives tore, cut, burned, and ate away at his flesh, and sometimes, his very soul.

His body shook as adrenaline coursed through every inch of him, and he held his breath to hold in the scream threatening to spill from his lungs.

He was under the blanket. He was lying on a bed. He was in the bedroom inside the inn. The rain was thudding against the window. The thunder was rumbling between the clouds as lightning flashed through the night sky. The scent of dust and wood filled his lungs, so strong he could taste it on the tip of his tongue.

"It's just the rain," came a soft voice from a few feet away.

The voice flowed over him like a warm embrace, easing his mind until the terror ebbed and the shuddering stopped.

Then he remembered who the voice belonged to.

It wasn't the voice of the woman who had slept beside him for more nights than he could count. It wasn't the voice of the first and only woman he'd confided in that he hadn't been able to endure the sound of thunder in three years.

The woman who sat with him and held him that night as the rain beat against the walls of his shack wasn't real.

She was a lie.

Everything she'd done was a lie.

It took everything Ronan had in him to sit up and face the woman whose face plagued his nightmares as memories of her holding his hand in the darkness forced themselves to the forefront of his mind alongside the nightmares.

She'd gotten her hands free from the bindings holding her wrists to the cot, and had pushed the sheets they'd laid over her down to her waist. She was sitting up when his eyes landed on her for the first time since he'd come into the room for the night. Concern was etched across her features, visible in her bright green eyes and the slight part to her lips. She held tightly to the edge of the blankets, her knuckles white as she gripped them with pure pain hidden in her expression.

It was the same expression he'd seen on his lover's face a hundred times. Even though her face looked different now, the expression was the same.

It made his heart hurt to see it for so many reasons, but he pushed the feeling away. It was another lie. He couldn't let her win whatever this mind game was. She was trying to manipulate him again, just like she'd done when she disguised herself as Margaid. He wouldn't let her win again.

"I was hoping you'd stay knocked out," Ronan muttered, keeping his tone emotionless as he climbed out of bed. He ignored his cane set beside the bed, and ignored the wave of pain that shot through his leg when he tried to apply pressure to it. It wavered beneath him, but he forced himself through it, and made the action look as normal as he could.

"Where are we?" Dealla asked softly. The concerned look hadn't left her face, but fear now hid behind her eyes.

Ronan didn't answer as he pulled the vial of sedative off the nightstand before uneasily making his way to where she sat on the cot. She didn't move away, even as he removed the cap from the needle and grabbed hold of her arm. Her muscles stiffened beneath his touch, and she sucked in a quick breath through her teeth. Her eyes darted between him and the needle hovering over her arm. She swallowed hard.

"Where are you taking me?" she whispered. She tried to keep the fear from her voice, but it seeped into her words, and her voice cracked at the end of the sentence.

Ronan clenched his jaw, even as the sound of her fear lodged itself into his heart like the most painful thorn he'd ever felt. Something new broke in him, and the truth spilled from his lips, despite the possible consequences swirling in his head.

"We're goin' to the Rayfait Mountains," he told her. There was very little she could do with the information unless she managed to escape and get back to her kingdom, but given that she got free of her bindings and hadn't tried to run, it didn't seem likely. And even if she managed to get away from them, she wouldn't be able to get to the Dragon Lord and have an army sent after them before they would be back at the castle.

Surprise flashed across her face. "Oh," Dealla said quietly. She glanced down at the vial of clear liquid suspended above her outstretched arm. "Is that going to knock me out again?"

"Yes."

She nodded and relaxed her arm into his hand. "Okay."

Ronan glanced at her, shock coursing through him. This had to be another trick, but he didn't know what she could gain from letting him inject the sedative. He shook his head, clearing away the confusion before dwelling on it for too long. There was nothing she could gain from this. Right?

"I really did love you," she whispered so softly Ronan hardly heard her.

Her words tore through him like the sharpest steel blade, and he shoved the needle into her arm, pushing down on the plunger before he second-guessed himself. She flinched as the clear liquid disappeared into her tan skin and he pulled the vial away.

Ronan let go of her arm, and Dealla lay back against the cot, surprising him once again. She stared up at the ceiling, waiting the few seconds it took for the sedative to have its full effect.

"You didn't love me," he snapped as he stepped away from her and tossed the needle back onto the nightstand. Fury raged in him, along with more hurt than he ever could've imagined. He wasn't supposed to feel anything for her. His feelings were supposed to disappear when her true identity was revealed to him. They should've been gone. "You kept me locked in a cell for months. You held the whip. You held the acid. You held the blades. And worst of all, you held the keys. Then, after all that, you disguised yourself and made me fall in love with you." The words were bitter on his tongue, and tears swam in his eyes despite himself. "That wasn't love, Dealla."

Her eyes were glassy when he turned back to face her. A single tear slipped down her cheek as she closed her eyes, the sedative finally taking its full effect. "I'm sorry," she whispered, so softly Ronan thought maybe he'd imagined it.

Chapter 33

They left early the following morning. The sun hadn't yet fully crested the horizon when their small group stumbled down the steps of the inn with Dealla's unconscious form tied to the cot. Only a few of the townspeople were awake for the day, and Caeden only counted three heads that turned to face them as they made their way back to where they'd left the dragon.

It was far fewer than he'd expected, and he felt more relief than he'd anticipated when they were finally deep enough into the forest that no one in the town could see them anymore.

The dragon waited for them exactly where they'd left her the night before.

Surprise flared through him when he saw she was still there. He hadn't expected her to leave, given that she'd stayed with them back at the castle, but they'd taken a risk when they'd left her alone in the woods. She could've easily left at any point, but she hadn't.

She was curled into a tight ball on the ground with her tail wrapped around herself so she could use the end of it as a pillow. Her bright orange eyes opened at the sound of them approaching, and when her eyes locked onto their group, her pupils shrank to small slits.

A shiver ran down Caeden's spine at the sight of it, but as quickly as she'd woken, her eyes dilated once again and she seemed to relax. She stood to her full height and shook the dirt and leaves from her body. She gave a loud, almost excited snort. Smoke billowed from her nostrils as she bent down and nudged Eryn with the end of her long snout, almost knocking her clean off her feet.

Eryn looked annoyed, but offered her a single light pat on the head before pushing her nose away.

"Let's get Dealla's cot up there and get out of here," Eryn said, turning back to face Caeden and Ronan as she moved to stand alongside the dragon.

The dragon took the hint and crouched down to the ground, stretching her wing out so Eryn could climb onto her back.

"You ready?" Caeden called up to Eryn once she situated herself on top of the dragon.

"Ready."

Ronan pulled his cane off Dealla's cot, and shifted from leaning his weight against the cot like he'd been since they'd left the inn and leaned onto his cane. He took a few steps back, but didn't say anything while Caeden and Eryn worked together to get the cot uneasily up the dragon's wing.

He'd only said a few words that morning, and Caeden was trying not to pry, despite the worry that was slowly strengthening the longer Ronan's silence lasted. He looked nearly as upset as he had right after he'd learned of Dealla's identity. Caeden was sure it had something to do with his night alone with the Dragon Lord's daughter, but now was not the time to ask. They wouldn't arrive back at the castle for several days, and come nightfall, Dealla would be awake with no way for them to easily get her unconscious again. By the time they returned home, Ronan would be much worse off than he currently was. There was nothing he could do to help, but that fact only made the worry intensify.

It twisted Caeden's stomach to watch his friend like this, and the fact that it would only get worse before he would get time away from Dealla was probably the worst part.

Caeden's arms strained beneath the weight of the cot as he heaved it up the side of the dragon while Ronan hung back. It wasn't as hard as he expected until he got to the halfway point, when the cot was nearly vertical right before Eryn was able to grab the other end of it.

"Careful, princy," Eryn said above him as the cot slipped down half an inch, just before she grabbed hold of it.

He didn't have the strength to respond while he lifted the stretcher higher again. It took another few agonizing moments before they got Dealla on top of the dragon, and by the time Eryn was getting her secured into place, Caeden's muscles were so strained he barely had the strength to pull himself up behind Eryn.

Ronan tossed the end of his cane up near Caeden's leg after he got himself situated on the dragon's back. He and Eryn held the majority of Ronan's weight from the other end of the cane while he pulled himself up in front of them. His jaw was set, and though Caeden only saw it for a split second before Ronan slung his leg over the dragon's back and turned away from them, he saw the pain etched into his features.

Caeden bit his tongue to keep himself quiet. None of them said anything before Ronan took the reins and flicked them lightly, signaling to the dragon that they were ready.

Slowly, she stood again. She crouched down slightly, her front so much lower than her back that Caeden slipped forward until his body was pressed nearly entirely against Eryn's. Then, before he had time to even consider moving back to his original spot, the dragon leapt into the air. Though he shouldn't have been surprised, he still instinctively wrapped his arms tightly around Eryn's waist to hold on.

Eryn's light laugh shook her body as they flew through the air, but the sound of it was lost to the wind. She placed her hand over his and gave it a squeeze. The gesture was small, but it made his heart flutter.

The town shrank beneath them as they flew higher until eventually, it disappeared entirely, and all Caeden could see was a blur of greenery beneath them as they flew over miles and miles of forest.

The flight to the mountains took them only another couple of hours, and throughout the whole flight, Caeden only spotted a few towns between the one where they'd spent the night and when they landed in the slick, icy rocks on the side of the Rayfait Mountains.

The towns were smaller than the one they'd spent the night in, and they passed two within the first hour of their flight before there was a long span where Caeden saw nothing but vast emptiness. The cold settled deep into his bones before he finally laid eyes on the third and final town they passed on their way to the mountains. It came and went quickly, and he shivered before pressing closer to Eryn.

All three of them were shivering by the time they finally saw the first flecks of snow drifting through the air, and the ground slowly turned from green to white as they flew up along the side of the mountains. It was another good fifteen to twenty minutes before they were high enough that a thick layer of snow half a foot deep coated the rocky terrain below. It took double that before they found a flat area with pine trees and foliage surrounding it.

Hopefully, the space would keep them hidden until night fell and they could find an entrance into the interconnected caves running through the Rayfait Mountains.

The dragon landed uneasily on the flattest part of the terrain, and the jolt of her feet sinking into the snow and connecting with the hard ground beneath sent a shock up Caeden's spine. She skidded to a stop that sent the three of them falling forward despite the saddle and the ropes they'd used to secure themselves to it.

"We're here," Eryn said dryly as she pulled herself into a sitting position again.

Caeden rightened himself and glanced around, following Eryn's gaze to the massive side of the mountain growing up from the ground ahead of them. Fear hid behind her eyes as she took in the snow covering most of the rock. Only a few patches of gray were visible between the breaks in the ice. Snowflakes fell around them, and the clouds overhead prevented them from seeing all the way to the mountaintops. From where they sat, the trees appeared entirely white, since most of them were only about half the height of the dragon's back.

A roar from somewhere above them echoed down the side of the mountain range, and the crisp air and general lack of vegetation did nothing to disrupt the sound.

A chill that had nothing to do with the cold ran up Caeden's spine, and he shivered. Eryn's entire body tensed.

Not once in his life had he imagined he would see the Rayfait Mountains with his own eyes, much less be halfway up the side of one of its highest peaks, but Eryn had been here before. She'd been abandoned on the side of this mountain range by people who were supposed to love and protect her.

Eryn shook her head, and her shoulders relaxed ever so

slightly. She slid off the dragon's back and to the ground beneath as if she'd done it a thousand times, before she helped Ronan do the same.

Caeden glanced at the mountain range beside them again. Only a few short months ago, his entire life was on a different path. He'd been trying to convince his father to grant him military training. He'd done very little outside of court ordeals and his occasional secret training sessions with Ronan. He'd hoped he'd be trained by now, but had never considered the court would allow him to leave on missions alongside his best friend and one of his kingdom's best Dragon Hunting warriors.

"Caeden?"

Eryn's voice pulled him from his thoughts, and he shook his head. Ronan was on the ground now beside her.

Caeden's face heated as he looked at the two of them. "Yeah?"

"I'm ready," Eryn said again, her eyes flicking to Dealla, who was still strapped to the cot securely tied down to the dragon's back. There was an edge of impatience in her tone, but he couldn't fault her for it.

She didn't have a jacket yet because their things were strapped to the cot along with Dealla, and he could see the goosebumps lining every inch of her skin, and the bright pink flush across her nose and cheeks from the cold.

Caeden shook himself again, and got Dealla's cot unhooked from the dragon's back. It slid back as he untied the ropes holding it in place, but he caught it before it slid too far and went plummeting to the ground. Slowly, he eased the cot over the side of the dragon's back as she lay crouched low against the powdery snow. Eryn caught it on the other end, and she and Ronan eased it to the ground as Caeden made his way off the dragon's back.

He landed uneasily in the snow beside Eryn, his knees buckling beneath the weight of his body when his feet took longer than his mind expected to hit the ground beneath the thick snow.

"What's the plan now?" Ronan asked as Caeden rightened himself and stood to his full height.

"Can I get a jacket before we start talking logistics?" Eryn hissed between clattering teeth. Goosebumps still lined her arms, and her whole body trembled from the frigid air surrounding them. She reached for the bag strapped to the back of the cot and hastily removed her large coat from inside before she pulled it around her shoulders. She grabbed two more coats from the pack, and handed them to the other two, who slipped them on just as quickly.

Caeden's heart clenched painfully at the sight of her bright red nose and cheeks as she shivered vigorously in her still-cold coat. Part of him wanted to wrap her up in his arms and hold her until her shivering eased, but he wasn't sure whether he should or not, given the circumstances. If they were alone, he wouldn't have questioned it, and he wasn't entirely sure why Ronan being there made him second guess something he would do without sparing it a thought any other time. Ronan knew he and Eryn had feelings for one another.

Ronan wasn't necessarily the reason he second-guessed himself, though. He wouldn't care, but he wasn't entirely sure whether Eryn would. She'd kissed him the night before when Ronan was standing nearby, but he hadn't been paying attention to them, and her kiss was quick. They weren't anything official, and though she hadn't seemed to care whether they showed physical affection before, something about holding her in the cold felt deeper than their occasional hand holding or their thighs touching when they were on the couch beside one another.

"We need Dealla to wake up before we can do anything," Caeden said, forcing away his confusing emotions and focusing on the situation at hand.

A dragon roared from somewhere deep inside of the mountains again, and Caeden jumped at the sound. Eryn's shivering ceased as the sound of the dragon's roar washed over them, and Ronan shuddered. The dragon beside them perked up at the noise, and she cast a forlorn glance up into the snow-covered peaks disappearing into the low-hanging clouds.

Ronan nodded slowly, his eyes flicking to the cot before returning to Caeden. "It'll be dark by the time she's up," he stated. "The second dose was more than the first. It's gonna take a while to wear off."

Eryn stepped around the cot to stand closer to the two of them. She was still shivering, but her teeth were no longer chattering, and Caeden felt a fraction of relief at the fact. His worry wasn't entirely gone, given that the woman beside him had lived through this kind of cold before. That fact alone brought so many more worries to the forefront of his mind. She said she would be fine, but he'd never known her not to put on a brave face.

"I brought a few candles with us," Eryn said, her voice coming out strained as she folded herself further into her jacket. "They won't be much, but they'll be enough for us to see when night falls."

"It'll be easier to travel by candlelight than to lug her around like that," Caeden agreed, nodding at Dealla over his shoulder.

Ronan gave a single, curt nod in response, his lips pressed together into a thin line. He didn't look at anyone when he responded, his eyes glued to the edge of the forest on the downward slant of the mountain ten yards away. "I'm gonna go find some firewood. Gonna need somethin' to light the candles."

He didn't give Caeden or Eryn time to respond before he turned on his heel and strode into the line of forest. His progress was slow, and Caeden contemplated calling after him when he watched Ronan slip a step and catch himself with his cane braced into the ground at the base of a tree. The slope in that direction wasn't steep, but he didn't love the idea of Ronan going off on his own.

Just before Ronan was out of sight, Caeden moved to run after him, only to be stopped by a hand gripping his upper arm.

"Don't," Eryn said softly, her fingers still wrapped around his arm, though her grip was looser now that he'd stopped and turned to face her.

He glanced between Eryn and where Ronan had disappeared, feeling torn between listening and ignoring her entirely to go after Ronan before he ended up hurt or lost.

"He needs some time alone," Eryn said, which Caeden had already gathered, but that didn't make him feel any differently about the situation.

"He's going to hurt himself," he argued. "Or get lost." He tugged his arm back lightly, but she held him firmly enough that he couldn't get out of her grasp without pulling her over in the process. She wrapped her other hand around his arm along with the first, and his heart skipped a beat as a rush of heat he hadn't been anticipating rushed to his face.

They'd spent the night in the same bed, pressed up entirely against one another beneath the single blanket, just like they'd done every night for the last two weeks, but her closeness still made his stomach flutter with nerves.

"He'll be okay," she said. She sounded like she was trying to convince herself as much as she was trying to convince him. "He won't go far. He just needs time to clear his head. He used to do it all the time when we were stationed together. It's how he copes when he doesn't have somewhere easy to sit and think."

Caeden looked after his friend again, the only sign that he'd ever been there his uneasy footprints in the snow. "I'll give him twenty minutes. If he's not back by then, I'm going to go find him."

"And I'll come with you," Eryn promised as a vigorous shiver worked its way through her body.

Caeden placed a hand over her ice-cold fingers encircling his arm and pulled her a step closer. He still wasn't sure whether it was a good idea, but Eryn didn't fight him when he pulled her body against his and wrapped her in an embrace. She shivered again, burying her face against his chest and slipping her icy hands beneath his jacket.

He shivered as the cold seeped through the thin shirt he wore beneath his jacket, and Eryn jerked away from him.

"Sorry," she whispered sheepishly, her cheeks reddening as she took a step back. She ran her hands up and down her arms as her shivering intensified again.

A small smile pulled at the corners of his lips as he watched her. Snowflakes had settled in her hair and clung to her lashes, somehow making her look even more breathtaking.

He took a step toward her and clasped both of her hands in his before tucking them around his waist beneath his jacket once again.

Eryn looked up at him, her eyes wide and her lips parted slightly as she stared into his eyes. Slowly, her hands relaxed against him, and she spread her fingers out against his back.

His breath hitched in the back of his throat as he watched her, and it had nothing to do with the cold seeping into his skin. There was something so incredibly intimate about the moment he'd found himself in. He'd kissed her multiple times, he'd fallen in love with her even if he hadn't told her so outright, and somehow this moment felt just as profound.

They weren't together. They had feelings for each other, but that was as far as it went. That was as far as it could go, given the circumstances of the world they lived in and their roles in it. He couldn't ask her if this was what she wanted when they didn't even know if they would live through the night with the dragons lurking inside of the mountains around them. But this didn't feel like they were simply two people harboring feelings toward one another anymore. This was something he could do forever. She was a speck of light in the darkness of the world. She was the hope he searched for when everything else felt lost. If there was one thing he wanted, it was to live through all of this just so he could continue to wake up beside her each morning and fall asleep beside her each night. He wanted to love her for the rest of his life.

But he couldn't tell her any of that. Not while they were on the side of the Rayfait Mountains about to venture inside in a couple of hours. Not with the war raging around them and no way of knowing whether either of them would come out the other end of it alive.

He couldn't. Not even as the words formed on the tip of his tongue and threatened to spill from his mouth.

So, instead, he settled for gently tracing his fingers along her cheek before he pressed a kiss to her lips that he wished could convey everything he wanted it to, but could never come close.

Chapter 34
Eryn

Eryn sat anxiously beside Caeden until Ronan finally returned what felt like hours later. He carried a small armful of sticks and branches with him, which they used to start a fire to keep the four of them from turning to blocks of ice in the hours of waiting ahead of them. They said little to one another as the sky slowly turned from pale blue to dim oranges and pinks, before darkness finally crept in around them. The sounds of the dragons inside of the mountains washed over them every few minutes as they waited, and Eryn's body stiffened each time. Her eyes flicked up to the tops of the mountains, half expecting to see the creatures flying down to engulf them in flames or swallow them whole, but there was nothing there each time she checked.

Fear worked its way through her, and she hadn't been able to force it away since they'd landed hours ago. She'd tried to ignore it and shove it back behind the wall she'd built up to contain her fears since she'd first agreed to travel up here, but it wasn't enough anymore.

She could hear them now like she could when she'd woken that morning years ago. It shouldn't have hurt so much to relive the memories, but they still lodged themselves into her heart.

She'd accepted long ago that her parents only did what they thought was best, but the hurt she felt never fully went away. Maybe it never would.

Caeden caught her eye when she finally pulled her gaze away from the mountaintops and turned her attention back to their group. Concern was etched across his features, but she was grateful he didn't say anything. She wasn't sure she could keep the emotions at bay if she had to see the worry in his eyes like she had the night before. She felt too safe with him, and every part of her wanted nothing more than to confide every last one of her fears in him. But that couldn't happen right now. They would be traveling up into those mountains soon, and all she needed was to keep the feelings at bay and push through this.

She'd spent her whole life fearing dragons, and even the mere thought of the mountains, but she was done letting that fear control her. She couldn't change the past, but she could decide that the memories haunting her wouldn't shape the way she lived now.

Eryn shook her head and climbed to her feet, leaving the other two to sit beside the fire as silently as they were before. Ronan hadn't so much as looked away from the flames since he'd first gotten the fire lit.

She grabbed the candles from the bag still strapped to Dealla's stretcher and kneeled beside the fire to work on getting them lit now that it was dark out and Dealla would be up soon. She'd remembered only at the last minute to pack holders for them to keep the hot wax from dripping onto their hands when they began their venture into the caves.

Eryn was halfway through lighting the candles and placing

them into their holders when Dealla let out a soft moan and tried to sit up on the cot. She didn't have much luck, given that the bindings were firmly wrapped around each of her extremities to hold her in place.

A smirk touched Eryn's lips at the sight of her struggle.

"You could've untied me a little," Dealla muttered, her voice raspy and slurred from the sedative that would have her groggy for at least a few hours before it wore off entirely.

"We heard how easily you got out last night. We weren't planning to take that risk again," Caeden said as he climbed to his feet and walked over to Dealla's cot. She glared at him when he came into her line of sight, and the hatred in her eyes for the man standing above her rivaled the amount burning in Eryn's chest for her.

"What the fuck are we doing here?" Dealla snapped, attempting to gesture with a hand to the snow-covered mountains surrounding them, though she had little luck.

Eryn lit the last of the candles and set them aside as Caeden untied Dealla's legs from the cot, and moved to do the same with her wrists. Ronan hadn't turned away from the flickering flames of the fire, but his shoulders had tensed.

"You aren't going to get far if you try to run," Caeden said, roughly pulling the ropes around Dealla's wrists in a sharp motion that ensured the jagged edges of the bindings bit into her skin when he pulled them away.

Eryn's smirk returned despite herself as she took in the red marks on the Dragon Lord's daughter's wrists.

Dealla hissed between her teeth, but it seemed less from the pain and more from annoyance, much to Eryn's irritation. "So, you've brought me up here to freeze to death, then?"

Eryn rolled her eyes. "Don't flatter yourself," she snapped. She clenched her jaw as she stared at the woman, annoyance and hatred burning so hot inside her that her body had turned rigid from the memories of everything Dealla had done. "You aren't special enough for us to make a trip up here just to dump you and let you die. You're going to navigate us to the stones."

Dealla let out a sharp, bitter laugh. "What did I ever do to convince you I'd help you with something like that?"

"Help us, or I'll slit your throat right here," Ronan said in a deadly whisper.

Surprise and pride hit her at once as Eryn glanced at him. It'd been a long time since she'd heard him use that tone with someone, and she'd never known him to unless he truly meant it. Nothing but surprise was written across Caeden's face when she turned back, and she wondered whether he'd seen anything like this from Ronan before, since he'd only fought beside him once.

Caeden's expression vanished as he yanked the other binding from Dealla's wrist, the rough rope scraping her skin and leaving a deeper red mark than the last. Once her hands were free, she sat up and gently rubbed her wrists.

Dealla smirked as she glanced between the three of them, and it made Eryn's blood boil. "Death doesn't scare me," she said in a tone far cockier than her darting eyes suggested. "And you know the kind of torture I'm capable of." Her words were casual as she snatched one of the jackets off the cot before tossing it over her shoulders. "There's a rule in Deovaria that you aren't allowed to deal that kind of torture unless you can take it. None of the tactics you can implement will make me do what you want."

Ronan climbed to his feet and stood directly in front of Dealla. He gripped her chin tightly before Eryn realized he'd gotten up at all. Dealla's breath hitched, but Ronan didn't seem to notice past the anger apparent in the set of his jaw. His gaze was hard as he stared into her eyes, and something in Eryn's heart broke for him at the sight.

"I don't need torture tactics to get information from you," he stated, so softly Eryn wouldn't have heard him if the wind hadn't slowed. "All I need is to see your face."

Ronan let go of her and turned away, and Dealla gave an audible gulp as soon as his back was turned.

Dealla may have been trained in torture, but she certainly hadn't learned how to deal with someone who had fallen in love with her and memorized her expressions, even if she had worn the face of a different woman at the time. Her features were different now, but her expressions hadn't changed.

Eryn wasn't there when they'd gotten the information from Dealla in the dungeon, but given the way Caeden and Ronan explained it to the court, it only could've been because Ronan could read her. Dealla had tried to use Ronan to get information, and instead, she'd created her own weakness. She couldn't hide the secrets she held as Deovaria's Princess from the man standing in front of her.

Ronan sat down beside Eryn next to the fire and moved to put out the flames.

Silence stretched between all of them for a long moment before Eryn cleared her throat. "Are we ready?" she asked, glancing between Caeden and Ronan, who refused to turn away from his work.

Caeden grabbed a piece of rope from the cot and grabbed Dealla by the wrists again. Dealla struggled against him, and Eryn moved to help him contain her, but she gave up trying to fight him when he tied her hands behind her back and pushed her off the edge of the cot. He didn't let go of her bindings.

He nodded once Dealla was standing in front of him. "We are."

Eryn glanced at Ronan again. He had put out the fire but was still kneeling on the ground. He shook himself before he climbed up to his feet, and Eryn handed him one of the candles she'd lit. She turned to Caeden and handed him one of the others, keeping two for herself.

Caeden pushed Dealla forward in the general direction they'd be walking in hopes of coming across a cave entrance as Eryn turned to the dragon lying in the snow nearby. The creature still set her on edge, but part of her felt bad leaving her alone again. The dragon could still leave at any point, but something told Eryn she wouldn't. She was loyal to them, even if Eryn couldn't wrap her head around how a simple stone could do that.

The dragon didn't owe them anything. She deserved freedom as much as any other living being, yet she'd been enslaved by the Dragon Lord, and though she wasn't sure why, it made Eryn's heart ache to think maybe they'd done that to her as well.

The dragon stooped so low that her head was a few inches away from being buried in the snow. She gave a single snort, and her eyes flicked to the mountaintops again before she looked at Eryn with a sadness she hadn't known dragons were capable of. It did nothing to ease the guilt welling in the pit of her stomach.

"You have to stay here," Eryn said softly, her words coming out strained despite herself. The creature scared her more than most things, but she shoved that fear away as she whispered the words. The dragon had done nothing to hurt them. Everything she'd done so far was only by the Dragon Lord's command, not her own free will, and Eryn couldn't hold that against her.

The dragon snorted again and plopped her head the rest of the way into the snow. She turned away from Eryn and wrapped her tail around herself like a pouting child.

Eryn let out a puff of air between her lips at the dragon's attitude, but reached forward to gently pat her on the side of her large head before spinning on her heel and joining the others.

Chapter 35

The four ventured along the side of the mountain for a couple of hours before they found the dark mouth of a cave tucked between two large rocks. It hid amongst the rocks in the darkness, and Caeden wouldn't have been able to see it without the candles they held. Even then, he did a double take before realizing that the cave wasn't simply the shadow of one of the stones resting on either side of it.

"Who's going first?" Eryn asked. Her voice was higher pitched than usual, and a shiver worked its way through her as she said the words.

Caeden pushed Dealla forward in front of him without answering Eryn's question. Fear worked its way through every vein in his body as he stepped toward the dark void ahead with his cousin bound in front of him. She had no way to plan a trap for them to walk into, given she'd been unconscious for the past two days and hadn't known anything about their journey until she'd woken up. But a small, irrational part of him still worried they were walking into something she'd set up for them.

He shook his head and pushed away the fear. Dealla had gone

as stiff as a board, but he forced her forward in front of him. She sucked in a breath and Caeden's eyes scanned the space.

The candle he held didn't provide much lighting in the dark cave, but he could make out the stone walls pressing in tightly on either side of them and the first few feet of uneven ground ahead. They would need to make their way through the cave slowly and likely walk in a single file line for the first leg of their journey in here, but he hadn't expected anything different. Though he hadn't known what to expect, either.

Eryn was close behind him and Dealla, and the soft thumping of Ronan's cane against the rock indicated he wasn't much farther.

"It's so quiet," Eryn whispered.

She was standing so close that Caeden felt her breath against his neck when she spoke, and it sent a shiver down his spine. Her words echoed against the walls and down the length of the cave ahead, though she hadn't spoken loudly.

Caeden tugged Dealla's arm roughly to ensure he had her attention. "Which way?" he asked, his voice just as soft as Eryn's, but his held an edge he'd never heard in his own tone before.

Dealla scoffed, but flinched when Caeden tugged on her arm harder.

She tried to keep her usual, unbothered composure, but the cracks in her mask became larger the longer she was awake and the further into their journey they got.

"You really think I'm going to know how to navigate these caves when I've never been here before?" she hissed, turning so she was nearly nose to nose with Caeden in the dark. The movement tightened the bindings around her wrists but she didn't seem to care.

He wasn't sure if she was trying to intimidate him, or if she was covering up her attempt to convince herself that she wasn't scared of the situation she'd woken up in.

Dealla rolled her eyes. "You are truly an idiot."

Caeden clenched his jaw, ignoring her insult and her lies. "I don't expect you to know exactly which way," he told her, his tone as cold as the air biting through their clothes. "But you know more than you're acting like you do. What are we looking for? Do we need to go east or west? I know you have the answers, so stop acting like you don't."

Dealla raised an eyebrow at him, a smirk pulling at the corners of her lips. "And you think I'll just tell you?"

"You will sooner or later," Ronan said beneath his breath.

Dealla visibly stiffened; Ronan's earlier words not forgotten. She lowered her gaze from Caeden's and stepped as far away from him as she could manage with his hand still wrapped around her bound wrists. Her eyes locked on the floor of the cave at her feet, and she refused to look back up.

Eryn scoffed, just as Caeden became entirely sure that Dealla knew exactly where they needed to go.

Dealla shifted uncomfortably, her head bowed low, even as her eyes flicked around the space. It was hard to see in the dim lighting, but her eyes went from Caeden to Eryn, then back to the walls surrounding them before returning to the floor. She looked everywhere except at Ronan.

That was when Caeden realized how they could get her to talk.

"Here," he said, moving Dealla until she stood only a few inches away from Ronan. She wasn't facing him when Caeden lifted her bound wrists and offered them to Ronan.

Ronan froze for a long moment, before he seemed to understand what Caeden was doing. He grasped the rope binding Dealla's wrists, and she took in a sharp breath. She glanced over her shoulder at Ronan, her eyes wide and frantic despite her clenched jaw.

Ronan had gotten to her when they were outside, and she was afraid he could read her as well as he'd said. It was an easy weakness to exploit.

"A river," Dealla blurted, and the corner of Caeden's mouth quirked upward.

He'd known she would crack, but he hadn't expected it to be that quick. She was terrified of accidentally giving the information away. So much so that she would rather blurt it out herself before Ronan could uncover something from her without her intending for him to.

"What was that?" Eryn taunted, amusement lacing her words.

Dealla glared daggers at her, but she refused to turn to face Ronan again. "It's a river," she said through clenched teeth. "The river to the center of the world. It draws magic from the depths of the earth, and anything that sits in the water long enough gets infused with its power. That's where the stones are from. It runs all throughout the mountains."

"That wasn't so hard, now was it?" Eryn said, the corner of her lips lifting.

Dealla refused to look at any of them as they ventured deeper into the caves, the candles doing little to light their path. They walked for what had to have been nearly half a day, until long after their feet and ankles began to hurt from the uneven ground and the jagged rocks covering it.

Caeden felt blisters forming on the soles of his feet just as doubts about whether they would find the river Dealla mentioned began to creep into his mind. They could spend a few days inside of the caves looking for the river, but none of them wanted to sleep a night in here with the dragons lurking around.

They stopped to eat after walking for several hours, and despite the irritated complaints he expected to hear from Dealla when they continued on their journey again, she kept her mouth shut.

It was another couple of hours when Eryn stopped walking behind him suddenly. She fell behind a few steps before Caeden noticed she was no longer keeping pace with the group. The other two noticed at the same time. Once their steps no longer echoed off of the cave walls, Caeden could faintly hear the sound of water dripping against stone.

He almost second-guessed himself, but it was too similar to the quiet thuds of the rain against the window at the inn.

"We're close," Eryn said softly, echoing the words resting on the tip of Caeden's tongue.

Dealla stiffened, and the relief Caeden felt from the confirmation lifted a weight off his shoulders that he'd been trying to ignore since they'd first landed.

They continued walking, the sound of the dripping water their guide through the maze of tunnels. The dripping was slowly drowned out by the sound of a flowing stream the further they got.

They followed the path around a sharp bend, their steps quick as they grew closer. Through the darkness ahead, a faint blue glow illuminated the rough edges of rock. It was dim compared to their lit candles, and when Caeden tried to focus on it, it disappeared entirely. He blinked quickly, and the blue hue was as clear as when he'd first noticed it.

"It can't be that easy," he breathed, as Eryn let out a long breath beside him and Ronan froze in his tracks to stare at the sight.

"You know of anythin' other than those stones that glows

blue, princy?" Ronan asked, a half laugh of disbelief slipping past his lips as he shook his head slowly.

Eryn nudged him gently with her shoulder, and smiled with a kind of thrill lighting her eyes that he'd only seen a few times before. "Don't say things like that out loud until after we know for sure we found it," she teased.

A smile pulled at the corners of Caeden's mouth, and he wasn't sure if it was because of the sparkle of joy in Eryn's eyes or because of the disbelief he felt at the possibility that they'd made it this far.

Slowly, the pale blue light grew brighter, and the sound of the river became nearly deafening as it came into view.

Caeden's eyes widened as he took in the glowing water as it flowed alongside the path they were on and disappeared around a bend up ahead that the path didn't follow. The water glistened and sparkled in its own light. It was identical to the light his mother's ring emanated.

His hand found the edge of his pocket where his mother's ring was safely tucked inside, and he ran his fingers along the jagged edge of it absentmindedly, transfixed by the sight ahead. How many others had the privilege to see something so beautiful? Very few knew the stream existed, aside from them, the Dragon Lord, and a select few of his followers. From what Caeden and the others had gathered, he doubted anyone else had heard even a whisper about this place.

If the river was mentioned in something as simple as a fairytale told to children late at night, hundreds, if not more, would've traveled to the mountains before now to see it, even if the magic it held wasn't a factor.

"Whoa," Eryn breathed, so softly Caeden hardly heard it over the running water.

Words couldn't do justice to the sight in front of them.

Caeden stood as the beauty of it took its time to fully register in his mind, and even longer for him to believe it was real and not simply a figment of his imagination.

The four of them stood in total silence for so long Caeden wasn't sure how much time passed before he finally shook his head and remembered why they were here to begin with.

He didn't say anything as he slowly stepped toward the water's edge and peered into the clear blue depths. There was an unspoken reverence in the air as the others joined him at the riverbank.

The water wasn't more than a few feet deep, and he could make out a few shining dots of blue at the bottom, along with a few that were purple and red. One tumbled slowly against the rock bottom, pulled along by the current until it got snagged on a particularly high point of stone.

He didn't give himself time to second-guess his decision before he pulled his jacket off and set it aside, easing himself over the rock edge and into the flowing water.

"What are you doing?" Eryn hissed, her tone less frustrated by his actions and more surprised.

Caeden was about to open his mouth to respond, but the words never left him.

The distinct feeling of the magic in the water washed over him so suddenly it nearly knocked him off his feet. It wasn't like anything he'd ever felt before, and he was sure he was only feeling a fraction of the magic's strength.

It flowed gracefully beneath his skin, leaving behind an almost tingling sensation. It was as if the water and its magic flowed straight through him rather than around him as it moved along the path it had carved through the mountains. He felt the magic's low thrum throughout his body, filling him with a warmth that spread from the tips of his toes to the top of his head.

Ronan and Dealla took in sharp breaths from the river's edge. When Caeden turned to face them, he was met with expressions of both fear and wonder as they stared straight at him.

"Caeden," Eryn said slowly, pronouncing each syllable of his name so clearly it made his heart skip a beat despite knowing her expression meant he should be worried. "You're glowing."

Caeden only stared at her, the words not registering in his mind. He could hear her clearly, but something about the magic working its way through him made it hard to focus on anything else.

"Caeden," Eryn said again, more urgent this time.

The fear lacing her words was enough to knock him from whatever trance the magic put him in.

He glanced at his hands, and his breath caught in the back of his throat. His skin was no longer the same color he was used to. Instead, it held a faint blue tint that matched the water, and when he removed his hand from the river, it emanated the same glow, though the light coming off his skin was much fainter than the light coming from the water.

"What's happening?" Ronan growled, so loud and sudden that Caeden flinched. Ronan gripped Dealla's arm tightly, pulling her so close their noses were nearly touching.

Dealla's face turned a deep shade of red, and she stumbled over her words repeatedly before she finally managed a coherent sentence. "The magic," she said quickly, the words coming out in a squeak. "The river infuses anything that goes into it with magic. The glow goes away when you aren't in the water."

Ronan loosened his grip on her just enough that she could step away from him.

"Like the stones?" Eryn asked.

Dealla nodded, a mixture of fear and anger mingling over her features.

"It feels…" Caeden broke off, unsure how to describe what he felt as the magic worked through him. "Natural," he settled with. "It feels like it's running through my body like it was always supposed to be there."

Confusion clouded Eryn's expression, but her shoulders sagged with something that resembled relief. "Just get the stones and get out quickly, okay?" There was a nervous edge to her voice, and her eyes never left his.

Caeden nodded and glanced at the blue specs sitting at the bottom of the river. "There aren't many," he told them, as he made his way toward one and nudged it with the toe of his shoe beneath the water. He counted only six in the small area the four of them could access.

"They'll have to be enough," Ronan muttered, as Eryn peered over the edge and into the water to count the stones. When she finished, her disappointment was evident.

How did we not see them?

Caeden stiffened as the words registered in his mind. They weren't crisp like the others' voices. These words were hazier around the edges, as if he'd thought them himself but in a different voice and in a language he'd never heard before but could somehow easily understand. They weren't exactly words so much as sounds originating inside of his own head.

I don't know, but I still smell them.

It was a different voice this time; deeper and rougher than the first.

We haven't been able to find them yet.

A third voice.

"We'll keep exploring the caves," Eryn stated, drawing Caeden's attention back.

"We can't," he said the words falling from his mouth as a

wave of panic settled over him.

He didn't know how it was possible, or how he knew with such certainty, but he was hearing the dragons. The dragons were speaking inside of his head. The dragons knew they were here. They knew they were inside of the mountains and they were searching for them.

The three turned to face him at once.

"Help me get the stones," Caeden said quickly, knowing they would argue before the words had even left his mouth. "The dragons are looking for us."

Chapter 36

Eryn's brow furrowed as she stared at him, and Ronan raised an eyebrow. Dealla's eyes went wide, and it only confirmed his suspicion.

The Dragon Lord knew how to control the dragons because he'd been here before. He'd been in this stream before. The magic flowing through Caeden's body was the same magic working its way through his uncle's veins. He didn't need a stone to control the dragons like his soldiers did. All the magic he needed was already inside of him. Whatever secret the magic in the stream held that possessed the ability to tame the dragons, he must have heard it from a dragon in the same way Caeden was hearing the dragons speak now.

Eryn opened her mouth, likely to protest, but Caeden cut her off before she could. "I can't explain right now," he told her. "We need to get the stones and leave."

The urgency in his voice was all she needed before he watched her push down her confusion and snap into action. "Come on," she said to Ronan, and tugged both him and Dealla into the water along with her as she stepped over the edge into the depths.

The three of them gathered the stones quickly. Eryn held tight to Dealla's bindings as they worked, though she didn't seem particularly eager to get away. Fear still clung to the edges of her expression, and her eyes darted around the cave, searching for any sign the dragons had found them.

Eryn and Ronan handed Caeden the stones they gathered, and he quickly tucked all six of them into his pocket alongside his mother's ring. They climbed back out of the river swiftly, their movements so rushed Caeden tripped and nearly fell against the sharp edge of a large rock at the riverbank.

Their scent is stronger this way, the second voice said, echoing throughout Caeden's head so loudly it could've been screamed into his ear.

He tripped again, this time losing his balance entirely and falling to the stone floor. Jagged rock bit into his palms when he caught himself, and blinding pain shot through his knees as they connected with the ground.

"Caeden!" Eryn was by his side before he had time to start climbing back to his feet. She grabbed his arm and supported half of his weight as he unsteadily rightened himself.

They have to be close. The third voice again.

Blood slipped down his fingertips and dripped to the floor beneath as pain coursed through his legs. He hissed between his teeth, but they didn't have time for him to wait for the pain to pass. The dragons were hunting for them, and they could move faster than the four of them could. Never mind that the dragons would know these caves as well as Caeden knew the halls of the castle.

"We need to leave," Caeden said, his voice breathy from the pain. "The dragons know we're here. They're trying to find us."

Eryn froze mid-step and turned back to face him. Pure fear

displayed itself across her features, but she pushed it aside quickly, setting her jaw with a new kind of determination he'd only seen from her when they'd been fighting against the Dragon Lord's armies.

She still held tight to his upper arm, supporting half of his body weight as they hurried through the twisting caverns back in the direction they'd come earlier in the day.

How did we miss them? It was the first voice asking again, this time sounding far angrier than before.

A shiver ran down Caeden's spine, and Eryn's entire body tensed in front of him. "Did you hear that, too?" he asked.

She glanced over her shoulder at him. Her face had paled since they'd started back from the river. He would've assumed it was caused by the physical energy they'd all expended from running, if not for the look of pure, undeniable fear that had returned to her face.

She opened her mouth to respond, but a split second passed before she snapped it shut and nodded her head slowly.

"They're talkin' about us?" Ronan asked from behind Caeden, his voice hardly a wavering whisper. "Those're the dragons? You're sure?"

"Yes," Caeden responded. He didn't know how he knew, or why he felt so strongly that it was the dragons they were hearing, but there was no question about it.

They paused in their tracks, the three of them sharing a weighted look as the full understanding of the threat hanging above their heads sank in. The dragons were hunting them. The four of them were inside the dragon's home—their territory—with nothing more than a few weapons to protect themselves against the thousands, if not tens of thousands, of dragons the mountain housed. They hadn't even had the foresight to bring lavender with them; not that they even could've, given that it would've affected the dragon they'd ridden to get here.

"How?" Eryn asked, turning her full attention to him.

He didn't have an answer for her, though. Aside from his certainty that they were hearing a conversation between multiple dragons, he was clueless about the situation they'd found themselves in.

"It's from the river," Dealla snapped, making Eryn jump before she spun to face the woman whose bound wrists she still held. Dealla bared her teeth when she spoke again, her words clipped. "Now can we get out of here before we're eaten alive? The stones aren't going to stop an entire army of dragons from ripping us apart if they have drakes with them. For a Dragon Hunter, I would expect you to know they won't have time to make sense of the magic over their bloodlust. It's the same as the lavender with those creatures, and I don't particularly feel like dying today."

More questions swirled through Caeden's mind as Dealla's words sank in, but he didn't have time to question her right now. They needed to get out of here, and they needed to do it quickly if Dealla's words were to be believed.

They hurried through the winding caverns, the pounding of their feet against the ground deafening in Caeden's ears. He wished that alone was enough to drown out the conversation the dragon's hunting them were having.

They can't have gotten far, the first voice snapped.

They were gaining ground quickly, but they'd spent hours wandering through the mountains before they'd stumbled upon the river. Even at the pace they were going, it would be hours before they reached the mouth of the cave where they'd entered.

"Are you okay?" Eryn called over her shoulder to Ronan, who was still at the back of the group.

Caeden turned to lay eyes on his friend, fearful of the state he would find him in after their hours of travel earlier and now the running, but Ronan was hardly breathing heavily when he turned around, and his cane wasn't supporting his weight. Instead, he held his cane at his side, the end not even touching the ground as he ran.

He had a bewildered look on his face and he kept glancing down at his leg, waiting for the moment it would give out and he would collapse. "I'm fine," Ronan called back, wonder dripping from his tone.

Caeden's heart rate pounded in his ears as he turned forward once again. Had the river's magic healed Ronan's leg? Or was his sudden ability to walk without his cane due to the adrenaline coursing through all of their veins?

It took them hours of running before they finally reached the cave entrance. It was light outside now, the sun so high and bright in the sky it was blinding as they stumbled on numb legs out onto the snow-covered ground.

At the very least, they'd been running long enough that they were dry when the icy air hit them.

Every inch of his body hurt, but he'd pushed through it for so long that it had turned to an odd combination between painful and numb. He'd only experienced the sensation once before, when he was held in the Dragon Lord's prison cell and paced for so long that he was sure he would die before he could bring himself to stop.

The dragon was waiting outside for them when they emerged. She looked around anxiously as they ran across the clearing to her, and she knelt in the snow so they could climb onto her back.

Hurry, hurry, hurry.

The words filtered into his thoughts as he climbed up her wing and positioned himself at the front on her back. Eryn followed closely behind, dragging Dealla up behind her. Ronan was the last to get up, his cane abandoned on the ground in the snow beneath. He glanced between the three already seated on the dragon's back. He stood there frozen for a split second as he seemed to realize the easiest place to get to would be directly behind Dealla.

A roar shook the ground, angry words piercing through Caeden's thoughts like the blade of a dagger slipping into his skull.

They have one of us with them. Don't let them get away.

It was a new voice this time, and the anger in the tone along with the way it pierced through his mind twisted Caeden's stomach into knots as he tied the rope around his waist and handed it back to Eryn. She tied it around herself before she pulled a dagger from its holster on her thigh and cut Dealla's bindings.

"Hurry!" Dealla called to Ronan, who snapped out of whatever trance he'd been in and climbed onto the dragon's back behind her.

"Grab the rope," Eryn said, handing it back to Ronan, as soon as she finished securing it around Dealla.

No time, no time, no time, their dragon seemed to whisper, though her words were so soft they hardly registered in Caeden's mind until she was crouching down again and preparing for flight.

Caeden gripped the handles on the saddle strapped to her back, clinging to them as she leapt from the ground and took off into the air before any of them were ready. Eryn grabbed him around the waist, a yelp escaping past her lips as she clung to him.

"Ronan!" Dealla screamed, so loud it could be heard clearly over the sound of the rushing air.

Caeden turned, and his heart stopped as he took in the sight of his friend dangling from the back of the dragon.

Ronan still held the rope that he, Eryn, and Dealla had tied around themselves to secure them to the dragon's back, but the dragon took off before Ronan had time to do the same or to grab onto one of the handles.

The rope slipped slowly between Ronan's fingers. Pain was etched into his features as he gripped it tightly, blood seeping between his fingers from the rough fibers cutting into his skin. He hadn't fallen far, maybe five feet away from where he'd been when he'd first climbed into the saddle, but the length of rope wasn't long. If he slipped much farther…

Caeden pushed the thought from his head.

"You have to land!" he shouted, hoping beyond anything that the dragon could understand him like they were able to understand her.

I can't. They're too close. I'm sorry.

"You have to!" Eryn yelled, fear and anger lacing her words as her hands shook around the rope she was trying to pull back. Tears shone in the corners of her eyes as the rope slipped between her fingers, her knuckles white around it as blood seeped between her fingers just like Ronan's.

I'm sorry, I'm sorry, I'm sorry, the dragon whispered, over and over again.

"Damnit!"

Before Caeden realized what she was doing, Dealla lunged over the dragon's back. She was still tied to both Caeden and Eryn, but the rope wouldn't hold her on the dragon's back if she went too far over.

Eryn dropped the rope so quickly Caeden almost missed it. She wrapped one arm around his waist again and reached for Dealla's ankle as Dealla tried to grab hold of Ronan. She missed at first, her fingers only grazing the tips of his, and she cursed again.

"I need you to climb higher!" Dealla screamed. Fear like Caeden had never heard from her before seeped into her tone. He couldn't see her face, but she sounded close to crying.

"I can't!" Ronan's words came from over the side of the dragon. He'd fallen so far now that all Caeden saw was his bloody hands as he held onto the rope.

Dealla reached further over the side of the dragon, and the weight of Eryn holding onto her pulled Caeden around the waist. He bit his tongue hard as he held tightly onto the handles on the saddle. If he let go, the three of them might not all fall to their deaths, but Ronan definitely would once he lost his hold on the rope. And if the dragon didn't land quickly enough, the others would follow soon after.

"Ronan, please!" Dealla's voice cracked when she screamed the words, and if Caeden hadn't been sure that she was crying before, he was now.

We won't get away in time.

The dragon's ominous words filled Caeden's mind as he watched Ronan reach up with a single, blood-covered hand. It was hardly an inch, but it was just enough for Dealla to grab his hand and pull him up beside her. Eryn heaved along with Dealla to get the two of them up onto the dragon's back, and the weight of Eryn's pulling nearly knocked the wind from Caeden's lungs.

Ronan collapsed into the saddle, bloody marks coating the leather from where his hands had touched the saddle on his way up. He was breathing heavily, his hair a wild, tousled mess on his head, but he was alive.

Caeden felt the relief of seeing Dealla tying the rope around Ronan's waist for only a split second before he registered the shadows flying in the sky around them. There were at least ten that Caeden counted behind them, and they were gaining ground quickly.

The dragon slowed her pace, trying to change direction and fly away, only to realize that more shadowed pairs of wings blocked their path.

We're trapped.

Chapter 37

The hazy black shadows of the dragons surrounded them. They crawled across the sky as if Caeden was seeing the world in slow motion. Everything dimmed as fear coursed through him, and his heartbeat pounding loudly in his ears was all he could hear.

The large creatures blocked out the sunlight as they closed in. Every breed of dragon Eryn had taught him about flew through the sky, creating a circle that closed them in on every side. There were Royal Talons of every color, drakes that bared mouthfuls of teeth, and curious wyverns whose movements were so graceful they looked less like they were flying and more like they were simply gliding through the sky. The only thing keeping those dragons from tearing them apart were the stones resting in the bag on Caeden's hip and the river's magic running through their veins.

Eryn's arms tightened around his waist. He placed his hand over hers and intertwined their fingers together without so much as a second thought. He gave her hand a gentle squeeze that he hoped was more reassuring than he was sure it was.

Trespassers. The dragon's voice was a deadly whisper in his mind, but it sliced through his head as painfully as the first time he'd heard the angry voice. The words came from a blue Royal Talon a few shades darker and at least fifteen feet taller than the one they rode.

Caeden opened his mouth to respond, but no words came to mind. What could he say to an angry horde of dragons? He couldn't lie and claim that they hadn't been trespassing, but no other words would form on his tongue.

The dragon flew closer until it was only a few yards away from the nose of the dragon they rode, and goosebumps that had nothing to do with the cold air rose on Caeden's arms. Its wings stretched out so far on either side of them that Caeden couldn't see anything but the large creature ahead unless he physically turned around.

Have they hurt you? the dragon asked. Its voice was softer this time—less like a knife cutting through his skull and more like a gentle caress, though the roughness around the edges and the anger hadn't disappeared.

It took Caeden longer than it should've to realize that the question was directed at the dragon they'd traveled with.

He couldn't make out her face, but her long pause gave him the odd feeling that she was just as confused by the question as they were. She only stared at the other dragon for so long that Caeden wondered whether she would even answer.

We can't kill them, the large dragon continued, his words still soft. *They've entered the river. Our magic flows in their veins. But we can still protect you. You can land, and we will keep you safe.*

No. Their dragon's voice was timid, but firm. *They haven't hurt me. They took me away from him and his enslavement.*

The words struck Caeden like a slap across the face. He didn't know what he'd expected the dragon to say, but it hadn't been that. They hadn't enslaved her like the Dragon Lord and his men had, but they had used her.

Guilt weighed heavy on his chest as he thought back to when Ronan first used the stone to tame her, then all of the times they'd used her as nothing more than transportation without so much as a second thought.

For the first time, despite the threat the dragons around them posed, the full realization that they were living, breathing creatures with their own fears and feelings sank in. They weren't fighting for Deovaria because they wanted to. They were stolen from their homes and trapped with the magic from the stones.

He'd thought of dragons as nothing more than bloodthirsty, mindless creatures until recently. Only after they'd learned about the stones had he considered that they were anything more than that. He hadn't considered whether they cared about their freedom. He hadn't known they would have feelings, or the kind of intelligence required to want those things. He hadn't taken the time to consider much of anything related to the dragons before now.

He wanted to apologize to her for everything they'd made her do since she first began traveling with them weeks ago, but now wasn't the time for that. As guilty as he felt, they needed to live. They could never put an end to the war with Deovaria—and maybe even the enslavement of the dragons—if they didn't make it out of here alive.

They saved you?

The question floated into Caeden's thoughts so softly it was nearly impossible to hear over his own racing thoughts.

Not exactly, their dragon said. *But I like them. They've been kind to me.*

He seemed to consider her words before he turned his piercing gaze to Caeden. Eryn's fingers tightened around his as the bright green eyes of the Royal Talon bore into Caeden's very soul. *Why have you entered our home? What is it you seek?*

Caeden swallowed hard, holding tight to Eryn's hand as if it were a lifeline. Nothing could've been enough to wash away the fear, but the feel of her hand against his gave him an ounce of bravery, even as his heart raced at an inhuman speed and adrenaline coursed through him. Every inch of him ached for an escape, but that wasn't possible with the hundreds upon hundreds of dragons surrounding them.

"We came for the stones," Caeden answered, his voice wavering against his will when he spoke the words aloud. He reached for the bag hanging at his hip and produced two of the stones tucked inside.

Anger flashed across the dragon's features, though Caeden wasn't sure how he knew what emotion he was seeing. *So you can enslave us like the rest of them?* the dragon roared inside of his head.

The voice radiated so loudly it sent waves of agony throughout Caeden's entire body. "No! We want to end the war with Deovaria. They are the ones enslaving dragons. Once we win, the dragons can be free of their control."

Then what purpose do the stones serve you if you have no intention of enslaving us?

"So Deovaria can't use the dragons against us. Dragons are the only reason they've lasted so long in the war, and the only reason that they are winning. If the dragons can't kill us because we have possession of the stones, then we take away their usefulness."

Caeden tensed in anticipation of the angry voice filtering into his head again, but the dragon remained silent this time.

"Deovaria won't continue to enslave the dragons if they have no use for them," Caeden stated, making his point as clear as he could. He didn't know for certain whether it was true, but they needed to get out of here. They couldn't give the stones back to the dragons, or he would be giving up their best hope of winning the war.

A strange sound that reminded Caeden of laughter filled his mind. *You ignorant child. If only it were that simple.* The dragon shook his head, clearing away the amusement that had lit his features for a brief moment. *Land. Let us continue this conversation.*

The dragon flew off before Caeden could respond. He gripped the edges of the saddle tightly as the dragon they rode followed after him. Most of the others surrounding them disappeared into the dense clouds.

They returned to the side of the mountain again a few moments later. Only three dragons aside from the one they were speaking with and the one they rode remained.

They landed uneasily in the snow, and Caeden and the others slipped off the dragon's back as gracelessly as they had the previous night.

What are your names? the dragon asked, as Caeden rightened himself in the uneven snow on his still-numb legs. Eryn clung to him, her hand wrapped firmly around his upper arm as her other sat positioned on the hilt of her dagger strapped to her thigh. Her fingers ran back and forth over the leather handle, but never fully grabbed onto it. Her eyes were locked on the dragon's neck, where a thin line of weaker scales was visible down his chest.

She'd taught him months ago about the places that a well-landed blade could kill a dragon, and the combination of her training and her fear of dragons seemed to be fighting against the part of her that knew no matter how well she landed her blade, they wouldn't make it out of here alive if she attempted to free them with violence.

"Prince Caeden of Aericora," Caeden answered, the words slipping from his tongue in the same manner he would've introduced himself to any high-ranking person to enter the castle walls back home.

The dragon angled his head at Eryn, his eyes trailing over her before they moved on to Ronan and Dealla. The two introduced themselves in the same way Caeden had, their voices slightly higher-pitched than Caeden remembered them being.

And you? the dragon asked, turning back to face Eryn again with a sort of familiarity lighting his eyes. *I recognize you. You were a small thing the last time I laid eyes on you. You've grown since then.*

"Eryn Gedding," she answered, her words clipped, despite her shaking hand now firmly wrapped around the hilt of her dagger.

Caeden reached to pull her hand away, but the dragon simply snorted hot air strong enough to pull the ends of their hair. Eryn's body tensed, but Caeden understood there was no threat behind the dragon's gesture. He was only amused.

You are a sight to behold, Eryn Gedding, the dragon stated, fondness slipping into his voice as if his memories of watching her suffer in the cold of the snow-covered mountaintops were pleasant.

Something about it made Caeden's blood boil, and he forced the anger at the sixty-foot dragon standing before them away before he did something he would regret.

I am Xalrum, the dragon told them, returning to their previous conversation without any further warning. *One of the nine elder dragons who guard the Rayfait Mountains.*

Xalrum looked pointedly at Caeden again. He paused just long enough for Caeden to recall where they'd left off before landing.

The stones hold magic from the river, Xalrum explained. *The river runs from the center of the world, as I'm sure you know, given you were seeking it out. The stones—much like everything else that enters the water—absorb the magic within. Dragons can't exist without the river's magic until we are fully grown. Until then, we need the magic of the river to grow into our own magic.*

Xalrum gave another huff of air that sounded like a dragon's version of a sigh.

I explained this to another human at one point. Anger, along with another emotion that Caeden couldn't quite place, laced the dragon's tone. *The man you now call the "Dragon Lord" spent years studying our caverns, and after some time, I believed him to be no harm. I shared the truth of the magic, and along with it, the weakness it can pose to dragons. I was wrong to assume he could be trusted. Not long after I last saw him, I learned he'd used the secrets I so foolishly shared to imprison and enslave my brethren.*

Caeden swallowed hard. He hadn't assumed his uncle had been told everything he knew about the stones and the river directly from one of the dragons dwelling inside. He'd only thought he'd overheard their conversations in the same manner Caeden had when they'd been inside of the river.

Those who hold the magic from the stream can occasionally harness the same powers the dragons have. But the magic comes with limitations when too much of it runs through your veins. All of you—and your Dragon Lord—don't have enough in your veins to do much, but you also don't feel the effects of the magic if you do something it does not approve of. Dragons are composed mostly of magic by the time we're adults, and the magic doesn't like to be used to destroy others who possess it. You all may still be able to hurt us, even with the small amount of magic in your veins, but we cannot hurt you or any who hold the stones. It's a weakness the Dragon Lord exploited, and has been for years.

Caeden thought back to the harnesses the Deovarian army made their dragon army wear; how the dragon they traveled with had permanent scarring along her sides from the contraption they'd pulled off of her after Ronan had tamed her. "Why explain all of this to us if the Dragon Lord already exploited it the last time you told someone?" Caeden couldn't help it when the question fell from his mouth.

At the same time Caeden said the words, Ronan asked, "How can people who use the stones have an advantage when neither should be able to hurt the other? The stones got a lot more magic in them than we do after bein' in there for only a couple minutes."

Xalrum seemed to smile at that, showing off rows of sharp teeth behind scaly lips.

The dragon they'd traveled with was the one who answered Ronan's question. *Not enough magic from the stones transfers into the human holding it. The magic the human gets from the stone is less even than what you now have in your veins from the river.*

Aubry is correct, Xalrum said, referencing the dragon who had spoken, though Caeden had no idea how he knew her name. *And we are explaining this because if you truly wanted the information, you have someone in your group who could give it to you just as easily.* Xalrum nodded in the direction of Dealla. The words weren't said with the same anger he'd had in his tone earlier, but there was an edge that hinted at the feelings he held toward the Dragon Lord, and likely his daughter as well.

Dealla stiffened, her hands clamping hard against the front of her thighs as her shoulders turned rigid.

It was obvious she knew more about the magic and the mountains than any of the others did, but Caeden hadn't expected her to know everything Xalrum was implying until he saw her reaction to his words. The Dragon Lord didn't trust his daughter as much as he should've trusted the person who would one day rule over his kingdom, but maybe that information alone hadn't felt like enough of a threat to warrant keeping from her.

With all of the lies the Dragon Lord had told his people, he was surprised that he'd trusted his daughter with even that much of the truth.

"You said when humans spend time in the river, they can have the ability to use the same powers the dragons can?" Eryn asked. Her hands still shook, but they'd fallen away from the hilt of her dagger now and instead both were looped around Caeden's upper arm. Her fear didn't show in her voice, despite her refusing to let his arm go.

Xalrum nodded. *And, if they have magic in their veins, then the stones can be used to amplify it. The three of you have a little now, maybe enough to make some use of with the right stone, but you,* he looked directly at Dealla, *likely have enough to harness a young dragon's abilities.*

Caeden glanced at her, the realization sinking in. The Dragon Lord had already been in the mountains before she'd been conceived, which meant he must have passed down some of that magical ability to her when she'd been born. Suddenly, it made sense why she was sent as the spy rather than anyone else.

"That's how you were able to disguise yourself," Caeden said beneath his breath, though he'd meant for her to hear the words.

Bewilderment played across Dealla's features, and she shook her head quickly to clear it away. She lifted her hand to touch the space on her neck where the necklace had always hung when she played the part of the Princess from Crevia. That space was empty now. "Is that why I only needed the one stone?" she asked Xalrum. "All of the others needed at least four, and they had to be blue."

Xalrum gave her an almost warm smile, if that was possible with the rows of jagged teeth he showed when he did it. *It was a red stone, I take it?*

Dealla nodded.

It would be difficult for you to craft the illusion, given your magic was likely weak before today, but yes. You likely had enough in your veins that you wouldn't need extra stones like others would. That was why a single stone worked for you. Red stones are the least powerful, but they're the easiest to use to craft illusions if you possess enough magic. Red is the color of illusion magic. Purple stones are the second most powerful, and contain the sort of magic used to control the elements. Blue stones are the strongest, and can be used to do either of the other things, but the lesser-known secret about blue magic is its ability to freeze desired objects in time. It's the same magic that allows dragons to live so long.

Caeden's heart stopped as the words washed over him.

Images of his sister frozen in a blue haze, her fear and anguish forever melded onto her childish features resurfaced in his mind.

He'd fought so hard to push the thoughts away. He could never entirely forget what he'd seen, though. He'd believed his uncle until he'd returned home and his father had talked sense into him. But what if his father was wrong? What if the Dragon Lord hadn't lied about everything?

If the blue stones could be used to freeze things in time, that meant that his sister was alive. The Dragon Lord had figured out how to harness that ability, and he'd used it to trap Amelia in space and time as an eleven-year-old girl.

She was alive.

She was frozen in time, but maybe that was better. He could get her out of there, and when he did, she wouldn't have had to live through all of the bloodshed and war everyone else had spent the past eleven years enduring. It would be hard for her. She would have to hear about their mother, but she could start fresh after all of this was over.

All of this to say, dear child, Xalrum continued, pulling Caeden from his thoughts, *as long as the stones exist, and as long as the human race knows our weakness, we will never be safe. I made the mistake of telling our secret once, and it will forever haunt us. Even if you don't mean us harm, there are others who will.*

Caeden nodded, understanding the words more than he wanted to. A similar weight to the one Caeden felt as the future ruler of a kingdom at war rested on Xalrum's shoulders. The only difference was that Xalrum's fight would never end.

"I swear we mean you no harm," Caeden said honestly, turning from Xalrum to speak to the other three dragons still standing behind him. "I can't guarantee your safety, even once we win the war, but I can promise I will do everything to help in any way I can. You won't ever be rid of the threat, but the Dragon Lord won't stop using the dragons unless they aren't useful to him. He's not the only horrible person who could harm you, but he is your primary threat right now. If we can defeat him, it won't mean you will live in peace, but it will rid you of the current dangers and suffering."

The dragon seemed to contemplate his words, looking between the three other dragons standing behind him before he turned to Aubry.

I see why you like them, Xalrum said, and Caeden remembered his father's words to him about how dragons liked determination and loyalty above all else.

Aubry nodded.

Very well, we will allow you to leave with the stones. His tone turned dangerous when he continued. *But mark my words, Prince of Aericora, if I hear that you are treating dragons in the same manner as the Dragon Lord, or even close to it, I will see that your entire kingdom is burned to the ground before you can form the kind of army Deovaria has crafted.*

Caeden swallowed hard, but didn't let himself cower at the threat. He had no intention of enslaving the dragons. Something had shifted inside of him since speaking with them face to face.

He'd never intended to hurt the dragons, but now he planned to do whatever he could to free those under the Dragon Lord's control. His people had suffered at the Dragon Lord's hands, but they weren't the only ones, and he would ensure the Dragon Lord could never hurt another living soul again, no matter what it took.

Chapter 38

Xalrum's words rang through Caeden's mind on the way back to Aericora. The dragon hadn't outright said so, but he'd heard the words he'd left unsaid in his threat. The other dragons, those the Dragon Lord had enslaved, were trapped there because the dragons in the Rayfait Mountains were too late to realize what the King of Deovaria had done.

The Dragon Lord's soldiers, much like Caeden's, knew how to fight dragons now. And though the dragons they'd enslaved couldn't harm those attempting to rescue them, the dragons from the mountains couldn't hurt the Deovarian soldiers who held their brethren captive either, since so many of them wore the stones.

How they'd missed it, Caeden could only guess, but somehow, they hadn't seen what the Dragon Lord was doing until it was too late.

Their flight back to Aericora took less time than their flight to the Rayfait Mountains, since they didn't plan to stop anywhere specific along the way. Instead, they made camp for a single night in the forest a few hours' flight from the castle to get in a short rest before they continued their journey.

Together, they gathered branches and sticks to light a small fire. They kept Dealla firmly tied between two trees, just close enough to the warm, glowing flames of the fire to keep her from freezing to death, but not close enough to be comfortable.

Ronan walked around without visible discomfort, and though he seemed as bewildered by it as Caeden was, he didn't dwell on it. Instead, he went about things as though nothing had changed. It could only be related to the time they'd spent in the river while trying to find the stones, but he didn't bring that up to Ronan. His friend would have put the same pieces together.

The same gloomy haze that hung over him since learning of Dealla still clung to him, and though Caeden wouldn't allow that to be an excuse to avoid topics with his friend for long, he would wait until they were back at the castle and Dealla wasn't around before he dared to bring up his leg.

They took off again before the sun crested the horizon. Ronan sat at the front, with Eryn right behind him, and Caeden and Dealla seated behind her. Dealla was bound with rope, and Caeden held her bindings still, even though she'd gone the whole trip without posing a threat to them. That didn't mean he trusted her any more than he trusted the Dragon Lord himself, though.

"What's that?" Ronan muttered, barely loud enough for Caeden to make out his words.

He looked up from where he'd spent the majority of their ride with his head resting against Eryn's shoulder, and froze when he noticed the thick cloud of black smoke billowing into the air ahead.

Fear seized him like a hand around his heart as his gaze followed the line of smoke to where his home sat in the distance.

"They couldn't have," Caeden whispered, his words falling

from his mouth as Eryn reached back to lace her fingers with his. "Not already. It's only been a couple of weeks. They didn't have time to regroup to launch another attack."

It was possible though, if his uncle's words were to be believed. Dealla had been planted at the castle for weeks before she'd kidnapped him. What if this was part of their plan? What if Deovaria had already planned another attack before they came the day of his betrothal ceremony? What if they regrouped while Caeden and Eryn were still hidden in the safe room, waiting for the fight to die down and for someone to find them?

"Caeden," Eryn said, her tone so stern it pulled his attention away from the sight ahead. She'd turned to face him, and he met her gaze, her bright blue eyes staring directly into his and grounding him in a way nothing else ever had. Among everything that happened, she was always there. He could always trust her to be there. "Even if that smoke is from another attack, which is highly unlikely given everything we know about their strength and army size, we can't do anything from all the way over here."

Eryn glanced around, her free hand reaching up to graze his cheek lightly as she searched for anything else to support her words.

"There aren't any dragons," she stated finally, looking back at him, and he realized as soon as she said the words that she was right.

Aside from the smoke billowing into the air, there were no signs that anything was wrong. No dragons circled the scene, and no sounds of a fight; there was nothing at all except for an endless cloud of black ash.

Caeden nodded slowly. It wasn't exactly relief he felt as the realization dawned on him, but it calmed his racing heart to an almost normal pace either way.

"There ain't any dragons, but it doesn't look good," Ronan said softly ahead. "There's still flames."

Caeden gripped Eryn's hand tighter as fear spiraled through him once again. What if they did more damage this time? What if more people were hurt? What if his father was hurt?

No dragons, Aubry said softly inside of his head, her voice like a featherlight caress.

"No dragons," Eryn repeated, squeezing his hand.

Caeden nodded again, unable to do anything else as he tried his best to calm his racing heart.

Caeden's ears rang even louder than the air rushing past as they flew the remaining distance to the castle. The thick cloud of ash and smoke burned his lungs the closer they got, but even as tears began to run down his cheeks from the soot stinging his eyes, he hardly noticed over the thrum of his heartbeat pulsing through his body.

"Looks like they got the fires out," Ronan said from the front of the dragon. He didn't turn to face them when he said the words. It would've been impossible to hear him speak if he hadn't yelled.

The fires were put out, which was evident by the lack of burning embers floating in the air and the disappearance of the orange hue that had hovered over the ground before, but the destruction from the flames was gut-wrenching.

The whole castle hadn't been burned, but from where they were, Caeden saw a large portion of the eastern towers had been burned nearly to the ground. One of the four towers had collapsed, leaving behind a pile of bricks and charred wooden beams.

In the grand scheme of things, it was one of the least important areas of the castle, and likely an area not many people were in, considering there was not much there other than the smaller throne room. The other rooms that burned were primarily servants' quarters, which were likely to have been vacant given the time of day.

It made no sense why they would've burned that part of the castle. After the first attack and the number of spies they'd hidden within their midst, the Dragon Lord and his armies would've known the chances of this attack making a difference in the war were limited.

Unless it was another tactic to scare them, but hadn't they already done that?

"What were you planning?" Caeden snapped, turning around abruptly to face Dealla, who wore a mask of confusion when he laid eyes on her. Her eyes were wide as she stared at the destruction that was Caeden's home.

She flinched, as if hearing his words knocked her from a trance, before she looked at him. She swallowed hard, forcing back whatever confusion she felt and shook her head. Her eyes flicked to the scene ahead of them again before she looked back at Caeden.

"How would I know?" she snapped. There was something hidden behind her expression that resembled fear, but between the anger and fear clouding his thoughts, he hardly noticed. "I've been locked away in your dungeon for weeks. Please, explain to me how I would've had any part in this?"

Her tone only made his blood boil hotter in his veins.

If it weren't for the fact that she was still useful, or for the mix of emotions he knew Ronan had for her, he would've shoved her off Aubry's back and let her fall to her death.

The wreckage of the attack grew clearer the closer they flew to the castle, twisting Caeden's heart painfully as he saw the horror on the faces of his people as they tended to hundreds of wounded servants. He felt it mirrored on his own face, but he pushed it away as they landed in the ash-covered courtyard, barely a few hundred yards from the destruction.

From here, the smoke was still thick, but the charred walls of his home were harder to see past the still-standing towers. The shouting and screaming that reached him as wounded were wheeled away to the infirmary was far harder to ignore than the smoke singeing his lungs.

Screams rang through the air and pierced straight into his soul as he slid from Aubry's back and ran up the front steps. Ronan and Eryn were right behind him with Dealla dragged between the two of them.

The front doors were held open. Bodies shoved past one another as stretchers—some empty and some with half-alive servants with bloody and burned skin—rolled down marble floors.

Relief flooded him when he saw most of them were alive, even as their screams and wails filled the air, and he watched them writhe in pain as they gripped their injuries, tears spilling down their soot-covered faces.

"Your Highness!" a voice called to him as the face of a woman he recognized all too well was wheeled past.

Her body was badly burned. Half of her hair was singed off, along with most of her skin, leaving her skull visible beneath as blood pooled around her head. Her ribs were crushed in; a bloody mess of tissue spilled out onto the stretcher she rested on.

Teafa.

The woman who had taken care of him and his sister when they were children. Who had reprimanded him as much as his parents. Who cared for him and loved him, who taught him how to read, who tucked him into bed most nights before his parents came down to kiss him goodnight.

She sucked in a ragged, heaving breath that shook her entire body, but her eyes were glazed over and lifeless. Any of those breaths would be her last, and there was nothing even the best healers could do.

She was as good as dead.

Another person he loved, another person who'd done nothing to deserve the Dragon Lord's wrath, had died at his hands.

Caeden clenched his hands at his sides, his nails biting so hard into his palms that blood coated his fingertips. A hand rested on his shoulder, and despite everything, the feel of Eryn's touch chipped away some of the blinding anger and rage. It wasn't much, but he relaxed just enough to feel the sting of his pierced palms as he unclenched his fists.

"Your Highness!" the voice shouted again, and Caeden turned to find a frantic Muire running toward them.

"That traitorous bitch," Dealla muttered behind them.

Before Caeden could consider her words, Muire was standing in front of him, her chest heaving with ragged breaths and her eyes darting to the endless array of chaos.

"You're back already," Muire stated, confusion and surprise lacing her words. They weren't back late, but they were far from arriving home early. She shook her head, seeming to realize that fact for herself.

"What happened?" Caeden asked, his voice calm despite his pounding heart and bloody palms taunting him with the lie in his tone. "Did the Dragon Lord do this, too?"

Muire nodded so vigorously her head could've been knocked clean off her shoulders. "No one saw them, but the east towers went up in flames and the whole castle shook. We don't know how they did it without anyone seeing the dragons, but it's the only thing that makes sense."

Eryn's hand tightened around his shoulder, and she took in a breath like she wanted to say something, but Muire pushed on before she could.

"The King and Queen of Crevia arrived this morning. They were supposed to meet with the king in half an hour in the smaller throne room. The Dragon Lord seemed to be planning to kill them all."

"But they're okay?" Caeden pressed.

He'd known his father was corresponding with Crevia since they'd learned what happened to the real Margaid, but why had he been meeting with them? Their daughter was dead, but that itself wouldn't typically warrant the royal members of another kingdom to travel to the kingdom their daughter was on her way to, especially not while they were at war. Unless they blamed Aericora for their daughter's death, and this meeting was only a precursor to a much larger outbreak of fighting.

Muire's eyes widened, as if she was remembering a crucial detail.

"They're all okay?" Caeden asked more forcefully as panic swelled in his chest.

"The king and queen are safe," Muire said carefully, her words slow and stilted, as if she was forcing them out past a lump in her throat. "But Aillin… Your Highness, he was badly hurt."

The world around him tilted, the edges of his vision blurring as those words settled over him like a thick cloud even blacker and more suffocating than the smoke outside. His heart pounded so loudly in his ears that her next words were hardly audible.

"He's in the infirmary, Your Highness. I haven't heard an update from the healers since he was first transported there… but it doesn't sound good."

Not his father.

The Dragon Lord had taken too many people already.

He couldn't take his father, too.

"Take her to the dungeons," Caeden bit out to the nearest guards, who were wheeling a stretcher toward the destruction.

Neither guard hesitated before dropping the stretcher and running over. They grabbed hold of Dealla's bound wrists when Caeden gestured toward her.

"Ensure she is safely locked away and don't leave her side. I'll send a member of the court to inform you when it is safe to leave her alone."

Both guards nodded. "Yes, Your Highness."

Caeden didn't hear the words clearly. He was already running through the halls toward the infirmary.

His heart pounded as fast as his feet against the stone floors as he ran through the hallways. Someone's steps echoed behind him, but he didn't turn to see who was following.

He wove past countless castle staff, each one with more blood either dripping from their bodies or coating their hands from helping someone else than the last. The doors to the infirmary were propped open, and Caeden squeezed his way past, dodging bodies as his eyes scanned each of the occupied cots, hoping beyond anything that he would find his father out here and not in one of the rooms at the back that were reserved for only the most life-threatening cases.

A new surge of panic made his legs feel like lead when his gaze landed on the last cot at the back of the infirmary. His father wasn't in here.

No.

It couldn't be that bad.

It couldn't.

Even as his mind raced with the lies he tried to tell himself, he didn't believe them. He'd gone through this already. He'd lived through his mother's and sister's deaths. He knew his father was only human, and as easily hurt as anyone else around him. The veil of innocence that fooled him into thinking no harm could come to those he loved was ripped away years ago.

Three rooms sat at the back of the infirmary. The doors to each were open, but only a few people rushed in and out of two of the rooms, while ten to fifteen worked inside of the third, determination mingling with panic on each of their faces.

That was the room his father was in.

No one else would warrant that kind of attention, no matter how severe the injuries.

He needed to go into that room. He needed to see his father, if he was even still alive, but his legs wouldn't move. No matter how hard he tried to step forward, even if only far enough to peer inside, he couldn't.

"Caeden."

Eryn's voice was soft when it reached him, her fingers grazing his shoulder as gently as her words.

People moved around them, but he hardly noticed as tears blurred his vision, slipping down his cheeks until they fell onto the collar of his shirt.

"What if he's gone?" Caeden whispered. They were laced with every ounce of fear winding its way through his body until he felt like he couldn't breathe, and he hated himself for letting that fear show when his father spent so long teaching him to keep it concealed when it mattered.

"What if he's not?" Eryn said, squeezing his shoulder lightly.

A nurse ran out from inside of the third room, her eyes landing on Caeden and Eryn standing in the center of the infirmary. Her eyes widened before she turned and ran back inside.

"The prince is here!"

Her voice carried throughout the space over the sounds of misery and anguish.

"Hurry and bring him," another voice called, this one belonging to a man.

Eryn's fingers tightened on his shoulder, and when he glanced at her, the wide-eyed look on her face confirmed what he'd assumed. "Go," she said quickly, releasing her hold on him. "He's alive."

Those words struck something inside of him, and finally, he was able to move. He ran to the doorway of the third room, rounding the corner right as the female nurse tried to exit, presumably to find him.

Surprise flashed across her face, but it was replaced almost instantly, turning serious in a flash. "Your Highness," she said carefully, and Caeden's heart sank. "He isn't well. The burns are too severe. We've tried to slow the bleeding, but he's barely holding on. He's not going to make it."

The tears, still wet and hot on his cheeks, burned his skin as they flowed even faster from his eyes. Her words lodged into him like a knife straight through his heart, tearing him apart from the inside out as another person he loved was ripped away. The room spun, his vision darkening around the edges as his eyes landed on his father. He breathed in uneven, ragged breaths, but he was still breathing.

Charred, black skin marred his body; white bone was visible beneath deep burns. Blood flowed in a steady stream from his injuries. His chest was mostly unmarked, aside from a few scrapes and a thick layer of ash and dirt, but everything from his stomach down was burned. Countless bits of debris from the attack were lodged in his abdomen—pieces of rock and brick stuck between bloody, shredded flesh. Bandages were wrapped around most of his body, but his blood had soaked them through already.

Even after the nurse said the words, seeing him lying there, crimson coating the white sheets of the cot, was what made the realization settle over him.

His father would not live to see the sunset in a few hours.

"Caeden," his father rasped, his voice so weak it hardly carried over the sound of the nurses working to replace the dressing on his wounds, though it wouldn't help.

They couldn't stop the bleeding.

There was nothing they could do, even as they continued to make every attempt to save him.

Caeden didn't think as his feet carried him to the side of his father's cot, the nurses working on him parting to allow their prince through. To allow the man on the cot to have his son stand by his side as the life drained from his body.

He knelt on the floor beside his father, and Caeden gripped his hand tightly, the blood oozing between his fingers through the rough bits of charred flesh.

His father's face swam before his eyes. Silent tears worked their way down Caeden's cheeks despite every attempt to keep them at bay until his father was no longer around to see him cry.

The king blinked at him, tears running down his own face as fast as they were on Caeden's.

He was going to die.

The fear, and the certainty of it, circled on repeat in his head, the weight of it crashing into him again and again as he clenched his father's hand, like that would be enough to keep him there. To keep him alive.

"I love you, my son," the king rasped, the words like a vice around Caeden's heart.

"I love you," he whispered past the lump in the back of his

throat. "Don't go." Despite every attempt, his voice still hitched on a sob.

The words were a desperate plea to the universe.

He felt like a child again. He was sitting outside while the castle guard told him he needed to speak with his father. Only, now his father was the one dying. And he wasn't hearing from anyone that it was happening. He was seeing it with his own eyes. He could feel it in the slowed beating of his heart where their wrists pressed against one another.

A smile broke out across the king's face, and he wheezed out a breath of air Caeden was sure was meant to be a laugh. "I wish it were that easy," his father said. He coughed suddenly, and blood rushed from his abdomen faster than before. A collective gasp from a few of the nurses filled Caeden's ears, but all he could do was focus on how much paler his father was now than he'd been before. His father blinked rapidly, attempting to clear the hazy look in his eyes as his breathing became rougher.

"You'll make a good king." His father squeezed his hand weakly, and Caeden gripped his harder in return, clinging to his cool fingers like a lifeline.

He wasn't ready to hear those words. He never wanted to hear those words. He'd known since he was a child that he would have to, but he hadn't wanted it to be like this. He'd hoped it would be because his father was too tired and simply ready to hand over the crown. Not that he would be bleeding out on the same cot where he would take his last breath.

"I'm not ready for that," he whispered. He hadn't considered before how ready he was to lead his kingdom. Now that he was faced with the inevitable fact that he would be king by the time the sun rose over the horizon tomorrow morning, he knew he wasn't ready yet. He wasn't ready to lead his people. He was too focused on his need to defeat the Dragon Lord. He was too focused on everything he'd lost, not on what they had ahead of them. Only recently had he truly considered the struggles his people were going through. Only recently had it begun to matter.

He'd been selfish. He'd been so absorbed in his need for revenge that he hadn't put effort into the one thing he'd known all his life he would eventually be responsible for: the entire kingdom of Aericora.

"That look tells me you're more ready than you believe," his father said, a gentle smile pulling at the corners of his ash covered lips. "And you have good people around you who will help you." His gaze trailed behind Caeden, where Eryn stood a respectable distance away with her head bowed and her hands clasped awkwardly in front of her.

Red spread across her cheeks, highlighting her eyes as she stepped toward them. She stopped when she was standing beside Caeden, her arm brushing against his, still unsure what to do with her hands.

Caeden had seen her nervous a handful of times—most of which while they'd been in the mountains—but her discomfort now was different. That was fear he'd seen in her expression when they were in the snow-covered mountaintops. There was still fear in her expression now, but confusion and uncertainty hid in the way her eyes darted around, as well.

"Take care of him for me when I'm gone," the king said, the smile not leaving his face.

Eryn's face turned a deeper shade of red, but she gave a single, firm nod in understanding. "Of course, Your Majesty."

The king's smile grew as he looked between the two of them. "I've always liked you, Miss Gedding." He laughed lightly. "Even when you were screaming at me."

Caeden glanced up at her again, remembering the time he'd

gone to his father's study to speak with him, only to overhear Eryn in the middle of a screaming match with the king.

She swallowed hard at the comment. "I'm sorry for that, Your Majesty," she whispered.

His father laughed again. "None of that," he said with an attempted wave of his blood-covered hand. "I'm only sorry I didn't get to know you better. I'm glad it was you."

"I'm sorry?" she asked, confusion lighting her eyes.

"I may have arranged it," the king carried on, not seeming to have heard her, "but none of them were right. He didn't look at them the same way he looks at you."

Caeden felt his face heat as the words left his father's mouth.

His father squeezed his hand again, another ragged cough shaking his body. His eyes found Caeden's again, but it took him longer this time, and he seemed unable to make his gaze focus.

"I wanted to see you happy, Caeden," his father said, his words ragged around the edges, and far harder to understand now than they were before. "You haven't been happy since you were young. That's all I've ever wanted for you. I'm glad I got to see that for a brief while before my end."

The words ripped Caeden's heart apart like nothing else ever had. It was one thing to hear of his mother's and sister's deaths, but this was different. He was glad to have the time with his father, but it hurt so much more this time. This was real. Too real.

"I love you, Dad," Caeden whispered, barely able to force the words past the lump of sorrow and pain lodged in his throat.

The king didn't respond.

Chapter 39

The clock ticked loudly on the opposite end of the desk as Caeden stared blankly at the lacquered wooden surface. A stack of papers sat beside him that appeared to have been hastily looked through before being cast aside. Except for those papers, everything else in his father's office was the same.

There was a fire lit in the hearth. The picture his sister painted when they were young still sat on the bookshelf beside the empty box his mother's ring was in for years. The books were stacked on the shelves in the same order they'd always been. The chairs hadn't moved an inch in the room to his left. It even smelled the same; the scent of old leather-bound books and incense.

His father's ring with the king's crest etched into its surface sat on the desk in front of him, taunting him with the truth of the world he'd found himself in. He hadn't yet dared to replace the ring he'd had for years with the one symbolizing his new title yet.

Caeden's eyes were dry and his face stung after he'd wiped the tears from his face more times than he could count.

His father was gone.

His body was taken from the infirmary to make room for others who were injured during the attack.

Caeden still had to meet with the court after everything that happened. And the king and queen from Crevia. He would need to speak with them regarding it too, along with what they knew about what had befallen their daughter.

Caeden rested his head in his hands, feeling the full weight of the responsibility placed onto his shoulders only a few hours ago. His tears only stopped an hour ago, and he'd just begun to feel the same numbness toward the situation that he'd experienced the last time one of his parents died.

Eryn had sat with him the whole time, her arms wrapped around him while he'd sobbed uncontrollably. She'd taken him up to his room, where they'd sat for hours in silence. The realization hit him over and over again with the same weight as it had the moment he'd looked up to see his father's eyes glazed over and lifeless. When he hadn't responded, it only took Caeden a second to realize that his father's grip on his hand had gone limp and that his ragged, uneven breathing had stopped.

He'd come to his father's office while Eryn went to find them something to eat. She knew where he was, but he appreciated that she'd taken her time to return. Her arms around him were a comfort he hadn't known he'd needed. He wanted to sit with her longer—to never leave the confines of his room until he met the same end as his father with her lying beside him.

But he couldn't do that. He couldn't even have until tonight to come to terms with what happened.

They were attacked by Deovaria again. Their neighbors were here to discuss the murder of their daughter while she'd been on her way to Aericora.

And their king was dead.

Caeden, a man who had never realized until today that he was so far from ready to hold the title was now Aericora's King, a weight that sat so heavy on his shoulders he struggled to breathe beneath it.

A knock came on the door to his father's office.

No. His office.

The weight on his shoulders increased ever so slightly with the addition of that realization as he turned his gaze from the ring atop the desk, and he sat up straight in the chair. "Come in."

The door creaked open slowly, and a young servant who didn't appear much older than Caeden peaked her head around the door before she slowly entered the room.

Caeden nodded in greeting, but couldn't make any words leave his mouth.

She swallowed uncomfortably, her eyes darting to the blood stains marking the front of his shirt before they traveled up to his face. She bowed her head politely before she spoke. "The court is asking for a meeting, Your Majesty," she explained.

Caeden flinched at the title, even though he'd known he would hear it long before he was ready. It was another weight he wasn't yet prepared to carry, and it lodged straight into his chest to be called by the title that was once reserved for only his father.

He rightened himself quickly, sitting up straighter in the chair and forcing back the new flood of emotion that threatened to send tears rolling down his cheeks again. "Please inform them that I will meet them tonight at midnight. They can take up any grievances they have with me tonight, but I need time to prepare."

The servant nodded. "Yes, Your Majesty. I will relay the message."

With that, she turned on her heel and strode from the room. She closed the door softly behind herself, leaving Caeden alone once again in the large room that somehow felt like it was closing in around him a little more with each passing second.

Caeden's shoulders slumped as soon as the door shut, and he fell back against the chair with a deep sigh. He couldn't put off meeting with the court and the King and Queen of Crevia, but he would push it back as far as he could. He needed to get his head on straight before he spoke with any of them. Breaking down into a pile of tears wasn't an option. He wasn't sure what all his father had spoken to Crevia's rulers about yet, and he would need to get a rundown of that from the court when they met tonight, along with everything else related to his new position and his father's death. He would arrange a meeting with the king and queen the following morning, and hope he wouldn't offend them by making them wait.

He sighed again and sat up in his chair before his eyes fell on the pen placed neatly into its holder on the desk. Caeden swallowed hard as he picked the pen up and found a piece of parchment tucked into one of the many drawers on the backside of the desk. He laid it in front of him and wrote a brief letter addressed to Crevia's rulers, apologizing for the delay and explaining that he would meet with them the following morning. He quickly explained the death of the king, and hoped that small explanation in itself would keep them from being too upset about the holdup. He folded the parchment into thirds before setting it aside.

His eyes fell on his father's ring again, and he suppressed another wave of emotion. He quickly used one of the candles to melt a small circle of wax, and used the ring to stamp the king's crest on the front of the folded parchment.

The door to the office opened slowly, and Caeden glanced

up to see Eryn slipping inside before he removed the ring from the wax, leaving behind a perfect replica of the seal. He'd seen that crest stamped onto more letters than he could count, but he'd never been the one to leave the mark behind. He'd had his own, one that had belonged to his father before he'd ascended to the throne and claimed the title of king, and the change in the mark made a lump form in the back of his throat.

"What's that?" Eryn asked, her voice so soft he hardly heard her from the opposite end of the space.

Caeden didn't take his eyes away from the seal as Eryn's footsteps came further into the room and around the side of the desk to stand beside him. She laid her hand gently on his shoulder, and he leaned into her touch. "A letter to the King and Queen of Crevia," he explained as he finally pulled his gaze away from the crest and turned to face her. He couldn't bring himself to meet her eyes, and rather than try, he slipped an arm around her waist and pulled her close enough to rest his head against her chest. The scent of lavender filled his lungs, and he let out a slow breath, relaxing into her.

"That's a good idea," she said, her fingers intertwining in his hair as she pulled him closer. "Have you set a time to meet with the court?"

She asked tentatively, as if worried that single sentence would crush him beneath its weight. Caeden was grateful to her for it, though. If not for the servant that came in, he would've continued to put it off. She knew that, and he appreciated the gentle push, even if it had been dealt with while she was gone.

"I'm meeting with them at midnight tonight."

He lifted his head just enough to meet her gaze. She gave him a small smile and rested her hand on his cheek, her thumb tracing the raw skin with a sadness hidden deep in her eyes.

"Can you be there?" he asked, every ounce of pain and

sadness making his voice come out strained. He swallowed hard, hating the words before they left his mouth. "I'm scared to do this alone."

Her eyes softened, and she bent down slowly to kiss him in a way that made his heart race. Her kiss was tentative and gentle, a promise hiding in the warmth of her lips. She pulled away slowly, meeting his eyes with a depth in her gaze that he felt mirrored in his own. He hadn't recognized that look in her eyes until recently, and knowing now how much love that single look held sent a wave of warmth flooding through him.

"Always," she whispered, still close enough that her lips brushed his when she spoke. She rested her forehead against his, her arms tightening around his neck, holding him close. "I'm always here for you, Caeden."

The weight of those words felt like a blanket draped over his shoulders to block out the cold night air.

The question he'd wanted to ask her since he'd first admitted to her that he was falling in love with her formed on the tip of his tongue again. He wanted her in every sense of the word, and he wanted to be hers, even if they didn't live to see the sunrise the following morning. If they were killed in this war, if they met the same fate as his mother, his nursemaid, his father, or even a fate akin to his sister's, he didn't want to have missed the chance to ask her.

But there were so many things hidden beneath that single question now. He'd been handed the rule of an entire kingdom. His father died only a few hours ago. They were in the middle of a war that could tear them apart in more ways than just death. How could he ask her to be his with all of those things attached? How could he place the weight of those things onto her shoulders when he was struggling beneath it himself?

"Thank you," he whispered, forcing down the longing to ask

her that single question even as it tore at his heart to do so. He took her hand in his and brought it up to his lips, pressing a kiss to her knuckles that made her cheeks turn the slightest bit pink in the dim firelight. "I love you, Eryn Gedding."

Eryn sucked in a breath, the flush on her cheeks darkening. A small smile pulled at the corners of her lips. "I love you, too."

Despite everything in the world around them—the raging war, the lingering fears he worried would never be suppressed from when he was held in the Dragon Lord's cell, the fate he'd learned his sister had lived in for the past eleven years, the death of his father, the weight of his new role as Aericora's ruler—hearing just those words from her was enough to make everything feel momentarily okay.

Chapter 40
Eryn

The court filed into the office late that night. Eryn expected to hear muttered complaints fall from their lips as they passed by, given the late hour, but to her surprise, they all remained silent as they found places to either sit or stand around the room. The king's death would have a large effect on them as well, but something about their silence put her on edge. She didn't trust them to not attempt to pull something with the state Caeden was in.

They knew he was upset, and despite only being present for a few court-related things, she knew how these people worked. The only one she could trust was Ronan, but he stood in the back corner with the same dark cloud hanging over him. His eyes were downcast, and though he didn't appear to have had anything to drink, he didn't look mentally present either.

Uncomfortable silence filled the space, and Eryn fiddled anxiously with the dagger strapped to her thigh. Caeden cleared his throat and stood after what felt like an eternity before he turned to address the room.

"As you're all well aware, my father was killed during the attack that took place earlier today," Caeden stated, his voice carrying clearly through the room. His tone was even. Not an ounce of the heartbreak she'd seen cloud his expression since they'd watched his father slowly succumb to his injuries made its way into his words.

The gathered group nodded in unison.

Pride warmed her chest as he addressed the courtiers and advisors with all of the strength a king should have, even as her heart broke, knowing he had to push down all of those feelings to do what his new position required.

He was King of Aericora now.

The thought sat heavy on her chest, and she had to remind herself to breathe.

Caeden was king.

The man she'd been brought here to train, the spoiled prince she never could've imagined she'd end up caring so much for, the man she'd fallen in love with, was Aericora's king.

They hadn't talked about where their relationship—whatever exactly it was—went from here. He'd told her he loved her only just earlier, and she'd told him she loved him too, but that didn't mean she could spend the rest of her life within the palace walls.

She couldn't be a queen.

Could she?

Did she even want that?

She hadn't questioned any of it until now. The responsibilities of a queen couldn't be much more difficult than the things she'd been through on the battlefield, even if they would be vastly different. But she'd never been afraid to lead before. She'd never questioned whether she could. Yet, suddenly, the thought of even speaking to the group in front of her felt entirely overwhelming.

"With the war raging," Caeden continued, pulling Eryn's attention from the downward spiral her thoughts had taken, "I don't know when we will have time for a ceremony for me to properly ascend to the throne, and that's far from the biggest thing currently on my mind. I hope you will all agree with me that said ceremony can wait, or even be overlooked altogether, since it is nothing more than a formality."

"It's a tradition," Muire said simply, as if the thought of ignoring a tradition was the biggest insult she'd ever heard.

Eryn suppressed the urge to roll her eyes.

"It is," Caeden agreed, far calmer than she ever could've managed. "But given the circumstances, I ask all of you to truly consider where I'm coming from. We don't have the time or resources to put something like this on with Deovaria only a few miles from our doorstep. We need to put our resources into defeating them, not on an overly extravagant ceremony."

Murmured chatter filled the room; half of the court members agreed with their king, and the other half leaned toward Muire's argument.

Eryn opened her mouth to speak, but her earlier doubts resurfaced, and she swallowed down the words she'd wanted to say.

Ronan raised an eyebrow at her from the other end of the room. It was the first thing she'd seen him do that indicated he was paying attention to the conversation, and she almost wished he hadn't seen whatever expression she'd let slip onto her face.

She shook her head slowly, hoping no one but him would see. She didn't want to talk about her doubts and she didn't want him to ask. He had too much going on already, and he didn't need to worry about her confusing feelings because of the man she loved on top of it all.

"What about the king's funeral?" a courtier, whose name

Eryn couldn't recall, asked. He was middle-aged with salt-and-pepper hair. Of the court meetings she'd attended, she'd never heard him speak before. Usually, he kept his nose down while scribbling notes onto a pad of paper, occasionally looking up long enough to nod or shake his head in response to things others said.

"The funeral will be small and happen relatively quickly," Caeden answered. "My father didn't want anything large." The look on his face was grim, and Eryn wondered how many times he and his father spoke about the possibility of his death and what the aftermath would look like.

The courtier nodded. Rather than respond, he instead went back to scribbling notes on his pad of paper.

"How will we announce this change to the people?" Muire asked, an edge to her voice that Eryn raised an eyebrow at.

She expected strife from the court because of Caeden taking over the throne. She knew he would rise to the occasion easily, but that didn't mean the court wouldn't make it difficult. Not to mention the power struggle they would be having amongst themselves with a new leader stepping in. Muire was the obvious favorite of Caeden's father, but that didn't mean she would be Caeden's go-to for advice, which was likely the source of the sharp edge to her tone.

Most of the court likely already knew, much like Eryn did, that the chances of Ronan being Caeden's primary trusted advisor were high, which wouldn't help matters given Ronan's reputation around the castle.

There was an obvious answer to Muire's question, but Caeden didn't let the irritation in his eyes seep into his tone when he said the words Eryn would've preferred to say while flicking the woman in the forehead to emphasize what a waste of time it was.

"The same way we would've informed them of a proper ceremony," Caeden stated simply.

Muire bit the inside of her cheek, her eyes blazing, but she suppressed her frustration quickly.

"I'll handle getting things ready for my father's funeral. Neill, will you handle sending out word to the towns about the king's passing?" The youngest of the courtiers, though he was still a few years older than her, Caeden, and Ronan, looked up. "If you can get the letters worked up, I can get them signed tomorrow morning."

"Yes, Your Majesty," Neill said quickly. "I'll have them ready and on your desk in the morning."

"Perfect."

Eryn shifted uneasily, her fingers finding the pommel of her dagger before she ran them back and forth over the smooth surface as the room grew silent again. The death of the king and Caeden's ascension to the throne were the two most important things they would discuss during this meeting, but every part of her itched to hear how they'd gotten here. She wanted to know how Deovaria had orchestrated another attack, and if the attack had been successful enough to kill the king, why they retreated. None of it added up, and if sitting with Caeden earlier in the day wasn't the most important thing on her mind, she would've sought out the court long before now.

The silence stretched on, and the court murmured amongst themselves. Most of the chatter had to do with the death of the king, but Eryn couldn't make out what any of them said well enough to discern if they were discussing anything else.

She glanced at Caeden as the chatter grew louder. He'd turned away from the court members and instead stared blankly at the top sheet of parchment in a stack his father left behind. He was making himself look busy by staring at the paper, but tears shone in his eyes.

Eryn's heart clenched painfully.

He had to bring up the details of the attack. They needed to discuss it, but he'd already talked about the matter of his father's funeral, even if it was briefly. It was something else entirely to discuss how his father had died; the steps that led to him lying bloody and burned on the cot where he took his final breaths with his son by his side.

She didn't hold any love in her heart for her own parents after all of these years, but she could imagine the pain if it was Caeden or Ronan on that cot. She wanted to reach out and touch him; to hold him until every last bit of pain was gone.

But she couldn't do that here. Not in front of the court when they hadn't yet spoken about what they were to each other, and certainly not when the court would be having its own internal struggle.

The bubble of doubt flickered in the back of her mind again, but she pushed it away as she cleared her throat. The court members turned to face her, and Caeden glanced up.

"How did the Dragon Lord attack?" she asked, surprised when her words didn't come out strained. Her nerves stood on edge, but her words came out clearly, and that alone helped loosen the tightness in the back of her throat.

Muire was the one to respond. "We aren't entirely sure. Our best guess is that the dragons swooped low overhead and dropped explosives. Or launched a combination of large boulders and fire to break apart the castle walls and then burn everything inside. We haven't found anyone who was outside during the attack who survived, so we are simply taking guesses." She said her words quickly, a hint of fear hidden beneath them as a shiver ran through her body.

The other court members nodded in agreement, glancing at

one another as if looking for confirmation.

Eryn frowned.

That didn't make any sense.

"Why did the Dragon Lord retreat?" Caeden asked, before she could untangle her thoughts and make sense of the mess of information. "He killed the king. It doesn't make sense for them to retreat after that. And even if they didn't know of the king's condition, they destroyed almost a quarter of the castle. Why would they leave?"

Muire opened her mouth, but Fionn beat her to answering. "We've been trying to figure that out. So far, we haven't found a reason. Unless they only planned to cause us distress and hoped it would hinder our ability to fight against them somehow. Their strategy doesn't make sense."

"It doesn't look like anythin' was dropped," Ronan murmured, voicing the same thought Eryn had, but Muire was already speaking again and no one but her and Caeden seemed to hear him.

"We've been trying to determine the exact reason for their attack since it happened," Muire said. "They attacked a generally unused section of the castle. It was simply chance that the king was there since he was having a last-minute meeting with the king and queen from Crevia. Since discussing it, we've determined that Deovaria wouldn't have had any way of knowing that. I think it's best we assume they were simply trying to scare us, much like last time."

"Why did they meet there and not in my father's office?" Caeden asked. He'd fully turned away from the papers on his father's—his—desk, and the tears that were shining in his eyes a moment earlier were gone. All that remained was confusion laced with an anger burning deep inside that rarely grew hot enough to display itself across his features.

The court members glanced at one another, as if searching for the one of them who held the answer.

After several long moments, Fionn shrugged. "He didn't discuss the decision with us. It makes sense that he would want to make their meeting more formal, though."

Eryn frowned. The king and queen from Crevia arrived quickly. Their entire meeting was last-minute. It wouldn't have surprised them to meet with Aillin in his office.

Caeden only nodded in response. If he had any of the same questions circling in his mind, they weren't visible in his expression. "Were they here to talk about Margaid?"

"That was our understanding," Fionn answered.

"What had they talked about previously? Do they know about Dealla?" Worry seeped into the edge of Caeden's tone, but nothing else hinted at his emotions toward the situation.

It hurt to watch because Eryn had found that dark, quiet place inside of herself more times than she could count. She'd lived in that numb, emotionless void that helped her through the hard times for far longer than she should've. It was hard to come out of, even when the pain eased on its own. She only hoped he wouldn't struggle to come out of it like she had.

"We don't know that either," Muire answered. "The king has been corresponding with them since before you left for the Rayfait Mountains. We only found out a couple days ago that they planned to come here to discuss things further."

Caeden nodded again. "Okay. I'm meeting with them in the morning. If my father didn't already, I will inform them of everything we know about Dealla and what she says was the true fate of their daughter."

The court turned to one another, quiet chatter filling the space again as they spoke amongst themselves. Doubt was written across all of their faces, but Eryn couldn't make out the words they said to one another. Ronan raised an eyebrow at the group, but didn't involve himself in their discussion.

"Alone?" Muire practically squeaked.

Eryn wanted to laugh at the look of shock that passed over her features. Aillin had relied on her heavily, and as far as she'd seen, he'd done very little without Muire present. Especially affairs like speaking with the king and queen from Crevia about the murder of their daughter and the woman who took her place to garner information to defeat them in the war.

"No, I won't be alone," Caeden answered as a flicker of confusion dawned on Eryn. "I'll have Miss Gedding and Ronan there with me."

It was strange to hear herself called that while everyone else here was on a first-name basis with one another. It was even stranger to hear it from Caeden, since he'd rarely ever spoken about her without using her first name. But everyone here knew nothing more about their relationship than that she was his trainer and traveled with him to keep him safe. Everything else they'd seen—including how she'd gone after him when he was kidnapped—wouldn't have made them second-guess a thing. Especially since the king had given her the order to do so. It was her job to protect him, and all they would've seen was a dutiful soldier protecting the future king.

Those words sent the court into another hushed conversation, and Eryn couldn't help it this time when she rolled her eyes. "We're all right here," she said, before giving herself time to think better of it. "If you have complaints, feel free to express them to us. It's not like we can't hear you, anyway."

All eyes turned to her, and her hand landed on the hilt of her dagger again, gripping it until she was sure her knuckles had turned white. Ronan snorted a laugh she didn't expect to come from him.

She truly wasn't cut out for the role of a queen. Not when she couldn't hold her tongue over something as simple as the court having a discussion about them in front of her.

The thought made her doubts resurface, and she glanced at Caeden. Would he be mad that she'd spoken up rather than attempting to be more polite? He'd never seemed to dislike how she handled things before, but he was the king now. He couldn't ignore it if she stepped out of line.

Caeden's lip quirked upward, something like pride shining in his eyes, along with that same look he'd given her so many times; the look of someone who loved her. She'd felt that look mirrored on her own face just as many times.

Her heartbeat quickened, and she turned away from him before her treacherous face heated and gave away her feelings for the king in front of his entire court. She needed to talk with him; needed to know what exactly was going on between them.

She loved him.

She knew that as truly as she knew her own name, but she needed to know that he wanted her like she wanted him. That she wanted to be with him, even if these things—the court meetings, the parties, the fancy dresses, the political nonsense—came along with it.

She looked over the faces of those in the room, passing over Ronan and his knowing smirk quickly but not so quickly that she didn't offer him a warning glare before moving on.

"We are simply concerned that the new king is choosing the people with the least experience in this court to deal with a situation that needs to be handled extremely delicately," Muire answered, while everyone else in the room shied away from Eryn's question.

Eryn shrugged. It was a valid concern, but that didn't make her like the way Muire had been acting this entire meeting.

"You are more than welcome to attend as well," Caeden told her. "But I don't want the entire court present when they hear their daughter was murdered in the woods because she was traveling here. It may have been an agreed-upon arrangement, but I would like to avoid making them feel outnumbered. As you already stated, this situation needs to be handled delicately."

Muire clenched her jaw, but nodded. "I will be there."

Eryn raised an eyebrow at the woman. Her behavior wasn't surprising, but it was still annoying. Despite everything that happened, they were still at war, and now wasn't the time for more strife to come up between them. Infighting wouldn't help them defeat the Dragon Lord and his armies, especially not when it was over something as simple as who would be present when speaking to another kingdom's rulers. Their king would be there. In any other scenario, that would be more than enough.

"Very well," Caeden said, moving on to conclude their meeting. "The four of us will meet with them in the morning, and I will arrange another meeting to discuss how it goes. I will handle my father's funeral, and we've agreed that, at least for now, there will be no large ceremony for it, or for my taking over the role of Aericora's king. Once the war with Deovaria is over, we can discuss the matter further, assuming we are all here to do so."

Chapter 41

Ronan

A knock came at the door, and Ronan downed what remained of the glass of whiskey in his hand. He let out a breath and replaced the glass on the counter. He reached for his cane that he always kept propped against the counter when he came into the kitchen, only to curl his fingers into a tight fist when he remembered he no longer needed it after their trip to the mountains.

A second knock reached him, and he shook his head before making his way to the door. He turned the knob and pulled the door open to reveal the same woman he'd gone out of his way to talk to on his way back from the court meeting earlier in the day.

After the king's death—along with everything else over the past weeks—even if he wasn't sure this was the best idea, he needed an escape. The whiskey hadn't been appealing until he saw the smoke swirling into the air from the back of the dragon while the woman who should never hold his heart sat behind him.

"Hi there," the woman said, her voice lower than he remembered.

Through the drunken haze permeating his mind and fogging his thoughts, words didn't leave his mouth when he gestured for her to step inside.

He couldn't recall the woman's name. All he knew was that he'd never seen her in the castle before, despite being well acquainted with the other staff.

The woman offered him the kind of smile that told him this was far from her first time sneaking around late at night with less than innocent thoughts swirling through her head. She looked him up and down, taking in his lack of a shirt and low-waisted pants. The left side of her mouth twitched up a fraction of an inch before she pushed back the hood of her cloak and stepped past him.

Deep red hair flashed across his vision, and the scent of lilacs drifted in as she passed him.

It wasn't supposed to be lilac.

It was supposed to be an earthy scent. Like the forest after a rainstorm.

He bit the inside of his cheek as he shut the door, forcing away the thoughts of the last redheaded woman he'd invited into his home. Forcing away the disappointment he felt when he turned to face her, and the beautiful gold sheen Margaid's hair always had in the flickering candlelight wasn't there.

No. She wasn't real.

She wasn't Margaid. The woman who had worn that face, who smelled like rain, who wore the curly red hair, was Dealla. The Dragon Lord's daughter. The woman who imprisoned him and tortured him. The woman who tricked him. His kingdom's enemy. *His* enemy.

None of those things pushed away the longing for the smell

of her hair or the feel of her touch.

Ronan kept himself from shaking his head to clear his thoughts as he turned back to face the woman. He expected her to be standing in front of him when he turned, and he blinked a few times before accepting that his eyes weren't playing tricks on him when he didn't find her there. He glanced around the room, only to realize that she was sitting on the couch.

Naked.

He licked his lips uncomfortably, a wave of adrenaline he hadn't expected to feel rushing through him when he looked at her.

The woman in front of him—was Natalie her name?—lay facing up on the couch, her top half propped up on her elbows as she peered at him with thick eyelashes coated in a touch too much makeup.

"I can't be here long," she said, angling herself on the couch in a way that pressed her breasts together, which only succeeded in drawing his attention to the curves and dips of her body.

The angle created the illusion of two perfectly full breasts. Every time he'd seen a woman naked and splayed out before he hadn't considered the different aspects of their body. Every woman he'd been with was perfect in their own individual way.

But those were the thoughts of a man who'd never before experienced perfection. Those were his thoughts before he'd been with *her*.

The woman before him was beautiful by every definition of the word, but she wasn't perfect. She was an inch too short. Her breasts were a size too big. Her hair was too dark. Freckles didn't dot her cheeks and nose. Her eyes were the wrong shade.

"No one ever can," he answered, not thinking over the words before they fell from his mouth.

The woman frowned.

He couldn't keep himself from shaking his head this time.

That was the wrong thing to say. He was supposed to say something flirty. He was supposed to tell her that he didn't need long to satisfy her in all the ways she wanted. He couldn't find those words right now though, and he was thankful when the woman shook her head and the smile she'd had before returned.

"So…" she drawled, drawing out the word as she patted the sliver of empty couch beside her bare hip. "Are you going to take those pants off and join me or not?"

Those words should've been attractive.

Those words should've made his blood boil with lust.

Instead, he was indifferent to hearing those words from her mouth. When she'd said them, he hadn't been able to think of anything but her. When she'd been the one naked on his couch, he hadn't stood in the hallway thinking about another woman. Everything but the thought of her fell away entirely.

Ronan bit the inside of his cheek again.

Could he do this?

The woman was watching him, but no words formed on the tip of his tongue.

Forget about her.

He wanted to scream those words to himself. He wanted her to disappear from his memory. He didn't want to remember how she felt in his arms. He didn't want to remember exactly what she'd looked like lying in the same position as the woman who now lay on his couch.

Ronan shoved away the thoughts, forcing them back into the smallest corner of his mind, and walked around the couch to stand before the woman waiting for him.

"How 'bout a little of this first instead?" he asked, pulling the same smirk he'd grown so used to wearing onto his face as he let his fingers trail up along her bare leg to her stomach.

The woman shivered beneath his touch.

He knelt on the floor beside the couch, his gaze traveling over her skin and the goosebumps that flared out over it.

"I said I can't be here long," she repeated, gasping when his fingers traveled lower and he made a circle with his fingertips around her belly button.

"I'm sure you'll come up with a good excuse," he whispered before he leaned over and pressed his mouth to the side of her neck. He kissed her skin lightly, drawing an irritated grumble from her that again, should've done something to him.

"Ronan," she grumbled irritably, a plea hiding beneath her tone as his fingers traveled slightly lower, but not as low as she wanted them to go.

He moved up the side of her neck, leaving featherlight kisses along her jaw until his mouth met hers with a kind of hunger he didn't feel. Their mouths moved together in an uncoordinated, sloppy way, and again, he expected to feel something.

But her mouth felt wrong against his. Her skin was too cold. Her lips didn't dip into that perfect V shape he'd never known he'd needed to feel against his own to enjoy a perfect kiss.

Ronan pulled away so quickly he fell back against the glass coffee table. He was dimly aware that the corner of it pressed into his spine, but through his drunken haze and the adrenaline screaming at him that every bit of this encounter was wrong, he didn't notice the pain.

"I can't do this," he said quickly, pulling himself to his feet. He grabbed her cloak from the edge of the couch where she'd laid it and handed it to the woman whose stunned expression gazed up at him.

A pang of regret flashed through him as she slowly took her cloak back, her mouth opening as if she wanted to say something before she snapped it shut again.

"I'm sorry," he whispered, running a hand through his hair as he turned away from her. "You're not her. I can't. I'm sorry."

The woman didn't say anything as she put her cloak back on and left. He didn't watch her go, even as the regret swirled inside him. Instead, he went to the kitchen again and grabbed a full bottle of whiskey before uncapping it and pressing the bottle to his lips.

He waited in the kitchen, gulping down mouthfuls of the bitter, brown liquid until the last of his self-respect was drowned away by the alcohol; until he was long past sure the woman was back inside of the castle. He grabbed his own cloak from his bedroom. He struggled to fasten the pin at his throat through the thick fog of the alcohol, before he pulled the hood over his head and slipped out into the night.

Chapter 42

The hours after the meeting with the court dragged on; seconds ticked into minutes that slowly turned to more hours than Caeden intended when he finally glanced at the clock. It was only a couple of hours until the sun would be up.

Caeden sighed and continued flipping through the papers he'd found around his father's study. He couldn't bring himself to sleep. Not with everything weighing heavy on his mind after the day's events.

He needed to understand what his father was working on when he died so he could speak with the King and Queen of Crevia and get everything from the attack sorted out. Once he was done with all of that, he would figure out a way to put an end to this war once and for all. They'd wasted enough time with Deovaria. If the Dragon Lord was making reckless attacks, it would make them harder to predict, and Aericora would only lose faster. He needed to get his sister out of his enemy's hands, and he needed to get his people off the battlefield and back into their homes.

Most of the documents littering the office were months old,

with occasional newer ones scattered throughout. He'd read each briefly, surprised when he uncovered letters that were sent back and forth between Aericora and Crevia, Nozac, and Drura regarding his betrothal that had brought them soldiers and ended with Crevia's princess dead.

Caeden stared at the letters regarding his betrothal for a long time, reading over his father's words agreeing separately to each kingdom. They specified which princess would be brought over from each kingdom: Ceana, Kylana, and Margaid.

His stomach tightened as he read each of their names scrawled in his father's perfect penmanship. He hadn't ever liked the arrangement, aside from the fact that it gave him Eryn as a trainer. That was all he'd focused on while the three women were in the castle, though. The idea of marrying a woman he didn't love made his stomach twist, so he'd opted to think about it as little as he could, which resulted in him treating the princesses like they were unimportant when he should've given them every ounce of his attention.

He'd acted that way because he couldn't see past getting the training he'd always wanted, but that was no excuse, and probably the poorest decision he'd ever made. Maybe if he'd paid them more attention, Dealla wouldn't have been able to spin her web of lies. Maybe, if he'd done the job he was supposed to as Aericora's prince, he would've picked a woman that wouldn't currently be sitting in their dungeon.

Caeden sighed and set the letters aside. He reached into the drawer by his left knee and pulled out two sheets of parchment. He wrote a brief note and an apology to both Ceana and Kylana. He wanted to explain his actions, how he'd been so naïve, and immature enough to think that a few months of training would undo everything that happened to his loved ones and somehow make him able to help his people defeat the Dragon Lord. But none of that would do any good. They both knew he'd focused his attention on his training, so he opted instead for a simple, sincere apology to each, though he likely wouldn't get a response from either. He folded each piece of parchment into thirds before stamping them closed inside of separate envelopes with the king's crest.

He pushed them to the edge of the desk to be sent off the following morning before he sat back in his large chair, his eyes trained on the angles of the crest he'd stamped into the wax.

Training hadn't gotten him any closer to killing the Dragon Lord, and that weight fell onto his shoulders with a sort of calm clarity he'd never felt before. Learning the skills had made him more reckless than he should've been. Going to the front lines before they were even close to the end of the war, and then traveling to the mountains rather than staying here like he should have.

The latter may have resulted in him keeping his life, but that didn't mean it wasn't still reckless. He'd known the risks, he'd known it wasn't his place as the prince and Aericora's then future ruler, and he'd known that his responsibilities were more important than anything else. That knowledge should've stopped him without a second thought, but it hadn't.

He turned his attention back to the stack of papers on the desk. He picked through them until he reached the last of the letters regarding his betrothal. Beneath those, he found a single letter from one of the towns nearest Deovaria's border.

The words he read on the page made a nauseating feeling climb up the back of his throat. The letter explained the state the town was left in after an attack from Deovaria struck too close to them. Thousands of wounded soldiers were dying in whatever cots they could find to lay them in. They were short on people to tend to the wounded, but even worse was that they didn't have the supplies they needed to try.

The king's crest marked the letter, but there was no way for Caeden to know what the response had been without digging through his father's thousands upon thousands of papers to find it.

The towns and their missing supplies would be a project for the following day. He intended to send the supplies to Dalelry like he'd promised, and look into the past shipments to ensure nothing was getting overlooked, but that couldn't happen tonight.

He set the letter back down on the desk. None of what they did in the war was working. He knew it as well as everyone else who had lived through the past eleven years. They were no closer to winning this war, but it needed to end. He needed his people to be safe, and he needed his sister to be back home where he could figure out how to undo the Dragon Lord's magic.

Even if that meant the Dragon Lord lived to breathe once all of it was said and done.

Before giving himself too much time to think about whether doing so without speaking to the court was a good idea, he pulled a third piece of parchment from the drawer and scrawled a quick note to his uncle:

This war has gone on long enough. Your people are suffering as much as mine. It's time we end this. I propose a final, fair fight between my men and yours to limit the lives lost. There will be no bloodshed anywhere before we meet on the battlefield. You may pick where and when, but I want my sister brought to me alive and well prior. In exchange, I will give you Dealla. Whichever kingdom is first to surrender, wins the war. If you agree to these terms, tell me a time and a place and prepare for your blood to stain the end of my blade.

Nerves ate at Caeden from the inside out as he wound his way through the halls toward his bedroom. He hadn't spent a night in his room alone since before he was taken by Dealla and held as the Dragon Lord's prisoner. He wasn't sure he'd be able to do it tonight still, but Eryn would already be asleep, and he couldn't wake her in the middle of the night because he hadn't yet gotten over his fear of being alone in his own room.

He could stay in his father's old room, given that it would be expected of him to move over there soon anyway, but even though he'd claimed his father's office as his own already, there was something very different about claiming his bedroom, too. It felt even more intimidating than spending the night in the room he'd been kidnapped from.

His heart thudded loudly in his ears as he rounded the final corner to the hall his bedroom lay down, along with his father's, which would remain empty until he grew brave enough to spend his nights there.

Eryn sat on the floor a few paces ahead of him when he turned the corner, and his heartbeat quickened at the sight of her. She leaned against the wall with her head lulled to the side, her chest rising and falling in deep, even breaths. Her hair fell across her face, shielding her from sight, but he knew her eyes were closed beneath the glossy black strands.

She'd waited for him. Waited so long she'd fallen asleep when he was gone for hours longer than she'd likely expected.

His chest tightened at the thought of her on the cold stone floor for hours. He should've known she'd be waiting. She hadn't left him to sleep alone since she and Ronan got him out of the Dragon Lord's prison, and she hadn't said anything that indicated tonight would be any different.

Everything was different tonight, though. Maybe that was why the thought hadn't crossed his mind.

Caeden knelt on the ground beside Eryn and carefully brushed the loose strands of her hair from her face. The love he felt for this woman was close to making his heart burst straight through his chest as he stared down at her, taking in her closed eyes and parted lips as she drew in another slow breath. She truly was tired if she hadn't woken to the sound of him approaching.

A small smile formed at the corners of his lips as he leaned in to press a gentle kiss to her forehead. She stirred lightly when his lips brushed her skin, and her bright blue eyes fluttered open.

"Hey," he said softly as she blinked up at him and glanced around. He didn't move his hand from where it had fallen against her cheek.

She sat straight, no longer using the wall to hold herself up. "How late is it?"

"The sun will be up in a couple of hours."

Eryn frowned. "And you're just getting back?"

He was thankful for the surrounding darkness so she couldn't see the blush threatening to turn his cheeks scarlet. "I wasn't ready to..." His words faltered and he let the unfinished sentence hang in the air between them.

There were so many ways he could finish it, but none of them were right. He wasn't ready to come back up to his room. He wasn't ready to be alone in the dark with a closed door separating him from the rest of the world. He wasn't ready to face the events of the longest day of his life. He wasn't ready to face his thoughts. He wasn't ready to face the tears.

He just wasn't ready.

Eryn seemed to understand everything he didn't say, and only offered him a gentle smile that tilted the left side of her mouth up just a hair before she climbed to her feet.

"You didn't have to wait for me," he told her, following her lead and standing straight.

Pink flared across her cheeks and down her neck. She shook her head in response. "I know I didn't need to," she said, an edge hiding beneath her voice, suggesting she was insulted that he thought she wouldn't even if she didn't need to.

The smile that had found its way to his face before returned. He opened the door to his room and gestured for her to go inside before he followed closely behind, shutting the door softly behind them.

Caeden found his way to the wardrobe and pulled out a change of clothes as Eryn sat down on the edge of his bed. She took off her shoes and slid her leggings off, leaving her in only a severely oversized shirt that fell midway down her thighs.

His gaze followed her progress as she pulled the leggings over her ankles and dropped them to the floor, his heart pounding in his chest. He would've liked to see her take the shirt off, as well, so he could lay eyes on the soft skin beneath that he'd only dared to graze with his fingers a few times.

He'd been tentative with his touches, even when they'd spent so many nights lying beside each other in the same bed, but it helped to remember that whatever this was between them, it wasn't anything certain. Even if he'd fallen in love with her more times than he could count.

It had been easier before, when she'd always been fully dressed. She'd never slept without pants on until now. He hadn't had to worry about his hands accidentally brushing against the skin of her thighs or hips. He'd imagined it enough times, but it couldn't have happened unless he crossed a line he wasn't ready to.

Eryn tilted her head to the side half an inch, and Caeden felt his face heat when he realized she'd caught him staring.

He fought the urge to clear his throat awkwardly. "I'm going to go wash up and change," he told her, stumbling over his own words slightly. "I'll be quick."

Eryn nodded her head. "Okay," she said softly.

Caeden walked to the other end of the room and into the washroom connected to his bedroom, before closing the door behind himself. He drew a quick bath before he changed out of the clothes he wore and climbed inside. He washed quickly before he stepped out and dried off. His clean pair of pants waited for him on the countertop beside his dirty clothes, and he pulled them on as quickly as he'd gotten undressed, not wanting to keep Eryn up any longer than she'd already been. She didn't sleep well through noise, and though he wasn't being particularly loud, it would still be enough to keep her awake.

He drained the water in the tub before he picked up the pile of dirty clothes and exited the washroom into his bedroom.

And then dropped them when his eyes landed on the woman sitting on the edge of his bed. His jaw nearly fell open at the sight of her sitting there. She'd taken off the shirt he'd wished more than once that he could pull over her head, leaving her in only her bra and underwear.

He stared at her, shamelessly taking in the curves of her hips and breasts and the way the orange candlelight illuminated her skin.

Caeden swallowed hard when he finally looked up and met her gaze.

"I know it's late," Eryn said slowly, easing off the edge of the bed so she stood fully in front of him. "And I know today was already… a lot." She cringed at her own words, but something about the sound of her voice was enough to drown out everything that had happened in the last twenty-four hours.

He opened his mouth to say something in response, but no words came out as he took in the sight of her, unable to tear his gaze away.

Eryn took a few tentative steps closer until she was standing only a foot away from him in the center of the room. "I want to be with you, Caeden," she whispered, her gaze heavy on his. "I want to be with you in every single way. I love you with all of my heart, every fragment of my soul. I want this"—she gestured around them without breaking away from his gaze—"if it means I get to be with you. I want to spend every night with you beside me, every moment with you around, every breath with my love for you consuming me. I want you. I want to be yours."

Words entirely failed him as he stared into her deep blue eyes. Those words were everything he'd dreamed of hearing from her, but nothing could've prepared him for the way they made his heart race.

Those words took every broken piece inside of him and carefully stitched them back together. They took the hurt, the pain, the worry, the doubt, the ache, and the agony he'd felt all day, and every day since he'd first been told that his mother and sister were gone, and they washed it all away.

Caeden stepped closer, closing the distance between them until only a few inches remained. He lifted his hand slowly, letting his fingers graze the side of her cheek as he gazed into her eyes, allowing himself to be swept away by the sight of her. "I'm yours, Eryn Gedding," he whispered, resting his forehead against hers. "I've always been yours. Until the last rays of sun fall across this world, I'll be yours."

Eryn's lips crashed against his the second the words left him, and his heart leapt inside of his chest as she wrapped her arms around his neck and pressed her body against his. The warmth of her bare skin seeped into him as his hands found her hips and he pulled her closer, deepening the kiss as she tugged him toward the edge of the bed. She lay down against the mattress, pulling him with her before she kissed him again, deep enough to draw a moan from his lips.

Caeden pulled away, just enough to leave kisses along her jaw and neck before he pulled her against him and held her close. "I love you," he whispered against her skin, the smell of her filling his lungs and instilling that same sense of calm in him that it always had.

The words didn't even graze the surface of the feelings he held for her, but they were as close as he could ever get. Maybe, if he said them to her enough, they would eventually mean what he'd wanted them to the first time he'd said them.

Eryn wrapped her arms around his neck and sighed as she relaxed into him. "I love you, too."

Chapter 43

Dealla

Dealla startled awake at the sound of uneven footfalls against the dirt-covered brick. They were slow, and each step dragged against the floor, as if the person making their way closer was half asleep. She'd only just begun to sleep through the night while the sounds of rats crawling past her echoed and the occasional bugs crawled over her skin, but she'd been trained to wake to even the slightest variation from what she would typically hear.

The steps grew nearer, and she pressed herself into the corner of the cell, hoping the shadows would conceal her presence. It wouldn't do much good if whoever came down here was looking for her, and the thought made her heart pound faster.

So far, she was left alone down here unless someone brought her food, but she'd already gotten her allotted two meals today. She was Deovaria's princess, on top of everything else she'd done. She'd been waiting for someone to come and take out whatever hurt and pain the war had caused them on her. She'd been waiting for someone to wander down here and beat her senseless for something completely beyond her control, simply because they were at war.

It wasn't until the shadowed edges of a man came into view and she took in the outline of his curly hair and broad shoulders that she realized who had come to see her.

Dealla swallowed hard as Ronan stepped closer to her cell, nearly tripping over his feet far more times than she could count in the time it took him to walk the length of her cell. He peered inside, but the shadows must have hidden her better than she'd given them credit, because he turned away quickly and moved to the cell across the hall.

He made it a few steps past the wall separating her cell from the one beside it before he finally lost his balance entirely and crashed down hard against the floor.

"Ronan!"

His name flew from her lips before she could decide whether she wanted him to find her sitting there or not. She was on her feet just as quickly, pressing the full front of her body against the bars keeping her caged before she realized that she couldn't get to him even if she was entirely sure that was what she wanted.

Ronan lay motionless on the floor for several moments, and her heart raced as she watched him. Had he hit his head when he fell? Would he be able to get up on his own? She couldn't get to him. She was trapped within the confines of her cell, and no one would hear her if she screamed for help.

Finally, after what felt like far longer than the few seconds it was, he climbed unsteadily to a sitting position. He gripped his forehead with a hand, his gaze passing over her a few times before his eyes finally settled on her face.

Dealla's heart ached when she saw the sweat coating his forehead and upper lip, and the flush spreading across his cheeks and neck. He was drunk. Far more drunk than she'd ever seen him, even when they'd spent their nights together.

Ronan glanced around the hallway again, as if trying to recall where he was as he rubbed his forehead with the palm of his hand.

"You're in the dungeon," Dealla told him, her voice soft. Her hand slid down the rusted metal bars caging her in as she sank to her knees, her eyes not leaving his face. "You're drunk." She couldn't keep the worry from making her voice waver.

Ronan shook his head and climbed to his feet. He didn't give any sign that he'd heard her before he came up to the edge of her cell and sank to his knees in front of her.

In the dim light, she couldn't make out much before, but now that he stood a few inches away, his gaze level with hers, she could see the sheen of tears glistening in his eyes.

Her heart shattered at the sight.

It didn't seem possible for this same man to break her heart into even more splintered shards, yet every time she looked at him, every time she saw that beautiful face, her heart broke a little more.

He'd done nothing to her. Only offered her the kind of love she wished she could've accepted, but knew she never could when her goals should only ever lead to his eventual death. But that only made it hurt worse.

She'd felt nothing for him when he'd only been another prisoner in that dark cell; another prisoner to torture in a means to an end. But this cruel world had a way of playing games with even the darkest of souls, and hers was no exception.

He'd fallen in love with her. She'd fallen in love with him.

And she'd watched his face when he'd learned the truth.

She'd watched the blissful world of lies she'd spun shatter before his eyes as the truth—that once again, even if only metaphorically this time, she'd twisted a knife into his flesh—crashed into him with all the force of the whip she'd cracked against his skin.

Tears she hadn't expected burned as they spilled down her cheeks. She had no right to feel anything after everything she'd put him through. She couldn't call this feeling love when she'd so easily tortured and manipulated him.

But that's what this was.

As cruel as it was for her to feel it, she loved him, and that alone felt like she was dangling another blade above his head.

"Why'd you save me?" Ronan asked, and those simple words were a blade of their own, slicing straight through the shattered pieces of her black heart.

He shouldn't need to ask. In a perfect world, he would know why she'd leapt over the back of the dragon in a useless attempt to pull him to safety. In a perfect world, if she let her true feelings for him slip through her lips, she wouldn't be tearing another hole in his heart.

Dealla reached through the bars, her fingers moving of their own accord as her hand fell against the side of his face. Her thumb ran over the warm, wet skin of his cheek as she wiped away the tears. "I can't answer that question," she whispered, her voice broken.

His tears fell faster, but he didn't turn away. There was a clarity in his gaze behind the haze shining in his eyes, and she knew he understood what she could never bring herself to say.

"How can you love me?" he asked. His tone wasn't cruel or demanding. He said the words gently, a kind of plea hidden beneath them that threatened to pull the oxygen from her lungs and leave her a suffocating husk on the floor.

"I didn't want to hurt you," she whispered. "Even back in the cell, I didn't want to hurt anyone. I didn't..." She choked back a sob burning the back of her throat. The words she had to say wouldn't ease his pain, but she needed to say them. "I didn't want to fall in love with you. You were a means to an end. A way to complete my mission. It shouldn't have happened, but I let you in. I let you see real parts of myself and I lied to myself that I was only doing it to get information from you. I didn't realize how far I'd taken it until it was too late. I didn't realize that you had real feelings for me either, until I cared too much about what you having those feelings would mean when you found out."

Ronan leaned against the bars, his forehead connecting with the rusted metal. He reached up with a hand and placed it over hers where it still rested against his cheek, his fingers intertwining with hers as if their hands were perfectly made to fit together.

"You're all I can think about," he confessed. "Even after everythin', all I see is you when I go to sleep. I hear your laugh in my livin' room. I see your lips pressed against my glasses. Your barrettes on my bookshelves. Your dresses across my floor. I smell you on my clothes, feel you against my skin. You're everywhere." He took in a shaky breath and let it out, his eyes returning to hers again briefly before he turned away. "I wanna be able to hate you. I wanna forget about you. I wanna move on, and yet, here I am. I want your memory gone, yet I wanna break down these walls and run away with you where this war means nothin' to anyone."

Those words. Those perfect, painful, traitorous words may have finally been the last thing to break her heart beyond repair.

Because how could he want that after everything she'd done to him? How could he stand here before her and tell her that simply being far enough away from the war would be enough to move on from everything she'd done?

"I would never let you do that to yourself," Dealla said softly. "You don't deserve to be with someone like me. You never have. You deserve so much more than my dark, twisted soul could ever offer you."

His fingers tightened around hers, and his beautiful hazel eyes lifted just enough to meet her gaze with the kind of weight that could've pulled her soul from her body. "Maybe we can find the light together."

More tears stung her eyes, welling up again at the hope she heard in his voice. "What if there's no light to find?" she asked, her voice cracking as a hiccup escaped her throat. "What if all that's left is darkness?"

The traitorous words left her before she knew for sure whether she wanted him to hear them. She hadn't voiced her doubts about everything she'd spent her life working toward achieving. Her father's dark longings weren't her own, and the parts of her she knew were good had suffered at her own hands when she'd pushed them away time and time again to complete the tasks she'd known were cruel. But the Dragon Lord was her father. She'd wanted to believe in him. She hadn't begun to believe he was past redemption until she'd heard the dragons speak about him in the mountains.

He'd killed hundreds of thousands—even if not all by his own hands—in the war with Aericora, but that was a means to an end. Aericora's people suffered too, and their king failed to help them, as far as she'd seen with her own eyes. But it wasn't until she'd heard the dragons speak about his cruelty toward them as well—toward creatures who did nothing to deserve his hatred—that she'd truly thought through her life and the things her father made her do in the name of a just cause. The same cause she'd spent years growing weary of.

Caeden's mother betrayed her father. She knew that was

where his animosity came from, but he'd painted a picture of a cruel world that those living in Aericora suffered in everyday. Aericora's people were starving in places, suffering and dying when their kingdom was rich enough that no one should ever have to, but how much of that happened after the war started? How much of it had her father lied about in the same way he'd tried to spin lies to Caeden? Had his own actions caused those words to become reality?

Surely not all of it was a lie, but how much of it was?

Ronan reached through the bars and ran his fingers along her cheek until his palm rested against the back of her neck. He pulled her forward gently until her forehead rested against his through the steel bars.

A heavy sigh escaped her when his warm skin touched hers. It shouldn't have felt so perfect.

"Then let me into the darkness with you," Ronan whispered. "I don't believe you're as cruel as you think. I don't believe you're heartless. I believe you made mistakes because of the Dragon Lord's reign. It forced all of us to do things we didn't want to. But I also believe that, even if you don't wanna admit it, you're starting to see those mistakes."

It was as if he were reaching into the deepest depths of her and examining every thought and every doubt she'd ever felt. She hadn't said anything out loud, but she didn't have to with him. He saw everything as if it were written clearly across her forehead.

A painful, brutal sob tore through her throat despite every attempt to keep it tightly sealed within. Once the first one started, another followed, and her tears flowed down her cheeks in an uncontrollable wave.

She reached through the steel bars until both of her hands found either side of Ronan's face. He froze for only a split second before a quiet, shaking sob rocked his body. He reached through the bars with his other hand to cup her face like she held his, his thumbs wiping gently at the stream of tears falling from her eyes.

Several agonizingly long minutes passed. They held each other through the rusted bars of the prison cell until their sobs and tears slowly subsided.

Ronan's fingers traced along her raw cheeks once the tears finally stopped. He pulled away slightly so their foreheads no longer touched and looked at her with a hint of a frown drawing his eyebrows together.

"What is it?" Dealla asked, her voice hoarse.

"You feel the same," Ronan said softly, his fingers still running along her skin, causing a shiver to work its way down her spine. "You look different, but everythin' about you feels the same." He traced his thumb along her brow, then down to the tip of her nose before he pulled his hand back and his palm rested against her cheek once again.

"The illusion only made my face look different and my skin color a little lighter," Dealla explained carefully. "It was like wearing a mask and a wig and the wrong shade of makeup. But since it was only an illusion, when you touched me, you weren't touching Margaid's face. You were reaching through the illusion and touching me. That's why I only ever let you touch me in the dark or when you were already drunk."

"Hmm," Ronan mused, his fingers drawing patterns along her cheeks, then down the side of her neck. "I never noticed."

Dealla leaned into his touch and closed her eyes, relishing the feel of his skin against hers. She'd wanted to feel the touch of his hands ever since the day she'd accepted her father's orders. She mourned the memory of his skin against hers since she'd first slipped her cloak on that night and forced herself to leave the confines of her room to kidnap Aericora's prince and permanently shatter the illusion of everything she'd lived during her months here.

"You weren't supposed to notice," she answered.

The frown he'd worn a moment before returned. "Still," he whispered, his words so quiet she could hardly hear him, even with only a few inches separating them. "I thought I knew you well enough to notice those things."

Dealla closed her eyes again. Maybe it was bad to tell him the truth, but she couldn't help it when the words slipped out. She'd never been good at hiding everything from him, anyway. "You know me better than anyone else in my life ever has."

Chapter 44

Eryn stirred beside him, making the sheets rustle noisily as she buried herself deeper in the covers. She breathed a heavy sigh before she stilled again with the blanket pulled to her chin and a content look on her face.

A smile pulled at the corners of Caeden's mouth as he reached over and lightly brushed his fingers against her cheek.

Her eyes fluttered open at his touch, pools of the most stunning blue he'd ever seen gazing up into his eyes and making his heart skip a beat. "Good morning," he whispered, pressing a gentle kiss to her forehead.

Eryn yawned, a sleepy smile on her face. "Good morning." She snuggled closer to him beneath the sheets and pressed a kiss against his neck before letting her head rest against him between his shoulder and his chest. "How did you sleep?"

Caeden wrapped his arms around her, holding her close as he ran his fingers along her arm beneath the blanket. She shivered beneath his touch, but didn't pull away. "I've never slept as well as I do with you beside me," he whispered into her hair.

Eryn snorted a laugh and lifted her head up just enough to look at him with a raised eyebrow. "When did you get so sappy?" she teased.

He grinned. "Around the same time you stopped referring to me with those nicknames you enjoyed so much."

Eryn poked him lightly in the chest, a smirk pulling at the corners of her lips. "I could start again, if that's what you want. Though some slight alterations may be in order."

Caeden's face warmed at the reference to his new title, even as his chest grew tight. His father was gone, and it hit him like a ton of bricks all over again.

He forced away the feelings welling up as thoughts of his father lying on the bloody cot slowly turned to thoughts of his sister still trapped in the Dragon Lord's hall of trophies. As if she weren't a living human being.

He'd get her out of there soon. If his uncle didn't take him up on his offer, he'd find another way to win this war quickly and get Amelia to safety.

"Hey," Eryn said softly, placing her palm against his cheek so that he would meet her gaze. "Where'd you go?"

He offered her a forced smile, and placed his hand over hers without breaking eye contact. The words he wanted to say felt lodged in the back of his throat, and he had to swallow down the lump that formed twice before he could speak. "This is what you want, right?" he asked softly.

Surprise flashed across her features, but it only lasted a second before she shook her head and refocused on him. "What do you mean?"

"This," he said again, gesturing quickly at the room around them, as if that would somehow make his meaning clearer. "Me." He swallowed hard again. "Are you sure you really want to be with me? This is all my responsibility now. I don't know what I'm doing and I don't know how I'm going to do it, but I have to lead this kingdom and make decisions for all of us regarding this war. And when all of this is over, I'll still have the responsibility of every single person living within Aericora's borders."

Eryn bit her lip, but didn't say anything, so Caeden continued.

"If you're with me, even if we keep this a secret and don't announce anything to the court or the kingdom, that weight will eventually fall to you if this is what you want." Caeden sighed, his next words feeling even heavier on the tip of his tongue. "I'm in this forever if you'll have me, Eryn. But that means you have to want to be a part of ruling this kingdom, too. You have to be okay with one day being the queen standing next to me. I'm…" He froze again for a split second, then shook his head and forced the words out before letting them hang there too long. "I'm giving you an out right now, if you want it. Everything that happened these past few weeks has been a lot, and I'm not trying to say you don't know what you want, but I wanted to give you the option to change your mind because none of this is over, and for me and whoever is with me, it never truly will be."

His heart pounded loudly as silence fell over them. He waited for her to say something, but she only sat there quietly, her eyes gazing into his while she seemed to mull over his words.

Then, after what felt like an eternity, a smile pulled at the corners of her lips and she laughed.

Actually laughed.

The sound surprised him so much he jumped as her loud, boisterous laughter echoed throughout the room.

She gripped her side tightly, as if fighting to get herself under control. Eventually, she sucked in a deep breath. She nudged him in the arm playfully. "What do you mean, 'you're giving me an out?'" She scoffed, another giggle escaping her before she could stop it. She reached up to cup his face in both of her hands and pressed her forehead against his, all manner of teasing disappearing. "I don't want an out, Caeden," she said softly. "I said I wanted you, and I meant it. I never wanted to be a queen or a ruler, but I'll learn. I've trained the most stubborn soldiers, and court is different, but I'll learn. I was worried about it at first, but… I'll figure it out and I'll get used to it. I can learn to deal with Muire and her need to hear her own voice if it means I get to be with you. I'll learn how the court works, and I'll get better at being there. If that's the only sacrifice I have to make to spend the rest of my life with the man I love, then so be it."

Eryn grinned up at him, and he felt his heart rate speed up as he listened to her.

This woman, this incredible, breathtaking, stubborn, headstrong, beautiful woman was willing to learn to navigate what most would find the most infuriating situations and people just to be with him. He would've gone to the ends of the earth for her, but there was something entirely overwhelming in the best way possible about knowing she was willing to do something like that for him.

"I love you, Eryn," he told her, the words holding the deepest, rawest parts of his soul out for her, yet they didn't even scratch the surface of everything he felt.

Those few words, those words that were supposed to mean everything, meant so little compared to the depth of emotion he felt for the woman sitting beside him.

A gentle knock came on the door then, and Caeden startled at the sound of it.

Eryn smirked up at him, but her smile softened almost immediately, and she pressed a kiss against his cheek. "I love you, too," she whispered, not loud enough for whoever stood on the other side of the door to hear.

There was a note of amusement in her voice, and he internally groaned at the timing of whoever stood outside.

"Your Majesty?" a voice called from the other side of the door, mild irritation hiding in the edges of their tone. "The king and queen from Crevia are waiting. Are you up yet?"

Caeden groaned again—this time out loud—when Muire's voice echoed throughout the room.

Eryn tossed an annoyed glare at the door, then rolled her eyes when Muire knocked again.

"I'm up," Caeden called, unable to keep his tone from holding the same irritation Muire's had.

"Breakfast will be served after the meeting," Muire hurried to say through the closed door, all business, despite how she could've just woken him up. "We don't want to keep the king and queen waiting much longer. I don't know how upset they'll be already, given the conversations we are expected to be having with them."

"Bitch," Eryn muttered as she slung her legs over the side of the bed. Caeden watched her despite himself, his gaze shamelessly taking in every inch of her bare skin as she picked up the clothes she'd discarded onto the floor late the previous night and slipped them back on.

A smirk hid in the corners of his mouth at Eryn's biting comment. He was glad he wasn't the only one who noticed Muire's way of speaking to him lately. She'd almost taken him more seriously when he was only the prince wanting to travel to the field to attempt to single-handedly fight dragons than she did now that he was the king. She'd never spoken to him as if he were an incompetent child until yesterday, even when that tone should've been warranted.

"Thank you, Muire," he responded, keeping his tone even

this time. "I'll be there in five minutes. Please apologize to them for the delay."

He wasn't sure what delay he was talking about, considering they weren't supposed to meet with the king and queen for at least another hour given that the sun was barely above the horizon, but he didn't feel like uncovering the reason for the sudden change right now. If he was already running late, he didn't have time to worry about it until later, anyway.

The light clicking of Muire's heels against the floor as she retreated down the hall drifted into the room beneath the door as Caeden climbed out of bed and selected a new set of clothes from the wardrobe.

Eryn came up beside him and pressed a kiss against his bare shoulder as he gathered his change of clothes. She laid a hand against his arm. "I'm going to go get changed and I'll meet you there," she told him.

Caeden nodded before he wrapped his free arm around her waist and pulled her into a quick embrace. "Thank you," he said into her hair, though he wasn't entirely sure what he was thanking her for in that moment. There were so many things to thank her for, he could've spent the next hour only brushing the surface.

Eryn wrapped her arms around his neck, and held him close for a few long seconds before she pulled away. "Always," she said, and he couldn't help but wonder how he'd gotten lucky enough to have such a wonderful woman in his life.

The king and queen from Crevia sat across from Caeden, Eryn, and Muire in the sitting room in his office. He wasn't sure where Ronan was, but considering the sudden timing change, he doubted Muire took the time to inform him given her feelings toward the castle's Head of Security.

The servants brought coffee and tea for each of them, and they sat in tense silence for several moments after the door was firmly closed.

The king and queen, along with Muire, sipped their drinks while Eryn swirled hers thoughtfully in her glass. The two were dressed in comfortable attire, the king wearing a simple coat over a button-down shirt and thick dress pants while his wife wore a fairly unembellished floor-length silk gown in the same shade of red that most of their late daughter's clothes had been. He could see the resemblance the two of them had to the disguise Dealla had worn. The queen's bright red, curly hair matched what the real Margaid's must have looked like, and the king's face shape was nearly identical to his daughter's.

Caeden glanced down at the glass in his hand, but couldn't bring himself to drink the bitter coffee inside. Instead, he set it aside. He cleared his throat uncomfortably, catching the attention of everyone in the room. "King Brine, Queen Moira, I apologize, but I'm not the most informed regarding the reasons for your visit," he said, speaking to each of the two in turn. "I've spoken with my advisors, and they informed me that my father was corresponding with you about your daughter, Princess Margaid, and the…unfortunate circumstances we believe may have befallen her." He tried not to cringe at his own words as they left his mouth. "I'm not sure how true any of it was. I am only aware of what I was told by the spy we encountered from Deovaria, and what she told me regarding your daughter. But those were the words of a trained liar, and I can only hope they were just that."

He no longer had a shred of doubt that the real Margaid had been killed in the forest on her way to Aericora. But he couldn't prove it to the king and queen, and it served no one's best interest for him to openly admit he'd taken Dealla's word as truth. Especially not in front of the mother and father of the woman she'd murdered in cold blood.

Caeden felt Eryn's stiffness beside him. Her fingers twitched where they sat awkwardly clasped in her lap, wanting nothing more than to grip the hilts of her daggers to prepare herself for a fight, even if it would never come to that sort of thing.

There also wasn't any reason to suspect Crevia's rulers held anything against them for the fate of their daughter. So far, they'd been nothing but polite and respectful.

Moira's fingers tightened around her glass and she clenched her jaw, but she didn't say anything.

Brine's outward composure remained relaxed, but his white knuckles matched his wife's as he set his glass down on the coffee table to his right before turning to face Caeden again. "I didn't believe your father at first when he told us that our daughter was killed by a Deovarian spy, but we've found evidence his words were true," he said solemnly.

Caeden's heart skipped a beat. So many feelings rushed through him so suddenly that he hoped he was keeping his face more placid than it felt. "I'm very sorry for your loss," Caeden told him, since no better words existed.

"I'm sorry for yours, as well," he responded.

Caeden only nodded in acknowledgement and accepted the words, hoping they could move forward with the conversation before the lump in his throat turned into a sob and he broke down into a pile of tears during one of the most important meetings he'd ever been in.

The king pressed his lips together in a thin line while he searched for a way to say the words on the tip of his tongue. After a moment, he cleared his throat. "Princess Margaid was murdered in the woods on the way to Aericora. She was still inside our kingdom's borders when she met her end. Your father mentioned that the spy disguised herself as Margaid, and that story is consistent with what we found." Brine's eyes were glassy, and he blinked a few times before he spoke again. "Her body was found in the woods a hundred yards away from a stream. Only bones and a few of her undergarments remained, which wasn't enough to identify her from initially, but after further inspection, our search party found an ankle bracelet beneath one of the socks she still had on, and my wife was able to confirm it was the same one she'd given to her before she left."

None of the words Brine uttered were surprising, but Caeden's heart still clenched painfully for the suffering the man in front of him and his wife were going through. He'd been feeling a very similar kind of agony from the death of his father.

The part of him that wasn't an emotional wreck realized it was in Aericora's best interest that Margaid was killed within her home kingdom's borders. Crevia couldn't place any blame on them, since they'd agreed to the arrangement in the first place and Aericora had nothing to gain from murdering their daughter.

"I'm truly sorry to hear that," Caeden said again. "We were hoping the information was wrong, but in any case, my father and the court agreed it would be best to inform you of our speculations, regardless of the lack of evidence."

"We appreciate how forthcoming you were," Moira whispered into the edge of her mug, her hazel eyes meeting Caeden's over the rim as she sipped its contents.

"If there's any assistance at all that we can offer you, don't hesitate to inform us," Muire interjected, and Caeden gave her a sideways glance as Eryn balled her hand into a tight fist against her thigh.

As much as he wished they could offer any kind of support to the king and queen, the court hadn't agreed to that. Muire was bringing this up on her own, at least as far as Caeden was aware. At the very least, it was never discussed with him, and if the court discussed it prior to him returning from the mountains, none of them mentioned it. But the change in leadership meant things like this needed to be discussed again before being brought up so easily.

Aericora was weak, and they didn't have endless amounts of money or supplies to offer to other kingdoms right now. Not given how their money and aid were going missing when it was being sent to the towns, and especially not with where they stood in the war. If things were looking up, even the slightest bit, Caeden wouldn't have batted an eye at her words, but it was out of place, given the circumstances tightening around them.

"Yes," Caeden said tightly, despite doing his best to keep his voice neutral. He chose his next words carefully. "We are more than happy to do what we can to help."

If there was anything offensive about his choice of wording, Brine and Moira didn't seem to notice. Instead, they nodded politely before Brine turned to Caeden again, as if Muire hadn't been the person speaking to him.

Caeden relaxed slightly, even as Muire's lips turned down into an irritated frown when the king turned away. Her treatment of him, along with how she was voicing things that either undermined his leadership, or implied she had a final say in matters was getting on his nerves. It also wasn't like her, at least not from what he'd seen. Maybe she was like this with his father, but she'd never been like this with him. She'd been favored, and his father listened to most of what she said above the others, but she wasn't quite like this when his father was in charge. It was good that whatever doubts she had about him weren't thoughts the rulers of their neighboring kingdom shared.

"On the contrary," Brine was saying, "we'd like to offer our assistance to you. We've already sent you soldiers, which we've learned now were not warranted, but that is not due to a fault on your behalf or ours. I would like to review your documents regarding your army and kingdom since the war began, and if I see any chance that our forces may be enough to put Deovaria back in its place, we will offer you the rest of our army to help overpower the Dragon Lord."

Keeping his expression neutral felt nearly impossible as Caeden took in Brine's words. Eryn cleared her throat beside him to cover up her own surprise, even as her raised eyebrows gave it away.

"I will arrange that immediately," Caeden told him with a nod. The hope he felt threatened to spill over into his voice.

Brine opened his mouth to respond, but Muire cut him off. "Your Majesty," she hissed, an edge to her tone that reminded Caeden of a parent scolding a young child. "Shouldn't this decision be brought to the attention of the court?" She said the words beneath her breath, as if somehow that would keep the two sitting across from them from hearing.

Eryn tossed the woman a glare before she seemed to remember they were in a meeting with another kingdom's rulers. She swallowed hard and plastered a look of indifference onto her face that Caeden struggled to keep on his own. Moira already noticed though, and was looking at Eryn with a raised eyebrow.

"I don't see a reason to involve the court," Caeden answered carefully.

He didn't want to explain in front of Crevia's rulers how weak Aericora was without their help, but Brine and Moira could've already guessed that given the arrangement that led to their daughter's death in the woods. Never mind that he would be giving them the documents that would provide them with the same information.

"We're losing this war—everyone can see that—and the aid they are offering would be more than enough to end the Dragon Lord's tyranny if we can hit them with that force all at once." He turned away from Muire and her stunned expression at his clipped words, and back to the king and queen. "I will get the documents for you to review myself, and have them to you by this evening. You are more than welcome to remain here while you look them over and either provide us with your decision while you're here, or once you've returned to Crevia."

Muire's gaze bore into the side of his head, but Caeden ignored her and kept his attention on the two sitting before him. He'd have to speak with her later once he decided how he wanted to deal with this situation.

There was no reason for her to question him in front of Crevia's rulers. The court would agree with him in a heartbeat, and his decision would be the final say either way. Still, her questioning him so openly was a bad look.

"Perfect," Brine said, moving to stand while his wife replaced her empty mug on the coffee table before doing the same.

Caeden followed their lead, straightening the front of his shirt as he did.

Moira offered him a smile with so much sadness hidden behind her eyes it almost made him stumble back a step. "Thank you for meeting with us so quickly. I can't imagine it's been easy transitioning with the way everything happened." She said the words gently, but the soothing effect she seemed to hope they had only wedged itself painfully into his chest.

Eryn laid a hand on his arm so gently he barely felt it through the fabric of his shirt. Moira raised an almost imperceptible eyebrow at the gesture, glancing between the two of them quickly before she turned her full attention back to Caeden.

He swallowed down the emotion threatening to build to an uncontrollable degree inside of him. "I can't imagine the past weeks have been any easier for you," he said, offering her a sympathetic smile matching the one she wore.

Moira nodded solemnly. "They've been far from easy," she agreed. She glanced at Muire who was in the process of straightening her floor-length dress and gave a slight frown before she turned back, the expression vanishing from her face. "You seem like a good king," she told him honestly, which surprised him since it wouldn't normally be entirely appropriate.

Brine cleared his throat uncomfortably, signaling his wife to stop talking in case she ran the risk of insulting someone, but Moira ignored him.

"You're still very young, and you'll face difficulties because of it, but you seem like you will do well by Aericora. You seem like a good man, and you seem to have the best interests of your kingdom at heart." There was something strangely motherly about her tone, and if not for the oddly comforting feeling they managed to lay over him, he would've found them strange.

Caeden nodded in response, unsure what he could say. "Thank you," he told her. "It was very nice meeting both of you."

Eryn nodded beside him.

"You as well," Brine and Moira said at the same time.

Caeden moved to open the door for the two royals to pass through, and everyone in the room exchanged quick goodbyes before they disappeared into the hallway.

Chapter 45

Caeden massaged his temples as he stared blankly at the untouched pile of papers he'd gathered an hour ago. He had yet to begin flipping through them since finding each of the labeled boxes he'd wanted and setting them into a stack.

So far, he'd spent his day since breakfast poring over documents for Brine and Moira to review. Nothing he'd found looked helpful to his kingdom's cause, considering they were running low enough in both funds and military that the King and Queen of Crevia might opt to simply stay out of it and hope the Dragon Lord would be satisfied once he won the war against Aericora. They didn't know about the stones though, and Caeden wasn't sure if he was willing to share that secret outside of those in his kingdom who already knew. Only the court along with the generals and those they assigned to be on the lookout for the gems knew what they could do, and he wanted to keep it that way.

His uncle had already hurt the dragons, and he didn't want to give anyone else ideas about doing the same. Moira and Brine didn't seem like the type to do what his uncle had, but he also didn't know them, and he wouldn't gamble with the lives of the dragons if he could avoid it.

An overly optimistic part of him hoped that once the war was over, if Aericora won against Deovaria, his sister would be safe, his kingdom would be flourishing, and the dragons could be freed from human control once and for all.

If it truly came down to it and Brine and Moira decided against helping his kingdom with only the information he'd selected to give them, then he would come clean about his worries and explain their plans to collect and use the stones to their advantage. But he hoped it wouldn't come to that.

After collecting the documentation earlier in the day, he sent Fionn to hand it off to the king and queen. Neither gave any indication whether they would review the documents and provide Aericora with an answer before they returned home though, and that only intensified Caeden's endless pool of anxiety.

Finally, after spending a few more quiet seconds staring at the worn edges of the pages in front of him, Caeden straightened and lifted the top sheet. After everything happened with his father's death, he hadn't taken the time to look into the one thing he'd been meaning to when he returned; he needed to know whether the town leaders had been telling the truth, and whether his father and the court had taken care of their people like he thought they had.

He would have to find the documents specifically from Dalelry, but he would need to separate those from the rest as he made his way through the stack.

He read over the first parchment. It was a letter from a town near the border, requesting more medical supplies. The letter dated back eight years, only a few short years after the war first started. The letter was stamped with his father's crest and signed with the same signature he'd seen his father write on more documents than he could count.

The next was a receipt of his father's response, also dated, signed, and stamped by his father. The one after that was the acceptance letter from the town, informing the king and the court that the supplies had been received.

The documents in the pile continued in that fashion, with an occasional correspondence originating with a letter from the castle asking if there was any additional assistance they required.

He was halfway through the pile, and the doubts he'd had slowly subsided the further he got. He wasn't sure what he'd dreaded finding, but it seemed like the town's leaders had lied. There was no good reason he could surmise for why they would lie so blatantly, but the letters he found suggested that every request from every town, including the ones from Dalelry he'd come across so far, had been met with a response stamped and signed by his father, and received gratefully.

Until he found one that hadn't been stamped at all.

It was a request for aid from a station just outside of a town Deovaria overtook a few months ago. They'd needed soldiers and more weapons, but their request had been ignored. His father hadn't stamped or signed this letter, and there was no receipt of a response ever being sent.

Caeden's chest tightened as he read the letter over again, then turned it over to make sure it hadn't simply been stamped incorrectly somehow. There was nothing. No sign at all that it ever made it to his father's hand, despite being in a pile of his letters.

His father got hundreds of letters a week since the beginning of the war, though. It wouldn't be surprising if he found a few more that were missed, though the thought made an uneasy feeling settle into the pit of his stomach.

His father wouldn't have let something like this slip through the cracks. So, how had he managed to miss a letter that resulted in Deovaria claiming a large chunk of their land?

Caeden shook his head. It was unlikely his father missed something like this, but it wasn't impossible.

He pushed the doubts aside and set the letter in a separate pile, away from the one he'd started beside his original stack. Then he continued riffling through the papers, the weight of the lingering doubt pressing heavily against his chest.

He found another letter from Dalelry after that. It dated back four years, and it was signed and dated by his father. They'd requested gold and supplies, and his father had sent it out the following day.

A knock came on the door to the office, and Caeden jumped.

"Your Majesty?" Muire's voice asked as she slowly opened the door and peeked inside.

Caeden set the letter down in a separate stack before he glanced up, doing his best to keep the wave of emotions he felt from showing on his face. "Yes?"

She glanced at the stack of papers in front of him before she turned her attention back to him. "It's late," she commented. "And no one has seen you for dinner. I figured I'd bring you something to eat." She opened the door wider and produced a covered tray that had likely been waiting for him for hours.

Confusion bubbled inside of him. It was odd that she'd bring the food herself rather than send a servant to do it for her, but he shook his head to clear the thought away. This was probably an attempt to make up for how she'd acted earlier during their meeting with Brine and Moira, which was enough to lift a little of the weight off his shoulders. If she was trying to make up for it, then he wouldn't have to figure out how to confront her.

"Thank you," he told her.

She nodded and came into the room before she placed the tray down on the edge of his desk. Her eyes flicked to the stack of papers again. Black soot hid beneath her nails still from the attack that took place the previous day. "Is there anything else I can assist you with?" she asked.

Caeden shook his head. "Not tonight."

She nodded again before she turned and left the room. The soft thud of the door closing felt like a relief with the stack of papers still looming in front of him. He glanced at the tray of food, but he couldn't convince himself to eat before he finished going through the papers. It would be there in another hour when he finished, and it was already long past cold, anyway.

He riffled through the stack again. He hoped that would be the only instance of a missed letter, but it didn't take long for that hope to dwindle.

Twenty more papers sat stacked on top of one another before he found another letter lacking his father's signature or stamp.

The weight on his chest grew heavier as he stared down at it.

This one was dated from later in the war, which was odd, given that the stack was ordered by date and he should've been looking through things from earlier, not only two years ago. Everything else was dated back around four years.

Again, this letter asked for supplies to be sent to a specific location in the field, and it had been ignored. Deovaria hadn't overtaken this town, but they had burned half of it to the ground and cost Aericora hundreds of soldiers.

Caeden set the letter aside with the first one, and forced himself to ignore the dread welling inside. That would be the last one. If he didn't find any more, he could attribute it to his father being busy and missing it.

If he found another, though…

He shook his head. He wouldn't consider that yet. He wouldn't consider that the rulers he'd worked beside for most of his life, the father he'd trusted was doing everything in his power to ensure every single one of their people was well cared for, had opted to simply ignore pleas for help from their dying people.

But that wasn't the last of the strange, unmarked letters in the pile.

He found two more before he made it halfway through what remained in front of him, but even as his hope shattered, those letters weren't the ones to catch his attention like the third and final one he laid eyes on.

This one was another request for assistance, this time for nothing more than gold from Dalelry so they could distribute it to their people and help those who couldn't fight move away from the battlefield's lines that were growing closer to their town. His father signed and stamped the letter, and had written a formal request for nine thousand gold to be sent to the town.

None of that caught his attention, though.

It was the letter after the request that caught his eye.

This one was a different sort of request, also stamped with his father's crest, but the signature looked wrong. The angles weren't sharp enough, and the little swirl his father did at the end of his name went entirely too far.

The letter requested a reroute of the money to an address in a town on the other side of Aericora.

The request was met with a response stating the money was already delivered to its original destination and asked for further clarification, and they were told to send another nine thousand to the other town. It was also stamped with his father's crest, but with the same false signature.

Bile rose in the back of Caeden's throat as he stared at the strange signature scrawled onto the parchment. He knew his father's signature better than he did his own. It was identical on every paper his father ever signed. This one was very close, but those minor details caused the same level of dread he'd only ever felt when he was on Aubry's back and saw the billowing smoke and lapping flames consuming his home to well inside of him.

He looked into Dalelry's correspondence more after that, and what he found only made it so much worse.

Each time they made any request over the past two years, it was only for gold, and each time, it was rerouted to the same town on the other end of Aericora. It had only ever made it to Dalelry twice. But those two shipments *had* arrived, and one of them was received only a few months ago. Which wasn't what the town leaders had told him. They'd said they hadn't received anything from Aericora in years. They'd also claimed Aericora wasn't answering them, but the castle never received a letter from them saying the shipments weren't delivered. Shipments were always rerouted without any further correspondence from the town leaders in Dalelry.

After another few hours, he found that two other towns had similar correspondence. They would request gold, the castle would send it, it would be rerouted to the same town on the opposite end of Aericora without any record of the original town being notified of the change or having requested it, and that would be the end of the transaction.

The king's crest was stamped onto each piece of paper, but he knew beyond any doubt that his father wasn't the person to sign the requests.

Someone else in the castle did that.

And the town leaders must have worked with them to do so, or they would've contacted the castle to let them know they never received the gold. The only benefit for the town leaders would be if whoever was in the castle rerouting the money was paying them off, but he couldn't find any record of that. Not that he expected to.

Whoever was rerouting money and hiding the requests for aid likely wasn't another one of Deovaria's spies, considering the address they'd sent the gold to. But someone inside of Aericora's castle walls was making moves against their own kingdom that had resulted in the deaths of thousands of Aericora's people.

Caeden sighed and sat back further in his chair. He pushed the papers aside and pulled the tray of food closer. It was entirely cold now, but after the added hours of searching through the papers, he didn't care with the hunger gnawing at him from the inside out.

His head spun from the unanswered questions, and he massaged his temples, attempting to keep the headache pounding between his ears at bay before he pulled a forkful of the food to his lips.

Someone had been redirecting money and hiding requests for aid from his father for years.

Someone had been inadvertently helping the Dragon Lord get closer to winning the war.

Caeden's eyes widened, and he spat the food from his mouth, his heart pounding.

That flavor.

He recognized that flavor.

The realization crashed into him with so much force he lost his grip on the fork and it clattered noisily against the desk beside the plate of poisoned food.

Chapter 46

Eryn

The entrance to the stable loomed in front of her as Eryn stepped closer. Her heart thudded at the idea of visiting Aubry alone, but she forced away the fear as she stepped inside and walked through the space to the back door leading to Aubry's small setup behind the stable. The dragon hadn't done anything to harm a single person in the time she'd been at the castle, or even when they were in the mountains. She wouldn't hurt her now.

The large blue dragon sat curled into a tight ball on the ground when Eryn exited the stable and entered Aubry's makeshift one. Her large orange eyes snapped open at the sound of Eryn approaching, and she shifted out of her comfortable ball so she could look at the Dragon Hunter.

Eryn stiffened, and she stopped a few yards away.

Aubry seemed to smile—if you could call it that—and she huffed out what Eryn could only assume was an amused snort.

If I wanted to hurt you, I would've a long time ago.

Eryn's shoulders relaxed, but her fingers still twitched

uncomfortably near the hilts of her daggers. "Did you recognize me, too?" she asked, having to force the words out past the wave of fear the possible answers to the question caused. "Is that why you followed me around on the way back from the field even though Ronan was the one who had the stone?"

Aubry lifted her head off the ground and eyed her curiously.

Was it possible the dragons had come to collect her in the mountains all those years ago after all? But if that were the case, why hadn't they killed her then and there? Their kind were already being tortured.

I was a child, just like you back then, Aubry told her, which wasn't an answer to Eryn's question, but she let the dragon speak into her mind without interrupting. *Xalrum told me to stay near the nest, but I smelled a human—you—and I ventured down the side of the mountain out of sheer curiosity. You were unconscious and didn't hear me. You were alone without even a lit fire to keep you warm, and you were shivering. I knew the fire had been lit earlier in the day from the burnt wood that remained, but it was out, and your parents' footsteps were already partly covered by the snow. I liked you, even before I knew anything about you. I tried to wake you, but you wouldn't budge. Even when I tried dousing you with water, you only shivered and remained asleep. Xalrum was so angry with me when he caught me lighting the fire for you, but I couldn't leave you alone to freeze after all of that. When we watched you wake up the next morning and slowly stumble your way down the side of the mountain after you realized you were left alone, he saw what I'd seen in you. You were a fighter, even as a young child asleep in a blanket. Anyone else would've frozen to death in the cold, but you were still alive. Even in such a deep sleep that you wouldn't wake, you clung to life.*

Eryn stood frozen.

No words could describe the emotions clouding her head after hearing that. Aubry was there that day. She'd found Eryn alone on the side of the mountain and likely saved her life. If

Aubry hadn't lit the fire for her, she would have frozen to death before anyone found her.

She'd spent her life afraid of dragons, killing them in a war they had no part in. They were only involved because the Dragon Lord learned to harness their magical abilities and imprisoned them.

But that wasn't what they were.

It wasn't what Aubry—the dragon standing a mere thirty feet in front of her—was.

She was kind, and something about that realization filled her with a wave of nausea for all of the things she'd done to dragons just like Aubry.

Eryn swallowed down the lump of bile in the back of her throat. She wanted to apologize, to say something to undo everything this war caused, but no good would come from her words. It wouldn't change what she'd done, or wash away the blood that would forever stain her hands crimson.

So, instead, she didn't say anything in response at all, and asked her the question she'd truly wanted to when she first stepped out into the cool night air. "Did the damage to the castle look like it was done by dragons?"

No one else within the castle walls would know the answer to her question. Ronan would've been suspicious of the attack too, but not in the same way she was. And no one else here was as familiar with dragon attacks as she was, either.

To Eryn, it didn't look like the damage came from a dragon at all, but she'd been wrong before. She knew better than to make an accusation like that without having proof, or at least someone who agreed with her.

And the only one she could ask who might know the true answer was Aubry.

The slight smile Aubry had on her face since Eryn first asked about Xalrum quickly faded. Something in her expression hardened, and her body went as rigid as Eryn's had when she first came out of the stable.

No.

The single-word answer sent a shiver down Eryn's spine.

There was nothing but certainty in Aubry's eyes, and she didn't turn her gaze away from Eryn's, as if the prolonged eye contact would somehow will the Dragon Hunter to believe her.

Eryn swallowed hard. "What do you think caused the destruction?"

Aubry fixed her with a look that reminded her of the expression she felt on her own face when someone asked a question she had to fight to avoid rolling her eyes at.

I think you already know the answer to that question.

"You're gonna be a queen one day," Ronan teased, cocking an eyebrow at her suggestively. His tone wasn't as lighthearted as she was used to when he'd said similar things to her in the past, but compared to his demeanor over the past few weeks, this was an improvement.

Eryn's face heated against her will. She swirled the tequila in her glass to distract herself from the bubble of nerves those words brought to the surface. She would do whatever was required of her if it meant she got to spend her life with Caeden. She would give her life for him. She would scale the Rayfait Mountains with nothing but the clothes on her back if she needed to. Being a queen one day was something she could handle.

"Maybe," she said, pulling her glass to her lips and savoring the taste of the bitter liquid on her tongue. She shouldn't have liked the taste of it as much as she did. She'd always had a weakness for it. Despite the work she'd put into ensuring she didn't fall down the same path Ronan had when they were younger, she still craved it every once in a while.

After her conversation with Caeden the night before, she was surprised she had managed to go a whole day without a drink to calm her nerves. The calm sense of bliss she felt every time she thought about the look on his face when she told him she would do anything to be with him wasn't something she'd wanted the alcohol to dull, though. It was the only reason she got through the day without a drink.

But the doubts had started again, as they always did, along with the stress of everything else that was going on in the world around them. The war still raged. The king was dead. They'd only retrieved a few stones from the mountains and they would hardly make a difference in the field. The king and queen from Crevia might send their soldiers, and if they did, that was enough to at least prolong the war like it had been last time, unless Aericora could organize a hard and fast attack against Deovaria, but that relied on the king and queen's interpretation of the paperwork they would review. Eryn hadn't laid eyes on the documents herself, but she doubted their chances were greater than fifty-fifty, and she refused to hope for something as monumental as the end of the war to come from such a simple decision.

Was this how easily their leaders made these choices? Was this normal for them? There was so much weight behind the decision Crevia would make; their own people would die, but it would surely mean the end of the war between Aericora and Deovaria if they chose to send their army, which would protect them from ending up in a war with Deovaria all on their own if Deovaria won against Aericora.

Eryn took another long drink from her glass.

Ronan watched her with an expression she couldn't place through her hazy thoughts when she pulled the glass away again. She contemplated refilling it, given that the mostly full bottle sat only a few feet in front of her on the coffee table, but thought better of it and set her glass down instead.

"You're his first, ya know," Ronan said suddenly, pulling her from the thoughts threatening to swallow her. She couldn't place his expression before, but with the alcohol in her system, she was sure the mask she attempted to wear had fallen away, and he'd read her as clearly as words on a page.

Eryn frowned before she remembered the conversation they'd had before she'd gotten lost in her head. Her face heated again, and she couldn't bring herself to meet his gaze. "I'm not," she told him.

She may have been, had things gone differently that night three years ago.

She'd been at the castle for a month of training, the last she needed to finally become a Dragon Hunter, when Ronan was on his mission in Deovaria. She hadn't known yet that the Dragon Lord had taken him and was holding him prisoner, torturing him for information.

Parties were held with royals from other kingdoms while she was at the castle, and she and the other trainees were invited to a masquerade ball the night the royals first arrived, only about a week before she and the other soldiers would be sent back to the field.

She didn't know for sure, but she assumed they were only invited to that party so none of the invited royals would stick up their noses at such low-ranking soldiers joining them. Still, it was an attempt at a thank you from the king for their service in the war.

Eryn hadn't asked Caeden if he remembered their conversation from that night, and she wasn't entirely sure she wanted to. It felt like a closely guarded secret, and she strangely liked it.

Their conversation that night was nice. She hadn't had many assumptions about him back then, and she'd started to think he was truly a nice man at heart. Their conversation was interrupted though, and despite him saying he would return, it rubbed her the wrong way when she saw him sneak out with another woman a few minutes later. She thought of him as nothing more than a spoiled royal after that, but he'd proven her wrong since then.

Ronan raised a curious eyebrow at her. "Whatcha mean?" he asked, taking a sip from the cup of whiskey in his hand. He stood at the kitchen counter, and it surprised her each time she glanced at him and realized that he wasn't leaning his weight against it or against his cane.

Eryn shrugged, weighing whether she wanted to divulge the information, before she eventually decided to explain.

Ronan grinned at her with what could've possibly been the widest smirk she'd ever seen on his face when she finished, and she worried it might split his face in two. "You know better than to assume things like that 'bout people, Reckless," he told her with a laugh.

She raised an eyebrow at him. "Do I?" she challenged. "Every example I've ever had of people sneaking out always led to one thing." She gave him a pointed look that made him laugh again.

"Ya know, that's fair. But that wasn't what happened that night. He'd bargained with her for some of her old trainin' manuals, and not in the way ya think. He arranged for her family to come to the party so she could see 'em. The party was the only good distraction to sneak 'em in and the only time she wasn't gonna be too busy to visit with them."

She hadn't expected to hear that.

Eryn relaxed into the couch, though she wasn't sure why that fact had such an effect on her. It hadn't bothered her before to think he'd been with someone else, or even multiple someones. "That sounds like him," Eryn said, hoping Ronan didn't notice the strange lightness she felt at his words.

She hadn't been with anyone else either, though that conversation hadn't come up and she didn't particularly care whether it ever did.

A knock came on the door to Ronan's shack, and they turned to face the sound as Caeden opened the door without waiting for a response. He offered them a half-hearted smile as he stepped inside before he closed the door behind himself.

His hair was a mess on his head, and he looked pale. The bags under his eyes had grown since earlier in the day, and the slump to his shoulders that wasn't usually there made her heart ache.

"Ya look like shit," Ronan commented.

Caeden shrugged, but the usual amused quirk of his mouth when Ronan said things like that wasn't there. Eryn frowned as he came into the living room and sat on the couch beside her. She wove her fingers through his, and he gave her hand a gentle squeeze in return. There was definitely something on his mind with the faraway look in his gaze, but she didn't attempt to broach the subject just yet.

The clammy feeling of his hand against hers worried her enough that she wouldn't be able to keep from asking for long, though.

"Need a drink?" Ronan asked. He already had a bottle of whiskey in his hand with the lid off, and was pulling a glass from the cabinet above the sink.

A smile touched Eryn's face when the corner of Caeden's mouth lifted.

"Yes," Caeden answered. "Or three."

"A'right, ya drunk," Ronan joked, a smirk on his face as he poured Caeden a glassful of whiskey.

Eryn snorted a laugh despite herself. "Like you can talk."

"I'll have ya know, I didn't have a single drink since we saved him from his psychotic uncle till last night, thank you very much."

Eryn rolled her eyes at him, doing her best to push down the sadness at the implications hidden behind his words. She didn't want to think about how upset Ronan had been for the past several weeks, or the things that had caused him to slip into such a deep state of depression that even his favorite crutch hadn't helped.

He'd had moments before when drinking only made his depression worse, but those moments were rare. Those moments were the only thing that stopped him from finishing bottle after bottle of whiskey since his injury.

He seemed better tonight though, and she hoped beyond anything else that maybe something had changed and things would be better from here on out, even if she didn't know what caused it.

Ronan came into the living room and handed Caeden the glass. Caeden took it with a confused look on his face, likely wondering like Eryn was what caused the shift in Ronan's demeanor. Unlike Eryn, he chose to question him about it.

"What happened?" Caeden asked, his tone cautious despite the bluntness of his words.

Ronan's eyes widened, and the blush hiding in his cheeks from the alcohol darkened, spreading down his neck and to the tips of his ears. He refused to meet either of their gazes as he turned and walked back to the kitchen.

Fuck.

Eryn sat bolt upright on the couch, her gaze pinned to the back of Ronan's head. She hoped he could feel the daggers she threw his way, yelling at him inside of his own head in the manner Aubry spoke to them about what an absolute idiot he was. "You didn't."

Caeden glanced between the two of them, confusion still written across his face.

Ronan's throat bobbed, but he made no move to respond. That single action was all the confirmation Eryn needed, though.

"You fucking…" Eryn ran her hand across her face, anger and confusion and a thousand other emotions flaring through her at once. "I don't have words for you right now."

Ronan sighed and poured himself another glass of whiskey. He stayed silent while he downed the glass. Eryn stared at him, waiting for an answer, and Caeden kept quiet and leaned back against the couch, waiting for the same thing.

"I…" Ronan paused, his face darkening to a shade of red Eryn didn't know was possible. "I still love her, even after everythin'," he admitted, his voice so quiet she hardly heard him.

Caeden's eyes went wide, and he visibly fought to keep his jaw from falling slack. "Dealla? You went to see Dealla?" The same bewilderment Eryn felt flashed across his face as he ran a hand through his hair. "Ronan, she tortured you. Then came here and used you to get information to destroy our kingdom. She lied to all of us about everything."

He hadn't said the words harshly, but Ronan still flinched. "It wasn't all a lie," Ronan said softly, still not looking at either of them.

Eryn wanted to scoff at that, but she kept her irritation at bay. What had that woman done to him to make him so blind? How could he say he still loved her when he'd never known the real her, only a fantasy woman who'd worn an entirely different face?

"She was a spy," Eryn told him gently. "The whole reason she was here was a lie."

Hurt flashed across Ronan's face, and he pressed his lips together before he shook his head slowly. "She lied 'bout a lot, I'm not sayin' she didn't." He took a deep breath and finally looked up at her, meeting her gaze with an unflinching determination that would've made her stumble back a step had she been on her feet. "But her feelings were real. I know ya don't trust her after everythin' she did, and I'm not sayin' I trust her not to do everythin' in her power to help her father destroy Aericora if she's let out of that cell. She just… she wants to do the right thing; she's just been tricked into believin' the Dragon Lord's side ain't the evil we all know it is."

"She still put Caeden in that cell," Eryn reminded him. "And tortured you when they were trying to get information from you."

"Not because she wanted to," Ronan whispered. He sounded so broken in that moment that tears nearly sprang to Eryn's eyes. "I know neither of ya are gonna believe me, but I saw the real her. I *know* the real her. She's not on our side and she's fightin' for a man she doesn't believe is evil, but she's good at heart, and her heart is what I fell in love with. Every broken, hurt, and twisted piece of it."

Caeden sighed and sank deeper into the couch, the weight of those words causing his shoulders to slump even more than whatever was already going on.

Eryn only stared at Ronan. Words refused to form on her tongue, despite the hundreds of things she wanted to say to him.

She couldn't argue with him, though. He wouldn't see the truth if she attacked him, and she hadn't seen their relationship behind closed doors. Maybe Dealla really had shared real parts of herself, but there was no way anyone could know that for sure. Maybe she was far better at being a spy than Ronan gave her credit for. She had been the one picked for the job, even if she said a large reason for it was because of the illusion magic and how it worked for her without the aid of any extra stones.

"I don't think you're wrong," Caeden said, surprising Eryn and making her contemplate smacking him across the face to shut him up. "She's scared of disappointing her father. All she wants is his approval. I can't say I know whether she truly wants to be good, but if you're right about that, I think that's what's keeping her blind to everything he's done. He's still her father, and anyone would want to be able to see the best in their parents."

There was so much weight behind those words that Eryn's heart clenched painfully. She squeezed his hand again.

She hadn't had a real conversation with the woman until after her true identity was revealed. While there were certainly aspects of her that both Caeden and Ronan could relate to, Eryn didn't share their blind spots when it came to the situation.

Maybe Dealla really had loved Ronan. She couldn't entirely deny that after she'd saved him from falling off the dragon's back, but that didn't mean she wouldn't use him or hurt him to help her father get what he wanted. Even if she did have a good heart like Ronan believed, that didn't mean she wasn't as brainwashed as every other Deovarian.

The three of them lapsed into silence. Ronan set his glass back down on the counter, the quiet ping of the glass hitting the granite deafening in Eryn's ears.

"What happened to you?" Ronan asked, directing his

attention to Caeden, who stared at the wall ahead with a faraway look in his eyes. He was paler now than when he first entered the shack, and he'd hardly taken a sip from his glass.

Caeden shook himself and looked down at the whiskey in his hand. He sighed. "I found something when I was going through the documents earlier," he told them. "Muire's been redirecting shipments of gold to an address on the other end of Aericora, and hiding other requests for supplies from my father so the shipments never got sent." He let out a light, disbelieving laugh and shook his head. "And she just tried to poison me."

Chapter 47

Fire lit Eryn's eyes when the words fell from Caeden's lips, and Ronan stepped away from the counter and into the living room. He sat on the edge of the coffee table with a confused look on his face.

Caeden glanced between the two of them before he drank more of the whiskey. It turned his stomach in a bad way with the poison he'd consumed earlier, but he didn't want to be sober right now. Part of him hoped it would dull his mind enough that the betrayal wouldn't sting as much.

"I'll kill her," Eryn practically growled. The fire and the fierceness in her eyes made him smile. Something about that look always made him fall a little more in love with her.

"What?" Ronan asked, nothing but pure disbelief in his tone.

Eryn's fingers tightened around the hilt of her dagger while Caeden tried to piece together a response that would make sense. The same sickness that claimed his father for a day when he was dosed with Muire's poison years ago had made Caeden weak, but he'd continued his search through his father's documents. There were so many more documents rerouting money that he'd lost count of the number he'd found. They were hidden in random boxes with letters that weren't even remotely related.

Muire's meddling had picked up considerably over the past couple of years.

Along with everything else, he'd also found hidden letters from the field requesting supplies, which was likely the main source of their struggles to communicate effectively with those fighting on the battlefield. Even with the assassins in the woods, they never could've been capable of doing the kind of damage Muire had done from within the castle walls.

When he got his thoughts together, Caeden relayed the information he uncovered to both Ronan and Eryn.

"Aubry and I talked earlier," Eryn said slowly, her anger still burning just as bright behind her eyes. The sudden topic change caught Caeden by surprise. "The attack didn't look like it was caused by dragons. I went to ask Aubry for her opinion since not many other soldiers here are familiar with dragons and what their abilities look like. She agreed that the damage looked different."

"What does that have to do with Muire?" Ronan asked, a frown making a crease form between his eyebrows.

"It was bombed," Eryn stated. "But the bombs didn't look like they were dropped. The damage looks like they were placed inside of the castle. Especially since they only blew up where the king was supposed to meet Crevia's rulers." She paused just long enough to let her words sink in before she continued. "Muire bombed the castle from the inside out. She killed your father, and now she's trying to kill you."

Caeden's head spun, the information making the headache pounding between his ears ten times worse than the poison already had.

"Dealla knew," Ronan whispered, so softly Caeden hardly heard him. He glanced up, his gaze falling on Eryn. "Muire was a spy."

Caeden shook his head, clearing away the fog from the headache as the confusion registered. "What do you mean? How would that be possible? We would've noticed if Deovaria replaced her."

Understanding lit Eryn's entire expression. "She was never disguised," she explained, despite the question being directed at Ronan. "She was here before the war. The Dragon Lord wanted your mother's ring long before the war started. He would've sent someone to try to retrieve it before starting a whole war over it. But that person would need to get close to the king and queen, so she had to become a member of the court."

"But after the war started, she already held the highest seat in the court beneath you and your father," Ronan added. "Dealla muttered something about her being a traitor when we got back. She was biding her time, waitin' for an opportunity for you and your father to be killed."

Eryn nodded. "She stopped giving the Dragon Lord any useful information and started rerouting shipments. Since she held so much power in the court, she would be the next logical ruler if anything happened to you and your father, especially since she already had the town leaders on her side. And with all of the money she rerouted at her disposal, she would look like a savior in the eyes of the people, and she would've been willing to negotiate something with the Dragon Lord, since he probably still doesn't hate her as much as he hated your father."

It made a lot of sense, even if it didn't answer the question of why Muire stopped helping the Dragon Lord before the war started. But if she was truly that power hungry, that could've simply been because she held more power by sitting on

Aericora's court than she did back in her own kingdom as a spy.

"She didn't argue when you wanted to go to the field," Eryn said, gesturing at Caeden with a hand. "She didn't outright agree, because that would look suspicious, but she didn't argue. You came back alive from that, but when we planned to go to the Rayfait Mountains, the chances of us surviving against all of those dragons were even lower. She probably thought at least a couple of us would die, especially since we took Dealla with. So, she planned to kill the king while we were gone. She wanted to wait to see what the Dragon Lord would do when we offered him Dealla because that would've taken the dirty work out of her hands. He didn't do anything crazy like attack the castle again though, so she resorted to doing it on her own. She already knew what not to do since she tried to poison your father last time, so how hard could it be to do it right this time?"

A sick feeling that had nothing to do with the poison running through his veins rose in Caeden's stomach. When she'd failed to poison his father the first time, she'd resorted to sabotaging them from the inside. She'd bided her time, hoarded tons and tons of their gold, so when the opportunity arose and the king and Caeden were killed, she could take over as Aericora's ruler.

Suddenly, all of Muire's inappropriate comments and undermining made perfect sense. He'd assumed it was because she thought he wasn't ready to rule, but it was because she'd waited years to steal his throne.

"But we did come back," Caeden said softly. A shudder ran through him when he said the words.

Eryn clenched her jaw and balled her free hand into a tight fist on top of her thigh that turned her knuckles a stark shade of white.

It was silent for multiple long moments. They glanced at one another, sharing a weighted look as yet another boulder of weight placed itself onto their shoulders.

"She's gonna try to kill you again," Ronan said softly. He said the words quietly, but they still echoed throughout the room. "Poison doesn't always have an effect on everyone who's dosed. She's gonna assume it just didn't work and she's gonna try again with somethin' else."

Caeden flinched despite himself. "I need more alcohol."

Eryn didn't say anything as she stood and took his glass from him, planting a quick kiss against his cheek before she disappeared into the kitchen.

"So," Ronan prompted, leaning uneasily back on his hands against the coffee table. "What are we gonna do 'bout… all of that?"

Caeden sighed. He wanted to sink so far into the couch that he could never come back, even if he tried. This was too much. He'd never expected being king to be easy, but he'd never thought too much about it. In his mind, until the war was won, things weren't going to change, and that included that his father would continue being the ruler of Aericora.

He slumped forward with his elbows against his knees and his face buried in his hands. "He's really gone," he whispered, all other thoughts falling away but of his father lying motionless with unseeing eyes on the blood-covered cot.

"He is," Ronan said softly, as if saying those words would cause a knife to strike him through the heart.

Tears welled in Caeden's eyes before he could even attempt to keep them at bay. He didn't want to cry anymore. Too many things needed to get done. A war still raged, and at this point, whether they won felt like it hinged on Crevia's decision to involve themselves or not. One of his advisors was trying to kill him. And on top of those things, the one person who may have known how to handle it—his father—was dead.

He wasn't even killed by the Dragon Lord. He was killed by a woman he'd trusted for years.

"How did all of this happen?" Despite the lump lodged in the back of his throat, his words came out steady.

"I wish I had an answer for ya," Ronan told him at the same time that Eryn returned to the couch and placed a hand on Caeden's back.

She had two glasses with her, one with water and one with more whiskey. She offered him the latter first, and he took it from her gratefully before he pulled it to his lips and drank half the glass, ignoring the way it turned his stomach.

"We're here for you, you know," Eryn said, as her hand trailed up to rest against his cheek.

Caeden leaned into her touch and let out a breath.

"Always gonna be, princy," Ronan agreed.

Despite everything, Caeden couldn't help the light laugh that escaped him at Ronan's use of what had been his nickname for years.

"Not very fittin' anymore, is it?" Ronan asked with a chuckle.

"Yeah, but please don't go and change it to 'king-y' or something," Eryn said, wrinkling her nose through the smile hiding in the corners of her mouth.

Ronan grinned with the same twinkle of mischief hiding in his eyes that Caeden hadn't seen from him in weeks. He wiggled his eyebrows teasingly.

Caeden snorted. "Don't even think about it."

Ronan rolled his eyes. "Y'all ain't any fun," he said, waving a hand at them dismissively. He stood and returned to the kitchen to get himself another glass of the amber liquid he'd already finished.

Caeden didn't love the idea of him talking with Dealla, but he couldn't deny that it had done Ronan some good. Whatever their conversation was, it had lifted the shroud of anger and depression he'd had for weeks. Caeden didn't see how it could end any way but badly, but for the moment, he was glad to see his friend somewhat back to normal.

Chapter 48

Caeden, Eryn, and Ronan met with the court, excluding Muire, the following morning. It took some convincing before they believed their claims about what Muire had done. The first argument was that anyone could've laced Caeden's food with poison, but the arguments died quickly when they paired the fact that Muire had brought the food to him with how no one else would've so easily been able to get their hands on his father's stamp to sign the letters. The day ended with Muire escorted down to the dungeon in handcuffs.

Dealla wasn't happy that she would have company from now on, but Caeden couldn't have made himself care how she felt even if he tried.

Over the few days that followed, they focused on uncovering everything Muire had done, and attempted to undo as much of it as possible. Caeden discovered more recent hidden letters requesting assistance from the castle, and made sure the supplies they asked for were sent out immediately. He hoped everything would reach its intended destination on time.

They sent a few trusted advisors who weren't typically

involved in court meetings to the three towns Muire was working with to embezzle the gold. For the time being, they wouldn't investigate too far into each individual town's leaders until they could fix everything at the castle from Muire's meddling, but with the advisors there to look over requests they wouldn't be able to continue moving money around.

The court gathered a few soldiers, and they were sent to the address Muire was rerouting the shipments to. It would be at least a week before the soldiers returned. There was no way of knowing yet if the gold was still there, but even if they could recover a fraction of what Muire had sent, it would help the towns near the border considerably.

In addition to everything they'd worked on since learning what Muire had done, the construction to rebuild the parts of the castle she'd destroyed was underway. It would be weeks, if not longer, before they fully repaired the destruction she caused, especially since good construction workers were harder and harder to find the longer the war went on.

Brine and Moira left to return home, and promised to inform them whether they would be allying themselves with Aericora officially and joining in the fight to defeat Deovaria once they spoke to their own advisors.

The matter of his father's funeral was also on the minds of most of the court. They agreed to a small, quiet ceremony, and with everything else going on, Eryn offered to get the details sorted out while Caeden focused on undoing Muire's damage.

The ceremony was held three days after Muire was imprisoned. It was a quick event that took less time from Caeden's day than dinner with the princesses had when he'd been in the process of deciding which to marry. His father would have wanted it that way, though. He hadn't wanted a large event, and there was no point in turning it into one.

"You okay?" Eryn asked late that night after they'd returned from the funeral and had climbed into bed. Her head rested against his chest, and she propped herself up on an elbow to peer down at him. The thick darkness surrounding them was more than enough to prevent her from being able to make out his expression.

Caeden nodded. "Thank you for arranging it," he told her. "He would've loved it if he could've seen it."

He could just make out the corners of her lips rising in the darkness. "I'm glad." She lay back beside him. "It wasn't as difficult as I expected," she whispered. "I'm not sure what I expected, but it went smoothly."

A smile pulled at the corners of his lips. She may not have wanted to rule a kingdom, but he had no doubt she would make an amazing queen for Aericora.

He leaned over to press a kiss to her forehead, but she lifted her head so that his lips fell against hers instead.

His heart swelled when his lips met hers. He kissed her deeply, wrapping his arms around her to pull her closer. He pulled away just enough to leave a trail of kisses along her cheek and jaw before he moved to her throat, breathing in the scent of her as she let out a heavy sigh and relaxed into him.

He held her tight, burying his face against her neck and relishing in the feel of her in his arms. There was nothing he wouldn't give to stay in this moment with her for the rest of his life. This perfect, beautiful woman was everything he could ever need.

"Caeden." Eryn's voice was an alarmed whisper as she shook his shoulder to wake him.

Fear crashed into him as memories of the night Dealla woke him only to kidnap him and lock him into a dark cell replayed as vividly in his head as when he'd lived through it.

Frantic knocking echoed throughout the room, but through his fear, he hardly registered it.

"I'm right here," Eryn told him gently, placing her hand against his cheek so he would look at her. Fear hid behind her eyes as the knocking continued, but the fierce determination he saw on her face every time they were faced with a challenge comforted him.

It took a moment for the real world to settle in around him. The feel of the bed beneath him, the warmth of Eryn's hand against his cheek, the scent of lavender, the darkness surrounding them, and the continued pounding of someone's fist against their bedroom door.

He nodded slowly, pushing back the fear as the knocking intensified.

"Your Majesty!" a terrified, breathy voice called from outside before they knocked on the door again.

Caeden pulled himself fully from the trance he was in and slung his legs over the side of the bed. "What is it?" he called as he hurried to the dresser to find a pair of clothes to change into. Eryn found her bag of things she'd moved from her room and pulled out a pair of clothes of her own. He could only vaguely see a few shadows through the darkness until Eryn lit a candle, and the faint orange glow produced just enough light to see by.

"The Dragon Lord," a voice said through the door.

Caeden's heart stopped.

The letter he'd sent.

He'd forgotten about the letter.

Panic laced the words of the woman on the other end of the door, and her voice shook. "He's here, Your Majesty."

Eryn froze, her entire body going rigid. She turned to face him, her bright blue eyes filled with a mix of confusion and pure fear.

He hadn't told her about the letter he wrote to the Dragon Lord.

He hadn't told anyone. Not even the servant who collected it from him to mail off.

Caeden swallowed hard, and Eryn's eyes widened. "What did you do?" she asked, her voice so quiet he almost couldn't hear how it wavered.

Now wasn't the time to explain, but she would walk into whatever this was with him whether he wanted her to or not. He knew better than to think she would stay here even if he asked her to.

"I sent him a letter," Caeden told her as he pulled on a pair of pants and a clean shirt. "I wanted to arrange a final battle to put an end to the war while hurting as few people as possible."

Eryn fixed him with a look that he couldn't entirely read in the darkness, but knew wasn't one of approval. "You didn't think to consult the court first?"

He had thought to, but he'd known he would send the letter regardless of what the court said. In hindsight though, mentioning it would've at least given all of them time to plan out their strategy if the Dragon Lord agreed. Or if he didn't.

Guilt weighed heavily on his shoulders.

His first week as Aericora's king and already he'd made a mistake he couldn't take back. What if the Dragon Lord was outside with an entire army? What if he brought hundreds of dragons to burn the castle to the ground once and for all?

His head spun as bile rose in the back of his throat.

How had he not considered those risks?

He could have just ended the lives of every single person

living in his kingdom with one stupid mistake he hadn't thought through.

His uncle could've seen his letter as a taunt. He could've interpreted it to mean that Aericora was truly weak enough for them to win the war with simply another attack on the castle.

"Caeden."

Eryn's voice sliced through his thoughts. He focused his attention on her again as she strapped her sword to her waist before working to tie her daggers to her calves.

"Your Majesty?" the voice called from outside the door again, even more frantic than before, if that was possible.

They were all going to die.

"Get your things," Eryn said slowly, enunciating every word. "We don't know what he wants. This could be an attack, or he could just want to talk. We need to be prepared for either."

Caeden shook himself, pushing away the fear coursing through every inch of him. He'd made a huge mistake, but there was no changing that now. He could only do whatever it took to ensure his people lived through whatever they would face outside.

"We'll be right there," he called to the servant on the other side of the door.

She didn't respond before he heard the sound of her feet pounding against the floor as she ran down the hall.

He and Eryn dressed quickly before hurrying through the halls toward the castle's front entrance and the courtyard. The servant hadn't told them where the Dragon Lord was, but no one would've dared to let the man inside, unless he'd forced his way there.

Hope bloomed in his chest the further through the castle they got. No screams reached them. Nothing was on fire. No loud crashes or bangs echoed in his ears. There were no signs anywhere that a fight was underway.

That didn't mean there wasn't one to come, though.

Eryn gripped his hand when they approached the front doors. Two guards stood there, one on either side. They glanced at one another nervously when the pair approached, before they pulled the doors open to reveal the last person Caeden ever wanted to see.

The Dragon Lord.

His uncle.

The man who killed his mother, imprisoned his sister in space and time, tortured his best friend, and tried to convince him to agree to hand over his kingdom and his people's lives in exchange for his father's death.

His uncle stood in the center of the courtyard. Two dragons loomed behind him in the darkness, and four soldiers stood on either side. Two held on to the dragons' reins, as if that would keep the enormous creatures under control if they tried to attack or escape. One held a white flag tied to the end of a short pole, its ends flapping lazily in the gentle breeze.

Wings beat overhead, and Caeden glanced Aubry flying above them. She watched the Dragon Lord and his small group intently as she landed twenty feet to Caeden's left. Her gaze never left their enemies as she spoke inside of his head.

What do they want?

The Dragon Lord laughed so suddenly Caeden nearly jumped.

"So, you can hear them now, too?" he taunted once his laughter subsided.

Caeden gritted his teeth. *I don't know*, he said to Aubry. *Thank you for coming.*

Aubry nodded so slightly that it was almost imperceptible, and he wouldn't have noticed if he hadn't waited for a response.

Luckily, his uncle didn't seem to hear the words he spoke to her, only the ones she said to him.

"Yes, we can," Caeden said to the Dragon Lord.

His uncle tilted his head, his large black and purple crown slipping to one side ever so slightly with the motion. "We?" He clicked his tongue. "Very interesting."

"What are you doing here?" Caeden demanded, his tone stronger than he felt. One command from his uncle and those dragons could kill everyone in the courtyard.

The Dragon Lord's lip quirked upward. "Don't pretend like you didn't invite me here, nephew," he chided, as if speaking to a young child.

Eryn scoffed. "Don't act like he did," she growled through her teeth, the words deadly. Her hand rested on the hilt of her sword, her fingers gripping it so tightly Caeden wouldn't be surprised if the metal bent beneath her touch.

"Keep your attack dog under control," the Dragon Lord said, tossing an irritated nod in Eryn's direction without bothering to spare her a glance. "This is supposed to be a polite meeting. If I get the impression she wants a fight," he shrugged a single shoulder, "well, I would love to see how quickly my men can put a sword through her chest."

"You'll keep your men in line," Caeden snarled. "If any of you lay a hand on her, I'll have you all killed before you can blink."

His uncle's smirk returned.

"Why are you here?"

The Dragon Lord rolled his eyes. "If I must spell it out for you, I'm here to accept your proposal. So polite of you to offer. Your father was never smart enough to attempt something so civil."

Caeden bit the inside of his cheek, and forced himself not to have an outward reaction to the comment.

"I'll be nice and allow you to decide where we'll meet, but I'll decide the date and time."

"Very well," Caeden agreed. He'd sent the offer to begin with. He didn't know if his people could win a fight like this, but the chances were higher than if they continued to drag this war out. The longer this went on, the weaker they got, and while Deovaria had lost soldiers, it wasn't as many as Aericora. Never mind the sheer number of dragons they still had at their disposal. "When will this be taking place?"

The Dragon Lord gave a feral grin, his eyes gleaming with something so wicked it made Caeden's skin crawl. "Four days. At sunrise."

Caeden's stomach felt like it sank through his body all the way to the ground at his feet.

Four days wasn't enough time to gather their armies to meet Deovaria with the kind of force needed to defeat them. And certainly not enough to organize a proper plan, or to decide whether they wanted all of their soldiers there or not, in case this was a ploy to get Aericora's soldiers in one place and simply go around to destroy the capital.

"Four days isn't enough time," Caeden argued. "Your army has dragons to move soldiers around quickly. We don't."

The Dragon Lord raised an eyebrow in Aubry's direction. "Looks like you have a dragon to me."

Aubry snorted irritably.

"We don't own her," Eryn snapped, more venom than Caeden expected to hear lacing her words. Her tone was protective, and even though Eryn had spent more time with the large dragon over the past few days, he hadn't expected that edge to slip into her voice.

"And even if she is willing to help us move soldiers, there's only one of her," Caeden added.

His uncle shrugged again. "Not my problem, nephew. Four days is the time frame. Either your soldiers meet us in four days, or mine will meet you at your front door. Your choice."

Caeden swallowed hard. Neither of those was a good option, but the threat in the Dragon Lord's words hung over his head like a dagger suspended on the thinnest of threads. It wouldn't be easy to get his kingdom's soldiers rounded up for a final attack in four days, but it wouldn't be any easier to get them here in preparation for an invasion either.

The end result would be the same, given the time frame. Either Aericora would win, or they would meet their end. At least, if they met the Deovarians in the field—as long as they won—their castle and capital wouldn't be destroyed in the process, and no innocent bystanders in any towns or who couldn't leave the castle in time would be killed.

He didn't hold much hope for their victory now that he'd laid eyes on the true level of destruction taking place, but he also didn't have any choice but to agree.

"Fine," Caeden bit out. "We'll meet you at sunrise in four days outside Tardide."

A grin spread across the Dragon Lord's face.

"Under one condition," Caeden continued. "As I already stated in my letter, you'll bring Amelia. You'll bring her to the field and you will hand her off to me before the fight. Sedate her if you'd like, but she better be alive. When we win, I want to ensure you don't have someone in position to slit her throat before we get there."

"Cocky little thing, aren't you?" the Dragon Lord taunted.

He didn't feel confident, but he wasn't prepared to let his uncle see that. The only hope he held was that he could send word to enough of his camps to meet Deovaria with most of their force, and send someone to Crevia to get a hurried response from the king and queen. Maybe the push that they would be meeting on equal ground would be enough to get Crevia to make their final decision.

Still, it might not be enough time for their soldiers to travel to the border between Aericora and Deovaria before the fight. He pushed that worry away for the time being. He couldn't prolong this fight, and he'd chosen the town closest in proximity to Crevia without allowing Deovaria to march on his kingdom.

The Dragon Lord remained silent for a long moment before he finally nodded. "Very well, but I assume that means you will hold up the other end of your bargain and that you will bring my daughter as well."

"How is a frozen girl equivalent to a trained assassin and murderer?" Eryn snarled, her hand falling to the hilt of her sword again.

The Dragon Lord shrugged. "One girl for another."

Caeden hadn't thought that fact through when he'd sent the letter to his uncle. He didn't like the idea of giving Dealla back given how trained she was, but it was part of the original trade he'd offered, and if it meant getting Amelia back, he would do it.

He nodded. "Amelia for Dealla."

"A fair trade, if I've ever heard one," the Dragon Lord said with a wicked grin. "I'll see you in four days, nephew."

His uncle said nothing else before he turned on his heel and mounted one of the two dragons standing stoically by. His eight soldiers followed before they flew off into the night.

Chapter 49

Ronan

The darkness pressed in around him as Ronan wandered through the damp halls of the dungeon. There was truth to Caeden and Eryn's words from the previous night, but he couldn't force himself to believe that there hadn't been more in Dealla's than they wanted to believe. He knew her on a deeper level than he could explain. They'd lived through very different circumstances. He'd been a soldier held captive, and she'd been his captor. But she was his other half. She understood him in a way not even Eryn and Caeden did.

And even if he would regret it, given the turn the war had taken earlier that night, he couldn't ignore that their souls bore the same set of scars, even if they'd come from different places.

He'd heard the dragons land on the other side of the castle hours earlier. He'd instructed the guards to prepare for a fight, and gotten everyone situated for one if it broke out. By the time he got to the courtyard, the Dragon Lord had already flown off with his goons.

He, Caeden, and Eryn had met with the court for hours

before he'd decided to come down here. Everyone was tired, and they agreed to a quick meal break, but he wasn't remotely hungry. If they were having a final battle with Deovaria in four days and Dealla was given back to her father to fight against him and his kingdom, he needed to see her before it happened.

He wasn't sure why it mattered, or what he would say when he got to her cell, but he needed to see her face. He needed to memorize the real features of the woman holding his heart. Her stature, and everything from her face down was the same aside from the tint of her skin, since the Princess of Crevia was paler than the tan woman beneath the disguise, but he needed to memorize her new features. He needed those to be branded into his mind the way the face of the redheaded woman she'd worn was.

The redheaded woman wasn't who he loved. He loved a curly-haired blond woman with the most vibrant green eyes he'd ever seen, the faintest splatter of freckles across her nose, dimples that formed on her cheeks when she smiled, and lips that dipped into a perfect V.

She didn't have the same face he remembered, yet she was just as beautiful as she was when she spent those long nights in his bed. He thought it was her features he was attracted to when he invited the staff member into his home—that another woman with red hair would be just as beautiful—but he was wrong. He couldn't explain what about her he loved, but he didn't care that she looked different now. She was the same woman whose heart he fell in love with, and she was just as beautiful, no matter how different she looked.

Dealla was pressed into the corner of her cell when Ronan stopped in front of the rusted bars and gazed inside. The light flickering from the candle in his hand gleamed against her golden hair, and highlighted the angles of her face.

She was asleep, but when the light washed over her, her eyes fluttered open. She groaned when she sat up, stiff from the awkward position against the wall. "Ronan?" she whispered. Her voice was hoarse.

"I brought you somethin' to eat," he said softly, hoping to avoid waking Muire. He'd never liked that woman, even long before she decided to poison his best friend.

Dealla perked up, squinting through the darkness to see the plate of food he held out for her. "Isn't it the middle of the night?" she asked as she climbed to her feet and came to the edge of her cell to take the plate from him.

"It is."

She frowned as she sat cross-legged on the floor with the plate balanced on her knee. "What are you doing here? You should be asleep." Her face fell suddenly, as if someone just told her Deovaria had lost the war. "Is it raining?"

His heart ached at hearing those words.

That was why he couldn't believe that loving her was wrong.

She may have caused that fear, but he would've acted in the same way if their roles were reversed. He would've done the same things to her back then if his king demanded it of him. It was her job. It was her duty to her kingdom, even if her kingdom was in the wrong.

But she noticed those things. It took Caeden nearly two years to figure out why he kept the candles lit throughout his home. She noticed immediately. She hadn't said anything until after he confessed everything about being held as her captive to her, but he saw the look on her face when she first saw the lit candles in the middle of the night. She knew long before he said anything.

"No," he told her as he sat on the floor just outside her cell so they were on the same level. It was still an odd sensation when he didn't have to lean heavily against his cane to get to the ground, and even odder still that he didn't have to endure the wave of agony he was so used to feeling shoot up his thigh.

She set her fork down before she even moved to eat the food. "Ronan," she said, an edge to her voice that told him she saw something on his face to indicate something wasn't right. "What happened?"

"Aericora and Deovaria are having a final battle to determine the outcome of the war in four days," he told her, holding her gaze through every word.

Dealla's face fell. "The end of the war?" she asked. Hope and dread mingled in her tone, and Ronan knew exactly what she felt because he was feeling the same. An end would mean one of their kingdoms would win, but the other would lose. She may be the one in the cell right now, but their places could be reversed in four days.

Or worse.

One or both of them could be dead.

Ronan nodded. "Caeden is gonna meet with the Dragon Lord before the fight. They're tradin' you for Caeden's sister."

Dealla's eyes widened before she sighed. She looked at the plate in her lap and picked her fork back up. She pushed around the eggs on the plate, but made no move to take a bite, even as her stomach rumbled in protest. "Oh," was all she said.

Eryn and Caeden's words from the previous night rang through his mind again as he reached through the bars and placed his hand on her knee, but he pushed them away. He loved her, even if that love would only break his heart over and over again. It was a small price to pay for the honor of loving the woman before him.

Dealla cleared her throat after a moment, and Ronan noticed the sheen of tears in her eyes when she met his gaze.

His heart cracked—the first break that would leave him

shattered beyond repair in the end.

"Will he take care of them?" she asked, so quietly Ronan hardly heard her. "If Aericora wins, will my people be safe?"

His shoulders sagged. "He's new to all this, but he'll do his best. He always has."

Dealla nodded slowly. "I know I don't have any right to ask," she said, "but will you make sure they're taken care of if we lose? You're Caeden's best friend. He'll listen to what you have to say. And they will need it. I…" Her voice cracked, and she broke off before she tried again. A tear slipped down her cheek and she looked back at the plate on her knee. "I don't trust that my father has been taking care of them. I had my doubts before, but after talking to the dragons… they're living creatures, too." She glanced up and met his eyes again, silent tears tracing down her cheeks and dripping onto the collar of her stained and ripped dress. "How could he do that to them? I know we're at war with Aericora. I understand where that death and torture comes from. I can't understand what the dragons did to deserve this."

Maybe he would regret this too in the end, but he nodded. "I promise, I'll do everythin' I can for them if Aericora wins." He swallowed hard. "Take care of them too, if we lose. You already know how I feel 'bout how your father rules."

A sad smile pulled at the corners of Dealla's mouth. "I think we're all starting to feel the same way," she confessed.

Those words.

Those were the words he had wished to hear above all else, long before now. The words that could begin to change everyone's opinion of her. The words that might free her from this cell and, maybe someday, bring her to the side of the war that didn't rely on brainwashing people into fighting over a petty thirst for vengeance.

But it was too late for that.

She was Caeden's bargaining chip. He wouldn't give up the chance to get his sister back for someone he still couldn't trust, even if she said those words.

Another crack tore through Ronan's chest.

Dealla placed a hand over his on her knee and intertwined their fingers together. She shifted over on the hard stone floor until she was against the bars, her shoulder resting against one of the rusted metal pipes keeping her securely inside of the cell.

Ronan shifted with her, so their arms pressed against one another through the six-inch gap. Her skin was warm against his, and a calmness he hadn't felt since those nights he spent with her beside him settled over him.

"Ronan," Dealla whispered. She bent down to press a kiss against his shoulder, and a shiver ran up his spine.

"Yeah?"

"Will you stay for a while? Before…" She didn't need to finish her sentence for him to understand what she meant.

Before the final fight.

Before they were on opposite ends of a war again.

Before they were forced to acknowledge that they were enemies.

He pulled her hand up through the bars and brushed his lips against her knuckles. "I would stay forever if I could."

The smallest smile formed on her face, and if he hadn't already been in love with her, that would have been the moment he'd given her his heart.

Chapter 50

Everything happened quickly once Caeden and Eryn worked up the nerve to reenter the castle after the Dragon Lord flew off with his soldiers. They assembled the court and met for almost three hours before they took a break for breakfast. They reconvened for another few hours after that.

They discussed not waiting for Crevia to respond, since they didn't have time for that anymore. They would send someone with Aubry to get an answer from them immediately. Ronan agreed to get Aubry ready for the flight, and he and Fionn would leave to get an answer before the following morning. The flight to Crevia would take Aubry most of the day one way, but they should be able to return midway through the night, and the court would meet the moment they got back.

If Crevia didn't agree to help them, they didn't have a high probability of winning unless their soldiers could collect enough stones from the Deovarians during the fight. So far, they hadn't heard of the soldiers having much more luck than they had been before Caeden and the others went to the mountains, and in order for that plan to work, they would need to collect them extremely quickly once the fighting began.

They resorted to having as many shipments of lavender as possible sent to the designated meeting place for the final fight, but the chances of enough getting there to inhibit the dragons' abilities were as slim as the chances of the stones being enough to turn the fight in their favor. With enough time to prepare, they could have gathered enough lavender to ensure the fight was in their favor, but the Dragon Lord made sure they would have a hard time doing that.

Once Ronan and Fionn returned the following night, regardless of Crevia's decision, Eryn would trade off with them and take Aubry along the border to inform the generals of their plans. They sent messengers on foot already, in case Aubry couldn't make the flight, or Ronan and Fionn were delayed, but the chances the messengers would get there so the soldiers would have enough time to travel to their new posts weren't high.

The court agreed they would spread their forces thinner along the border so the majority of their soldiers were at the meeting place when Deovaria arrived, and they would leave the castle fully guarded while they were away. Caeden, Eryn, and Ronan would travel to the field, leaving Fionn and Cormac at the castle in charge of the guards.

It was the first time Caeden questioned whether traveling to the field was the best option. He'd disregarded the concerns of the court in the past, regardless of how legitimate they were, but he was the king now. This was his home. Aericora was his responsibility. If the Dragon Lord attacked the castle and the capital rather than meeting them on the battlefield like they'd agreed, he would be leaving his kingdom in someone else's hands. But if his uncle held true to their arrangement, then he needed to be on that battlefield. If he wasn't there to trade

Dealla for Amelia, if the Dragon Lord truly meant to meet them on even ground for a final fight, he would send his soldiers on dragons to attack the capital, anyway.

After Ronan agreed to make the flight and he and Fionn left, they made further plans to share with their generals when they arrived in the field in two days' time. Hopefully, the single day they would have there before the fight would be enough to get everyone situated and prepared.

They couldn't make definitive plans, but they got a map laid out of where they would place soldiers in preparation for the fight. Eryn took point on the decisions along with other court members who had military experience, since Caeden was nowhere near as familiar with it as she was. They questioned her at every turn, but she took every argument in stride, explaining her reasoning until she guided them to an agreement that satisfied most of their points.

She was a phenomenal leader in the field, but it truly amazed him to watch her bring some of the most argumentative people to agreements on things that didn't leave half of them irritated.

"Everything happened so fast," Eryn whispered so softly Caeden hardly heard her over his racing heart that hadn't calmed since they were woken nearly twenty-four hours ago. "After eleven years, it's all going to be over."

There was fear behind those words, but also relief. Either they would win the fight, or they would lose. Either they would move on with their lives without the constant war raging around them, or they would die trying.

They lay in bed side by side, their hands clasped between them as they stared at the ceiling. Caeden had lost track of how long they'd been there like that, his thoughts swirling in his head so fiercely the rest of the world had fallen away except for the feel of her hand in his.

Eryn released his hand and propped herself up on an elbow as she turned to face him. The flickering candle on the desk reflected in her eyes. Worry was etched into every feature of her face, and she reached over to run her fingers against his cheek.

He closed his eyes and leaned into her touch, that small brush of her fingertips enough to ease the weight that pressed down on his chest so intensely he could hardly breathe beneath it.

"What happens if we lose?" he whispered. His voice wavered around the edges when he spoke the words he'd been thinking all day.

She kept her expression neutral, but he saw the fear that passed behind her eyes. "I don't know," she answered. She bent over and placed a gentle kiss against his forehead before she curled up against him, wrapping her arms around him. "What happens if we win?"

Caeden glanced at her. The same fear he saw hidden behind her eyes now displayed itself across her whole face, making a small crease form between her eyebrows and her lips pinch together. "Everything goes back to normal," he told her, but as soon as the words left his mouth, it struck him for the first time just how untrue they were.

That was his hope since the day all of this started. But even back then, even if the war ended in only a few short months, nothing would've been normal again. His mother was dead, his sister was frozen in time, and now his father had died as well. He was a king now, no longer the child he was when all of this began. Even if he got his sister back at the end of this, it wouldn't be like it was when they were young. She was still eleven, never mind everything that had changed since she last lived through a real moment in their kingdom.

Those thoughts circled through his head more times than he could count. Maybe it was why he decided to push the thoughts of his sister as far away as he could. How would she react to all of this? He couldn't leave her like she was now if they won against the Dragon Lord, but how could he explain everything that happened? How was he supposed to fill her in on eleven years she should've lived through on her own? How could he do that without breaking her entirely?

She was still a child. He'd lived through those eleven years and grown into an adult, but she hadn't. How could he tell a child that both of her parents were gone? That her younger brother was now ten years older than she was? That he now held the title their father had the last time she walked through the castle? That she was held prisoner where space and time didn't exist as a trophy throughout all of it?

Eryn sighed heavily. "Nothing will ever be normal again," she whispered, seeming just as lost in thought as he was. "I don't even know what normal is anymore."

Caeden wrapped his arms around her, forcing away the thoughts of his sister as he pulled her closer. She snuggled against his chest as he ran his fingers through her long, silky hair and breathed in the scent of lavender that made his heart skip a beat every single time.

Thinking too much about Amelia wouldn't change what he had to do if they won all of this. He would have to tell her everything. He could never keep that from her, even if he wanted to. But they didn't know yet if they would live through the next three days.

"Maybe this could be our new normal," he offered. His words were muffled through her hair, but he didn't pull away.

"What could?" Eryn asked, not bothering to look up at him when she spoke.

"This," he breathed. "Us. Here. Together." His voice hitched at the end, and he swallowed down a lump of emotion in the back of his throat. He'd already admitted his feelings for her. He'd already told her he loved her and they'd already said they would be together through all of this, but there was something about saying it aloud again, now that there could very well be an end in sight, that made his heart swell with more emotion than he could handle.

Eryn smiled against him, and that simple gesture alone was the most perfect thing he'd ever experienced. "It will always be us," she said. "No matter what happens."

A knock on the door echoed throughout their room, and Caeden tensed. He knew that sound would come since he first lay in bed with Eryn beside him. Regardless of whether that knock brought good news or bad with it, he'd dreaded hearing it.

He wasn't ready to hear what answer Ronan and Fionn got from Crevia, and he certainly wasn't ready to let Eryn go. He wouldn't stop her from leaving just like he wouldn't stay in this bed as if he hadn't heard the knock rather than attend the court meeting. Even if those two things were all he wanted.

"Your Majesty," a voice called through the door. He couldn't place who it belonged to, but there were so many people working inside of the castle that he'd only ever been able to discern a few of them from voice alone.

Eryn sighed before she lifted her head just high enough to look into his eyes. The same sadness he felt deep inside of his chest was mirrored in her eyes, and he contemplated holding onto her right here until the Dragon Lord came and burned them all to the ground.

She placed a gentle kiss against his lips, her hand sliding to the back of his neck to pull him close. His hands found her hips as they kissed, and a soft moan escaped her when his fingers dug gently into her skin, holding her against him to steal just an extra second before she slipped away into the night.

There was nothing he wouldn't give to hold her there like that forever.

Slowly, she let her hand fall away from the back of his neck and she pulled away.

A hole he hadn't expected to feel formed in his chest as she stared at him, a silent goodbye in her eyes even though they would only be apart for a few days. If everything went as planned…

Caeden forced the thoughts away. He would see her again. She would take Aubry and she would fly to each of the camps and meet with the generals before the fighting broke out in three days. But even as he wanted to believe that, three days was hardly enough time.

There was a very real possibility she wouldn't make it to their meeting spot before they faced the Dragon Lord.

And there was a very real possibility that whoever was there on the battlefield in three days' time wouldn't live to see the sunset the following evening.

"I'll meet you in the field," Eryn whispered, her lips brushing against his when she spoke. Her bright blue eyes stared into the deepest depths of his soul. "I'll be right by your side through the fight, and I'll be here with you for everything that comes after."

She kissed him again, slower this time, as if to convey the promise lacing those words.

"Eryn," he breathed. Her name felt perfect on his lips.

"Hmm?" She pulled away just enough to gaze into his eyes again, and the look she gave him made him fall in love with her all over again.

"Will you marry me?" he whispered, the words so soft he feared she wouldn't be able to hear them. "Once all of this is over, if we win, will you marry me?"

Eryn's eyes widened. She stayed silent, but it only lasted a beat before her lips found his again. She kissed him deeply, her arms wrapping around his neck again as she fell against him. "Yes," she said against his lips.

Caeden's chest could've burst with the joy and love he felt at hearing her say that single word. He held her tight, pulling her against him again and drawing another moan from her lips.

Another knock came on the door. "Your Majesty?" said the voice on the other end again.

Eryn pulled away, offering him an apologetic smile. "I'm sorry," she told him. Her eyes gleamed in the dim candlelight. "Yes, I'll marry you." She kissed him one last time before she climbed off the bed. She dressed quickly in a black tunic and leggings, carefully securing her leather armor and holsters over her clothing. A bag sat next to the bed that held the supplies she packed to take with her for her flight with Aubry.

"I'll be right out," Caeden called to the servant still waiting outside.

Caeden sat up, watching as Eryn wound the straps of her holster for her dagger around her upper thigh and carefully secured it into place. The edges of her dagger shone brightly in the flickering candlelight as she sheathed it.

"Eryn," he said again, partly because he wanted to feel her name on his lips again, and partly because he needed her to hear him say the words sitting on the tip of his tongue.

She turned back to him again. "Yeah?" Determination was written across her face, just like it was every time she was preparing herself for a fight.

"I love you," he told her. The words still weren't enough, but he needed her to hear them again. He needed her to hear them in case this was the last time he would ever say them to her. "No matter what happens, even if we both meet our end three days from now, I will always love you."

Eryn's expression softened, and a smile touched the corners of her mouth. "I love you, too," she said. "In this lifetime and the next." The corner of her mouth twitched upward. "But I better see you again before then, got it?"

Caeden grinned. He couldn't make that promise when there was no way of knowing whether he could keep it, but he nodded either way.

She finished getting dressed before she leaned over the bed to kiss his cheek again. "Be safe for me, please," she whispered, her lips trailing along his skin and making a shiver run down his spine.

"You too," he said, catching her by the arm before she could pull away entirely and pulling her into another deep kiss that left him missing her before she was even gone.

Eryn offered him one last smile before she slung her bag over her shoulder and left their room, her lavender scent hanging in the air in her wake.

He breathed it in, savoring the scent as it washed over him, before he climbed out of bed and got dressed to meet the court.

Chapter 51

Crevia would fight with them.

His heart hadn't stopped racing since getting the final decision from Ronan an hour earlier. They had a chance. It wasn't high, not with the number of dragons the Deovarians controlled, but their defeat wasn't a certainty with the added soldiers from Crevia.

The cell door groaned loudly as the guards entered Dealla's cell and placed shackles around her ankles and wrists. She kept her head bowed as the guards hauled her out from the confines of the small space.

Caeden stood outside as she was brought through the door, Ronan and Fionn standing by his side.

Ronan kept his head high, and Caeden glanced between the two of them, having expected their composures to be opposite.

Dealla glanced up long enough to meet Ronan's gaze briefly, and Caeden caught the smallest glimpse of sadness flash across her features before she turned away and refused to look up again. A quick glance at Ronan confirmed his expression had softened with the same sadness clinging to the down-turned slant of his lips.

Caeden knew Ronan had visited her more times than just the one he admitted to, and he didn't believe Dealla was trying to manipulate him again. She already knew she would be released to her father regardless of how Ronan felt about her. There was no reason for the sadness to pass over her face unless she truly meant it when she told Ronan she cared about him.

But that didn't change everything she'd done to him. It didn't change that Deovaria was her home and the Dragon Lord was her father, or that, if it came down to it, she would sacrifice any of them—Ronan included—if it meant her kingdom won this war.

"Make sure the dose isn't too strong," Caeden told the nurse standing beside the stretcher Dealla was being lowered onto. She had a glass vial of sedative in one hand and the syringe she would use to inject Dealla in the other.

The nurse nodded as Dealla laid down and the guards fastened her securely to the stretcher.

No one wanted to give her the opportunity to escape, but they also needed to ensure she was awake when it came time to trade her for Amelia. Caeden didn't trust his insane uncle not to ignore their agreement and fly to the castle to destroy it if he caught a glimpse of his daughter and assumed she was dead.

It wasn't likely that she would try to escape, but he wasn't any more willing to take the risk than he was willing to risk his uncle's wrath if he thought they'd killed her. At least with the sedative in her veins, she would be weak for the fight to come. She was a strong warrior, and it would only help them if she couldn't fight to her full capabilities.

The guards stepped away from Dealla's side, and she let out a shaking breath—another thing that Caeden hadn't expected to see from her—as the nurse approached her with the now half-full syringe of sedative.

Ronan visibly flinched as the tip of the needle slid into Dealla's arm.

He'd barely begun to believe that Dealla truly loved his best friend, but he couldn't deny the feelings Ronan had for her. Even if all he could see was Ronan getting even more hurt by her.

Dealla let out a heavy breath as her eyes fluttered closed, and her breathing turned slow and even. It only took a few seconds for the sedative to work its way through her veins and knock her out entirely.

"Let's get her in the wagon," Caeden said to the gathered group. "We leave in half an hour."

The guards nodded their understanding and wheeled Dealla away.

Caeden turned to Fionn, who still stood beside him. "Ronan has the guards on a pre-planned rotation," he told him. "All of the information is laid out for you in case you need it, and they've been made aware of the temporary change in leadership while Ronan is away. I trust you and Cormac have everything under control from here?"

"Yes, Your Majesty," Fionn answered. "We have everything we need. Hopefully, we won't need any of it." He said the last part lightly, but there was a darkness hidden beneath his tone that Caeden felt deep inside his very soul.

They would only need most of the information Caeden made sure to gather for them if Deovaria attacked the castle. They'd been on the court for years and knew how to take on the responsibilities Caeden would need of them while he was away without much instruction.

He had doubts about assigning someone to take his place while he was away, so instead, he'd opted not to at all, in case there were any more spies in their midst. Fionn and Cormac would share the responsibility of overseeing the guards since Ronan would be away, but the responsibility of ensuring the castle was taken care of fell to the entire court collectively. Important matters that were to be handled by the king alone would have to wait until he returned. If he returned at all.

Caeden and Ronan left the dungeon soon after, with Fionn following behind until they split up once they were upstairs. Less than half of the guards were gathered to travel with them, since they still wanted the castle itself to be protected. They waited outside when Caeden and Ronan entered the courtyard together. There were a few hundred of them in total, along with the twenty horses they could spare, as well as the wagon carrying Dealla's limp form.

Ronan gave him the smallest, almost imperceptible nod, and Caeden returned it before walking down the front steps to the gathered group with his best friend by his side. His heart pounded with an intensity he felt throughout his entire body, and his ears rang as he walked through the assembled soldiers.

Heads turned their way, and Caeden was met with eyes full of fear from each one of them. That same fear sat like a boulder on his chest, but he kept his expression neutral.

They were scared, and it was his job to put up a brave façade. Even if all he could offer right now was a straight face and to keep moving things forward.

Caeden grabbed the bridle of the horse waiting at the front of the group as Ronan stopped at the one directly beside his. The guard who'd held them took a step away, and Caeden let out a breath, every emotion he felt weighing him down just a little more with each passing second. He climbed up onto the horse's back and into the saddle.

If he were his father, he would have some encouraging words

to say to the gathered group. He would be able to lift their spirits as they marched to what could be all of their deaths and the death of their kingdom.

But his father wasn't here.

He was dead.

Just like so many of his kingdom's people were as a result of this war.

Caeden sighed and turned to face the group. He didn't have words as good as his father would've, but he needed to say something. These were his people; his responsibility was to them and always would be. If what he needed to do was offer them words of encouragement, even if he wasn't sure where to find them, he would do it.

The group of soldiers turned to look at him. They were set to leave any minute now, and they were waiting on him to give the final order for departure.

"Thank you everyone for being here, by our side, throughout this war against Deovaria," he said. A lump formed in the back of his throat, threatening to make his voice waver, but he swallowed it down before it got the chance. "All of us have seen things by now that we never wanted to, lost someone we never thought we would, and suffered in more ways than we thought were possible before all of this started. None of us knows what will happen three days from now, but Crevia is on their way to help us win this fight, and I have faith that we will prevail in the end. You are all good fighters; you are strong warriors and strong people. You have all been through too much in these past eleven years, and it's time for the suffering to end. It's time we put an end to all of this bloodshed and war. It's time we put an end to the Dragon Lord and his reign of cruelty."

Cheers were the last thing he expected to hear from the group of soldiers assembled before them. He expected silence, maybe a few nods of understanding, but the people before him held a fire deep within them that hadn't yet burned out.

Soldiers raised their swords over their heads as their cheers rang out, growing more boisterous and loud as more and more joined in.

Since his father died, Caeden hadn't felt the same drive to fight their enemies. He wanted to end the war—maybe even more so than he did before—but the revenge he'd wanted for years took a backseat to the needs of his people. His people didn't need him to fight alongside them until now. What they needed was a king, and he was the only one who could fill that role now that his father was gone.

But they didn't have the same shift in their lives. They had a new king, but they hadn't felt that change the same way he had.

Caeden met Ronan's gaze as he climbed onto the back of his own horse. A grin that Caeden hadn't seen in far too long pulled at the corners of his mouth. It was the same teasing, mischievous smirk he'd always enjoyed seeing from his friend.

Ronan turned to face the crowd and raised his sword along with the gathered soldiers.

Caeden grinned in return as a flame burst to life from the hot coal inside that had never truly burnt out since the day all of this began.

Crevia was on their way to the front lines. They may not arrive until after the fighting began, but he hoped it would still be enough. Eryn was flying ahead of them with Aubry to get the soldiers moved where they needed to be prior to the fight. They'd chosen to thin out the number of soldiers along the border, but they'd gone about it by shifting soldiers from one post to their next nearest and moving nearly all of the soldiers in close proximity to the final fight's location. Most, if not all, of the soldiers they'd assigned to meet them there would be able to make it. As long as everything went mostly to plan, they would be able to hold off Deovaria until the soldiers arrived from Crevia.

He'd lost his mother and his father to this war, but he was about to get his sister back. That would come with a multitude of difficulties of its own, but she was alive and she would be safe by this time three days from now.

They could win this.

Aericora and all of the people who lived within its borders could be free of the fighting and the death caused by the Dragon Lord.

A flicker of doubt still tucked itself away next to the flaming ember inside, but it was easier now to ignore as he stared out at the soldiers—his people—gathered before him as he reached for his sword and held it high above his head.

The sound of the soldiers' footfalls against the ground pounded in Caeden's ears hours after they arrived at the camp. The sun was beginning to crest the horizon when they finally arrived after walking nearly straight through. They stopped for only three half-hour rest breaks on their way. The fight with Deovaria would begin in only a day and a half, but everyone had needed some time to rest.

Samuel, a stocky general Caeden had met when he, Eryn and Ronan traveled to the field together months ago, was waiting for them when they arrived. He was in charge of the specific camp they would be gathering at for the fight, and Eryn had met with him first to prepare him for the influx of soldiers he would receive and the fight to come.

They didn't have enough supplies to house all of the soldiers comfortably, but the things they brought from the castle along with what Samuel could gather before their arrival meant that even though it would be a tight fit, every soldier would be able to sleep inside of a tent with at least a blanket.

It wasn't as good as Caeden wished he could give them, but there wasn't much he could do given the time frame. Had he been given a month, he would've found a way to ensure each soldier was as comfortable as possible before having to meet the Dragon Lord and his armies for the last time.

They got everyone situated as quickly as they could after they arrived, and had spent the remainder of the day discussing their minimal battle strategies for the fight with the generals all gathered into the largest of the camp's tents.

Shipments of lavender had arrived ahead of them, but it was less than half of what Caeden ordered. Not all of them had arrived yet, but there was no way to predict how many of them would before the sun rose in a day and a half.

They laid out a rough plan of where they would have soldiers waiting. There was a stream nearby, and soldiers would be stationed with buckets at the ready for when the Deovarians inevitably attempted to burn them all to death.

The lavender would be dispersed around the perimeter, but it would be thin. It would be enough to inhibit the weaker dragons, but not all of them. And if they were high enough, it would do nothing. He'd instructed them to hold off on the lavender until Aubry and Eryn arrived though, since it wasn't in their best interest to weaken her before the fight.

They wouldn't be able to avoid it during the fight, but there weren't many other options.

Whatever was left of the lavender would be worn by soldiers stationed the farthest away from the Dragon Hunters, since they would have the few stones they'd gathered from the mountains, and the protection they provided. Eryn would have his mother's ring, come the morning of the fight.

Caeden sighed and sat up, pushing the thin blanket covering him aside. A shiver ran down his spine as the cool morning air seeped into his bones, but he hardly noticed it over the thoughts and worries swirling in his head.

Ronan lay beside him, entirely unfazed by the cold and unaware of the looming fight as he slept peacefully.

They'd gone to bed a couple of hours ago, and despite Caeden's inability to sleep no matter how hard he tried, sleep claimed Ronan within a few seconds of his head hitting the pillow.

Maybe he would be okay once all of this was over.

Maybe he could move on from whatever it was that happened between him and Dealla and live his life without the heartache and the pain.

He deserved that. He deserved, more than most people, to be free of the war and to settle down and live a quiet life.

A gust of wind pushed in the edge of the tent, making the whole structure strain to one side, and the distinct sound of a dragon's wings beating through the air reached him through the paper-thin walls.

His heartbeat was deafening in his ears as he climbed to his feet and pulled a jacket on over the same clothes he'd worn since they left the castle. A loud thud echoed outside as the dragon landed not too far away from the tent he was in.

Avoiding accidentally stepping on the edges of Ronan's bedroll, Caeden tiptoed his way out of the tent. He pushed aside the tent flaps and stepped into the even cooler morning air awaiting him outside.

Aubry was already curled into a ball on the ground near the wagon where they left Dealla for the night with two guards stationed outside. The dragon huffed a single, long breath, smoke curling up into the air from her nostrils as she shifted to a more comfortable position on the ground, her eyes staying closed the whole time.

"Long flight?" Caeden asked her. He said the words aloud, though he didn't need to.

For a moment, even though he'd spoken aloud, he wasn't entirely sure she'd heard him until he saw her open a single eye and give him what he could only assume was a dragon's version of an irritated glare.

Aubry huffed again. *You're welcome*, she told him, in the most sarcastic tone he'd ever heard from her.

A small smile pulled at the corners of his mouth. "Thank you," he whispered back, and she seemed to relax at hearing those words.

She wrapped her tail so far around herself that it covered her face, which was enough to let him know she was done with their conversation. And she more than needed the rest after everything she'd done over the past couple of days.

Light footsteps against the grass caught his attention, and he spun to see Eryn standing a few paces away. Even in the dim light from the torches burning around the camp, he could see the dark circles beneath her eyes, and the way her easy smile came on a fraction of a second slower than usual. Her hair was tied in a messy bun on top of her head, but a few strands had fallen free and dangled into her face. And those eyes. He'd been indifferent to the color blue before he'd met her and gazed into the most perfect set of sapphire eyes to ever grace the earth. Now, he could say beyond any doubt that no color compared.

His breath caught in the back of his throat as he took her in.

Eryn's smile rose higher on the left side, and she tilted her head slightly. "What?" she asked, the grin not leaving her face, even as she raised a curious eyebrow at him.

"You're stunning, Eryn Gedding," he told her, the words heavy on his tongue. "There aren't words to describe how much I love just laying eyes on you."

Eryn's face turned red, but her smile grew wider. "Hi to you, too," she teased as she closed the distance between the two of them and laced her fingers together behind his neck.

The warmth of her body against his sent a shiver down his spine, and he wrapped his arms around her waist, holding her close.

"I missed you," she whispered, her breath warm against his lips. "I didn't think we'd get back in time, but Aubry can really fly when she wants to." Her mouth tilted up into a smile again before she pressed her lips against his, making his heart race.

For just a moment, the world faded away as Caeden pulled her closer and deepened their kiss, pulling the most incredible sound from her lips. For a moment, it was just them, alone, without Caeden's responsibilities as king, without the fight that would put an end to this war one way or another, and without the thousands and thousands of lives that would be lost by the time the sun set the following day.

For just a moment, Caeden felt peace like he hadn't felt in longer than he could remember.

The worries could wait another hour.

He pulled away from their kiss just enough to lay his forehead against hers, letting himself get lost in just her.

"I missed you, too," he told her. "Thank you for coming back safely."

Eryn snorted a laugh. She pulled away and reached to tilt his chin up to look at her. "You forget that your fiancée is the only soldier in the entire kingdom to make it inside of Deovaria's palace and back out alive again." She smirked. "Twice. I can handle delivering a message, you dummy pri—king."

Caeden heard her words, but they were dim through the pounding of his heart. "Say that again."

She raised an eyebrow at him. "You dummy king?"

He laughed, a kind of joy he'd never felt before warming his entire body as he took her hands in his and gazed into those stunning blue eyes that had captivated him even before he'd fallen in love with her. "No. Say you're my fiancée again."

Eryn grinned. "I love you, my fiancé."

Caeden wrapped her up in a hug again before lifting her up off her feet and spinning her around, her laughter echoing in the cool night air. He replaced her on her feet, and she beamed up at him. "I love you so much more," he told her, before he kissed her again, the warmth inside of him burning even brighter.

Chapter 52

They spent the remainder of the day preparing for the battle taking place the following morning. A letter arrived late that evening, confirming where and when they would meet the Dragon Lord to exchange Dealla for Amelia.

Dealla had woken in the middle of the day from the sedative they had given her. Ronan insisted on dealing with her, and though Caeden wasn't sure how he felt about Ronan being alone with her right before they would hand her over to their enemy, he'd agreed to it.

He'd heard their whispered conversation late that night since they hadn't given Dealla any more sedative. They spoke softly, so he couldn't make out their words, only the distinct sound of hushed whispers through the thin walls of the tent he and Eryn shared for their last night before the fight.

Caeden wasn't able to sleep as the hours ticked by, slowly but inevitably leading them straight into the fight that would either take his life and the lives of so many in his kingdom, or set them free from the Dragon Lord entirely.

They hardly spoke after relaxing comfortably into each other for the night, but Caeden didn't need to hear her voice to understand that the same worries—the same fears—weighed heavy on her mind too.

All he wanted was to be near her for the time they had left. He didn't want to give voice to the thoughts with how close it all loomed in front of them. No one could guarantee that by this time tomorrow, they would ever be able to lie beside one another again.

"We have to get up soon," Eryn whispered, breaking him out of his thoughts.

Caeden angled his head to face her, her bright blue eyes gazing into his.

How was it that just the sight of her could still take his breath away every time?

"I know," he answered, his voice soft, before he leaned in and pressed a deep, longing kiss against her lips.

Eryn moaned against him, and he pulled her close. She deepened their kiss as Caeden reached to cup her cheek with his palm. The damp streaks that traced down her face and wetted his fingers only made him kiss her harder.

He pulled away slowly, his eyes meeting hers again. Her tears were silent as they fell, dripping down onto the collar of the shirt she'd borrowed from him for the night and darkening the thin fabric.

Cracks wove their way through his heart as he framed her face in his hands and stared into her eyes. This woman before him somehow possessed the ability to heal his heart and break it entirely without saying a single word.

"It's going to be okay," he told her. The words felt like a lie as they fell from his tongue. He didn't know what he could say to ease her mind, though. No words would bring her comfort. Not with everything they were both feeling.

"You can't promise that," she whispered. Her voice was strained when she uttered the words he'd thought even before he spoke.

She was right, but he wished beyond anything that just this once, he could make a promise like that to her. Just to keep her safe and happy, to keep the tears from ever falling from her eyes again. He would trade his soul to be able to make that promise to her.

He ran his thumb across her cheek, wiping away the tears that hadn't stopped falling. "I promise that until my dying breath, whenever that is, I'll always stand beside you. I love you with every breath in my body, and I always will, now until the end of time."

The smallest fraction of a smile broke out across her face, and she fell against him, burying her face against his neck as her arms came around him, and he held her tighter. Tremors ran through her body, her tears hot against his neck.

Caeden held her tight until long after her quiet sobs eased and her tears dried. He didn't let her go even as the time ticked by and they were late getting up, and if he could've gotten away with stealing just one more second after the soft knock came on the outside of the tent, he would've.

"Time to go," Ronan murmured from outside, resignation and a deep sadness Caeden felt in his very bones lacing his words.

"We'll be right out," Caeden told him, before he buried his face against Eryn's hair, breathing her in one last time. He kissed her, hoping it could do better than words could to express how much he truly loved her and always would, before he broke away to get dressed.

♥ ♥ ♥

Dealla shifted uncomfortably, and Caeden's grip tightened around her bicep. Eryn held her other arm, and Ronan stood a few paces behind them. He'd been quiet this morning. Caeden only heard a few words fall from his mouth, and most things he said were short and to the point. Ronan was the one to rebind Dealla's hands behind her back, and Caeden wasn't blind to the wordless conversation between the two. They really did love each other, but that didn't make them any less enemies.

Dealla shifted again, and Eryn yanked her arm roughly, pulling her body against hers. The expression on Eryn's face could've sent the entire army marching toward them running, but Dealla only glared back. "What's your problem?" Eryn snapped, her face inches away from the other woman's.

Caeden released Dealla's other arm to avoid pulling it from its socket, and glanced back in time to see Ronan visibly flinch at the harshness of Eryn's treatment. He didn't say anything, but he was visibly fighting with himself to keep from stepping between them.

There was nothing he could do, though. She was about to be given to the Dragon Lord.

Caeden's heart pounded in time with the thunder of footsteps against the ground beneath their feet. The Deovarian army had arrived a while ago—around the same time the soldiers from Crevia surprised them with their early arrival after they'd woken up—stopping far enough away that when Caeden emerged from his tent that morning, he was barely able to make out their tents on the horizon. Now, they stood halfway between the two opposing sides, waiting for the Dragon Lord to emerge with Caeden's sister for their trade before they would separate again and wait for the upcoming fight to begin at first light.

"The bindings are biting into my skin," Dealla snarled

through clenched teeth. "Pardon me for shifting because my wrists are about to bleed."

Eryn smirked at her, but nothing but deep-seated hatred was visible behind her eyes. "I can make them tighter, if you'd like," she offered, her smirk turning into a wicked grin. She said the words sweetly, but nothing but venom dripped from her tone.

Caeden barely heard their exchange as dread beyond anything he'd ever felt tightened around him like a noose. He'd heard the footsteps long before the Dragon Lord and his two companions were visible. Now, they stood only a few hundred yards away.

They were still far enough that he couldn't make out their faces, but he saw the black crown with its glowing purple jewels gleaming atop his uncle's head.

That hardly held his attention, though. Not when compared to the stretcher hauled between the two soldiers accompanying the man wearing the crown.

A white cloth was draped over a small body, and it rose and fell steadily. No matter how hard he tried, he couldn't pull his gaze away from the sight.

She was alive.

Amelia was alive.

"Enough."

Ronan hadn't spoken the word loudly, but it still cut through the argument that Eryn and Dealla were having and pulled Caeden back from the combined relief and dread that threatened to drown him.

"They're coming."

Dealla and Eryn froze, both of their heads turning to the scene.

Caeden's eyes remained trained on the group approaching theirs, but Ronan's words still sent a shiver down his spine.

This was it.

They would trade Dealla for Amelia, then the fight to end the war would begin.

"Nephew." The Dragon Lord's voice sliced through him like a freshly sharpened blade.

Caeden straightened as the group stopped in front of him. His heart pounded wildly in his chest, but he kept his face neutral as he eyed each of them. His gaze found the stretcher again and lingered there for a beat longer than he intended. His uncle was smiling at him with an expression that made his skin crawl when he looked back up.

"Lovely morning, isn't it?" the Dragon Lord said in a tone so casual Caeden had to bite the inside of his cheek to keep from driving his sword through the man's heart before the fight even began.

Eryn had turned her scorching glare away from Dealla and onto him, and Ronan now stood straight, looking every part the soldier he was.

"She's unharmed?" Caeden asked, nodding to Amelia on the stretcher and choosing to ignore his uncle's attempt to get under his skin.

The corner of the Dragon Lord's lips curled upward. "Straight to business then." He reached to lift the sheet covering Amelia.

Golden ringlet curls spilled out from beneath the sheet, splayed at odd angles across the stretcher beneath her. Her eyes were closed, her lips slightly parted as she took slow, deep breaths. She was alive, and seemingly unharmed, aside from the sedative they gave her after waking her from whatever magical trance she had been under for the past eleven years.

Caeden's heartbeat slowed as he took her in, an aching pain crushing against his ribs. She looked exactly as she had when they were children, only now he was nearly double her age.

He forced away the fears that came along with her waking in an entirely different world than the one she'd lived in eleven years ago. None of that mattered if they didn't defeat the man standing before them.

Caeden nodded. He turned and motioned for Eryn to come forward with Dealla, and she did. "She's been held in a prison cell for the past month, but she has been fed and has been unharmed by any of my people."

Eryn forced Dealla to turn around, allowing the Dragon Lord time to look over his daughter with his own eyes. He briefly glanced at her, then made a motion with his hand signaling he was satisfied, and Eryn spun her back around.

"Shall we finish this, then?" the Dragon Lord asked, not paying his daughter another second of his attention as he turned to face Caeden again.

Dealla visibly gritted her teeth, but didn't say anything.

Caeden nodded. He grabbed hold of one end of the stretcher Amelia was on, one of the guards holding tight to the other end, while Eryn offered the Dragon Lord Dealla's other arm.

They made the trade at the same time, Eryn releasing Dealla's bound hands as the soldier released his hold on the stretcher.

Caeden pushed the stretcher behind him and straightened to his full height again. "The fight begins at sunrise," he stated, his voice even despite the emotions swirling through him so intensely he worried he wouldn't be able to take a single step without falling. "Not a moment before. Whoever wins the fight, be it by surrender or death, will be declared the winner of the war. If it's by death, whichever kingdom prevails will claim the losing kingdom as their own. If it's by surrender, we will discuss further what that will entail."

A slow smile spread across the Dragon Lord's face. "Very good, nephew." He gave a mock bow, his eyes not leaving

Caeden's as his gaze turned predatory. "I look forward to meeting you on the battlefield."

And without another word, he spun on his heel and strode back toward his camp, pulling Dealla along by her bound wrists.

Chapter 53

Dealla

Dealla stumbled after her father, his fingers biting painfully into her skin a few inches above the rope encircling her raw wrists. She clenched her jaw tightly as she righted her feet beneath herself after stumbling a few more times.

Anger flared through her as she glared at the black and purple crown resting atop his head. He never took that thing off.

Despite herself, once she could keep pace with her father, she glanced over her shoulder. Caeden and Eryn were working together to roll the stretcher back toward their side of the battlefield, but Ronan hadn't moved.

He stood tall, his back straight, and if she'd been anyone else, maybe she wouldn't have noticed the tears shining in his hazel eyes.

Her chest tightened, and she swallowed hard past the lump forming in the back of her throat.

She would never see him again.

Or worse, she would meet him on the battlefield.

What would she do if it came to that? Would she be able to

force her blade into his flesh again? She'd done it more times than she could count when he was her prisoner years ago. That hadn't been deadly, though. And she hadn't been in love with the man whose eyes now refused to turn away from hers then, either.

Could she do it?

Could she kill him?

She prayed it would never come to that.

Dealla held Ronan's gaze for a long moment, stumbling again as her father continued to pull her arm, but she hardly noticed. She could have fallen to the ground and it wouldn't have made her break eye contact with the man behind her; the man she loved so much more than she ever should have.

It took everything in her when she finally turned away from him to face what she always knew she would have to.

This was where she was supposed to be. She was a Deovarian. These were her people. She may have spent her weeks in that cell wondering whether this was worth it, and wondering why her father hadn't put an end to the death and suffering yet, but that's what they were doing now. This was the final fight; the final day of bloodshed.

And she would stand with her people through every moment.

All she'd ever wanted was for them to be safe, and that was exactly what the end of this war would do.

A line of soldiers waited for them when they reached the edge of the Deovarian camp. Heads bowed when her father passed, but their eyes glanced up quickly after to land on her face. Wide smiles spread across familiar faces, and Dealla felt a smile form on her own lips, despite the humiliation she felt at being dragged along by her father like a misbehaving child and not his military captain and the one who had trained more than half of the soldiers currently standing on either side of them.

Her father didn't release her arm until they reached the center of the large camp, after parading her around as if she were no more important than the lowest-ranking soldier in their army. He didn't say anything as he spun her around and sliced through her bindings with a swift strike from his sword.

The rope pulled so tight around her wrists before it finally snapped that she bit her tongue hard enough for the copper taste of blood to fill her mouth. It was better than crying out in front of her father, though. She'd made that mistake too many times before.

She fought the urge to run her fingers along her raw wrists, checking the damage the ropes had caused. Ronan hadn't wanted to tie them so tight, and it was her own fault that they'd been that way. She'd urged him to tie them tighter; to truly bind her. It would look bad for both of them if he left them loose and she didn't use that fact to break free before the trade and kill them all.

Truthfully, she wasn't sure why she hadn't taken the opportunity he almost gave her and kept her mouth shut. She was alone with Caeden, Eryn, and Ronan while waiting for her father to arrive. She wasn't sure she would've been able to kill Ronan, but she wouldn't have had a hard time killing Aericora's king, and she certainly wouldn't have thought twice about killing that godforsaken Dragon Hunter.

She chose not to linger on the thought, though.

"The weapons are inside of that tent," her father said, dismissively waving a hand in the direction of the tent to her right. He turned away from her without even bothering to ask how she was after being held captive for a month.

Anger flared through her, and she clenched her hands into tight fists at her sides.

Dealla's eyes landed on the black and purple crown resting

atop his head again as he began to walk away, the stones gleaming in the moon and firelight.

It struck her for the first time that he'd never told her she would ever inherit that crown. He'd never told her she would inherit any of Deovaria. She was his only heir, so it was a given that she would, but the fact suddenly felt like a burning coal settling into the pit of her stomach.

She was only a soldier in his mind. He'd used her as one since she was a child. She was given military training from the age of four, and it never stopped. He never bothered to do the training himself, or congratulate her when she outranked nearly every other general in his entire army and became the only logical option for the open spot as Deovaria's military captain.

She spent so long trying to impress him. When her rank hadn't done it, she'd thought training new soldiers would. When that did nothing, she turned to being his weapon. She stopped being on the front lines and started being the face he presented to his soldiers—and to his prisoners.

She was the face of war to the Deovarians.

She was the face of death to the Aericora prisoners they'd taken.

And still, it wasn't enough.

So, for the first time in her life, Dealla planted her feet firmly on the ground, and spoke to her father in a way she had never dared to before.

"Why have you not attempted to negotiate peace?" Dealla asked. Her tone was accusatory, which wasn't her original intention, but she refused to back down.

The Dragon Lord turned to face her, anger flashing in his dark green eyes. He stared at her for a long time, and she felt her resolve crumbling beneath his gaze, until he finally burst into laughter.

Dealla gritted her teeth. Of course, he was amused by her. She shouldn't have expected anything less.

"Maybe we could've negotiated for peace if they hadn't been the ones to betray me and this kingdom," he bit out, then spun on his heel and disappeared before Dealla could make sense of how that had ever been the case.

His sister abandoned her responsibilities. She'd been irresponsible, but that in itself wasn't a betrayal. They made an agreement that would've seen her as the Queen of Deovaria and left him to live his life as he pleased, but she fell in love with a man from a different kingdom—the only heir to the throne of Aericora—so she renounced her title and left.

She hadn't gone about it well, and everything fell into chaos for a brief moment since all she'd done was leave a letter waiting for Dealla's father to find when he woke the next morning to see his world turned upside down.

But how was that enough to start a war of this scale? She understood he was furious with his sister. She understood why he'd transferred that blame onto Caeden's father and Aillin's kingdom for the turn his life took, but how could he use that to justify so much bloodshed? How could he use it to justify the lives lost as a result?

There was also the fact that he wanted control of the Rayfait Mountains, which was why they went to war with Soborg in the first place, and why Aericora was next on the list, even if that was the smallest of the reasons he wanted to end Aericora.

Still, how far had her father slipped into his hatred to allow it to come to this? How mad had he become from festering in events of the past and what he'd wanted his life to become?

"How are you?" came a soft voice, startling Dealla out of her thoughts.

Nora, a soldier around Dealla's own age who Dealla had met

and befriended despite being her trainer nearly five years ago, stepped out from behind the side of the large tent.

Worry hid in the lines of her face, and her lips were pressed together into a tight line. Her eyes flicked to Dealla's wrists before they roved over the rest of her body, searching for any more signs of injury. When she found none, she met Dealla's gaze again.

"Ready to end this," Dealla said. The words came out tight as her mind drifted back to the man on the other side of the battlefield with the most gorgeous set of hazel eyes. She shook her head, forcing the thoughts of him away.

He was her enemy, and she had a war to win.

Nora eyed her suspiciously, and Dealla was sure she could see right through her. Instead of questioning her, Nora only grinned and held a pack out for Dealla to take. "Let's spill some Aericora blood," Nora said, a mischievous glint sparkling in her eyes as Dealla took the pack from her.

Dealla glanced into the bag, finding a pair of her usual black leather armor and tight clothing to fit beneath it.

Dealla forced herself to smile back. "Let's win this," she said, even as images of Ronan lying dead in the grass in a puddle of his own blood flashed over and over in her mind.

Chapter 54

Smoke billowing into the air was the first thing Caeden saw as the fight began. Eryn stood by his side as they watched tendrils of gray ash rise into the sky from the first low sweeps of a dragon above. They hadn't set flame to any of their camp yet, only the grass a hundred yards away from the edge, marking a distinct line that Aericora's soldiers wouldn't be able to pass until the flames died down.

The lavender meant that the first dragons who swept low enough quickly retreated, but now they flew higher in the air overhead and kept to the edges of the camp, just far enough that the flowers wouldn't inhibit their abilities.

Aubry was in the center of their camp, away from the flowers on all ends so that she wasn't affected. But she was also trapped within the border they'd set up. She was still tired after her past days of flying, so they'd positioned her next to the medical tent to keep the wounded soldiers who would be transported there as safe as possible.

Eryn gripped Caeden's hand tightly, their fingers intertwined. The sharp edges of his mother's ring bit into his skin from where it rested around Eryn's finger as the first soldiers barreled through the twisting orange flames.

Somehow, Deovaria had managed to use the stones to make their soldiers immune to the raging flames. The only assumption Caeden could make was that the trick came along with enough stones being held on a single person, in the same way that Dealla's illusion magic had only worked for others when they'd held enough.

In all of their preparation for the fight, Caeden had forgotten about that small detail. Those were the people they needed to go after for stones, as well. All he could do was hope his soldiers figured it out quickly.

Fear twisted inside of him, a vice tightening around his stomach as he watched his people take up arms against their enemies.

The Deovarians could run through the flames. They couldn't set their entire camp ablaze thanks to the lavender, but they could spew turrets of flame high above their heads that would be warm enough to harm some, even if the flames wouldn't be able to reach them. It would only harm Aericora's soldiers, not Deovaria's, if they chose to do something like that.

It was too late to take that into consideration, though. They were here. They were fighting Deovaria, and one kingdom would come out victorious by the end of today.

The soldiers who were given the responsibility of ensuring the flames didn't grow too high were already carrying buckets of water from the nearby stream to drown out the fires.

He hoped it would be enough; that his soldiers could fend off Deovaria, and that they could steal more stones to take control of some of the dragons.

Eryn's fingers tightened around his, and he glanced at her. She wore a smile, even as the clanging of swords hitting one another, soldiers screaming, and billowing flames echoed around them. "We've got this," she told him.

Part of him wanted to laugh. He wanted to believe her words, but the doubts that snaked through him held on tight, and he couldn't push them away this time.

Still, he forced a half-smile and squeezed her hand back. He nodded, but couldn't force words out as the Deovarian soldiers descended on them and they broke apart to lift their weapons.

His blade connected with a Deovarian's as it arched high above his head, a split second away from connecting with his shoulder. The loud clang of metal on metal vibrated through his entire body as their swords met midair.

This was it.

This fight would determine the fate of his kingdom.

And he would fight like hell to ensure his people lived to see another day.

Blades clanging together was all he heard as he lost himself in the strange sort of trance he'd fallen into the last time he fought against the Deovarians. He'd learned it fighting with Eryn, but the dance was different with every partner who met the opposite end of his sword.

The first soldier was slower; easy to fight against and beat. He sliced a gash so long into the man's leg that blood gushed onto the grass at their feet, the slick red on green creating a sickening sight as the man crumpled to the ground, agonizing screams tearing from his throat. The screams were drowned out by the swords and the crackling of flames as another dragon made a sweep over the camp, creating another border to keep Caeden's soldiers trapped on two sides.

The second soldier was much faster, landing blows so quickly Caeden barely kept up. The tip of his enemy's sword sliced into his skin, but the pain was a dull throbbing in the back of his mind that he ignored. A slow smile spread across the soldier's face as he backed Caeden up a few steps, then slashed out and nicked his thigh with the lightest brush of his blade.

Everything dimmed around him as the soldier backed him up further. Fear worked its way through his veins, and the stinging of the two cuts he'd sustained suddenly burned like a hot iron against his skin.

The Deovarian slashed out again, this time so fast Caeden's only option was to duck to the ground to avoid the strike.

His knee collided with the hard earth, panic settling like a burning coal into the pit of his stomach.

He realized the fatality of his mistake too late.

The soldier pulled back his sword again, the same, slow smirk pulling across his face.

Caeden's chest seized. He wasn't afraid of the pain. He wasn't afraid of death. He was afraid of what his death would mean for every single soldier—every single *person*—around him.

How would the Dragon Lord treat his people once Caeden's head was severed from his shoulders? Would he allow them to live out their lives as an extension of his kingdom? Would he enslave them? Starve them? Torture them?

The soldiers would all die at the very least. His uncle wouldn't risk leaving those who would fight against him alive; those who would rebel against his every command.

Eryn would die.

Headstrong, stubborn Eryn, who he'd never known to hold her tongue a day in her life.

Eryn, who had only fought against the Dragon Lord because of the horrible things he'd done. Who had been born a Deovarian and suffered through the atrocities the Dragon Lord was responsible for.

Eryn.

His Eryn.

The woman who had stolen his heart more times than he could count. Who taught him how to hold a sword in his hands properly. Who would've given him the most debilitating glare only a few months ago if he'd made this same mistake during their training sessions, and probably still an eye roll now that would make his cheeks flush red.

Caeden's heart thudded as the realization hit him.

In the split second before the soldier's blade struck him, he dropped his sword. He twisted to one side, throwing his leg out with the same technique Eryn had used to knock him clean off his feet so many times it was almost embarrassing.

It wasn't as easy as she made it look, and he underestimated the force required to pull the move off properly, but it still made the soldier stumble forward. He tripped over Caeden's leg, but caught himself on the other side as his sword hit the hard ground.

That was all the time Caeden needed to grab his sword again and rightened himself on his feet, though. By the time the soldier turned back around to face him, he'd launched his own attack, and he struck the soldier square in the stomach. His sword slid through the man's flesh as easily as a knife through butter, and he forced himself to ignore the blood pooling on the man's shirt as his eyes flicked down to the sword embedded in his middle, then back up to Caeden's.

Caeden pulled his sword free from the man's flesh, and his body fell to the ground, his eyes turning glassy and lifeless.

"Good save."

The voice struck him like a slap across the face. Not already.

Dealla stood behind him with her sword already in her hand. Blood was smeared across her cheek and down the side of her neck from whoever's life she'd ended before finding him.

She held her blade limply, the tip dangling an inch above the grass at her feet, but her knuckles were white around the hilt. She was ready to use it, but she didn't want to. Resolve was written across her face though, and he knew beyond any doubt that if she got the chance, she would sink her blade into his flesh without a second thought.

And no part of him could blame her for it.

Ronan, his best friend and only confidant for longer than anyone else in his life, was in love with the woman in front of him, and Caeden wouldn't hesitate to kill her. He wasn't so sure anymore that he would like the feel of his cousin's blood coating his hands, but he would still run his sword through her chest if he got the chance. An ounce of sympathy for her had found its way into his heart. He wasn't sure when it happened, but he couldn't deny that it was there, even if it wasn't enough to keep him from doing what he needed to win this fight.

Caeden opened his mouth to speak, but no words formed on the tip of his tongue. He shook his head, and Dealla smirked at him. Whatever doubts she had before were gone as she stepped toward him, lifting her sword.

The fighting around them rang loud in his ears as she slashed at him and he narrowly stepped out of range, shoving her sword away with his own. No soldiers looked their way, each one too engrossed in their own fights. He caught one Deovarian glance at them, but when her eyes landed on Dealla, her lip twitched upward and she turned back to her fight.

He pushed Dealla back with the full weight of his body, and she stumbled a step before she pushed off his blade and launched another attack. He blocked her again, gritting his teeth as the blades slid against one another with a high-pitched screech that made his head spin.

"Why are you still fighting for him?" Caeden asked, but over the sound of the fighting, he wasn't sure if she heard him or not.

He'd seen the doubt on her face before. He knew she loved Ronan. The chance that either of those things was enough to change her mind about fighting for her father was slim, but something deep inside told him to try.

Dealla bared her teeth. She forced him back again before raising her blade high above her head and bringing it down near his shoulder. Rage displayed itself across her face, her nostrils flaring and her jaw clenching so hard he saw her pulse in her temples.

She leaned into his blade, pressing the full weight of her body into his. "Because he is my king," she growled, her voice low. They stood so close he felt her breath against his face as they pressed into one another. Their swords were so close to cutting into each other that Caeden held his breath.

It was the wrong thing to do, but he couldn't help it when he laughed. Dealla glowered at him, but the hatred he expected to see in her eyes wasn't there. Doubt clouded her features instead, and the sympathy he felt for her only intensified.

He'd seen how she was with her father. She didn't respect him like Caeden had respected his. She was scared of him.

The realization struck him like a slap across the face. He'd seen the signs clearly before now, but he never fully put the pieces together. It was obvious that she wanted his approval—that he didn't see her for what she was capable of and she would do anything to prove it to him—but the thought that it was fear causing that was new. The realization that it was fear of her father and not just a fear of rejection made his heart clench, despite knowing he shouldn't allow himself to feel anything but hatred for his cousin.

He had to kill her, no matter how damaged she was. She may have been scared of her father, but she was still fighting for him.

She was still murdering Caeden's people to aid in the Dragon Lord's pursuit of overtaking Aericora.

Dealla's rage flared. She shoved him back with so much force he stumbled over his own feet. He barely managed to catch himself before tumbling to the ground.

She was on him before he was fully back on his feet, landing blow after blow against his blade. He barely kept up with her swift movements as his heart pounded wildly and his muscles ached.

Caeden backed up as she continued to swing at him with such force that all he could do was defend. She was better trained than he was, and though she'd been going easy on him before, she wasn't holding back now. He wouldn't be able to hold her off for long, and that alone sent another wave of adrenaline through him.

She swung out wide, aiming a strike for the left side of his ribs, and he readied himself to block it, but she shifted downward at the last second.

He saw the change a split second too late. He blocked it with the tip of his sword, but it knocked him off balance. His sword slipped from his grasp, tumbling to the ground mere inches away from his hand as he lost his footing and fell flat onto his back.

His spine connected with the dirt and his vision went black as pain radiated through his body. His lungs burned as he struggled to take in a breath for a painfully long moment. His ears rang as the world slowly came back to him. Too slowly for safety.

He could just brush his fingers against the hilt of his sword, but couldn't quite wrap them around it.

Dealla was on him in a flash, so quickly he didn't have time to decide how he could safely shift to grip his sword before her boot came down on his wrist. The tip of her blade hovered a hair above the tender skin of his throat, and Caeden swallowed hard, the small movement enough to cause the sharp metal to bite into his flesh.

His cousin's face stared down at him, her green eyes a mirror of his own. For a brief moment, the world around him dimmed, and he wondered where in their family history the trait of bright green eyes came from. His mother had given them to him and Dealla's father had given them to her, but who had passed the trait down to them? Was it their mother or their father who passed down the genetics that led to their grandchildren staring into each other's matching sets of emerald while one held a blade to the other's throat?

Dealla paused, her sword still hovering above his trachea. The uncertainty returned to her face, and she wasn't trying to hide the worried crease that had formed between her eyebrows.

"Dealla!"

Caeden turned a fraction of an inch to see Ronan running toward them.

Dealla's hands shook on the other end of the sword, the tip of the blade piercing his skin just enough for a bead of blood to slide down the side of his neck. Her eyes were hard as she stared down at him. She didn't want to kill him, but she would do it because it was what her kingdom commanded of her. Even if her warring emotions were clear over every part of her face.

The thud that reached Caeden's ears echoed far louder than it should have.

Ronan's pained grunt followed, and Caeden's heart sank to the ground beneath him as Dealla's gaze landed on Ronan a few yards away.

He turned before truly making the decision to do so, and bile rose in the back of his throat.

Ronan was on the ground, a dagger protruding from his

stomach. Blood seeped from the wound, spreading across his shirt like a red ink stain on parchment. Pain was written across every inch of his face as he gripped the shaft of the dagger where it stuck out of his flesh. His breaths came in short, shallow gasps, and his eyes flicked from the wound back up to Dealla. A soldier stood a few yards away from him, his hand wrapped around the hilt of a dagger identical to the one in Ronan's stomach as he prepared to launch an attack on another enemy soldier.

Anger flared like a white-hot flame inside of Caeden's chest. He didn't even register the biting pain of Dealla's blade as his fingers closed around the hilt of his sword and he knocked the tip of Dealla's away from his neck before she could turn to face him. Tears streamed down her face, but he didn't care. He slashed his sword into her arm, leaving behind a thick, red gash that bled as fast as the wound in Ronan's stomach.

He didn't expect to feel the guilt that washed over him when Dealla dropped her sword and clutched her arm with her other hand. Her eyes flicked from him to Ronan again before they came back to his face.

Caeden lifted his sword, prepared to strike her again, but the pain in her eyes made him pause. He'd seen it before, but it struck him this time far harder than he'd expected. He didn't want to hurt her.

She was a pawn in all of this. She was a pawn who caused so much pain for so many, but the man she loved was lying fifty yards away with a knife protruding from his stomach that likely wouldn't make it out before it killed him.

There was something about that look in her eyes that made a strange part of him believe, truly believe, that she wouldn't harm a single one of Caeden's soldiers. That even if her father ordered her to torture another person from Aericora, she would refuse.

He had no way to know for certain whether he was right or if he was only hoping to see the best in her when he looked at her tear-streaked face.

Dealla must have seen that he did as well. Another tear slid down her cheek before she turned, allowing Caeden the chance to strike her down—to kill her without even a fight if he wanted to—and ran across the battlefield toward Ronan.

And Caeden let her, despite the part of him wondering whether it was the right choice or if he would come to regret it.

"They'll all die eventually," a voice said from behind him, and Caeden didn't need to turn to see the face of his uncle to know it was him who stood there.

Caeden gritted his teeth, the raging flame of anger returning tenfold before he turned toward the Dragon Lord.

"One by one," the Dragon Lord continued, a sickening gleam lighting his eyes as he watched the anger Caeden couldn't keep at bay slip onto his face. "We'll pick them off one by one until everyone you care about, everyone you love, has met the same fate as your mother and father."

Chapter 55

Ronan

Sunlight reflected off of the pristine, sharp edge of the dagger as it soared through the air. Ronan saw it only a fraction of a second before it sliced into his flesh.

The jolt rocked his body before the pain registered, and a grunt escaped him. He tried to step back and catch himself against the impact of the blade sinking into his abdomen, but the pain that flared through every fiber of his body made his head spin so intensely that he couldn't even recall how to move his limbs.

Ronan tumbled to the ground. Blue sky and green grass swirled before his eyes, and it wasn't until his head hit the hard earth that he could tell which way was up and which way was down.

He expected to feel the pain of the impact radiate through his skull, but instead, it only increased the raging current of fire flaring in his abdomen.

His hand gripped the hilt of the blade as he glanced to see it protruding from his flesh. Blue and purple gems studded the hilt; silver metalwork depicting gentle vines and flowers twisted over the surface. How could something so beautiful cause so much pain?

That thought struck him even harder than the blade in his flesh, and his eyes flicked back up to Dealla. She stood over Caeden still, her blade pressed into his throat.

He loved her, despite knowing he shouldn't. He'd fallen in love with the woman who'd held a dagger to his throat. She'd twisted so many blades into his flesh, both physically and metaphorically, and yet, he'd allowed himself to love her despite it. He'd forgiven her for the pain she'd caused him.

Could he forgive her if she killed Caeden, too? Could he forgive her if after the body of his best friend was lifeless on the ground, she moved on to Eryn, his sister?

He tried to sit up, but another pained grunt escaped him when he found that he couldn't, and he fell back against the ground.

Dealla's gaze turned to meet his, and his heart ached as painfully as the dagger in his stomach.

He couldn't.

He could forgive her for everything she'd done to him, but he couldn't forgive her if she took them from him. He couldn't forgive her if she took the only other people he loved.

"Don't," he wanted to whisper, but fear lodged itself in the back of his throat, and he couldn't make himself mouth the words. He couldn't figure out how he would begin to try as the blood seeped through his fingers, slick and hot.

Tears streamed down Dealla's face, and he could see her warring with her own emotions behind the glassy sheen to her eyes.

Ronan watched through the hazy fog swimming across his vision as Caeden grabbed his sword from the ground and disarmed Dealla. The haze grew with each passing second, even as the fear that his friend would kill the woman he loved intensified.

He blinked through the pain, but the fire in his veins was too much to fight against as the blood continued to seep through his fingers. He didn't dare look back at the wound as his head suddenly grew so heavy he couldn't force himself to keep it up any longer.

He blinked again, but this time, when he opened his eyes, Dealla stood in front of him. Tears streaked down her cheeks, her breaths coming in short gasps that sounded more like sobbing than breathing. They were nearly as stilted as his own, and he tried hard to ignore what that meant for himself.

"You're okay," Dealla whispered. She reached for him and pulled him into her lap. One hand clasped over his, applying pressure to his wound that he couldn't keep up on his own anymore, and the other gently ran against his cheek. "You're—" A sob escaped her, cutting off her next words, but she caught herself midway through and continued. "You're going to be okay."

Ronan wanted to laugh, but he couldn't find the strength to. A smile touched his lips as her features swam before his eyes. Those beautiful green eyes, the light dusting of freckles across her nose, and the sharp V her top lip dipped into at the very center.

He'd wanted to kiss those lips for the rest of his life. He'd wanted to grow old feeling them against his own, feeling the warmth of her skin seeping into his. He'd wanted to figure this out somehow, find a way for them to be together despite the opposite ends of the war they sat on.

But this was the last time he would see her.

This was the last time he would lay eyes on the face of the

woman he loved. The last time he heard her voice. And the last time he felt her arms around him.

Maybe, someday—he hoped far from now—he would see her again. Maybe one day, in whatever world awaited him after this one, they could live out a lifetime of memories together that weren't tainted by the bloodshed and horrors of a war they'd never asked for.

Maybe one day, it could just be the two of them and nothing more.

"Ronan!" Dealla sobbed, her arms tightening around him suddenly when it became hard for him to keep his eyes open.

He blinked up at her, trying his best to clear the fog away, but it was impossible. The blood loss was too much. He'd be unconscious soon, no matter how hard he fought it.

At least now, his thoughts were dimming so much that the pain hardly mattered. At least now, he could focus on the feel of her for the last moments he had.

It took every ounce of strength he had left in him to lift his arm up to rest his palm against her cheek. She leaned into his touch ever so slightly, the warmth of her tears mingling with the blood still coating his hand.

It had dripped from his hand onto her arm as well, or so he'd thought at first. It took a long moment for his gaze to clear long enough to make out the large gash running the length of her upper arm, blood oozing from the wound and trickling down to her forearm, dripping to the ground beside them.

"You're bleeding," he whispered, the words coming out so slurred he wasn't even sure he'd said the correct ones.

Dealla laughed lightly, but nothing but pain was visible in her eyes. "Don't worry about me," she told him, stroking his cheek gently with the tips of her fingers. She bent forward to brush her lips against his, and Ronan sighed at the feel of her kiss.

It would be the last time he would kiss her, and he never wanted it to end.

The fight was still hours from over, and there was no way he could get the medical attention he needed, even if someone managed to get him to the medical tents.

No, he would die here.

He would breathe his last breath right where he lay, in the lap of the woman who should've killed him years ago.

The haziness grew thicker, and when he opened his eyes again to take in Dealla's face, his vision was so tunneled all he could see were her eyes and the sad tilt of the small smile still on her face. His heart broke as he stared at her, the blackness closing in slowly.

"I love you," Ronan whispered to her.

He saw her open her mouth to say something else, but whether the words ever left her mouth, he couldn't be sure as the cruel claws of death pulled him into darkness.

Chapter 56

The Dragon Lord held his sword loosely. The tip of the blade swung back and forth over the grass beneath as if he was entirely convinced Caeden wouldn't slide his own blade through his ribs right then and there.

His uncle's lip quirked upward, and his hand tightened around the purple gem-studded hilt of his sword.

Caeden gritted his teeth, forcing his expression into one of neutrality even as every fiber of his being protested.

"Why are you doing all of this?" Caeden snapped, his tone as hard as the steel blade in his hand. The Dragon Lord had already given him the answer to the question back when he was held prisoner inside of Deovaria's palace walls, but he needed to hear it again. He needed to hear once more that all of this death and destruction was for no other reason than petty revenge. He needed to hear it even as every muscle in his body tensed at what hearing those words could mean.

"I'm only giving all of you what you deserve after they took my life away from me," the Dragon Lord snarled, flashing his teeth as he said the words.

Caeden's heart thumped loudly in his chest.

Maybe at one point the Dragon Lord had tricked himself into believing this war would help his people, but he was blinded by nothing more than his anger now. He couldn't see past it enough to see that it was causing his own people to suffer.

Revenge was the justification his uncle used for all of the lives he'd taken; all of the worlds he'd destroyed.

Caeden's heart thudded loudly in his chest.

He was no better.

His want for revenge against the man in front of him was the same thing that had led to his father's death. If he hadn't been so convinced that being in the field as a soldier would ease the aching pain he felt from the loss of his mother and sister, he would've stayed at the castle. He would've spent the time he should've spent getting to know the princesses, and Dealla never would've fooled all of them for so long. The King and Queen of Crevia never would've been called to the castle, and things never would've so easily lined up for Muire to murder his father.

For the first time since he was nine years old, Caeden was in control of the surge of anger that flooded him. It wasn't the same, uncontrollable torrent that blinded him to the world. This was a gentle thrum in his veins.

The man before him was mad.

There was no other reason for all of this destruction than his need for revenge against Caeden's mother. Her death, the imprisonment in time and space of her daughter, and the death of the man she'd left everything behind for wasn't enough.

Even if he killed Caeden too, it wouldn't be enough.

He wanted his old life back, but he would never get that.

Even if he overtook Aericora, even if he tortured its people for the rest of his life, it wouldn't give him what he wanted.

And somehow, more so than ever before, Caeden knew he

would do anything to keep his uncle from hurting anyone else. The people of Deovaria included.

When he lifted his sword and lunged at his uncle, it wasn't because the burning coal of hatred in his chest was craving revenge. It was because he needed to protect his people. And he needed to protect those from Deovaria who had been nothing but pawns in a game they hadn't even known they were playing.

The Dragon Lord's blade met Caeden's midair. The metal clanging together was the only sound he could make out over the ringing in his ears.

He would kill him.

He would slide his blade into his flesh and make sure no one else suffered like those living in Deovaria, and everyone else who had fought in this war. Every single one of them had suffered at the hands of the Dragon Lord, all because he couldn't accept that his sister had fallen in love with someone who made it impossible for her to become Deovaria's next queen without joining the two kingdoms together permanently.

If she'd died, the result would've been the same. Colm, the younger of the two siblings born to the King and Queen of Deovaria back then, would have taken the throne in any other number of circumstances. It was his duty to do so, even if he hadn't wanted to.

"This isn't worth it," Caeden bit out as he leaned into his blade, attempting to force his uncle back a step, but to no avail. "They're all suffering, but it won't change anything. She made her choice a long time ago. It's not what you wanted, but it's your responsibility to make sure Deovaria is safe."

The words wouldn't get through to him. Too many years had passed, and his hatred was an immovable piece of his very soul by now. If he couldn't see long ago just how much he was hurting his own people, if he hadn't seen it when his people began turning over their children to the dragons in hopes that it would keep them from starving, he would never fully understand everything he'd put his people through. Either that, or he would never care enough to change it.

Caeden said the words anyway, though. Some part of them helped him understand the path he'd been on when he let himself get swept up in his decisions. He'd made so many poor decisions over just the past few months in the name of trying to get back at the Dragon Lord for taking those he loved. If only he'd opened his eyes to what he was doing then, maybe things would've ended differently. Maybe, he could've figured out a way to end this war years ago, if only he'd had his mind on his responsibilities to his kingdom rather than his selfish want for revenge. Maybe he would've sent that letter to his uncle years before Aericora's soldiers dwindled enough that he questioned whether they would come out victorious in the end.

It was too late for all of that now, though. He'd made those decisions, but now he would need to do better. Now, he would need to fight not only for what was taken away from him, but for his people, and what had been taken from them and the lives they'd lost.

The Dragon Lord bared his teeth and shoved Caeden so hard he stumbled back before he rightened himself. His uncle was on him again in a flash, his blade slicing through the air, its sharp edge glittering in the early morning sunlight.

It came down hard near Caeden's side, an aim meant to slice straight through his collarbone, but he ducked away just in time to avoid the blow. He slashed out with his own sword aimed at the Dragon Lord's thigh, but he blocked Caeden's attack as if it were nothing.

Caeden may have technically been fully trained, but he was nowhere near the skill level of the man before him.

The Dragon Lord smirked as he pulled his blade back, giving Caeden just enough time to righten himself from the force of the blades hitting one another. "You won't win this fight, little prince," he sneered.

Caeden swallowed hard at the word; the use of his old title struck him through the heart in a way he hadn't expected.

A deep chuckle rumbled through the Dragon Lord's chest, and a glint of mischief that was so unlike the one he always saw on Ronan's face sparkled in his green eyes. "My mistake. It's 'king' now, isn't it?"

Bile rose in the back of Caeden's throat as images of his dying father flashed through his mind, then images of Ronan with the blade sticking out of his stomach. He couldn't let the Dragon Lord get to him, but it was hard not to when the wounds those words reopened hadn't even had time to stop bleeding.

He forced the images away, along with the pain and sorrow that came with each one. The sadness would never go away entirely—he'd learned that after years of mourning his mother and sister—but it would ease. The pain he'd seen on his friend's face was hard to push away, but he couldn't let himself feel the full force of those emotions right now.

Ronan wouldn't have wanted him to, anyway.

He wanted this war to be over just as much as everyone else.

And, if this could end fast enough, there was a chance the blade embedded in his stomach wouldn't cause the end of his life like the fear lacing Caeden's veins knew it would, given enough time.

Caeden lunged forward again, but the Dragon Lord's blade met his, not even close to striking him. A jolt shot through Caeden's arms as the blades connected, and Caeden gritted his teeth against the pain. He slid his blade along his uncle's, leaning into the hit as he slashed at his ankles.

The Dragon Lord jumped effortlessly out of the way and forced Caeden's blade into the dirt. He kicked Caeden's shin, his boot connecting with his bone and sending a wave of pain flaring through his leg. His knee buckled, and if not for the fact that he hadn't heard a crack, he would've been sure it was broken.

Caeden's knee hit the ground first, with a hard thud that only added to the excruciating pain. He fought to keep himself upright, but another blow, this time from the hilt of the Dragon Lord's sword against his back, sent him falling to the dirt.

Fear mingled with the pain, creating a blinding haze that made his vision go black. When it returned, his chest was heaving, the stinging in his spine having hardly dulled. Caeden spun onto his back. The aching only intensified as he met his uncle's gaze.

The smirk still pulled at the corners of the Dragon Lord's mouth as he raised his sword high above his head.

Death awaited him at the end of that blade.

It beckoned to him like a soft thrum throughout his body, dulling the pain, the fear, the anger, and leaving behind nothing but an overwhelming sadness as he watched the blade arc through the air.

There would be no one left to care for his sister. There would be no one left to care for his kingdom, not once the Dragon Lord's blade ended his life.

He'd failed.

He'd failed his kingdom, he'd failed his sister, and…

Eryn.

He'd failed her most of all. Not just as her student who she'd poured hours upon hours of her time into training to ensure he would live to see it through a fight like this, but as the woman he loved. As the woman he only got to call his fiancée for a few days. She deserved so much more than this. She deserved a life not held within the confines of a war she had no stake in.

They all did.

But his death would mean hers, and that pained him so much more than anything else.

The Dragon Lord's blade arced through the air, the pristinely sharpened edge glistening brightly. Caeden watched in slow motion as it neared his chest.

He squeezed his eyes shut, waiting for the pain the strike would inflict. Waiting for the feel of the steel as it slid through his chest.

The hard strike of metal on metal cut through his ears so harshly he felt it in his bones, and his eyes flew open to see Eryn standing over him, her blade blocking the Dragon Lord's mere inches away from his chest.

Beads of sweat rolled down Eryn's face. Her jaw was set, and the anger and hatred flaring in her eyes made his heart race in an entirely different way than it was before.

"Get. Away. From. Him," Eryn bit out through gritted teeth. The muscles in her arms flexed, and Caeden wasn't sure if it was purely her natural strength or if it was the rage and adrenaline coursing through her that gave her the strength to lift the blade away from his chest. Whichever it was, she forced the Dragon Lord back so swiftly that even his uncle looked shocked as he stumbled back.

Eryn was on him again before Caeden had time to climb to his feet. He reached for his fallen sword while Eryn lunged for the Dragon Lord with a ferocity that he'd never seen from her before. Her moves were lightning quick, aiming strike after strike in such quick succession his uncle had no choice but to back up.

Caeden turned away from the scene for a split second, and

found the hilt of his sword on the ground.

"Nice try, girl," came the Dragon Lord's voice from behind him.

Caeden's heart stopped.

Every muscle in his body seized at the sound of Eryn's sharp intake of breath.

No.

He didn't.

He couldn't have hurt her.

Paralyzing fear overtook him, but he forced himself to lay eyes on the woman he loved.

Eryn's eyes met his when he turned around. She stood with her back pressed against the Dragon Lord's chest, his blade a fraction of an inch away from her throat.

Her breaths came in rapid, shallow gasps, but the fear Caeden should've seen in her eyes wasn't there. Instead, there was only a hardness behind her gaze; the kind of understanding that made his heart shatter like glass smashed beneath stone.

She was prepared to die.

Accepted that this would be her end.

His grip tightened so hard around the hilt of his blade that his fingers ached, but it was nothing compared to the anger scorching through his entire body.

"Hurt her, and I swear to you there is nothing you could do, nowhere you could go, where I won't find you and make you wish that Death itself would come for you," Caeden growled, the words slipping out before he had time to consider whether he wanted them to.

The Dragon Lord laughed so loud it could be heard clearly over the fighting.

His gaze hardened after a fraction of a second, and his laughter ceased. "Make your choice, little king," the Dragon

Lord sneered. "Surrender or I slit her throat. Your kingdom, or your girlfriend's life; which will it be?"

Caeden's heart pounded in his chest as wildly as the blades banging against one another around them.

His grip loosened on his sword, every muscle in his body screaming to kneel. Screaming to surrender to the man in front of him if it meant Eryn's life.

He couldn't lose her. She didn't deserve to die like this.

But when Eryn's gaze met his, her eyes pleaded with him. The promise he'd made to her all of those weeks ago came rushing back, and he hated himself for making it.

He couldn't do it. He couldn't surrender to the Dragon Lord and let him kill and torture so many of his people. But how could he watch the woman he loved, the woman who could make every single bad thing disappear with nothing more than a smile, the woman who stood beside him through so much more than she ever needed to, how could he watch her die?

Tears streamed down Eryn's cheeks as she gave him the tiniest, almost imperceptible nod, urging him to make the choice he'd promised he would—the only choice the King of Aericora could make.

Caeden's heart crumpled until there was nothing left but dust. Tears burned in his eyes as he gripped the hilt of his sword.

"She was going to be my wife," Caeden told him, his voice strong despite the lump in the back of his throat. "And she will always be the love of my life." He didn't look at his uncle when he said the words. His eyes remained locked on Eryn's, soaking in every agonizing second of the most beautiful sapphire he'd ever seen.

There were so many things he'd refused to promise her because he couldn't be sure that he could keep those promises, but this one he could. Even if his soul would shatter beneath the weight of the promise he'd made in the dark before the glinting blade was ever held to her throat.

The Dragon Lord rolled his eyes in response, but Caeden didn't need to say another word for his uncle to understand his decision.

Even as every bit of him protested, he refused to turn away from the sight as the Dragon Lord's fingers tightened around the blade against Eryn's neck.

Chapter 57

Dealla

Ronan was dead.

The thought circled through her mind on an endless loop that made Dealla's heart break over and over again. Tears streamed from her eyes, hot and wet as sobs wrecked her. He was still breathing, ragged breaths that shook his entire body slowly making his chest rise and fall.

But there was no way to get him the medical aid he needed. There wouldn't be enough time, or enough resources, to help him. He would be dead before she had time to return with supplies to even try to save him.

She clung to the limp form of the man she loved.

She hadn't deserved his love. Not after everything she'd done.

She would've spent the rest of her life trying to make it up to him. It never would've been enough, but she would've done it without a second thought because that was what he deserved. He deserved that and so much more than she could ever have given him.

And now she would never be able to try.

Something inside of her broke a little more at the thought, like a string holding together a worn cloth finally giving out, causing the whole thing to fall to nothing but shreds of what it once was.

Numbness like she'd never known before settled over her like a thick fog. Her tears slowed as she sat up and stared down at the man who held her heart.

Suddenly, the world around her seemed to clear, despite the numbing haze swallowing her whole.

She'd felt something like this before when she was younger.

It'd been a fraction of the numbness that now drowned her, but it was there.

Her lies to Caeden when she'd been disguised as Margaid and told him about seeing her mother's death hadn't been as untrue as she'd intended, even if she hadn't allowed herself to relive the memories when she'd been letting those words spill from her lips.

She'd suppressed the memories for so long that she'd almost forgotten the way her mother cried before her father slit her throat.

She'd almost forgotten how her mother looked to her with a broken-hearted apology hidden behind her crystal blue eyes, the cry of pain that she'd almost let escape when the guard forced her to her knees on the hard tile floor of the throne room, and the dark red blood that stained the floor twenty feet in front of where Dealla's throne now rested beside her father's.

She hadn't looked to that spot in years, as if it had never been there to begin with. The pain that had come with the thought had felt traitorous until now. Sympathy for the rebels was equal to a rebellion of her own, and she hadn't allowed herself to feel anything for her mother since that day.

Her mother had spent years undermining her father, attempting to hinder Deovaria's advancement in the war from inside the palace walls without the Dragon Lord finding out. There were countless Deovarians in the villages doing the same, but their acts were nothing compared to the things her mother did right under their noses.

She'd needed to die for her actions, or so Dealla was told.

And she'd believed every word her father said.

She'd believed the rebels were the enemy. She'd believed they were working for Aericora to get them all killed. She'd believed they were evil. That her mother was.

And she'd done so without even a second thought.

Dealla swallowed hard as she stared down at Ronan. His face was still twisted to reflect the pain from the wound, even after an air of peacefulness had settled over him when he lost consciousness.

Her father had brainwashed her. He'd tricked her into fighting against people who hadn't meant any harm. He'd started a war because one person made a choice he wasn't happy with, and now thousands were dead.

Maybe he'd even brainwashed himself. He'd said he was doing this for their people, but that was a lie. Maybe it was a lie he'd told her, but it seemed to be a lie he believed himself. A way to trick himself into thinking this war wasn't simply because he wanted revenge for the decisions his sister made.

And now, because of everything her father did, the man Dealla loved was dying in her arms.

No. Not her father.

The Dragon Lord.

A father wouldn't do this to his daughter.

A father wouldn't have turned her into a murderer at the age of twelve. A father wouldn't have made her feel worthless no matter how many of his enemies she tortured and killed. A father would never have been responsible for the death of the man his daughter loved.

The numbness turned to a sour pit of rage in her stomach, hot and heavy with so much sorrow it made her entire chest hurt.

How could he have done all of this to her?

Maybe at one point, the Dragon Lord had felt love for his daughter. But he hadn't seen her like that in a long time. She wasn't his child anymore; she was only a tool in his arsenal. She was the blade he used to strike down anyone who got in his way, no matter how much blood covered the steel or how worn its once pristine edges became.

She refused to be his tool anymore. She refused to be his murderer.

The edges of her soul were too worn. The very fibers of her being were too frayed.

She wanted this to end. All of this death, the pain, the torture that he'd put so many people through, including her.

Dealla lifted her gaze to where the Dragon Lord stood, fifty yards away from where she knelt on the ground with Ronan's limp form in front of her. The Dragon Lord held a dagger to Eryn's throat.

Eryn Gedding. She used to despise the very thought of the woman now standing painfully close to death. The man she too loved stood only a few feet away, as powerless to help her as Dealla was to help Ronan.

The hatred she used to feel for Eryn was gone. Now, all she felt was a twinge of regret. A sadness for the life Eryn had lost because of the Dragon Lord, much like she'd lost her own.

Dealla's gaze flicked to Ronan's face. Blood was smeared across his cheek, a clean streak running through the spot of red from where his tears had fallen only moments before.

She turned back to Eryn, who had tears of her own streaming down her face. Silent resolve was written into her features, as if she'd accepted the fate awaiting her. As if she'd accepted death itself.

But she didn't have to die. Not one of the soldiers surrounding her did.

There was only one.

Only one whose death would truly make a difference and end all of this.

Dealla was on her feet before registering that she'd even made the choice to do so. Her hand gripped the hilt of her sword with such ferocity it could've bent the metal beneath her palm.

She hadn't realized she'd made the choice until she was running. Until she pulled her sword from its sheath and ran the blade through the back of the man who she should've been able to call her father.

But there hadn't been a choice to make.

Not truly.

This was the only way.

This was the only way it would finally end.

A gasp left the Dragon Lord's lips as sticky, warm blood flowed over Dealla's fingers.

The tears that had stopped only moments before returned, and the numbness was drowned out by a pain that consumed her from the inside out.

The Dragon Lord's blade tumbled to the ground, and Eryn jumped away from him. Caeden rushed to Eryn's side, and they both stilled when their eyes landed on her.

Dealla could feel their gazes, feel the weight their stares held, branding the truth of what she'd done into her very soul.

But she didn't look at them.

All she could see was her sword in her hand, its blade driven so deep into the Dragon Lord's back that she couldn't make out an inch of the metal. Blood ran over her hands, firmly wrapped around the hilt of the weapon that had killed her father.

Chapter 58

Eryn

Eryn's heart pounded wildly as Caeden's arms came around her. She fell into his embrace, tears stinging her cheeks. She faced the man who'd held a blade to her throat mere seconds before.

The man who now stood with a sword shoved through his heart that protruded from his chest only a few inches away from where Eryn had been held against him. Her heart skipped a beat at the sight. She'd been so ready to accept death, but seeing now how narrowly she'd evaded it sent a shiver down her spine.

"I'm sorry," Dealla whispered, so softly the words hardly reached Eryn's ears. "You… you can't live. I'm sorry." Her voice cracked over the words, and tears flowed so quickly down her cheeks that they dripped steadily onto the collar of her shirt.

The Dragon Lord glanced at the sword struck through him, his eyes wide with a kind of panic that sent a primal wave of satisfaction running through her. It mingled with such a strong feeling of relief that she fell further against Caeden, unable to hold herself up.

"She killed him," Caeden breathed, his voice a disbelieving

whisper against her hair, just as the Dragon Lord's body fell to the ground in a heap.

A sob so loud it drowned out the fighting around them tore from Dealla's throat. She sank to her knees, her body trembling with grief as she crumpled over the limp form of her father, his eyes glazed and lifeless.

Caeden's grip on her loosened, and Eryn took a step toward Dealla and the Dragon Lord's dead form.

He was dead.

The Dragon Lord was dead.

A half laugh escaped her, even as the fighting around her continued, oblivious to the scene lying amid all of it.

They'd won.

Aericora had won the war.

The fighting would stop the moment Caeden stood over the Dragon Lord's dead body and proclaimed their victory.

Eryn turned to face him; to face Aericora's king, her fiancé, the man she loved.

And her heart plummeted straight through her stomach.

Caeden wavered on his feet.

He hadn't let go of her to get a better look at the Dragon Lord. He'd let go of her because an arrow had struck him in the side.

"No," Eryn breathed.

Caeden's hand gripped his side at the base of the arrow, blood seeping through his fingers.

"No. No, no, no!" Eryn screamed, the words flying from her mouth without her approval.

Caeden looked up at her, pain written across his features as he pulled his hand away from the bloody mess at his side.

He would die if they didn't get him help quickly. But would they be able to fix it? The realization that she'd never seen someone live through an arrow through their liver in the center of the battlefield hit her like a brick wall.

Caeden stumbled a step, but this time he couldn't keep himself up. His knee hit the ground first, and a grunt left him before he let himself roll onto his side with the arrow sticking upward.

Eryn was on the ground beside him, though she couldn't remember taking the few steps to get to him or when she'd lowered herself to the ground.

A small smile touched his face as Eryn wrapped her arms around him. The tears that had eased returned with a vengeance as she pulled his body against hers. He lifted his hand and placed it against her cheek, the warmth of blood—his blood—coating his hands sticky against her skin.

"You can't die," she told him. She said the words like a command, even though he had no way to ensure he stayed alive through this. "I can't lose you both in the same day."

She'd pushed the sight of Ronan to the back of her mind, but she knew what it meant that Dealla was over here with her sword plunged through her father's back rather than in a medical tent with Ronan.

Caeden's smile softened, his eyes not leaving hers. "Take care of them for me, okay?"

"No!" Eryn practically shouted the word. She pulled him closer and buried her face against his chest as his hand fell into her hair. "You don't get to say that. You're going to be just fine." She lifted her head just enough to look him in the eye. "You're going to be okay," she promised, but the lie in her words burned her throat. She had no way of keeping that promise.

His eyes searched hers, and the love she saw in them made her heart ache. "I love you, Eryn Gedding," he whispered, and she wished she could've paid more attention to the sound of those words rather than the trickle of blood that fell from the corner of his lips.

She'd never liked being referred to by her last name, and was quick to tell fellow soldiers to use her first name only, but when her full name fell from his lips, it was the most perfect thing in the world. Even before she'd fallen in love with him, she'd liked the sound of it.

"I love you," she told him, but his eyes were already closed when she was finally able to push the words out past the sob threatening to make her voice hitch.

"LAY DOWN YOUR WEAPONS!"

Dealla's scream pierced through the air like the most pristinely sharpened blade, and through her tears, Eryn turned to focus her gaze on the woman.

And dread hit her when her eyes found the crown resting atop Dealla's head.

The Dragon Lord's crown.

She should've taken it before Dealla had the chance. They should've claimed their victory the moment the Dragon Lord's body hit the ground.

They hadn't won.

They'd just lost.

Because Aericora's king was as good as dead, and the Dragon Lord's daughter, the heir to the throne and Deovaria's next rightful ruler, now stood above them with every ability to claim victory as her own.

The fighting around them stopped, and slowly, one by one, the soldiers paused their fights to turn their attention to the new Queen of Deovaria.

Dealla's gaze locked on hers, and Eryn's heart thudded loudly with every step Dealla took toward her.

She would kill Eryn next before she claimed her victory.

And Eryn couldn't even blame her. She knew the woman standing before her harbored the same hatred that Eryn felt for her.

Eryn swallowed hard when Dealla stopped in front of her and lifted her sword into the air. She made a show of holding it high above her head, turning so all of the soldiers surrounding them could take in the sight and watch as she used that blade to end Eryn's life.

At least she would die beside the man she loved. At least she wouldn't have to live this life without him.

Eryn closed her eyes and clung to Caeden's body, his shallow breaths coming in ragged gasps that told her death would come for him soon.

She waited for the strike.

Waited for the jaws of death that she'd evaded for too long to finally claim her.

A thud reached her ears as something landed on the ground beside her.

Heart still racing, Eryn dared to open a single eye. She was fully prepared to see Dealla's blade coming at her, but that wasn't what lay in front of her.

Eryn gasped.

Dealla, Deovaria's queen, had dropped her sword to the ground mere inches away from where Eryn sat.

Eryn glanced at her, bewildered as she took in the pure sadness on the queen's face.

Dealla fell to her knees, her head bowed, but her eyes never left Eryn's. "I, Queen Dealla of Deovaria, surrender to Eryn Gedding, Queen of Aericora. Let this war finally come to an end."

Chapter 59

Caeden groaned, the pain in his side overwhelming every other thought. It was sharp at first, but as he slowly gathered his thoughts, it dulled to a dim ache.

He blinked, clearing the fog from his vision, and glanced around the room slowly. He was in the infirmary in the castle.

Something crashed to the floor beside him, and he didn't have time to register what was happening when someone slammed into him, their arms wrapping around him hesitantly, but still with enough force that it sent a wave of pain flaring through him.

The feel of Eryn's arms around him and the way her lavender scent enveloped him washed it away just as quickly, though.

"You're awake," she whispered. Her voice sounded breathless when she spoke against his neck, and those simple words sent everything that happened crashing back into him.

The fight.

The Dragon Lord.

The dagger to Eryn's throat.

Her tears.

Dealla's sword slicing clean through her father's chest from behind.

And then the arrow that struck him in the side.

Ronan.

Bile rose in the back of his throat as images of his best friend with a dagger protruding from his abdomen flooded his mind. Eryn was safe, the Dragon Lord was dead, but Ronan…

He didn't know if he had it in him to ask what had happened to Ronan by the time the fight ended.

Eryn pulled away from him just enough to gaze into his eyes. Tears streaked down her pretty face, and he hadn't realized he was close to crying until her beautiful eyes blurred beyond the tears clouding his own.

"I love you," Eryn whispered, so softly her words hardly reached him.

He'd been so sure he would die when she'd held him while blood poured from the arrow wound in his side. He didn't think he'd ever get to see those sapphire eyes again.

Pain flared through every inch of him when he lifted his arms, but he didn't care as he held her close, pulling her back against him. He kissed her deeply, the feel of her lips against his enough to drown out every remnant of pain.

"I love you, too," he told her.

He wanted to hold her there until the end of time. Until everything around them crumbled to dust and they were nothing more than ivory bones.

After what felt like far too little time, Eryn pulled away again. She wiped the tears from her eyes with the backs of her hands, but made no move to stand up. Instead, she sat on the edge of his cot, her fingers intertwined with his as her thumb traced circles over the back of his hand.

She glanced behind herself quickly, and turned back with a

sheepish grin on her face that made his heart race.

A chair sat beside his cot. A blanket was draped over the back of the chair, and a book and pencil he was sure she was holding before he woke up were on the floor a few feet away, the pages of the book splayed out in every direction.

A smile pulled at the corners of his lips as he took in the sight. She'd sat beside him. He was sure it was far from the whole time, but there was something comforting about the fact that she'd made herself space next to him, and it made a warmth seep through his chest.

Caeden knew there were things they needed to discuss, but rather than ask the questions he knew he would have to, the two of them sat together in a silence that felt like a gentle embrace until Eryn curled up beside him on the cot and sleep claimed them both.

Eryn was still beside him when he woke again, but this time, they weren't alone. Ronan sat in the chair beside his cot, a thin sheen of sweat coating his face. Pain twisted his features, and he looked far paler than Caeden had ever seen him before. But he was alive.

Somehow, they were both alive.

Eryn must have seen the confusion across his face, because a light laugh escaped past her lips and she squeezed his hand gently. "It's because of the magic, you dummy," she explained.

Caeden frowned at her, until she gave him a gentle smile that told him in the most loving way possible that he was an absolute idiot, and the realization dawned on him.

"How's that possible?" Caeden asked, his eyes flicking between Eryn and Ronan.

Ronan shrugged in response and turned to Eryn for an answer. "I don't know," he answered. "I wasn't exactly conscious for most of all..." He paused before he made a gesture with his hand toward the room around them. "Everythin'," he finished, which only left Caeden more confused.

"Aubry explained it," Eryn told them. "Just like the water from the stream healed Ronan's leg, it kept you both alive. I don't understand exactly how, but since the magic runs through our blood from the stream, it somehow kept the bleeding under control enough that we were able to get you both medical attention in time. It's the same magic that helps dragons heal so fast." A blush hid in her cheeks. "And why I've lived through more things than I should have."

Caeden could only vaguely recall one of the many books Eryn had assigned him talking about how dragons could heal quickly from their wounds, but that wasn't a conclusion he ever would've come to on his own.

"That's a dangerous thing to know," Ronan mused, a glimmer of mischief twinkling in his hazel eyes. "Does that mean I ain't gotta worry 'bout what drinkin' too much'll do to my liver?"

Eryn tossed him a glare. "No."

Ronan only smirked in response, which meant he wasn't going to listen to what Eryn had to say about it.

Caeden couldn't help the grin that spread across his face.

The three of them lapsed into silence, and Caeden's thoughts swirled in his head. There were so many questions he needed to ask, but one in particular forced itself to the forefront of his mind, drowning out all of the others.

"Where's Amelia?" he asked, his voice so soft it hardly reached his own ears. He dreaded the answer that would come from it. He didn't trust the magic his uncle used on her. The Dragon Lord had given her a sedative after waking her from the trance she'd been in for the past eleven years, but there was no way to know whether she would ever wake up again. She may not have woken up at all after they removed her from the glass prison they'd kept her in.

Even if she was entirely out of the magic's hold and they really had only given her a sedative, what if the magic did something to her mind and left her frozen? What if she never truly came back?

Eryn's fingers found his arm, as gently as a feather against his bare skin. He turned to face her, and though he'd become as good at seeing past the masks she'd worn consistently when they'd first met, he couldn't read what he saw in her eyes now.

"She's awake," she said gently. "She's scared, but she's awake. She's in her room and hasn't wanted to come out. I helped her get her things unpacked yesterday after we returned home, but she hardly spoke." Eryn lowered her gaze, and her next words sounded forced. "She wants to see your father, and I didn't have the heart to tell her yet that he's gone. I figured you would want to do it."

Caeden's heart squeezed painfully. He didn't want to be the one to break the news to his sister, but he appreciated that Eryn had waited so he could be the one to do it. She would learn everything that happened either way. The proof was all around them, and there was no point in trying to hide everything that changed if Amelia was ever going to have a chance at a normal life again.

Caeden swallowed down the lump of emotion threatening to make his words come out hoarse before he spoke. "Thank you." He took Eryn's hand and squeezed it gently, the cool metal of the ring his mother once wore pressing into his fingers.

His gaze flicked to it, and he couldn't help the smile that touched the corners of his mouth as he took in the sight of the sapphire stone against her skin. He would need to have a new one made for her, now that everything was over. Unlike when his father had given him a replica to give to the fake princess, it felt right for the ring to be on Eryn's hand. His mother had wanted his future wife to wear the ring, and no part of him believed his mother wouldn't have adored Eryn if she'd gotten the chance to meet her.

Caeden turned to Ronan, who watched them closely. There was another thing he needed to ask, and the look on Ronan's face told him he was waiting for the answer to the same question. He must have only woken up recently, as well.

"What happened to Dealla? How did everything end?"

They clearly hadn't lost the war, or he would never have woken up in the infirmary, but that left a lot of questions to be answered.

"She's upstairs," Eryn answered, which was the last thing Caeden expected to hear.

Ronan's eyes lit up with a mix of excitement and confusion. He started to climb out of his seat, but flinched when he moved and seemed to decide it wasn't a good idea. That would likely change when he found out exactly where Dealla was currently residing, though.

Eryn explained to them how everything ended. How Dealla claimed control over the Deovarian army, and how she'd surrendered. Her cheeks turned pink when she explained how Dealla referred to her as Queen of Aericora, but it only made Caeden's heart skip a beat.

They weren't married yet, but she was his queen, and that alone was the most incredible thing in the world.

"She came to visit you," Eryn continued, turning her

attention solely to Ronan, who had been still with an entirely unreadable expression on his face the entire time she'd been speaking. Eryn swallowed hard. "I got to talk with her a bit. She's… not so bad."

The words seemed to pain her, and it was enough to make Caeden laugh, even despite the pain that surged through him when he did.

Ronan's cheeks turned the slightest bit pink. "I really do love her," he said softly. "I meant it before, and it's not gonna change."

"She's…" Eryn stopped herself and stared at Ronan for a long moment; at the man who she'd fought side by side with on the battlefield for years, who she'd been raised with—her brother.

The same thought still circled through Caeden's head along with the confusion over how Ronan could love someone who did so many horrible things to him, but he pushed that aside, and he could see when Eryn did the same. It wasn't either of their place to decide what was right for Ronan, or even for Dealla. They may never have made the same choices, but somehow, despite everything that happened between the two of them, Caeden couldn't deny that they did truly love each other, and he knew Eryn wouldn't be able to deny it either.

"She's up by my old room," Eryn told him. It wasn't what she'd first intended to say, but the way her lips tilted upward ever so slightly told Caeden she was happy she'd said those words instead.

Ronan smiled back, a sense of warmth and acceptance passing between them. "Thank you, Reckless."

Eryn rolled her eyes. "Nothing to thank me for, you idiot," she told him, a grin hiding in the edges of her expression.

Ronan smirked. "It was only preemptive since I know you're

gonna help me get outta this chair in a minute."

Caeden snorted a laugh while Eryn grumbled a half-hearted string of insults beneath her breath. She stood to help him out of the chair either way, though. "Miss the cane yet?" she joked as she helped to support most of Ronan's weight against her while he righted his feet beneath himself.

"I ain't ever gonna miss that old thing," he told her.

It took him a few long moments to stumble his way out of the infirmary, but he managed to do so without falling, and by the time he was to the doors, he was hardly struggling at all.

Caeden focused his attention on Eryn as she turned to face him. "You're next," she told him. "Amelia is waiting for you."

Chapter 60

Ronan

The halls were dark all the way to the room where Eryn used to spend her nights. There was no sign that she'd come back to the space since before she began sleeping with Caeden. Dealla was down that hall, but as a silent protest, the servants seemed to have opted to leave her in darkness.

The only way Ronan could tell which of the doors led into Dealla's room was from the dim candlelight flooding out beneath the small crack between the bottom of the door and the tile floor.

A wave of nervousness crashed into him as he stopped in front of her door. There was nothing left to keep them apart. Not really. Her betrothal to Caeden was most definitely off, even if the rest of the kingdom didn't already know the entire story. But they were no longer at war with Deovaria either. He wasn't sure what the exact result of the end of the war was, but that likely wouldn't be discussed in detail until Caeden was back on his feet and ready to meet with the advisors, anyway.

But something about that sent a new wave of worry through

him.

She was the Queen of Deovaria. Not only was he from the kingdom she'd been at war with only a few days ago, he was nothing more than a soldier. He wasn't someone a queen would ever be with.

Ronan had to push the worries away before he raised his arm to knock on the door, the pain more manageable now that the medicine the nurse gave him had kicked in.

The door swung open just as his knuckles were about to connect with the hard wood.

Dealla stood in front of him.

Ronan stared at her, surprise flashing through him as he took her in. Either she'd been waiting for him, or her timing had been perfect. There wasn't any surprise on her face though, only a gentle smile laced with a hint of fear hidden behind her eyes.

"Hi," Dealla said.

"Hi."

Her eyes trailed down his body before they rose up to meet his again. The bandaging covering his stomach was thick, and he knew she could see it clearly beneath his shirt. The way her throat bobbed with a hard swallow when her eyes lingered there for a beat longer than anywhere else only confirmed it. "How are you feeling?"

A grin spread across his face against his will, and he shrugged casually. "Absolutely wonderful."

Dealla raised an eyebrow at him, the corner of her mouth quirking up. "The way you flinched just now definitely shows it."

Ronan shrugged again, but didn't say anything in response. Dealla didn't seem to know what to say either as a heavy silence filled with so many unspoken things fell over them.

"Are you okay?" Ronan asked. Eryn had told him what she'd

done. How she'd killed her own father so she could surrender to Eryn and officially end the war.

It didn't matter that her father was evil. Even if she was no longer blind to it, he had still been her father.

Dealla's gaze fell to the floor, and she sighed. "It needed to be done."

"That ain't what I asked."

She peered up at him through thick eyelashes, her bright green eyes shimmering with the start of tears that weren't there before.

Ronan swallowed hard as he watched her rub them away with the backs of her hands. He wanted to reach out to her, to hold her like he'd done so many times before, but something felt different now that everything was over. There were too many unanswered questions, and he needed to know that she still wanted to be with him as much as he wanted to be with her before he would do that.

Dealla offered him the kind of sad smile that made his heart twist inside of his chest. "I will be," she told him. "Eventually." She wiped at her eyes again, clearing away the last of her tears before she stood straight and stepped aside in the doorway. She gestured inside. "Do you want to come in?"

Ronan didn't so much as hesitate when he stepped past her and into the room. The space was small, compared to most other rooms in the castle, but it was still considerably larger than his shack outside. It was sparsely decorated; only a few paintings hung on the walls that he was sure had been there long before she occupied the room. Clothes hung in her open wardrobe against the wall to his right, and unlike the lavish dresses she'd worn when she was disguised as the princess, these were simple, and he could make out quite a few pairs of pants hanging between the cloth dresses.

"Eryn brought them for me yesterday," Dealla explained, noticing where his gaze had drifted. "She's not so bad, once you get to know her a little."

That was the way most people described Eryn, but it sounded like high praise coming from the woman who had fought with her as her enemy.

"She said pretty much the same 'bout you," he told her.

A slight smile turned the corner of Dealla's mouth upward.

"What happens next?" Ronan asked softly. She wouldn't have much of an answer, but he needed to ask the words. He wanted to be with her, wanted to spend the rest of his life with the woman who had once held the keys to his cell, but who had also been the one to sleep beside him and ease his every worry with nothing more than the brush of her fingertips.

"I don't know," she answered, her eyes glued to the floor and the few feet of space separating them. Her left hand lifted to her throat, as if she expected to find the ruby necklace that had disguised her, but her fingers closed into a fist and fell back down to her side when she remembered she hadn't worn it in weeks. "They aren't truly my people anymore, but I want them to be safe and cared for. I know Aericora will take care of them, but I will miss them."

Ronan heard the words she didn't say; how she couldn't go back simply because of politics. If the people of Deovaria—specifically those in the palace—were at all sympathetic to what her tyrannical father had done, they could use her. They could threaten her life or anyone she cared about and make her be the face of a new war. The Deovarians couldn't know most of the reasons behind what the Dragon Lord had done or they never would've followed him, but at the very least, the court knew he wanted to overtake Aericora. And whatever lies he'd spewed to convince them that Aericora needed to be defeated had clearly been enough. If any of them were half as mad as Dealla's father had been, they would have no problem using his daughter as the face of whatever their next insane plan may be.

He wished he could say something comforting, but no words formed on the tip of his tongue. Instead, he took a few, tentative steps closer to her.

Dealla's gaze met his, and his breath caught in the back of his throat. She was the most stunning woman he'd ever seen. She wore a different face than when he'd first met her, but the woman he loved was still there.

And the last of whatever doubt he'd had faded away.

He closed the distance between them, his hand coming up to rest on her tear-streaked cheek before he wiped them away with his thumb.

She relaxed into his touch and the air of uncertainty that surrounded them disappeared entirely.

Dealla lifted herself onto her tiptoes and pressed a gentle kiss against his lips that made his heart feel like it would melt straight through his chest. His hand lifted to the back of her neck and tangled into her hair as he pulled her closer, deepening the kiss and drawing a moan from her lips.

Her hands cupped either side of his face, and she pulled away slowly to look him in the eyes. Silent tears rolled down her cheeks as she stared at him, her eyes drifting across every feature of his face as if she was committing him to memory.

"I thought you were dead," she whispered, her words hitching with a sob before her arms fell around him and she buried herself against his neck.

Pain flared through him when her body fell against his, but it was nothing compared to the ache in his chest at hearing her say those words.

Ronan held her close. "I'm right here," he whispered.

She pressed a kiss to the side of his neck, the remnants of the tears falling down her cheeks wetting his skin. "I love you," she told him. "I'll always love you, and I'll spend every day for the rest of my life telling you just how much, if you'll let me."

Her words made his heart skip a beat. "Was that a proposal?" he asked. He'd meant the words to come out like a joke, but there was no hint of it in his tone. He was entirely serious, and she seemed to realize that too when she pulled away to look at him again.

It wasn't until her gaze met his that he realized just how much he hoped it was. He wanted her. For the rest of his life, he wanted to be with her, and only her.

"No," she said, and he felt the oxygen drain from his lungs until a smile spread across her face. "This is."

Before he had time to register what she was doing, Dealla knelt to the ground in front of him, her beautiful green eyes gazing up into his with so much love that it made his chest ache in the most incredible way.

"Ronan Atkyn, will you marry me?" she breathed, as if the words were the most sacred of promises. As if there were so many promises beneath them that the words themselves could never do it justice.

"Yes."

He said the word too quickly, but there wasn't a single doubt in his mind when he did. There was no other answer. Only the one he'd given her.

Dealla smiled up at him and climbed back to her feet. She cupped his face in her hands and kissed him, not quite rough but not quite as gentle as she had earlier either. This too, was a promise. A promise that just like he would, she would stand beside him for as long as she lived.

And his heart swelled with the overwhelming sense of love

he felt when he kissed her back, his kiss laced with every last one of those same promises.

"I love you, Dealla," he whispered against her lips.

No one else had ever made him feel the same way she did, had ever made him want for anything more in life than a quick evening in bed and a bottle of whiskey.

But she did.

He wanted to spend his nights beside her, wanted to wake with her still next to him every morning. He wanted to live his life with her, have children with her, grow old still standing beside her. There were so many things he'd never considered wanting in his life until he'd met her, and with her, he wanted every last one of them.

"I love you, Ronan."

Chapter 61

Amelia was in her old bedroom, where Eryn said she hadn't yet left in the two days since they'd returned from the battlefield. She hardly spoke to anyone, likely because she was still confused by everything Eryn told her would need to wait until she could speak to Caeden.

Eryn knocked on the door twice, and the sound of light footsteps against the floor echoed from inside.

Caeden's heart rate sped up at the sound. Even her footsteps sounded the same as they had eleven years ago. He hadn't realized how distinct they were back then. He'd heard that same sound at least once a day when he'd gone to find her as a child.

Eryn didn't wait for a response before she pushed the door open, revealing the face of the eleven-year-old blond girl inside who looked exactly the same as Caeden remembered her. She was smiling with the same too-wide grin he remembered like the back of his hand when she looked at Eryn, but it faltered when her eyes drifted to Caeden, and he couldn't help it when he winced.

She looked him up and down, her eyes taking in every detail

right down to the bandaging beneath his shirt and the crooked way he stood to compensate for the pain.

"Caeden?" she asked suspiciously when her eyes returned to his. Confusion was written across her face. She didn't try to hide it the same way anyone else would. Instead, it was written plainly across her features in the furrow of her brow and the way she tilted her head to the side.

Caeden opened his mouth to respond, but a lump had lodged itself in the back of his throat, and it was impossible to force the words out past it. He closed his mouth, only able to nod in response.

"You're an adult." The words weren't a question, and he wasn't sure why that surprised him. Eryn must have told her a few things, including that she was frozen in time for eleven years while a war raged between their kingdom and the one that had taken her hostage.

A breathy laugh escaped him before he could think better of it.

Amelia's gaze drifted over him again, this time landing on the ring encircling his finger. Her eyes widened, and she looked up at him. "You can't wear that," she told him, as if they were still children and they would get in trouble if their father found him wearing the ring they were never allowed to play with. "Only the…"

She froze mid-sentence. She was still a child, but she had never been oblivious.

"King can wear it," Eryn finished, when it became clear neither of the two siblings would say it.

Caeden swallowed hard. There were so many things he needed to tell her. So many things he wished she would never have to know, but were inevitable.

"Do you want to sit?" he asked her. "There are a lot of things

I need to explain."

Amelia nodded slowly.

"I'll leave you two alone," Eryn said, and slipped out the door before Caeden could respond.

Amelia moved to the bed. Fresh white sheets covered it now rather than the painter's cloth that was there for years. The walls were finished, and now that everything was mostly unpacked, it looked like a real room again.

"Can we start with who she is?" Amelia asked, glancing back at the door Eryn had disappeared through before she turned back to him again. "Why has she been the one checking on me this whole time and not Teafa? Or you? Or Dad?"

Caeden sat on the bed beside her slowly, doing his best to keep from hurting his side, as inevitable as it was. He glanced up at the door. "She's my fiancée," he answered, the words tight.

Amelia glanced at the door again, then back at him. "Your fiancée?" she repeated, as if the words sounded foreign on her tongue. "You're getting married?"

Caeden nodded.

She stayed silent for a long moment, seeming to let the words sink in. "Where's Teafa? And where's Dad? Does he know about…" Tears shone in her eyes and she swallowed hard. "Does he know what happened to Mom?"

The question hit him like a slap across the face and he flinched, but telling her about their deaths and that their mother's death was what had started the war to begin with was only one of the mountain of things he needed to explain.

They talked for far longer than he'd intended. He explained how the war had broken out after her capture and their mother's murder. He told her about his training, how Eryn came to the castle, and about Margaid who turned out to be Dealla. He told her about being kidnapped, where he'd learned she was still alive. How they'd learned about the ring and traveled to the mountains where they were told about the magic that kept her frozen in space and time. About the explosion that they'd returned to, that Muire was responsible, and that it resulted in the deaths of both Teafa and their father.

Amelia listened as if the information didn't hurt her in the way her hands gripping the fabric of her dress and the tears rolling down her cheeks suggested.

He explained how they captured Dealla, and how the final fight was arranged. How he traded Dealla to get her back, and everything Eryn had told him about how the fight had ended in their victory.

She didn't say anything when he was done. Only nodded her head and moved closer to him on the bed so that she could lay her head against his shoulder.

The sudden contact made him flinch, but only for a brief second as the surprise flashed through him. He wrapped his arms around her small frame and held her close. She cried against him, and he felt when the tears started to fall from his own eyes as the pain from everything they'd lost hit him as if for the first time again.

But the Dragon Lord was dead this time.

He may not have been the one to end the life of the man who caused all of this, but he no longer cared. He thought he'd wanted revenge for the past eleven years—sought it out as though it was the only option—but that wasn't what brought him peace. It was knowing his people were safe. Knowing that those he loved who still lived would grow old in a world where they weren't fighting for their lives every single day. He had been so caught up in wanting the Dragon Lord's death that he hadn't stopped to think about why he craved it so badly. He'd thought all he needed was to sink a sword into his heart and everything would be solved, but that was a naïve thought.

This wasn't over yet.

His people weren't at war any longer. They were as safe as they could be for the time being, but there was still so much that needed to be discussed; so many decisions that needed to be made to ensure they stayed that way.

He didn't think that sitting inside of the castle would get them anywhere in the war, but it had. The letter he'd sent was what arranged the final fight. The conversations he had with the rulers from Crevia had resulted in them having enough soldiers. And now, the meeting he would have with the advisors this evening would be what ensured his people lived the rest of their lives in peace.

The responsibilities he held weren't more important than the job of every soldier that got them to this point, but it couldn't be pushed to the side either. This was equally important, and as he held tightly to his sister, one of the few people he cared for most in the world, he wished he could've seen that years ago.

Caeden and Eryn met with the court shortly after he left Amelia's room. He'd invited Amelia along, if she wanted to see more of what was happening, but she only shook her head and said she needed time to process everything. Which he fully understood, but it only made his heart ache more for her.

"How are we moving forward with this?" Fionn asked, gesturing around them as if it were a clear indicator that he meant how they would deal with finalizing the war.

Dealla sat at the table beside Ronan, who'd made himself comfortable on Caeden's left while Eryn sat to his right. Her hands were hidden beneath the table, but he saw when her arms flexed and she shifted, and he knew she was fidgeting with her dagger in her lap.

Caeden took a breath before he spoke to the court. They wouldn't like what he had to say, just as they hadn't liked when he told them he wanted Dealla present for the meeting. Regardless of how the court felt, there was no doubt in his mind that his plan would result in the best outcome for both kingdoms.

"Dealla will rule over Deovaria," Caeden said firmly.

Several courtiers and advisors opened their mouths to speak, but Caeden raised a hand to silence them before they could protest.

Dealla froze, her eyes wide.

"Deovaria's people have suffered enough. Just as our kingdom has suffered, so has theirs. They've been through two wars in the past fifteen years, and they are scared and confused. We don't understand what they went through under the Dragon Lord's rule, and we don't know how many of them truly believe he was doing something noble. If we invade their land and claim them as part of Aericora, we can't know how many of them will rebel. I want peace for our kingdom, not to be suffering through more fighting. And I want peace for Deovaria, as well. I don't know what kind of future they are looking at, but I trust Dealla will know how to handle it far better than we ever could."

The court did argue, but they came to their decision far faster than Caeden expected.

Though some were still reluctant, they would let Dealla rule over Deovaria. Aericora would have no say in their political affairs, though they would be allies moving forward. The only stipulation Caeden had for Deovaria and for Dealla to enforce was that the dragons would be freed, and she hadn't so much as opened her mouth to disagree.

The papers to make it official were drawn up quickly, and pens were handed to the rulers of both kingdoms to sign the document.

"Thank you," Dealla whispered, as they both bent over the paper to scrawl their signatures together across the bottom.

"I meant every word I said," Caeden told her as he finished signing his name.

She smiled over at him before she placed her pen to the paper and drew her signature alongside his.

Chapter 62

Caeden sat with Eryn, Ronan, and Dealla in Ronan's living room late that night. The meeting with the court hadn't run long, but by the time he left Amelia's room earlier, it was already well into the evening. The sun set hours ago, and the chirping of the cicadas outside drifted through the ajar window to Caeden's left.

Eryn laughed at a joke that either Ronan or Dealla had told, but Caeden missed whatever it was while his thoughts drifted back to everything that happened earlier in the day. It was harder now that the whiskey flooded his veins to keep them at bay. He hadn't yet had much to drink, but it was enough to make his thoughts hazy around the edges, which made it harder to suppress those he would rather avoid.

They didn't all fit on the couch together, but it was far from the first time Eryn had opted to sit on the coffee table rather than the couch. She sat across from him, Ronan to his right, and Dealla on the other side of Ronan.

A half-empty bottle of whiskey sat on the coffee table along with everyone's glasses, and a bottle of tequila that only Eryn was drinking from sat beside them all.

Eryn's fingers grazed over the back of Caeden's hand where it rested against his knee, and he glanced over at her. She'd moved to sit on the very edge of the coffee table, a smile on her face and a blush across her cheeks that highlighted her stunning blue eyes in a way that made his breath catch in the back of his throat.

"We have something to tell you two," Dealla said, her words slurred since she was currently on her fourth glass of whiskey.

Ronan glanced at Dealla, who gave him a single nod as if to tell him the words needed to be said.

Caeden glanced at Eryn, who looked just as confused as he felt.

"When Dealla goes back to Deovaria, I'm gonna go with her," Ronan said softly, his words hardly above a whisper.

Caeden's eyes widened. He couldn't say he was surprised by their decision, but he was surprised they'd made it so quickly.

"That was fast," Eryn commented, speaking his same thoughts aloud.

Ronan and Dealla glanced at one another again. "That's not all of it," Dealla whispered.

Ronan clenched her hand tightly, as if willing himself to say the next words. "We may also have gotten engaged."

Caeden and Eryn stared at the two of them for a long moment. He was supposed to say something in response to that, but his thoughts were too hazy after everything that day, and words failed him.

He was genuinely happy for them, even if he couldn't figure out how to put into words how to tell them so. He wanted happiness for his friend. It was all he'd ever wanted for him since he first met him years ago. He more than deserved to finally get it.

Caeden wanted that for Dealla, too. He wouldn't have been

able to say anything of the sort a week ago, but after everything she did to end the war, he could say it with certainty now.

Eryn was the one who spoke first. "Congratulations," she told them. Caeden had expected her voice to sound tight around the word, but she sounded genuinely happy for them. She turned to Dealla, a mischievous smirk hiding in the corners of her mouth. "Break his heart and I'll kill you. And you know I can."

Caeden snorted a laugh.

That was more like it, even if the words were said as a joke.

Dealla laughed, and if Eryn's words had gotten to her at all, she didn't show it. "Maybe, but you'd have to work for it, Dragon Hunter," she fired back. She squeezed Ronan's hand again, nothing but love in her expression when she turned to face him. "But it's good I don't ever plan to."

Caeden and Eryn stayed in the shack with Ronan and Dealla late into the night. They would be leaving in the next couple of weeks, and as happy as Caeden was for his friend, it was hard to imagine what it would be like in the castle without him.

"Do you know yet who you're going to hire to replace him?" Eryn asked. She was propped up on her elbow beside him on the bed, peering down at him with those bright blue eyes, curiosity making them twinkle alongside a glimmer of mischief. "Aubry already said she wanted to stay, and my vote is to hire her, but I don't know how well she'll fit in the shack."

Caeden snorted a laugh, and he smiled up at her. "I think she would do well, but she could probably use some help."

"Agreed," Eryn joked. "Maybe we can find her a drake companion? Someone to do her dirty work?"

"Actually," he said, sitting up so they were eye level with one another. "I have someone else in mind."

Eryn raised an eyebrow at him. "Do you?"

He nodded. "I know you'll be busy already with court matters once we're married," he started, and he loved the way her eyes widened with surprise. "But I can't think of anyone who would be better for the job. Even Aubry, just don't tell her I said so. You would still have to attend court meetings, which I know you don't enjoy, but it would generally be more from the standpoint of the castle's Head of Security, rather than Aericora's Queen. Not that you wouldn't still have responsibilities as both, but it might be something you would enjoy more. Plus, even though it won't be frequent without a war, there would still be occasional groups of soldiers brought here and they would be yours to train."

A smile broke out across Eryn's face, so wide he wasn't sure it could get bigger if she tried. "That sounds perfect," she told him. "But I'm keeping Aubry, if she'll let me."

Caeden laughed. For someone who'd been so afraid of dragons weeks ago, it was nice to see how relaxed she'd become with Aubry, even if that didn't translate to every dragon.

Eryn lowered herself just enough to press her lips to his, making his heart race as quickly as it had the first time they'd kissed. "I love you," she whispered against his lips.

"I love you too, Eryn Gedding," he whispered. The words didn't convey the depth of what he felt for her, but he was beginning to wonder whether anything ever could. She was everything to him. She was the reason he lived, the reason he breathed, and there was no way to convey just how much he meant it to her with words alone.

Rather than try, he held her close when she snuggled up next to him again. He breathed her in, the familiar scent of lavender drowning out everything but her. Her warmth seeped into him as they laid there together, and for the first time he could remember, everything felt perfect.

About the Author

Mase Evans is a fantasy and romance author who enjoys a story that immerses readers in new worlds full of fun characters, adventure, and swoon worthy love stories. She primarily writes fantasy romance books, with occasional outliers, that are geared toward younger adults.

She grew up in Houston, Texas with her younger siblings and began writing at the age of 10, finishing her first full length novel when she was 14. She continues to live in Texas with her husband and her three fur babies.